RANDOM HOUSE

LARGE
PRINT

**Also by Richard North Patterson
available from Random House Large Print**

Balance of Power
Protect and Defend
Dark Lady
The Final Judgment

CONVICTION

CONVICTION

A NOVEL

Richard North Patterson

RANDOM HOUSE
LARGE PRINT

Although the case law discussed in these
pages is real, **Conviction** is a work of fiction, and
names, characters, places, and incidents are the
products of the author's imagination or are used
fictitiously. Any resemblance to actual events,
locales, or persons, living or dead,
is entirely coincidental.

Copyright © 2005 by Richard North Patterson

All rights reserved.
Published in the United States of America by
Random House Large Print in association with
Random House, New York.
Distributed by Random House, Inc., New York.

**The Library of Congress has established a
Cataloging-in-Publication record for this title.**

0-375-43468-2

www.randomlargeprint.com

FIRST LARGE PRINT EDITION

10 9 8 7 6 5 4 3 2 1

This Large Print edition published in accord with
the standards of the N.A.V.H.

For Gina Centrello
and
Nancy Miller

From this day forward, I no longer shall tinker with the machinery of death. . . . Rather than continue to coddle the Court's delusion that the desired level of fairness has been achieved and the need for regulation eviscerated, I feel morally and intellectually obligated simply to concede that the death penalty experiment has failed. . . . The basic question—does the system accurately and consistently determine which defendants "deserve" to die?—cannot be answered in the affirmative. It is not simply that this Court has allowed vague aggravating circumstances to be employed . . . relevant mitigating evidence to be disregarded . . . and vital judicial review to be blocked. . . . The problem is that the inevitability of factual, legal and moral error gives us a system that we know must wrongly kill some defendants, a system that fails to deliver the fair, consistent, and reliable sentences of death required by the Constitution.

—MR. JUSTICE BLACKMUN,
dissenting in **Callins v. Collins**

Justice Blackmun begins his statement by describing with poignancy the death of a convicted murderer by lethal injection. He chooses, as the case in which to make that statement, one of the less brutal of the murders that regularly come before us—the murder of a man ripped by a bullet suddenly and unexpectedly, with no opportunity to prepare himself and his affairs, and left to bleed to death on the floor of a tavern. The death-by-injection which Justice Blackmun describes looks pretty desirable next to that. It looks even better next to some of the other cases currently before us which Justice Blackmun did not select as the vehicle for his announcement that the death penalty is always unconstitutional—for example, the case of the eleven year old girl raped by four men and killed by stuffing her panties down her throat. . . . How enviable a quiet death by lethal injection compared with that! If the people conclude that such more brutal deaths may be deterred by capital punishment; indeed, if they merely conclude that justice requires such brutal deaths to be avenged by capital punishment, the creation of false, untextual, and unhistorical contradictions within "the Court's Eighth Amendment jurisprudence" should not prevent them.

—MR. JUSTICE SCALIA,
concurring in **Callins v. Collins**

It is tempting to pretend that [those] on death row share a fate in no way connected to our own. . . . Such an illusion is ultimately corrosive, for the reverberations of injustice are not so easily confined. . . . [T]he way in which we choose those who will die reveals the depth of moral commitment among the living.

—MR. JUSTICE BRENNAN,
dissenting in **McCleskey v. Kemp**

PART ONE

THE TRIAL

ONE

IN FIFTY-NINE DAYS, IF THE STATE OF CALIFORNIA HAD its way, the man inside the Plexiglas booth would die by lethal injection.

Teresa Peralta Paget paused to study him, the guard quiet at her side. Her new client stood with his back to them. He was bulky, the blue prison shirt covering his broad back like an oversize bolt of cloth. A picture of enthrallment, he gazed through the high window of the exterior wall at the San Francisco Bay, its water glistening in the afternoon sun. She was reluctant to distract him; the man's sole glimpses of the world outside, Terri knew, occurred when his lawyers came to see him.

The others were out of it now; the last set of lawyers had withdrawn after their latest defeat. The final desperate efforts to keep Rennell Price alive—what she thought of as the ritual death spasms ordained by the legal system—had fallen to Teresa Paget. This was their first meeting: but for his solitude, she could not have picked her client out from the other men huddled with their lawyers in the two rows of Plexiglas cubicles.

It resembled, Terri thought, an exhibit of the damned—sooner or later, in months, or more likely years, the impersonal, inexorable grinding of the machinery of death would consume each one in turn.

But perhaps not, Terri promised herself, this one. At least not until she had burnt herself down to the nerve ends, sleep-deprived from the effort to save him.

To her new client, she supposed, Terri might appear a mere morsel for the machine, insufficient even to slow its gears. She was small—barely five feet four—and slight, with olive skin and a sculpted face, which her husband stubbornly insisted was beautiful: high cheekbones; a delicate chin; a ridged nose too pronounced for her liking; straight black hair, which, in Terri's mind, she shared with several million other Latinas far more striking than she. There was little about her to suggest the steeliness an inmate might hope for in his lawyer except, perhaps, the green-flecked brown eyes, which even when she smiled never quite lost their keenness, or their watchfulness.

This wariness was Terri's birthright, the reflex of a child schooled by the volatile chemistry which transformed her father's drinking to brutality, and reinforced by the miserable first marriage which Terri, who had no better model, had chosen as the solution to her pregnancy with Elena. Her personal life was different now. As if to compensate for this good fortune, she had turned her career down a path more arduous than most lawyers could endure: at thirty-nine, she had spent the last seven years representing death row inmates, a specialty which virtually guaranteed the opposition and, quite frequently, the outright hostility of judges, prosecutors, witnesses, cops, governors, most relatives of the victim, and by design, the legal system itself—not to mention, often, her own clients. Now that stress and anxiety no longer waited for her at home, Terri sometimes thought, she had sought them out.

What would be most stressful about **this** client was not the crime of which he stood convicted, though it was far more odious than most—especially, given certain facts, to Terri herself. Nor was it whatever version of humanity this man turned out to be: her death row clients had run the gamut from peaceable through schizophrenic to barking mad. But this client represented the rarest and most draining kind of all: for fifteen years, through a trial court conviction in 1987, then a chain of defeats in the California Supreme Court, the Federal District Court, the Federal Court of Appeals, and the United States Supreme Court, Rennell Price had claimed his innocence of the crime for which the state meant to kill him.

No court had considered this claim worthy of belief or even, in the last five of these proceedings, a hearing. As far as the State was concerned, its sole remaining task should be to dispatch three psychiatrists to advise the Governor's office, within twenty days of the appointed date of execution, whether her client was sane enough to die: one of the niceties of capital punishment, Terri thought sardonically, was the State's insistence that the condemned fully appreciate that lethal injection would, in fact, be lethal.

She nodded to the guard.

He rapped sharply on the Plexiglas. With a twitch of his shoulders, as though startled, the black man inside the cage turned to face them.

His eyes were expressionless; for him, Terri thought, the highlight of her visit—a view of the bay—was already over. With a resignation born of fifteen years of meeting lawyers in these booths, he backed toward the door and, hands held behind his back, thrust them through an open slot.

The guard clapped on his handcuffs, closing them with a metallic click. Then Rennell Price, shackled, stepped away from the door.

The guard opened it, admitting Terri.

The door shut, and Rennell stood over her. As he backed to the slot again, waiting for the guard to uncuff his outthrust hands, Terri had an involuntary spurt of fear, the reflex of a small woman confined with a hulking stranger who had, in the estimate of twelve jurors, done a terrible thing to someone much smaller than she.

She held out her hand. "I'm Terri Paget," she told him. "Your new lawyer."

His expression was somewhere between sullen and indifferent—she might as well have pronounced herself an emissary from Pluto. But after a moment, he looked up at her and said in a monotone, "My name Rennell."

She searched his eyes for hope or, at least, some instinct to trust. She saw none.

"Why don't we sit," Terri said. "Get acquainted a little."

With a fractional shrug, her client turned, slid out the orange plastic chair on the far side of a laminated wood table, and sat, staring past Terri. Settling across from him, Terri saw the inmates in the next two cages huddled with their lawyers, lips moving without sound.

Rennell's face, Terri decided, was more than inexpressive—it had no lines, as if no emotion had ever crossed it. She reminded herself that he had been only eighteen when convicted, now was barely thirty-three, and that the fifteen years in between had been, were this man lucky, mostly solitary, and unrelentingly the same. But not even Terri's presence—a novelty, at least—caused the line of his full mouth to soften, or his wide brown eyes to acknowledge her.

Terri tried to wait him out. Yet the broad plane of his face remained so impassive that he seemed not so much to look through her as to deny her presence. It was hard to know the reasons. But one of the hallmarks of an adult abused as a child, Terri reflected, was an emotional numbing to the point of dissociation—a willful process of going blank, of withdrawing mentally from this earth. Jurors often thought such men indifferent to the crimes their prosecutors described so vividly; in the case of **this** crime, that could hardly have helped Rennell Price.

"I've taken over your case," Terri explained. "Your lawyers at Kenyon and Walker thought you deserved a fresh pair of eyes."

This drew no reaction. Mentally, Terri cursed her predecessors for their absence, the ultimate act of cowardice and desertion—leaving her to build a relationship with a sullen stranger, the better to save his life, or prepare him to die. Then, to her surprise, he asked, "You know Payton?"

"Your brother? No, I don't." Terri tried to animate her voice with curiosity. "How's he doing?"

"Fixing to die. They're going to kill him. Before me."

Oddly, Terri thought, this last detail about Payton seemed to carry more dread than his own fate. "How do you know?" she inquired.

He slumped forward on the table, not answering. "I can't be there," he said dully. "Warden told me that."

Struck by the answer, Terri chose to ignore its unresponsiveness. "What else did she tell you?"

"That I can pick five people. When my time come."

Five witnesses, Terri thought, granted the condemned by the grace of the State of California. But from what Terri knew, it would be hard to find five people, outside the victim's family, who gave enough of a damn to watch. Rennell Price's death, if it came, would be a very private affair.

"You don't have to worry about that yet." Pausing, Terri looked hard into his eyes. "We'll have a lot of help—my husband, Chris, who's a terrific lawyer, and a team of investigators to look into your case. You'll meet them all soon. We'll be doing everything we can to save your life."

For almost half that life, he had heard this—Terri could see that much in his face. And each time, she already suspected, whoever said it had been lying.

Slowly, his eyelids dropped.

"I didn't do that little girl," he said. "Payton didn't do her."

The denial sounded rote, yet etched with fatigue. "How do you know about Payton?" Terri asked.

"He told me."

What to make of that, she wondered. As either a reason to believe his brother or a statement of truth, it was implausible to the point of pitiful, and she could not divine if this man knew it. "Who do you think 'did' her, Rennell?"

He gave a silent shrug of the shoulders, suggesting an absence of knowledge or, perhaps, a massive indifference.

"The day she died," Terri persisted, "can you remember where you were?"

"I don't remember nothing."

As an answer, it was at least as credible as the alibi the defense had offered at the brothers' trial. But one or the other could not be true, suggesting—unhelpfully—that neither was.

Terri simply nodded. There was little else to ask until she combed the record, little purpose to her visit beyond starting to persuade Rennell Price—against the odds, given his life lessons—that someone cared about him. "I'll be coming to see you every few days," she assured him. "Is there anything you need?"

Rennell gazed at the table. "A TV," he said at last. "Mine's been broke for a long time now."

"Before it broke, what did you like to watch?"

"Superheroes. Especially Hawkman. Monday through Friday at four o'clock."

She could not tell if this commercial announcement was a statement of fact or suggested an unexpected gift for irony. Whatever the case, given the size of his cell and the cubic footage limitations on his possessions, a new TV would not bankrupt the Paget family. And fifty-nine days of Hawkman was not too much to ask—though it was not easy for Terri to imagine the waning existence which would be measured out, hour by hour, in images on the Cartoon Network.

"I'll get you a new one," she promised.

Her client did not answer. Maybe, Terri thought, he did not believe her. Even when she stood to leave, he did not look up.

Only as the guard approached did Rennell Price speak again, his voice quiet but insistent.

"I didn't do that little girl," he told his lawyer.

TWO

"To look at his reactions," Teresa Paget told her husband and stepson, "most people would wonder if there's a human being inside. But I began to wonder if he's retarded."

Chris's mouth formed a smile. "Or maybe just antisocial. In the Attorney General's Office, that means just smart enough to feel no remorse."

The three of them—Terri, Chris, and Carlo—sat on the deck of the Pagets' Victorian home in the Pacific Heights section of San Francisco, three tall glasses resting on the table in front of them. In the foreground of their sweeping view, Victorians and Edwardians and red-brick Georgians crowded the hill, which descended to the Italianate homes of the Marina District. Beyond that, the bay was still crowded with boats in the failing sun of a late Saturday afternoon, their sails swelling with a steady wind, which on the Pagets' deck calmed to a fitful breeze. Though the panorama relieved Terri's sense of claustrophobia, so intense in the Plexiglas booth, it heightened her consciousness of the surreal gap between Rennell's existence and her own, intensified by the familiar visages to either side of her.

At fifty-five, Christopher Paget remained trim and fit, the first streaks of silver barely visible in his copper hair, the clean angles of his face as yet unsoftened by age. Wealthy by inheritance, Chris carried an air of sophistication and detachment which never obscured, at least for Terri, his devotion to their reconfigured family: her thirteen-year-old daughter, Elena; their seven-year-old son, Kit; and, as always, their newest legal associate—Chris's son Carlo, fresh from Yale Law School at the age of twenty-five.

If anything, Carlo appeared more blessed than Chris. His mother, of Italian descent, had been a beauty, and Carlo had dark good looks which Terri had seen stop women on the street. Among Carlo's many graces was that he seemed unaware of this. Unlike Chris, who superficially did not appear so, Carlo was idealistic, a sweet and loving soul—all of which, Terri knew, had everything to do with Chris himself. That was part of what had caused Terri to fall in love with Chris. So here she was, the daughter of a struggling Hispanic family, sitting in a beautiful house in a beautiful city with two men who, by all appearances, had been showered with God's favors since the moment they were born.

It was not quite true, of course. Chris's parents were unloving and alcoholic socialites whose wasted lives had ended in a car wreck. Carlo had been the by-product of an affair, the miserable and unloved son of a single mother who despised Chris too much to let him raise Carlo—until the moment, fearful that the stunted seven-year-old child would become a damaged adult, Chris had given her no choice. It was this sense of life's underside that had given Chris the capacity to understand, at least as much as he could, what it was like for Terri to grow up in a household where her father raped and brutalized her mother, indifferent to what their daughter saw or felt. That this experience had led her—with whatever emotional crosscurrents—to comprehend the lives which so often created death row inmates, and to feel that representing them was recompense for her own escape, was something that Chris still strove to understand; that their law firm would subsidize her efforts, and that Chris would help, was a given. Which was why Carlo—preserved in his idealism, Chris wryly remarked, by an absence of student loans—had chosen to join them.

They drank iced tea; though it was close to the Pagets' accustomed cocktail hour, the conversation was too purposeful for that. "Still," Chris ventured, "it's a strange crime."

Only after a quick glance at Terri did Carlo turn to him, and she was acutely aware of the sensitivity toward her that, for a moment, delayed his question: "Strange in what sense?"

"That it would involve both brothers. It's a matter of shame—if you put a nine-year-old boy on the fifty-

yard line at Notre Dame stadium, and packed the seats
with pedophile priests, none of them would move.
Child molesters tend to act alone."

This remark, with its echoes from her daughter
Elena's past, reminded Terri that walling herself off
from the nature of Rennell Price's alleged crime might
be far more difficult than she had made herself believe.
Then Chris reached across the table and touched her
hand. Quietly, he said, "You don't have to take this
case, you know."

Pensive, Terri curled her fingers in his. "The Habeas
Corpus Resource Center is jammed, and they're out of
volunteers. So it's me or no one." She faced Carlo.
"About child molesters," she told him baldly, "your
dad's right. Elena could tell you that. But Rennell Price
still claims he's innocent. That's where we have to
start—and quickly."

This settled the matter, as Terri had known it
would. After another glance at his father, Carlo
nodded.

"So," she continued, "we have to look at the facts as
if no one ever has before. Review the police reports,
the physical evidence, the witness statements, the trial
transcript. Track down the key witnesses—could they
have been mistaken, we'll want to know, or have had a
motive to lie? Both happen more often than you'd
think."

"What about the cops?"

"If they're willing. Same with the prosecutor **and**
Rennell's trial lawyer—we'll want to know why they

made the choices they did. That will be far more touchy for defense counsel."

Carlo raised his eyebrows in inquiry. "Because we'll second-guess him?"

"More than that," Chris told him. "We have to prove that Rennell Price's trial lawyer was so incompetent that his client was denied the effective assistance of counsel granted by the Sixth Amendment. It won't be easy, given that some courts have ruled that even sleeping through your client's trial is not enough to qualify. Damned few lawyers will admit they were worse than **that.**"

"If we can prove Rennell Price is innocent, why should it matter?"

Terri suppressed a rueful smile: framed against the panoply of sailboats, his crew-neck burgundy sweater carelessly draped over his shoulders, Carlo still seemed innocent himself. But so had she been.

"Later on," she promised, "I'll induct you into the wonderland of death penalty jurisprudence. For now, take my word that the State of California can claim that even compelling new proof of this guy's innocence doesn't bar his execution—at least, taken alone. If the trial was fair, then they'll say his execution is constitutional. Even if the verdict may well have been wrong."

"How can innocence not matter?"

"Because that's the law—you'll find out soon enough. Rennell Price was convicted of an awful crime, and fifteen years later, he's still alive. He's become an overdue debt to the victim's parents, and the

State of California is determined to collect on their behalf."

Saying this reminded Terri of how solitary Rennell was—and of why she must distance herself, as much as possible, from the fact that the victim had suffered a death which caused Terri to cringe with guilt at what her own daughter still was forced to live with.

"So we'd better hope he **is** retarded," Chris remarked to Carlo. "That's the good news, if there is any. While you were holed up cramming for the bar exam, the Supreme Court decided in **Atkins v. Virginia** that we no longer execute the mentally retarded. The trick, if Terri's right, is **proving** that she's right with respect to Rennell Price. Otherwise," Chris added sardonically, "or so the argument goes, we'll be flooded with claims of retardation filed by crafty middle-aged inmates who suddenly can't tie their own shoes.

"That means we need to show who Rennell was at age eighteen, and how he got that way—his parents, relatives, brother, friends, home, neighborhood, educational and medical histories, mental profile. Everything that ever happened to him, an entire social history in fifty-nine days."

The task was so daunting that Carlo, feigning a careless shrug, simply inquired, "So where do we start?"

Restless, Terri stood. "By going to the office," she told him with faux good cheer. "Right now. We'll start by reading reams of paper, then tracking down the cops."

Now Carlo looked genuinely startled. "What if I have a date?"

Chris laughed aloud. "Ask her to come to your place late," he suggested helpfully, "and hope that she'll stay over." Abruptly, his eyes grew serious and, in his wife's appraisal, a little sad. "Until you save Rennell Price, or the State of California kills him, life as you know it is over. After that, it will merely never be the same. I know that from living with Terri."

THREE

"KIDS," CHARLES MONK SAID SOFTLY. "TO ME, THEY were always the worst. Never quite got used to it."

Fifty-seven days to go. Perhaps that was why, Terri thought, Monk's words had a valedictory tone; perhaps it was just the reflective melancholy of a veteran homicide inspector who, freshly retired, had the freedom of acknowledging emotions which for too long had been a luxury. Then she wondered if the melancholy was her own, more about the daughter she knew than the children Charles Monk had seen.

They sat at a sidewalk café in North Beach, the early morning pedestrians—tourists and schoolkids and office workers headed for the Financial District— passing by their table. The morning was bright but a little chill; Monk stiffened, a wince briefly disturbing the granite angles of his seamed brown face, and then stretched one leg in front of him. "Knee," he told her with resignation. "Vietnam."

"Want to go inside?"

Monk slowly shook his head. "Not if I can help it.

Just make me feel like an invalid. Worse than that—retired."

Terri smiled. They had been adversaries, sometimes bitterly so, but never enemies. Monk was smart and honest, a legend on the street; he seemed willing enough to talk with her, maybe because he was bored, more likely because he was satisfied with the integrity of his work. For Monk, the execution of Rennell Price was a given—the recompense, too long delayed, for what he had seen fifteen years before.

"Let's start from the beginning," Terri requested.

It had been late September, the waning of the baseball season, and the Giants were playing a Thursday night game at Candlestick. Through Monk's windshield, the circular glow of klieg lights rose from the bowl of the stadium.

It sat on a promontory jutting eastward into the San Francisco Bay, the ill-advised project of a mayor who seemed never to have visited at night, when the stiff winds buffeted your face and chill fog seeped into your bones. A cop waved Monk past the barrier erected to divert the flow of traffic, and Monk's headlights found the parking lot closest to the bay.

He parked beside the water. Stepping out, conscious of the shadow of the stadium a quarter mile behind him, the thin cries of deluded fans carrying in the cold, damp air which made this such a miserable place to play—or watch—a ball game. Or for Monk to be now.

Pulling up the collar of his windbreaker, he crossed a strip of sand and underbrush to the low wall of rocks which edged the bay. Far across the water were the glistening lights of the Oakland hills; a few feet from him, in the black shallows of the water, the new medical examiner, Liz Shelton, dressed in a down jacket and hip boots and clutching a flashlight, braced herself against the current as she scrutinized a dark form which had washed up against the base of the rocks. A lab technician knelt beside it.

"Didn't know you fished," Monk said.

Liz glanced up at him. Her dirty-blond hair was tied back off her neck, and her level gaze was somber in the moonlight. "Fly-fishing," she answered and moved her flashlight toward the shadowy form.

Captured in its yellow glow was the bloated face of a child who appeared to be Asian. Long black hair, swirling in the water, marked her as a girl.

Monk peered down at her. He could not see her legs; though soaked with water, her wool sweater appeared dark green. As her hair swirled again, Monk caught the glint of what might have been a silver barrette.

"Who found her?" he asked Shelton.

"Samoans. A bunch of them were sitting on the rocks, drinking beer."

Which figured; in Monk's reckoning, they were about the only folks scary enough, or maybe just dense enough, to hang out here in the dark and cold. Monk's knee had begun to throb.

"How long she been in the bay, you think?"

Shelton peered at the body with narrowing eyes, as if trying to see the child beneath the bloated mask. "Two days, maybe."

Beside the victim, the criminologist studied her for signs of trauma. In terms of external evidence, it was all he could accomplish now, and perhaps ever: a floater in the bay would have all sorts of stuff on it, from seaweed to the residue of toilets, and there would be little way of telling where any of it came from. Far better if she'd been wrapped up in a blanket and dumped in Golden Gate Park.

Monk looked up again. "How long dead?" he asked Shelton.

"Not sure. Maybe about the same."

"Any guess on cause?"

"Not yet."

Monk stared down at the victim. More quietly, he asked, "Think it's her?"

Shelton considered this. Monk did not need to explain: two afternoons ago, in a crack-infested section of the Bayview District, the nine-year-old daughter of Cambodian immigrants had vanished after school. She had stayed late for extra help with English; she had left alone; and as of now, her teacher was the last person who claimed to have seen her. In the photographs shown on television, the girl, named Thuy Sen, appeared grave and delicate.

"I'd say I hope not," Shelton answered, "but then she'd just be someone else's daughter."

Turning from the body, Monk gazed out at the sloping hills of the Bayview District, their light and shadow some distance beyond the stadium. "Why," he wondered aloud, "would Cambodians decide to settle in Bayview?"

"It's like Bogart said in **Casablanca,**" Liz responded wearily. "They must have been misinformed."

After Liz took charge of the body, transporting it to the Hall of Justice, Monk had gone to his office and begun calling the plainclothes cops who were searching for Thuy Sen.

The lead cop was in a sports bar in the Marina District. Above the din of voices and the Giants game, he told Monk where things stood.

They had done it by the numbers—cruised the neighborhood, searched her house, broadcast her description to operations, called hospitals, interviewed her teacher and, of course, her father, mother, and sister. "You know how it is in the Bayview," the cop told Monk. "Ninety-nine percent of the kids just decide not to show, or Mama lets 'em run around loose. Maybe nine or ten o'clock she'll get curious about where the kid might be. But Cambodians are different."

From blacks, you mean, Monk thought but did not say. "The parents have any ideas?" he asked.

"Nope. Last time they saw her she was heading off

to school with her twelve-year-old sister. Sis's job was to walk her to school every morning, and home every afternoon. This time she didn't—she seems pretty much of a mess. You can see the parents staring at her—they don't need to say a word."

Monk found himself studying the picture on his desk, his wife and their two daughters. "How are **they**?" he inquired. "The parents."

"Mom's jittery and anxious, can't sit still. Dad's, as they say, inscrutable. But they say they had no problems with Thuy Sen—no acting up, no conflicts, no hanging around with drug dealers or bad kids on the street. Her teacher agrees; as far as she knows, the girls keep pretty much to themselves."

"What does Sister say?"

"Not much," he answered, "except that they took the same route every day from home to school. We've been knocking on doors to ask if anyone saw her. Nothing yet."

In the bar, Monk heard a ragged chorus of cheers—the Giants, he guessed, had just done something good. "When she left for school," he asked, "did they say what she was wearing?"

"Yeah—a plaid skirt, Mom says. And her favorite green wool sweater."

By the time Monk caught up with Liz Shelton, the victim was on the autopsy table, her eyes shut, her naked limbs rigid and pitifully thin under the harsh light of an overhead lamp.

Monk gazed at her. "So?" he asked Shelton.

"No evidence of a beating, no obvious indications of brain damage. The only bruises seem to be post-mortem."

"What about penetration?"

"No sign of it, vaginal or anal. We'll take swabs, of course. But I doubt we'll find anything."

"Any guesses?"

Touching one side of the girl's face, Shelton extended her forefinger and gently opened an eyelid. At the edge of the sightless brown eye were starbursts of red.

"Like she was strangled," Monk observed.

Gently, Shelton removed her hand from the child's face, closing her eyelid again. "Except that there's no external evidence of that. It's like she maybe choked on a sandwich. That's why we perform autopsies."

Monk nodded. "I'll call the parents," he said. "See if they can ID her."

Shelton emitted a sigh. She was new on the job, Monk thought.

Monk and his partner, Rollie Ainsworth, sat in Shelton's office with Thuy Sen's father, mother, and the police translator, a petite young woman who had fled the Cambodian killing fields.

As had the Sen family, Monk learned in the ghastly form of small talk which occupied their anxious waiting. The mother, Chou, had lost her parents to the murderers of the Khmer Rouge; the brother and two sisters of Meng, the father, had been taken by the government and never seen again. Both seemed traumatized anew—the woman trembled, and the father, sitting stiffly in a chair, stared at the wall with foreboding.

"How did they get to the Bayview?" Monk asked the translator.

The young woman, reluctant, turned to the father and uttered words which sounded to Monk like a question. After a moment, Meng Sen answered in a monotone.

"His great-aunt was already there," the translator told him. "She wanted family around her."

When Liz Shelton was ready, Monk led the Sens to the glass window. The translator lingered behind.

The window was covered with curtains. Though it was intended to minimize shock and cut off the odor of death, neither, in Monk's experience, was much help at moments like this.

From inside, Shelton slowly drew back the curtains. The child lay on a gurney, draped in a white sheet.

The parents gazed at her. It was the mother who broke first, emitting a muted shriek, hands covering her face. For what seemed a long time, the father did not react. Then he closed his eyes, still silent, and nodded.

Thuy Sen did not play near the shore, Monk learned through the translator. She did not swim, and did not like the bay. The water was too cold.

After a few minutes, Monk told the woman to take them home.

It was midmorning before Shelton finished the autopsy, and Monk had barely slept before returning to her office.

"She choked to death," the medical examiner said baldly. "But not on a sandwich. On semen."

Monk said nothing. Briefly, it struck him that Thuy Sen's older sister was in for a lifetime of guilt and anguish.

"We found semen in her mouth and throat and airways," Shelton continued. "One male can ejaculate three to five milligrams. More than enough to choke a nine-year-old girl."

Monk considered this. "Anything to show she didn't volunteer?"

"No. But judging from what you know, how likely does that seem? Even over there."

Monk answered with a shrug. "What else?" he inquired.

With a tentative air, Shelton steepled her fingers, resting them against her chin. "There was a hair snagged in her barrette. For all we know, it came from the bay, and hair identification by ethnicity is hardly an exact science. But more likely than not it's Negroid."

Again Monk said nothing. Neither needed to comment on the inflammatory images this might summon, even in San Francisco—a nine-year-old girl choking to death during forcible oral copulation with a black man. Whoever the sperm donor turned out to be, Monk's job was to find him.

For some moments, Terri had not touched her coffee.

" 'Him' turned out to be 'them,' " Monk said with quiet emphasis. "We found them both."

FOUR

MONK STUDIED THE LEMON RIND FLOATING IN THE
tiny cup of espresso, incongruous in his paw of a hand.
"Should have ordered a double," he observed. "Less
rind, more caffeine."

Terri emptied her own cup, cold now, its contents
bitter on her tongue. "Tell me about Flora Lewis."

They didn't find a witness for two fruitless days,
spent going door-to-door in the crack-ridden streets of
Bayview, hilly and sunny and stark, where black kids
loitered on the pavement from childhood until, in
their twenties, half the boys were dead or in jail. To
outsiders, it was a foreign country—taxi drivers
wouldn't go there, cops blew off domestic violence
calls rather than stick their necks out, and the whole
mess was sitting on a Superfund site, with exposure to
buried poisons as toxic as the lives of many who were
born there.

Once it had been a place of hope, its white, blue-
collar residents joined during World War II by African

American shipyard workers who remained there, thinking the jobs and sunny weather—best among the city's microclimates—might presage a better life than whatever they'd left behind. The jobs vanished; many blacks remained, predominant now, mingled with pockets of Tongans and Samoans, a few Asians, and remnants of the white home-owning classes—stranded in the houses they still owned, Monk knew, by an economy which otherwise had passed them by. Some, like Flora Lewis, saw Bayview as a prison.

She lived two blocks south of Thuy Sen's accustomed route to school. Cracking open the door of her tiny Edwardian home, she peered above a door chain at the two black men—Monk and Rollie Ainsworth— who had come there unannounced. Only when Monk thrust out identification and stated their purpose did Lewis let them in.

The next thing she did seemed odd. Going to the window, she craned her neck to peer out, one palsied hand drawing open lace curtains, her frail body still bent away from the window to conceal herself from view. When she spoke she did not turn.

"I'd have moved," she said, "but all I've got is my social security and my parents' house."

Glancing at Ainsworth, Monk saw his partner's shrewd, round face appraising her and concluding, as Monk had, that silence was best. "They live across the street," she told them.

Uttering this non sequitur, her voice was parched. Her eyes maintained their vigil. "Who?" Monk asked.

"The Price brothers, two boys, if you could call them that. Cars squealing up at night, men and trampy-looking girls streaming in and out, music getting louder all the time and more obscene." Her tone became quieter, to Monk, etched with bitterness. "It always felt to me like anything could happen—their grandmother locked up like a prisoner, the boys with no one to control whatever impulses they had."

"Tell me about them."

She faced Monk now. Behind her wire-rim glasses Monk saw hesitance and fear, and a grimace deepened the seams of her face, drawing down her mouth. "The older one's named Payton," she said. "Quick-moving, with a bad mouth, who thinks he's clever. Used to be bright-eyed and almost pretty-looking—you watch them turn cruel, over time, and it would break your heart if you could believe they still had hearts of their own. But the younger one scared me from the time that he was four or five. You could see he'd be a hulking brute even before he became one.

"Even more than his size, it was his expression. It never changed. You just looked at him, and saw no feeling." Her eyes closed. "I can only imagine . . ."

"Imagine what?"

Silent, Lewis shook her head. When her eyes opened again, she said softly, "She was there. With them."

"How did you know it was her?"

Reflexively, her eyes sought out the television to one corner of the cramped room—an ancient couch, a coffee table, photographs of a woman and man who must have been her parents. Though tense now, Monk forced himself to remain patient, calm.

"She was Asian." Lewis hesitated, then finished. "It was the day before her picture was on the news."

Ainsworth glanced at Monk. "Tell us exactly what you saw."

Lewis paused, as if to summon an image in her mind. "They're sitting on the porch with one of those big, boxy radios blaring this chanting kind of music—Payton all jittery with his head snapping from side to side. The big one, Rennell, is staring at the sidewalk like he's been hypnotized. Minutes pass with him not moving.

"Then **she** comes by."

The last phrase held a fateful certainty. "Can you describe her?" Monk asked.

"Asian," she repeated simply. "Straight black hair, and even without seeing her face I can tell by how she carries herself. Eyes straight ahead, fixed on the sidewalk, like they do. Acting like she doesn't notice them."

"But they noticed her."

Flora Lewis bit her lip. "It was the big one," she said with quiet anger. "Rennell.

"He stands. I see his mouth open, calling out—it's like a pantomime, because I can't hear him with all that barbaric chanting from their radio. But I see the girl hesitate for the briefest moment before she's moving again, still not looking up.

"That brings the big one off the porch. His mouth

opens again, calling out." Lewis turned back toward the window, staring through the curtain as if at the remembered Asian child. "I can only imagine what he said. Suddenly, she's frozen there—petrified, more like it. Then she turns to face him.

"He comes down off the porch, towering over her. Payton's still twitching back and forth in his chair. She's standing with her back to me—you can see her glancing from one to the other, guessing at who scared her worse.

"Then Rennell says something else to her. She looks up at him, slowly shakes her head." Lewis finished in a monotone. "So he just reaches out and takes her by the arm."

Monk felt his own sense of foreboding. "And then?"

"Slowly, Rennell pulls her forward. She stumbles, like she'd been trying to stay rooted on the sidewalk. After that she just lets him pull her toward the house.

"Her shoulders are drooping now. But the thing I remember most is her looking up at the porch at Payton, and him standing. Like what's about to happen involves **him** now, too." Lewis slowly shook her head. "Then the big one says something to him, and Payton opens up the door."

Lewis stopped abruptly. After a moment, Ainsworth asked, "What happened then?"

"Rennell leads her to the porch, then puts his hand on her back and pushes her toward the door. I remember her stumbling on the doorsill. Then Rennell steps in behind her, and I can't see her anymore. He was too big." A mist clouded Lewis's eyes. "The last thing I saw was Payton closing the door behind them."

Monk and Ainsworth stayed quiet, letting their unspoken question fill the silence. "I'm afraid of them," she murmured with muted shame. "When I saw her picture, I told myself they'd find her. But not like that."

Monk thrust his hands in his pockets. "If the girl was Thuy Sen, by the time you saw her picture she was dead. All you could have done you're doing now."

But not without a house call from us, he thought to himself. **And maybe not if you'd called us when the big one pushed her through the door.**

"It would help," Monk said, "if you could remember what the girl was wearing."

The old white lady looked more grateful to him than she deserved to feel. "A plaid skirt," she answered. "And a dark green sweater. As long as I live, I'll never forget."

Monk and Ainsworth stood with a burly plainclothes cop in the squad room of the Bayview station. "Shit," Larry Minnehan said.

Monk shrugged. "If the girl **was** Thuy Sen, she wasn't taking her usual route. You started looking where you should have."

"I meant about this old lady. She damned well should have called us. Now all we've got is another fucking homicide."

Monk nodded toward an oversize bulletin board on the cinder-block wall behind Minnehan. "So tell me about the brothers Price."

"They're fungible, man. Like a lot of these gang-bangers." Turning to the board, Minnehan contemplated roughly a hundred mug shots of young men organized by gang affiliation, with typed notations of their more salient characteristics—arrest records, whether they were in prison or dead, maybe even who had killed them. A wall of blank eyes staring from blank faces which were all black.

"This one's Payton," Minnehan told Monk, pointing out a picture at the right side of the board.

Moving closer, Monk began committing the face to memory. It was more memorable than most: thin and handsome, close to refined, with a glint of irony rarely found in such photographs, whose subjects tended to prefer stone-cold indifference. "Payton's the supposed mastermind," Minnehan said. "Runs a network of dealers."

"Crack?"

"Natch. But I give him this—he's not hooked up with any gang. A true small businessman, with the kind of entrepreneurial spirit which makes this country great."

Ainsworth studied the photograph. "Not easy, down here."

"Payton's a nervy bastard," Minnehan responded. "A real survivor. You know what dealing crack is like in the Bayview. A lot of scuffling and hustling on the street—fractious, paranoid, and violent. We're like the Balkans for black folks."

Monk gave a short, mirthless laugh. "How's Payton work his business?"

"The usual way. Buys powder cocaine from a dealer, in kilos, and then turns it into rocks.

"But his dealer's only going to sell powder in significant quantities. So there's economic pressure for Payton to keep selling enough rocks to buy the next batch of powder, even if he has to sell them on consignment.

"He sells through a franchise of twenty or so street dealers—juveniles, people someone vouches for, anyone he thinks he can trust at all. That insulates him from the danger of hanging out on the corner drinking beer and mingling with the crackheads, maybe getting killed for the rocks or cash in his pocket." Minnehan tugged his Notre Dame sweatshirt down over the small protuberance of his belly. "You can sell a dozen rocks for maybe one fifty. Payton will want the money up-front. But if someone says he's short till Monday, and Payton's under pressure, he'll maybe have to trust him. For that you need muscle, a collector. Just what Rennell was born for."

Listening, Monk felt a weary familiarity, the inevitable arc in the lives of the two boys who had grown up across from Flora Lewis. Crack was the first business kids learned in the Bayview. It is tough to sell powder cocaine on the street—the customers are cynical, and can't be sure what they're getting isn't cut with sugar or salt. But any twelve-year-old can take powder, combine it with baking soda and water, then cook it into rocks a buyer can sample and **know**—from the first rush hitting his bloodstream—that it's the real deal. And so kids become both dealers and users—smoking crack for pleasure, dispensing crack for business, and trading crack for sex for the rest of what is likely to be their very brief lives.

"Payton have a girl?" Monk asked.

"Nice-looking boy like that? Always. Plenty of coke whores to go around, even if you look like a fucking gargoyle. Some of these sweet young things would suck the chrome off a trailer hitch."

"So what they need with a nine-year-old Cambodian girl?"

Minnehan shrugged. " 'Cause this whole fucking place is depraved, with a capital D. No rules, no limits, no respect for life or anything which might grow up to have a pussy. Add the crazy sexual rush which comes from smoking crack and see if guys like Payton and Rennell bother with these fine distinctions."

The mention of Rennell reminded Monk that he had not seen the man who, if Flora Lewis was right, had led Thuy Sen to her death. "Show me Rennell," he directed.

Minnehan jabbed at a picture. "Right here. Piss-poor protoplasm for sure."

Monk took it in. Not much to see, he thought—a round, expressionless face, eyes even deader than normal.

"Let's run 'em in," he said. "Both of them."

FIVE

ON THE WAY TO PICK UP PAYTON AND RENNELL, THEY
cruised down what passed in Bayview for the business
district, Third Street—do-shops, thrift shops, liquor
stores, check-cashing businesses, barbecue and soul
food restaurants, corner stores run by Arabs too smart
to live there, made prosperous by the total absence of
chain groceries. There was suffocating unemployment;
most of those with straight jobs left the Bayview to
work, and the most vigorous signs of economic life
were the crack dealers loitering at the corner of Third
and Palou. There was a culture of hanging out on the
porches and front steps, as Flora Lewis said the Price
brothers had done, or on the streets drinking beer, especially on warm nights, when it felt good to be outside, even if the streets became a nightmare after dark.
The other hub of social life lay in a plentitude of black
churches—when temporal life is so hard, Monk knew,
the hope of a hereafter spent somewhere other than
the Bayview holds a certain appeal.

For sure it beat the public housing—Stalinist stucco
complexes from the fifties and sixties, their street signs

riddled with bullet holes, festering with crime and violence and living arrangements as mutable as the white powder mixed with baking soda. Not all of it was quite that grim: there were old Edwardians and Victorians amidst the plain one-story homes, and on sunny days, like this one, the streets sloping up and down the hills could present a sudden sweeping vista of the bay—dazzling, Monk felt certain, to the dockworkers who had come there from the rural South. But the residue of the shipping industry was a few shabby warehouses and this endless supply of young street hustlers on a treadmill to nowhere good and, perhaps even sadder to Monk, who dearly loved his own two daughters, young women with nowhere else to turn for love or solace. Too many of these stunted men had far too little of that to give—the subculture which had spawned the Price brothers ran on adrenaline, in a here and now that was brutal, direct, and violent, with no sense of consequence, no "friendships" but with the people they used, no family but the illegitimate kids they had left with girls more cunning than smart.

Payton was twenty-two; Rennell barely eighteen. Monk already knew the rhythms of Payton's days and nights—constantly changing his meeting places; packing a gun or bringing along his brother for protection; searching for dealers among juveniles effectively immune from law enforcement, indifferent to the fact they might get killed; telling would-be snitches that he'd burn down their mamas' houses if anything in his life went bad; keeping cash under the bed or at some woman's or anywhere but a bank; stealing cars because he couldn't buy one, then beating the rap by saying he'd borrowed the car from some other dude without knowing it was stolen. The elements of a life built around loud music, sex, cars, and guns bought out of the back of a stranger's trunk, spent in a world where bus drivers cruising down Third Street called in robberies in progress, and the corner store sold glass pipes or one cigarette at a time so you could hollow it out to smoke a rock you'd just bought on the street. A life spent living—or dying—in the moment.

At this particular moment, it was Payton Price's bad luck to be home.

The house was a shabby Victorian on Shafter Avenue owned by Payton's grandmother. He stood in the doorway, lean, well-muscled, and more handsome than his picture, with seen-it-all eyes which held surprising flecks of green and, in their absolute determination to give nothing, perhaps the faintest hint of fear.

Blocking the door, he looked from Monk to Ainsworth to Monk again. "You got a warrant?" he demanded, hostility etched with disdain.

Caught doing your home chemistry, Monk thought. "We just dropped by to talk."

"What about?"

"The Cambodian girl who washed up in the bay."

A split-second glance at Ainsworth. "Don't know nothing about that," Payton said flatly.

"Then there's no problem with talking to us, is there?"

Payton turned his stare on Monk. "Only problem's my time you'd piss away."

Monk held his gaze. "Then maybe we'll talk to your brother."

This time Monk was certain he saw fear. After a moment, Payton shrugged. "Let's get this over with, man."

"First," Monk answered, "you can tell me where to find Rennell."

They stuck Payton in a bare room with bare walls in the bowels of Robbery and Homicide, a videocam staring down from one corner and a tape recorder on the laminated table in front of him, the two cops letting him think for a while about the sullen hulk of the brother who waited in the interrogation room next door. Leaning forward on the table, Payton propped his chin on one cupped hand, elaborately bored. But his body was rigid; Monk sensed a perpetual vigilance, perhaps never more than now, though it was hard not to wonder when this man had last enjoyed a dreamless sleep.

Monk slid a photo of Thuy Sen across the table. "Ever seen her?"

Payton made a show of studying her face, his squint a parody of concentration. "Don't know," he said, pausing to gaze back up at Monk. "Pretty much all look alike, don't they?"

Monk summoned a faint smile. "You see that many little Asian girls?"

The glint of irony vanished. "Not saying I saw this one."

Monk sat back, hands clasped behind his head. "I'm only asking," he said amiably, "because we hear she was at your house the day she disappeared."

The incredulous smile this summoned did not change Payton's eyes. "That's bullshit."

Monk appraised him. In a casual tone, Rollie Ainsworth interjected, "That's just what someone said."

"Who?"

Now it was Ainsworth's turn to smile. "Can't say. You know how it is."

"Well, they're fucked up, man."

"Because she wasn't there?" Monk asked. "Or wasn't there that day?"

Payton sat up, folding his arms, glaring straight at Monk. "What would I want with some Asian kid not old enough to bleed?"

That the disclaimer carried sexual overtones only fed Monk's suspicion: at his request, Liz Shelton had suppressed the sexual aspects of Thuy Sen's death. "What would **anyone** want with a nine-year-old girl? But someone did."

"Not in my house," Payton answered with a trace of arrogance. "Got all the grown-up pussy I need, whenever I need it. For whatever I need."

Monk gave him a slow-building smile. "Good for you, son," he answered in a tone of laconic amusement, and then placed one thick forefinger on the Asian girl's picture. "So this girl was never in your house."

Payton paused briefly before answering with calm conviction, "If she was, man, I sure as hell didn't know about it."

No, Monk thought, **you're not stupid. Maybe just smart enough to fuck up.** "Any idea where you were last Tuesday afternoon?"

Silent, Payton gazed at the tape spinning on the table between them. "If I'd known it was so important," he said after a time, "maybe I'd have noticed."

"We know you're a busy man," Ainsworth said in his most pleasant voice. "But please do take your time."

Payton's face went blank again. "Don't have that much time."

"We're going to give you some," Monk assured him. "While we visit with your brother."

For whatever reason, Monk sensed, this worried Payton more than what had gone before. "Rennell and me got to go," their quarry insisted.

"We'll try to keep that in mind," Monk said. He did not wait for an answer.

Arms resting on the table, Rennell Price made the room seem smaller. His face was fleshy, his features flat and indistinct, as though nothing was quite in focus. There was a gap between his two front teeth, both stained a dull yellow, one edged with a bright gold crown. Unlike his brother, he stared at the girl's photograph with a stony blankness.

"Remember her?" Monk asked.

The silence stretched with no sign of an answer; again, unlike Payton, Rennell seemed indifferent to the impression he made on Monk and Ainsworth, or even to their presence. "Yeah," he finally said. "I think maybe I seen her."

Monk reined in his surprise. "Where?"

The same pause occurred, Monk was noting, before each answer—silence did not seem to trouble Rennell Price. "Maybe at a store."

"What store?"

Silence.

"You don't remember?"

Lazily, the big man shook his head. Though he no longer stared at the picture, he did not look up at Monk.

More sharply, Ainsworth asked, "She ever at your house?"

This time his silence was followed by a single stubborn word. "No."

You, Monk decided, **are the weak link.** He could almost smell Payton's fear through the wall between them.

Learning forward, Monk spoke quietly. "Because someone says you took her inside your house the day she disappeared."

For the first time the dead zone which was Rennell

Price's eyes showed defensiveness and a veiled hostility. "No way."

"What about last Tuesday, Rennell?"

"No."

This time the monosyllable had come quickly, as did Monk's next question. "Where **were** you last Tuesday?"

The big man shrugged, indifferent once more. "Most days I sleep."

That much Monk believed. "Were you sleeping last Tuesday afternoon?"

"Probly." Rennell said this with a lassitude which seemed to have seeped into his bone and brain, bespeaking days that were endlessly the same. To Monk, he seemed so divorced from humanity as to be beyond reach.

This same thought seemed to have struck Ainsworth. With a quiet, lascivious undertone, he inquired, "When you saw her at the store, Rennell, did you think that she was pretty?"

This time Rennell did not move or speak.

"Her name was Thuy Sen," Monk said in an even tone. "Is there anything else you can tell us about her?"

To Monk's surprise, Rennell Price gazed up at him, though his face held no emotion. Then, very softly, he answered, "I didn't do that little girl."

So how do you know she was "done"? Monk wondered. He said nothing to Rennell.

S I X

Monk had begun watching the street traffic and the neighborhood stores, a grocery and vegetable stand and delicatessen with salami hanging in the window, stirring to life as they talked. Observing was his habit, Terri supposed.

"I suppose it occurred to you," she said, "that Flora Lewis saw what she wanted to see. Or maybe didn't see it at all."

Monk turned to her. "You mean used me to rid her of these two black crackheads **and** their boom box, sort of scoop up the garbage?"

"Something like that."

Monk smiled faintly. "Something like that is why we went back to see her."

They drove back to the Bayview in the morning. Crack dealers stay up at night and sleep in late—they didn't want the Price brothers to see them and then torch Flora Lewis's house with her still in it.

Their questions started simply, parsing her story

into microscopic details: the time she first saw Payton and Rennell on the day Thuy Sen vanished; where precisely she was standing; whether she was wearing her glasses; how long it was until the Asian child appeared; how much longer it took for the girl to disappear inside. Then, what the brothers were wearing—a red windbreaker and blue jeans for Payton, she said, a black hooded sweatshirt and maybe matching sweatpants for Rennell. Now and then, Monk or Ainsworth would repeat a question to see if her answers were the same. At length, Ainsworth placed six mug shots on the coffee table in front of her.

"Recognize any of them?" he asked.

"Of course," she answered with asperity and jabbed a palsied finger at two photographs. "This one's Payton. **This** is Rennell—the one that grabbed that child off the street."

"Can you tell me again what she was wearing?"

"Of course—plaid skirt and a dark green sweater."

"Is it possible," Monk asked carefully, "that you remember her clothes from the description on TV?"

Lewis plucked at a pleat of her flowered dress in a gesture of irritation. "I **saw** her. What I least remember, Inspector, is the description on TV. I was too shocked."

"We have to be thorough. I'm sure you understand the importance of that."

The tacit reminder that this was a homicide investigation which could become a murder trial seemed to give Lewis pause. When Monk placed Thuy Sen's school photograph beside the two black faces, she studied it with quiet sobriety.

"Is this the girl you saw?"

Lewis bit her lip. "You know, I just can't be sure. I **think** so. But I don't remember ever seeing her pass by before—or any Asian girl. From here to the sidewalk it's hard to pick up features."

"But you recognized Rennell and Payton."

"Because they were facing me, and I've seen them all their lives. They live there, after all."

"But you say other young men come there, too."

"That's true."

"Could one or both of the men you saw with the Asian girl have been one of **them**—a visitor—instead of Payton or Rennell?"

In the dim light of her standing lamp, Lewis's mouth pursed, and then she shook her head decisively. "No. I can even tell you how Rennell Price walked toward that little girl, with the kind of lumbering menace he always has. Like he enjoys what his presence does to people."

Monk pondered whether to raise the matter of race, then chose a more neutral question. "The other young men that visited the brothers—can you identify any of them?"

Lewis stared into some middle distance, considering the question. "I don't **know** them, or even know their names. Maybe one—the tall one with the light blue, beat-up Cadillac. Seems like he's always parked out there when there's any space to park."

"Ever see this man up close?"

"No. Just through the window."

"Think you'd recognize his picture?"

Lewis's eyes narrowed in thought. "Without seeing it, I don't know."

"But you didn't see his car that day."

"Not that day, no." Lewis paused, then added with emphatic distaste, "All I saw was those two brothers."

Watching her, Monk decided to change course. "Do you remember the last time, Miss Lewis, you spoke with either Payton or Rennell?"

Lewis's shoulders twitched. "A long time ago."

"Years?"

"Several years. Ever since I saw what they'd become."

"Was there a particular incident?" Ainsworth asked.

Lewis hesitated. Then she said, "Payton called me a vulgarity."

"Recall the nature of it?"

She folded her arms. "I was carrying a bag of groceries. The bottom dropped out, and a melon burst all over the sidewalk." Her voice filled with indignation. "Payton and Rennell were sitting on the porch. But neither lifted a finger to help. Instead, Payton laughed and said, 'Serves that nosy old bitch right.' "

"How old would you say Payton was?" Monk inquired.

"Thirteen, fourteen."

"So that was eight or more years ago. When was the last time you saw one of the brothers up close?"

"I don't know, Inspector—I cross the street to avoid them, and keep my eyes straight ahead." Her tone became quiet. "Like I saw that little Asian girl do."

"So it's been years since you looked Rennell or Payton in the face."

"Maybe **that's** been years. But I see them most afternoons across the street, preparing to do their filthy business."

"What business would that be?"

"Selling drugs, Inspector. Turning other boys into **them.**"

Monk considered this. "While all that's going on, what's their grandmother doing?"

"Mrs. Price? I barely see her anymore, except looking out on the street from the second-story window." Lewis's tone assumed a measured compassion. "She always seemed like a decent, churchgoing woman. I still see her walking to church on Sundays, sometimes with a flower pinned to her dress.

"Years ago, maybe we'd stop and talk. But now I think she just stays locked up on the second floor of the house, hiding from those boys and their lowlife friends. Sometimes I wonder how their music sounds to **her.**"

Monk was silent. The sense of kinship which he heard seemed to make Flora Lewis pensive. "I suppose," she reflected, "that those brothers have turned us both into recluses. Eula Price only goes to church, and I only go to the corner store. So we don't speak anymore."

"Do you have any black friends, Miss Lewis?"

"I don't have **any** friends, now. The ones I had are dead or gone."

"Did they include black folks?"

"To talk to."

"To invite to your house?"

Lewis looked him in the eyes. "No. Does that make me a racist?"

"What you are for sure, ma'am, is a witness. What about friends or acquaintances who are Asian—at any time."

"At **all** times," Lewis said flatly, "I'm civil. Have been my entire life, to anyone who deserves it. But I can't say that I've had Asian friends."

"Just how long have you lived here, Miss Lewis?"

"I was **born** here. If you're curious, that adds up to seventy-two years. Thirty-three with my parents, thirty-nine alone, twelve since I retired from teaching school."

She had lived here by herself, Monk calculated, since World War II, the time that Bayview had begun to change. "How does this neighborhood seem to you now?"

Lewis sat erect. "Like a nightmare," she said harshly. "Except that I don't wake up." Abruptly, her voice trembled, and a film of tears glistened in her eyes. "My parents left me this house out of love, to be my safety and security. Now I can't escape it."

Monk drew a breath. "I'm sorry, ma'am."

Lewis paused to compose herself. "Don't be. Just

believe the truth of what I've told you." Once more, she laid her finger on the mug shot of Rennell Price. "This one's Rennell, the one who pulled the Asian girl off the street. The other one, Payton, closed the door behind her. Lord knows what they did to her."

Monk and Ainsworth stopped for coffee at a dingy soul food restaurant on Third Street. No one else was there.

Ainsworth took a sip of coffee. "So?"

"So I'm pretty damned sure **she's** sure of everything she thinks she saw. I'm also pretty sure Thuy Sen died inside that house."

"Me, too. Why not get a warrant?"

Monk shook his head. "Let's poke around a little—whatever we'd find at Grandma's house is likely to still be there in a day or two. I keep wondering about how Thuy Sen got from the house to the bay. Sure as hell didn't walk there, and the brothers don't own a car."

Ainsworth propped his chin on folded hands. "Wouldn't be smart to swipe a car for **that,** would it."

"A tall guy in a light blue Cadillac," Larry Minnehan repeated. "That would be my man Eddie Fleet."

He turned to the bulletin board and pointed out a mug shot, glancing at the notation beside it. "You're in luck, guys—no overnight change in status. Eddie's still not dead."

Monk studied the photograph—close-cropped hair, flat features, full mouth with one corner twisted in disdain. Even from a head shot Monk could guess that Fleet was tall and rangy. "Tell me about this guy."

"A real waste of talent—before crack got to him he was a playground hoops legend. But you know the story—all innates, no character." Squinting, Minnehan called upon his memory. "I'm remembering girlfriend violence, a concealed weapons charge, a couple of assaults, a dope-dealing rap that got kicked for illegal search and seizure. Typical lowlife résumé."

"What's he got to do with the Prices?"

"He's Payton's jack-of-all-trades, majordomo, and chauffeur. God help us if the State of California took away this asshole's car, 'cause then he couldn't drive Payton where he needed to go. **Then** where would the Bayview be." Minnehan cocked his head. "You thinking Eddie might fit in this somewhere?"

"He'd give us someone else to play with." Monk thought for a moment, then asked Minnehan, "Rennell have any girlfriends you know of?"

On the way back to the Hall of Justice, Ainsworth pondered this. "You think Payton's covering for his pedophile brother?"

"Too fancy a concept for him to get his mind around," Monk answered. "But it's funny Minnehan never saw Rennell with any women. I'd have given odds he'd be a daddy by now." He turned their car down Bryant Street. "It would make more sense if Rennell wound up alone with her. That's how these creeps like it."

"What's in it for Payton?"

"**He's** no respecter of women, either. Maybe Rennell wants what he wants, and Payton just wants his muscle happy. What's Thuy Sen to either one of them?"

The toxicology report was waiting on Monk's desk. He passed the report to Ainsworth. Thuy Sen had died clean—no crack cocaine in her system. Though this was only what Monk expected, he had learned that you could never be too jaded. In the Bayview, girls scarcely older than Thuy Sen traded oral sex for crack.

Putting down the report, Ainsworth asked, "What goes next—warrant, or Fleet?"

"I keep thinking about that Cadillac," Monk answered.

"Eddie Fleet," Terri said now. "Anyone's dream witness. No wonder you went looking for him."

Monk regarded her impassively. "That's what we get in our business—scumbags who know about other scumbags. You were expecting Kofi Annan?"

SEVEN

LARRY MINNEHAN AND HIS PARTNER, JACK BRESLIN, drove Monk and Ainsworth out to look for Eddie Fleet.

Their unmarked car entered Double Rock, a public housing project so lawless that cops who went there feared being shot. "Came out here last week," Minnehan said, "to pick up a guy for a probation violation. Walked into his kitchen and the fucker jumps out from behind the refrigerator and tries to shoot me in the face."

"What happened?" Ainsworth asked.

Behind the wheel, Minnehan kept tautly watching the street as he drove. "Pretty much blew his kneecap away. He's off the street for a while."

Not that it much mattered, Monk thought. The dingy stucco buildings spewed an endless supply of young men warped by Double Rock into dead-enders before they could make the choices they never believed they had. The place they lived in looked like a training ground for prison: even the graffiti-scarred buildings, some with windows boarded up, had addresses—like

F-7: 1840–1860—which reminded Monk of a prisoner's ID number. As they passed one parking lot, a gangly teenage boy, urinating on someone else's car, called out to Minnehan, "Don't give me a ticket for pissing, man."

Minnehan, laughing, gave him a jocular version of a papal blessing. "That's Lance," Minnehan explained. "He's a Crip, and stupid as a rock. Whoever owns that car will probably do him for us." Breslin kept his eyes on the street.

A block later the car slowed to a stop beside a gray-bearded man in a Yankees cap cooking burgers on a grill. Breslin rolled down the window. "Hey, Globetrotter."

The man glanced warily at the two strangers in the back of the car. "Hey, man. What's happening?"

"Nothin' much. Just looking for Eddie Fleet."

"Eddie? Haven't seen that boy for a while. Heard he took a job being President of Microsoft."

A corner of Breslin's mouth turned up, though his eyes didn't change. "If he gets sick of it, Trotter, and comes back here, you might mention dropping by our office. We've got an opportunity for him."

The man nodded. It would not take long, Monk knew, for word on the street to spread.

"Fucking waste," Breslin said as the car pulled away. "Man used to play for the Globetrotters before the white powder got him. Now all he can afford is crack." They kept on driving, eyes combing the sidewalk idlers for the guy who looked back at them a little too long, or avoided looking at all, or maybe just started walking faster—the small signs of psychic disruption at the otherwise routine appearance of an un-marked car.

Two blocks later it happened. From the backseat, between the broad shoulders of the two cops, Monk saw a tall man slide from inside an old blue Cadillac and swiftly head for the door of an apartment in a one-story complex. "Step on it," Breslin said.

Minnehan did, snapping Monk and Ainsworth against their seat. Tires squealing, they pulled up in front of the complex; Breslin leapt out of the car before it stopped and covered the twenty feet to the door before the man could get inside. By the time the three others came up behind him, Breslin had his quarry by the scruff of his sweatshirt and was pressing his face against the door. "Give me trouble, Eddie, and I'm gonna be truly pissed."

Fleet said nothing. Jerking him three steps to the sidewalk, Breslin held Fleet upright while Minnehan searched him. In the bright afternoon sunlight, three women and a small boy walked by with their eyes straight ahead, their silence the only sign they had even noticed a black man being frisked by two white cops.

This gave Monk time to look Fleet over. He was perhaps six foot five, with close-cropped hair, cleft chin, and a broad face whose most remarkable features were a nose which appeared to have been flattened—perhaps by a flying elbow in a Darwinian game of playground hoops—and large brown eyes, which just before they assumed an unusually persuasive look of otherworldly detachment had raked Monk's face with a swift, keen glance. Monk had never seen Eddie Fleet before, but he understood at that moment that Fleet knew who he was—Monk's reputation on the street, held with a mixture of awe, fear, and respect, was that of a man who could be trusted but never crossed. By the time this piece of street theater was over, word would begin spreading in the Bayview that he had picked up Eddie Fleet.

"You keep Eddie company," Minnehan directed Breslin. He climbed up the stairs, Monk and Ainsworth following, to knock on the door Fleet had tried to enter.

It took several more knocks until a young woman answered, clutching the front of her white robe. She was in her early twenties, Monk guessed, with one eye swollen half shut in her scared, pretty face. It was Eddie Fleet's notion of foreplay, Monk supposed.

"Mind if we come in," Minnehan said. Though it was phrased like a question, the woman knew that it was not one: she lived in public housing, and any problem with the law could get her thrown out. In her world Larry Minnehan had more power than the President.

Her name was Betty Sims, and she turned out to be no housekeeper. She backed away from them into a cramped three-room apartment with sheets strewn across the couch and floor, CDs scattered all over a small kitchen table, and what looked like a couple of days' of dirty dishes in the sink. The chicken cooking on the stove seemed to Monk a sad gesture toward domesticity, as did the incongruous Chinese painting above the couch. The woman's one unblemished eye as she watched them was frightened and sad and deeply resigned, and Monk could feel her shame and helplessness at being exposed to the judgment of strangers.

Minnehan left to search her bedroom. With a nod to Betty Sims, Monk followed.

Her bureau was covered with cosmetics and empty beer bottles. Minnehan yanked open the top drawer, revealing a treasure trove of frilly bras and panties with the sales tags still on them.

"Girl's an underwear klepto," he observed.

Ainsworth was studying a framed picture on the bureau: next to the carousel in Golden Gate Park a slight woman stood beside a fleshy, smiling man. "Demetrius George," Ainsworth said. "Last time I looked, he was a suspect in a gang murder."

"Still is," Minnehan said. "Let's ask Betty."

Betty Sims sat on the couch now, shoulders slumped, knees pressed together beneath her half-open robe. Minnehan held the picture out to her; his other hand, Monk saw, held a wad of tinfoil plucked off the top of the bureau.

Betty's gaze flickered from the photo to the wad of foil. "Who's the lucky girl with Demetrius?" Minnehan asked.

Betty glanced back at the picture. "My cousin, Cordelia. Cordelia White."

"What's her address?"

Betty told him. "Know where we can find Demetrius?" Minnehan asked her politely.

She shook her head. "Maybe Cordelia does."

Without asking anything more, Minnehan took out his cell phone and directed someone at the station to visit Cordelia White. Then he opened up the tinfoil and showed Betty Sims two rocks of crack cocaine— maybe forty bucks' worth, Monk thought. Enough to get her tossed out in the street.

"Who this belong to, Betty?"

She looked away, silent. Minnehan appraised her swollen eye. In a gentle tone, he asked, "Eddie do that to you?"

She hesitated, then shook her head, no longer looking at Minnehan. Still speaking quietly, Minnehan said, "If you can, Betty, stay away from him. Guys like Eddie don't get better."

The words were followed by silence. In an affectless tone, she asked. "Am I going to be in trouble?"

Minnehan studied her with a look akin to resignation. "The crack?" he answered. "No. That's Eddie's now."

They left her sitting on the couch. Closing the door behind him, Minnehan murmured, "Demetrius and Cordelia. Almost sounds like Shakespeare."

Monk and Ainsworth put Eddie Fleet in the same room they had used to question Payton Price.

He sat staring at the wall, eyes as blank as poker chips. The bulky gray sweatshirt he wore, far too thick for such a day, was meant, Monk supposed, to create the illusion of a body mass to go with the attitude.

"Minnehan took your last two rocks," Ainsworth said. "I don't think he likes you beating up on Betty. I don't think he likes you, period."

The tacit threat induced only silence. Monk placed the photo of Thuy Sen between them. "Ever seen this girl, Eddie?"

Seconds passed before Fleet looked down. Then he gave an almost indiscernible shake of the head.

"Was that a no?" Ainsworth asked skeptically.

This time Fleet shrugged. "I never seen her."

" 'Cause my friend Inspector Monk has. He saw her floating in the bay."

Fleet neither moved nor spoke. "The thing about a body," Monk told him conversationally, "is it just lies there. Most uncooperative kind of person you'll ever know.

"Now it's one thing, Eddie, to murder somebody in **his** house—you just leave him there. But killing someone at your own house is a whole different deal. As long as the body stays there, it's incriminating.

"So you got to move it. That's how this poor child wound up in water way too cold to swim in."

How long, Monk wondered, could Fleet go without seeming to breathe? "The whole problem," Monk continued, "comes down to transportation. How do you get little Thuy Sen where she won't take herself? You drive her." Monk softened his voice. "Unless you don't own a car.

"Don't own a car, Eddie, then you've got to borrow one."

With this, Monk fell silent. Moments passed before Fleet slowly raised his eyes. With a touch of melancholy, Monk said, "You got anything to tell me, son?"

Fleet stared back at him. This time the frozen look of his eyes struck Monk as more than attitude.

In the silence, Monk reached into his wallet and pulled out a card, laying it beneath Thuy Sen's picture. "Time may come you need to talk. If it does, I can do more for you than any lawyer can. But it's way better to seek me out before somebody else does."

For another long moment, Fleet gazed down at the card. Then he reached out and slipped it into the front pocket of his sweatshirt, the reluctant, surreptitious movement of a man whose head doesn't know what his hand is doing.

Abruptly, Monk informed him, "That's it, Eddie. Inspector Ainsworth will call a car to take you home."

The last thing Fleet wanted, Monk knew, was to be dropped off in the Bayview by a squad car. But he seemed to have lost the gift of speech.

Ainsworth left. Glancing at his watch, Monk gave himself five minutes with a man who would no longer look at him at all. Then he stood and said comfortably, "Let's see if your ride's here."

Ainsworth was waiting outside. Together, they walked Fleet out the door and down the dim, tiled hallway to the elevator.

As they approached, one of the elevator doors rumbled open. Breslin and Minnehan stepped out. Between them were the Price brothers.

For an instant, Payton looked startled, then managed a subdued "Hey, man."

Fleet nodded as they passed, his brief glance meeting Payton's. But when Payton looked away, Rennell still stared at Eddie Fleet, eyes wide with surprise in his sullen face.

EIGHT

"LIKE PULLING THE WINGS OFF FLIES," TERRI OBSERVED in a clinical tone. But beneath this she felt a chill: at this point in Monk's narrative, Rennell Price's fate had already begun to feel inexorable. "You were pretty sure the brothers killed her, then."

Though Monk eyed the Italian delicatessen across the street with seeming idleness, his voice turned cool. "You mean, did I commit myself to their being guilty, then look for the evidence to match?"

"Something like that."

" 'Fraid not. All I was convinced of then was that they were scared of Eddie Fleet."

"Both of them?" Terri asked quietly. "Or just Rennell?"

Monk pondered this. "I didn't see the difference," he answered with a shrug. "Turns out they both had reason."

Monk and Ainsworth put the brothers in separate rooms, then worked on each in turn.

The questioning was taut now. Payton had nothing more to say; clearly fearful, Rennell kept repeating, "I didn't do that little girl." But each pause between denials seemed longer.

None of this mattered. All that mattered at the moment was happening before the nearest convenient judge. So when Monk offered the brothers a ride home, it was with an incongruous amiability.

They sat in the backseat, silent. "By the way," Monk said over his shoulder, "we just got a warrant to search your grandma's house. Hope she doesn't mind—it's the best way of checking out your story."

In the rearview mirror, he could see Rennell turn to glance at Payton, who kept staring at the back of Monk's head. As they stopped at a traffic light on Third Street in the borrowed squad car, some gangbangers on the corner gazed at Monk and the two brothers. By the time they reached Eula Price's house, the forensics team was already there—the neighborhood, Monk figured, would soon be humming with tension.

"We'll be talking with your grandmother," he told the brothers. "We'll get some other folks to hang around with you."

Monk seated Eula Price on the porch between Ainsworth and himself.

Worriedly, she turned her head from one cop to the other. She was a large woman with venous legs: though judging by her face she could not be much past sixty, her body seemed a burden on her heart. Her other burden in life, Monk perceived, was the brothers. She was clearly respectful of police, and he guessed that his visit tapped into some nameless but pervasive dread about what the boys would come to.

The sight of Thuy Sen's picture seemed to convert the dread to fear. "Ever seen this girl?" Ainsworth asked.

"Only on TV." She paused, then added softly, "That poor child."

"But you never saw her here?"

Eula Price's throat worked. "No."

"Where do you sleep?" Monk inquired.

Slowly, she turned to face him. "Upstairs."

"And the boys?"

"They sleep downstairs."

"Do you eat together?"

"We used to. Then they started keeping different hours." She hesitated, and Monk could hear the sadness in her voice. "I got the bedroom set up to cook my own meals."

Monk recalled Flora Lewis's image of this woman gazing out her second-story window. "When did the boys come to live with you?" he asked.

"When Payton was eleven," she answered quietly. "Rennell was only nine. But they both were trying so hard to be little men."

To Monk, her last phrase bespoke a long-ago tragedy. "How was it that they came to live with you?"

"Athalie, my daughter-in-law—she stabbed my son Vernon with a knife." She began gazing out at the street, at nothing. "They put her in an institution. Been there now for eleven years."

Monk could think of no response. "When did you move upstairs?" he finally asked.

Her eyes shut. "Four years back."

"Why was that, ma'am?"

"The boys got bigger."

Monk waited for a moment. Almost gently, he asked, "Do you know how they earn a living?"

She folded her hands in front of her. "Odd jobs, they tell me."

"Not selling crack cocaine?"

Eula Price was quiet and then turned to him, tears welling in her eyes. "My health just ran down," she said wearily. "Every day, I pray to the Lord to lead my boys down a righteous path. I tried so hard, and now I pray so hard . . ."

Her voice trailed off. In the silence, Monk heard other voices—the crime lab team, going through the first floor of what once had been her home.

After Monk watched her retreat upstairs, each step slow and painful to watch, he sought out the head of the three-man crime lab team.

"What you got?" he asked.

The man, small and lean and precise, adjusted his glasses as he took his mental inventory. "Some stuff just for the finding," he answered. "The makings for crack cocaine, some remnants in the sink. Condoms—good for crack whores." The man handed Monk two magazines. "Plus pornography for inspiration."

Monk riffled their pages. They were less than he had hoped for—long on sadism and aggression but devoid of photographs that might suggest a taste for children.

"What else?"

"Some clothes that more or less match your eyewitnesses' descriptions, though they're kind of generic. We think this room may be more interesting."

Monk paused to look around the living room—the green walls were dingy, the carpet and couch were worn and stained, and the sooty fireplace, which did not look like anyone used it now, was filled with empty beer and soft drink cans. The sole, incongruous remnants of what Monk supposed was Eula Price's more gracious household were the painting of a beatific, pale Jesus and a lacquered coffee table, which retained a dull sheen beneath its mars and nicks.

It also retained, Monk saw at once, fingerprints—on his hands and knees, a technician studied the dust he had scattered with a laser light. Nearby a plump female technician had put down her ultraviolet lamp and begun slicing out a rectangle of carpet.

"She found what looks like fresh semen stains," the crime lab guy told Monk.

"Semen mixed with saliva," Terri amended now. "I read the crime lab report. But without DNA technology, the most it proved is that someone had oral sex with someone else. There was nothing to link the semen to Rennell, or to Thuy Sen's strangulation." But Terri was not as impervious as she tried to seem—once more, she imagined her own daughter, and then, too vividly, the painful image merged with what had happened to Thuy Sen. And she had read the whole damning report.

Monk completed its narrative for her. "Black hairs consistent with Asian ethnicity. A green fiber which matched Thuy Sen's sweater. A partial of her fingerprint on one corner of the coffee table. All we had left to prove was that she'd died there."

"So you went back to Eddie Fleet."

Monk's laugh was short and unamused. "He angled his way back to us," he said with weary disdain. "Human nature."

NINE

Monk and Ainsworth sat side by side in an inter-rogation room, a tape recorder between them and Ed-die Fleet.

"So why'd you call me?" Monk demanded curtly.

Fleet mustered a smile which combined nervous-ness with bravado, displaying a row of gold teeth—a status symbol behind which, Monk supposed, the enamel was rotting away. The smile faded in the face of Monk's impassive stare. "Had somethin' to run by you," Fleet ventured at last. "Call it a hy-po-thetical."

Monk was not certain whether the satiric twist given the last word was intended to obscure Fleet's dif-ficulty in enunciation. But it did not conceal his fear, or the guile which had driven him here.

"Spit it out."

Fleet fidgeted, trying out the smile again. "Not that it happened this way, understand. I'm just wanting to hear what you might think."

Monk said nothing. Silent, Fleet watched the tape keep spinning.

"Can you turn that damned thing off?" he asked.

Monk did. "So?"

Fleet glanced at Ainsworth, then tried to look Monk in the eyes. "S'pose somebody asked to borrow my car the day that girl disappeared."

"Somebody?"

A trapped, furtive look crept into Fleet's eyes. "This can't get out, man. You can't tell no one."

Still Monk stared at him. "I can't tell 'no one' about something that 'somebody' asked you that maybe never happened. You call so I can watch you tap-dance?"

Fleet looked away. Finally, he said, "What if I said it maybe was Rennell."

"Maybe? I'd say we need a warrant for your car. You just went and gave us probable cause."

Fleet's ancient blue Cadillac Eldorado smelled like sweat and cigarettes and pot. Payton's prints were on the passenger-side dashboard, Rennell's on the handle of the right rear door.

The rough gray carpet in the trunk compartment was spiky and matted. Caught in its fibers was a strand of green wool; the portion cut out by the crime lab yielded a mixture of semen and saliva. There were also traces of urine—as Monk well knew, corpses often leak.

They picked up Fleet and the brothers again, sepa-rately, then stuck them in three rooms. Monk's message to each was simple: whoever talks first does best. But Payton was stone silent, and Rennell kept repeating in a monotone what Monk now thought of less as a mantra than as a life raft—"I didn't do that little girl."

In the fourth hour of questioning, Monk came back to Eddie Fleet with the same relentless patience. "We know she was in your trunk, Eddie. We know that she was dead. Sooner or later someone's gonna tell me how she got that way. When he does, this thing is over."

Fleet hunched in the chair with folded arms. "Was she dead when you first saw her," Monk inquired, "or were you part of how she died?"

Fleet's lips parted, as if to speak. Then his jaw clamped tight again.

"Don't know about my friend here," Rollie Ainsworth said in a tone of deep sincerity. "But in my heart and soul I don't believe you killed Thuy Sen. Maybe I'm wrong, but you don't seem like the type to me." His voice hardened. "The thing we know for sure is that you had a part in it."

The room felt hot and close now: the first sheen of sweat began appearing on Fleet's forehead. Monk and Ainsworth contented themselves with watching.

At length Monk asked, "You know about accessories?"

Fleet did not answer. Only his body, tense with anticipation, betrayed him.

"I'm not talking about do-rags, Eddie."

Slowly Fleet looked up at him. "I'm talking about murder," Monk continued softly. "So let's see if you can follow what I'm telling you.

"With murder there's only three types of accessories. First there's accessories before the fact. They're the worst ones—they know a murder's gonna happen, and don't do anything about it. Maybe they even help things along.

"Then there's accessories **during** the fact. Want to guess who they are?"

Fleet barely seemed to breathe. "I'll tell you then," Monk said in a conversational tone. "They're present when the murder happens, and still don't lift a finger to stop it. You with me so far?"

Still Fleet was silent. "You're with me," Monk said. "You're a real smart young man, and I just know you're with me. So you know damned well if you're one of the first two kinds.

"Course maybe that's why you're so quiet. If I were an accessory before or during, I'd have a whole lot to think about."

A trickle of sweat made Fleet's left eyelid flutter. He was too proud or scared to wipe it. "Want to hear the rest?" Monk inquired.

Almost imperceptibly, Fleet nodded. "Okay," Monk said. "Last one's an accessory after the fact. That's where the victim's already dead, and you help cover up. Maybe like getting rid of the body.

"That's the least culpable kind of accessory." Sitting

back, Monk gave him a slow, appraising stare. "Don't know where you fit in, Eddie. But all three of us know there's a slot for you. Sooner or later we're going to decide which one you are."

In the silence, Fleet's light brown face glistened beneath the fluorescent lights.

"Thirsty?" Ainsworth asked.

After a moment, Fleet nodded again. Companionably, Ainsworth said, "I'll get us all a Coke." He left Monk staring at Fleet.

With mild interest, Monk wondered if Fleet would meet his eyes. For a moment Fleet seemed ready to try, then looked down again.

Ainsworth came through the door, which was still ajar, clutching three cans of Coke.

Monk accepted one, then placed the second can in front of Eddie Fleet. Ainsworth took a swallow of his and leaned against the wall. Still quiet, Fleet studied the cool red cylinder, beading with its own sweat as he watched.

"Maybe," Ainsworth suggested, "we should leave you with your thoughts. Maybe you'll figure things out before Rennell or Payton does."

Monk stood abruptly. Before Fleet could form an answer, they closed the door behind them.

In another interrogation room, feet propped on the table, Monk and Ainsworth drank their

Cokes while they observed Eddie Fleet on a video monitor.

Fleet was slumped forward, face in his hands. The inspectors kept watching with the casual interest of anthropologists studying an all-too-familiar species. "Sort of sluggish," Ainsworth remarked. "Quiet, too. Not like Ralphie Menendez."

Monk emitted a laugh. Left alone after absorbing Monk's dissertation on the degrees of murder, Menendez had muttered on videotape, "Goddam, fifteen fucking years"—repeating the minimum sentence for murder in the second degree.

"Ralphie," Monk said nostalgically. "Hardly left us anything to ask."

"At least he was entertaining. I'm getting fed up with these three." Ainsworth turned from the monitor. "So which one we go back to?"

"Fleet." Monk nodded toward the video cam. "Look at him."

On the monitor, Fleet's hands were cupped over his mouth, as though he were about to vomit.

"You ready to help us out?" Monk asked.

Eyes averted, Fleet nodded.

"No rehearsals," Monk said curtly, switching on the tape recorder.

For a time, Eddie watched it spin. Then he gathered his thoughts and began to speak. Listening,

Monk had to give him this much—Eddie Fleet could tell a story so vividly that Monk could see it happening.

The knock on Eddie's door had sounded heavy, urgent.

Eddie was alone. One eye shut, he peered out through the keyhole. In the night outside stood a massive form which could only be Rennell.

Eddie cracked open the door. "What is it, bro'?"

"We got need for your car."

Somehow Eddie knew that "car" included him. Beneath Rennell's accustomed monotone he heard an urgency close to panic, and the big man's feet shifted from side to side. In Rennell this passed for jitters, Eddie thought—he must be high on crack.

Eddie fished his car keys from the drawer where he kept his Saturday night special, taking the gun as well.

In the six-block ride to the brothers' house, Rennell said only, "This is trouble, man."

He would not say more. But whatever Eddie had imagined was erased from his memory once Payton, eyes bright with crack and panic, yanked him inside.

Lying on the floor was a small Asian girl with spittle coming from her open mouth. It took a few seconds for Eddie to absorb that she was dead.

"What the fuck...?" he whispered.

Payton backed one step away. From behind him, Rennell said dully, "Choked on come."

"Whose come?"

When no one answered, Eddie felt himself begin to shake. "You make her do this? That's a kid, man."

A spark of anger flashed in Payton's eyes. "No time for this shit," he snapped. "We got to get rid of her."

Fleet stared down at the girl as though he'd been asked to pick up a dead rat. "No way, man. Not me."

Payton's fevered eyes shot a peremptory glance at Rennell. From behind him, Fleet felt the big man pin his arms back in a hammerlock. He cried out, Payton's half-crazed face two inches from his.

"Shut up," Payton hissed. "You trying to wake up Grandma?"

They forced Eddie to pick up the child by her hands.

Her fingers were stiff and cold. Drool kept dribbling from her mouth, like she couldn't keep the come down. Eddie felt the bile rising in his throat.

Payton took her feet; Rennell cracked open the front door. Jittery and silent, they edged out the door in the cool night air.

No cars.

They dumped her on the sidewalk while Eddie

fumbled for the trunk key. When they dropped her inside the trunk, he smelled the pee.

Payton told him to drive down the hill to India Basin, pull into Shoreline Park.

Payton sat beside him, Rennell in back. When they entered the darkened park, Payton signaled Eddie to stop.

They looked around. To the left rose the stacks of a massive power plant; another car was parked close to the water. Through the windshield, Eddie saw a small orange cylinder inside, the glow of what was probably a joint passing from hand to hand.

"Not here," Payton said tightly.

For a moment, he started chattering about the warehouse district of Potrero Hill. Then Eddie reminded him of the homeless who camped out there.

All at once, it seemed, Payton remembered the tallow plant.

They turned down an unmarked road past the shadowy forms of warehouses. Through the driver's-side window, cracked open to help him keep from vomiting, Eddie caught the stench of burning fat and animal remnants. No one else would be here.

Silent, Eddie clamped his jaw against his own fear and nausea.

On the spit of land where the road ended was a construction site, sand and gravel sitting in piles like burial mounds. To the left was a channel of brackish water. The wreck of an old barge was grounded there, next to a neglected wooden pier, which stuck from weeds and sand into the water. Across the channel was an outpost of the Port of San Francisco, the black skeletons of loading cranes towering above. Eddie heard no sounds at all.

"Get her out," Payton directed.

Eddie sat there like he was paralyzed. Only when Payton opened the car door and barked something more did Eddie force himself into the chill, toxic air.

Curtly, Payton nodded toward the trunk. He seemed to have come down off his high.

With renewed dread, Eddie opened the trunk.

The child was still curled stiffly, her posture frozen. "**You** do it," Payton told his brother.

To Eddie, the order carried the edge of reproof. In silence, Rennell lifted the dead child.

Payton angled his head toward the channel. "Out there."

Rennell started toward the water's edge. Following, Eddie thought his lumbering shape resembled that of a monster in a horror film. Their feet crunched stunted shrubbery.

They reached the sand at the edge of the channel. "Dump her in the water," Payton said.

Corpse cradled in his arms, Rennell walked to the pier, testing it with his weight.

The beams creaked. Shaking his head, Rennell backed off.

"In the water," Payton repeated. "We want her away from here."

Like an automaton, Rennell stepped out into the channel.

Right away, Eddie saw that its current was swift— Rennell staggered sideways, clutching at the nearest piling, the girl's body tucked beneath one massive arm. He righted himself, then began edging farther out, to where the ruined wood tumbled into the water.

Almost gently, he laid the body on the surface of the channel.

At once the current began sweeping her away. The last Eddie saw of Thuy Sen was strands of long black hair, swirling away in dark, moonlit water.

Surprising tears sprung to his eyes. "Let's get high," he heard Payton say.

"He was shook up," Fleet finished now. "Don't think he meant to do it. Don't even know if he **did** do it." He puffed his cheeks and exhaled. "Whatever, you got to feel sorry for her."

You're a real humanitarian, Monk thought. In his flattest voice, he asked, "The brothers like doing nine-year-olds?"

Fleet moved his shoulders. "They were high, man—do crazy things when you're high."

"That all you know?" Ainsworth asked.

Fleet turned to him. "It is," he said fervently. "I swear it."

"So you wouldn't mind taking a lie detector."

Fleet faced Monk again. "**You** want me to?" he asked.

Not really, Monk thought—they didn't need a murky polygraph. With a shrug, he said, "Up to you, Eddie."

Fleet seemed to consider this. "Yeah," he said finally, "I guess it's okay."

You just passed, Monk thought.

"Best to keep you around," he said. "You don't want to be out on the street."

The next thing Monk did was call the Coast Guard. Suppose, he asked, you dumped that nine-year-old girl at the foot of that tallow factory. Two days later might a floater end up on the rocks near Candlestick Park?

Sure, came the answer. That's how the current goes.

Monk put down the phone. "First Payton," he told Ainsworth. "Then Rennell."

T E N

"IT DOESN'T LOOK GOOD FOR YOU," MONK TOLD PAYton. "No good at all."

Hands clasped in front of him, Payton said nothing. His eyes drilled Monk's from a tight, staring mask.

"We're willing to hear your side of the story," Ainsworth interjected. "But we know Thuy Sen died in your house. My friend and I keep wondering if you're covering for your brother."

Payton's grip on himself was so taut that Monk could see the tendons in his forearms straining. "Whatever you do," Monk said, "is fine with me. You can take your chances, or you can tell us what happened."

Payton's stare still locked Monk's, and then he slowly drew a breath. "Man," he answered with weary defiance, "I don't have to tell you shit."

"We know she was there," Monk said sadly. "We know it, and you know it."

Rennell shifted in his chair. His demeanor, silent

and sullen and self-absorbed, reminded Monk of an adolescent being chastised for some minor offense.

"We found her fingerprints, Rennell. So tell me how they got there."

Rennell's gaze darted to a corner. Monk watched his fear grow like a living thing.

"She like your sound system?" Ainsworth asked.

Still Rennell did not answer. "Sometimes," Monk proposed, "like when you smoke crack, maybe things happen you didn't mean to happen. You think that's possible?"

Rennell's brow furrowed. "Sometimes," he responded to Monk's surprise.

"Is that what happened with Thuy Sen? Maybe 'cause you were smoking crack?"

Rennell stiffened, silent once again.

"Son," Monk said softly, "we know it was you who put her in the water."

Rennell looked up at him, mouth half open. "No way..."

"You carried her out," Monk continued. "Because the current was fast, and you were the strongest. And because your brother told you to."

Rennell's gaze broke. Eyes focused on the table, he shook his head with silent stubbornness.

"We know she was at your house," Monk said in a reproving tone, "and we know you dumped her body. It's time for you to say what happened in between."

Rennell was still now.

"I mean," Monk amended quietly, "what happened **before** you went to get Eddie Fleet."

The worry in Rennell's face was palpable. His gaze darted past Monk, as if searching the barren room for help.

"No one here but us, Rennell. No one but you can tell us why you did that with Thuy Sen. Not even Payton can tell us that."

Rennell shifted in his chair. At length he asked, "Payton, what he say?"

"Time for you to be a man, son. Time to tell us for yourself what happened."

Rennell crossed his arms, staring at the wall.

"You didn't want for her to die, did you?"

Still the big man did not respond. Then, slowly, he shook his head. "No."

Tense with anticipation, Monk prodded. "You just wanted her to make you feel good."

Rennell's eyes shut. In a dull monotone, he asked, "What Payton say?"

"Why does it matter?" Monk said coldly. "Was Payton the one who killed her?"

"No," Rennell answered with surprising swiftness. "No way."

"No," Monk agreed. "It was you. But you didn't mean for that to happen."

"No."

"I didn't think so," Monk said reassuringly. "You were holding her head down. When she started choking, you didn't know what to do."

Rennell bent forward. "I didn't do that little girl," he said with quiet vehemence. Then he just sat there, seeming gradually to detach himself, until Monk and Ainsworth left him alone.

"Did you begin to wonder," Terri asked sardonically, "if Rennell wasn't maybe a little slow?"

Over the rim of his second cup of espresso, Monk gave her a look of sour amusement. "How slow do you mean, counselor? So slow he couldn't remember what he'd done?" He put down the cup. "For sure Payton was what passed for the family brains. This boy wasn't swift, though mostly he was as scared as he had every right to be. But he knew what he'd done, and he sure as hell knew that 'doing that little girl' was a bad thing to admit to. Don't have to be Einstein to do murder."

"Let's pretend we're the defense," Lou Mauriani told Monk and Ainsworth. "Lay out what you've got."

It was their good fortune, Monk thought, that Mauriani was the Assistant D.A. tracking the case— gray-haired, round-faced, and congenitally affable, Mauriani had keen blue eyes and an equally keen sense of the absurd, coupled with lightning swiftness of thought and a deep seriousness about doing his work well. In twenty-seven murder prosecutions, Mauriani had never lost.

Monk set down his coffee mug on a corner of Mauriani's cluttered desk. "First, we've got Rennell pulling a girl dressed like Thuy Sen into the house, with Payton closing the door behind them—"

"By virtue," Mauriani interposed dryly, "of a cross-racial ID, from all the way across the street, by a scared old lady who hates them both. If I'm the defense, I'm thinking this pillar of Bayview's vibrant white community saw exactly what she wanted to."

"We went back to her," Monk responded without rancor. "She's as solid as anyone like that can be. The forensics bear her out."

"The fibers, hair, and fingerprints," Mauriani amended, "put Thuy Sen in the house. But only Flora Lewis makes her playmates Payton and Rennell."

Ainsworth nodded. "True. But we also found clothes which more or less match what she says they were wearing—"

"Uh-huh. Them, and every third guy in the neighborhood. So what happened inside the house between her and whichever two guys these were?"

"That's where they forced her to have oral sex," Monk answered. "We found semen and saliva."

"Whose semen? Whose saliva? Suppose Payton or Rennell says they've lost track of all the age-appropriate young women who've blown them in the living room. Saves on condoms, after all."

"Semen," Monk countered, "is what choked this girl to death. We've got Liz Shelton for that. And we know Thuy Sen was dead when she left the house."

Mauriani gave them a beatific smile. "Ah, yes, on

the word of the honorable Edward Fleet. I can't thank you guys enough for the chance to share **him** with twelve of our fellow citizens. Let's see—crack selling, gun peddling, and a social life spent slapping women silly. No wonder he couldn't wait to help us out."

Ainsworth flashed a grin. "You've put on worse, Lou. We've brought you most of them ourselves."

"And proud of it." Mauriani's smile faded. "You know the problem, Rollie. Fleet's a dirtball, and he admits to helping them dump the body. The only reason he's talking is so we can help him save his ass. If I'm the defense, I go after his credibility like hell won't have it—maybe imply **he's** the one who did her, and we're kicking him loose. There's no forensics that tells us whose 'weapon' killed her for sure."

"We know that," Monk said patiently. "But we've taken Eddie through this, over and over. From beginning to end, his story makes sense. They needed a car; Fleet had one. We found semen and saliva on the carpet; Fleet saw drool coming from her mouth. He says Payton forced him to help dump the body; forensics puts her in Fleet's trunk. Fleet says Rennell dumped her by the tallow plant; the body washed up where the Coast Guard says it should have. Logic and the evidence corroborate his story."

"What about its internal credibility. Any cracks?"

"Nope. Fleet doesn't try to say too much, or to be too helpful—like telling us who asphyxiated Thuy Sen. He didn't see it, he says, and no one told him."

"That's also the missing piece. No confession, or no witness to her death."

Monk fought back his annoyance. "You need us to go back at the brothers again?"

"No. We've got more than enough to take them to the Grand Jury." Amusement surfaced in Mauriani's clear blue eyes. "After that, they'll have **two** defense lawyers—one dedicated to Payton's interests, the other to Rennell's. We'll let them sort out this last piece by themselves. Maybe they'll even play Cain and Abel."

"So Mauriani indicted him," Terri said. "Then the media got hold of death by oral asphyxiation, and made sure everybody in the jury pool knew everything about it."

"No help for that, counselor."

"No help to Rennell, for sure. Both brothers became these scary black predators, kidnapping the daughter of Cambodian refugees and using her for sex." Terri leaned back in her chair, studying Monk's expression. "I was in law school, and it felt like I saw Thuy Sen's face every day for weeks. And theirs, staring out from the mug shots with no expression in their eyes. I was planning to be a defense lawyer, and I hated them anyway."

And that was before, she did not add, what happened to Elena.

"Yeah," Monk retorted with an edge in his voice. "Pretty rough on those boys, people learning what they'd done. Kind of like it was for Thuy Sen's parents."

This silenced Terri. For a while, they both sat there without speaking, Terri fighting back the images of what had seared Elena's soul.

"Early on," Monk ventured at last, "you wanted to do defense work. When I was young, I thought about that, too."

"I guess you got over it."

"Not over what made me consider it. Being a black man, I'd had occasion to ponder the fact that life wasn't fair. I pondered it in Vietnam, watching black men sent by white folks to kill Asians and sometimes dying instead, and I pondered it when I came home and saw too many of my friends drifting into trouble for lack of much else life offered them. I thought maybe I could defend them, get some a fairer shake." His voice remained soft. "Maybe you didn't know I came from the Bayview."

"No," Terri admitted. "I didn't. So what changed your mind?"

Monk's gaze grew distant and reflective. "More like I recalibrated my thinking. A cop can make the judgment on whether something is a case or not, try to make sense of it all. Whatever notion of justice he has, without the cop there'd **be** no case.

"The people I grew up with were struggling in their world, trying to survive. I thought maybe I could make that world a safer and fairer place—make the righteous cases, and let the rest go. Maybe even save a

few young men and women by steering them right."
Pausing, Monk shrugged, gazing back at Terri. "Like a
lot of notions, life complicated it some. The more I
lived it, the less sure I became of what justice really
was. You just do the best you can. Like you're doing
now, I guess."

"What I'm doing now," she answered, "is trying to
keep the State of California from killing someone else.
That includes figuring out how Rennell Price lost the
lottery." She gazed at Monk, curious. "That day with
Mauriani, did you think Rennell would end up being
sentenced to die?"

Monk gave her an ironic smile. "Not in San Francisco," he answered flatly. "That took some doing of its
own. Payton's work, mostly. Maybe with a little help
from the lawyer."

ELEVEN

IT WAS KIT'S BIRTHDAY.

Christopher Peralta Paget, officially age seven, sat at the head of the Pagets' candlelit dining table, his piece of chocolate angel food cake now reduced to rubble. To his left sat his parents, to his right his thirteen-year-old sister, Elena—dark and slight like Terri, with round, expressive eyes—and his brother, Carlo, Kit's hero. With an expression of deep well-being, Kit contemplated the cake sitting on its pedestal, the familiar faces in the candlelit glow.

"I love my birthday," he announced to his parents. "Thank you for creating me."

Briefly, Chris smiled at Terri. "No trouble," he informed his younger son. "Just another day at the salt mines."

As Kit looked from one face to the other, seven-year-old merriment crept into his eyes; without being sure why, Terri saw, Kit knew that the exchange was funny. Except, perhaps, to Elena, who rolled her eyes in disgust.

"I know," Terri said to her with gentle wryness. "Unthinkable." But, though she could not acknowledge it, Terri knew too well that this involved far more than teenage squeamishness. Terri had once done these embarrassing things with Elena's father, before she discovered the unspeakable things Ricardo Arias had forced on his own daughter. Some trace of that would stay with Elena forever, as everyone present knew but Kit. Once more, cringing inside, Terri imagined Thuy Sen with Rennell Price, her client.

With the grace that characterized him, Carlo draped his arm around Elena's shoulders as though nothing notable had happened. "It's like earthquakes," he advised her. "You just put it out of your mind."

Terri wished she could.

Afterward the two Paget men sat in the living room amidst the bright modern paintings, drinking coffee.

"Nice birthday party," Carlo said. "Kit's pretty funny."

"He is." Still pensive about Elena, Chris glanced up the stairs. "I should put him to bed pretty soon. It's getting to be story time."

This was Chris's nightly task: Kit was the only one of the children he had helped raise from the beginning, and he savored the rituals of parenting in a way a younger man might not.

"What are you reading him?" Carlo asked. "I still remember **James and the Giant Peach**."

"Not violent enough. His current favorite is **Greek**

Myths for Children. Incest, fratricide, and behead-
ings—in cartoon form, with funny captions."

"You're serious."

"Completely. Sorry you missed out on it."

Terri entered the room. "Kit's ready," she told her
husband with exaggerated weariness. "At last." Turning
to Carlo, she asked, "Did you hate having your hair
washed?"

"Always," he answered with a smile. "Still do."

Terri sat beside her husband. "Sorry to interrupt,"
she told him, "but there hasn't been time to ask Carlo
about Rennell's grandmother."

At once Carlo was somber. "Waiting for God to call
her home. She's not got much to show for her last two
decades on earth."

Surprised, Chris turned to his son. "She's still alive?"

"Barely," Carlo answered.

Eula Price was morbidly obese now, and plagued
with diabetes. She lay in her bed, a massive form beneath white sheets with, Carlo was certain, legs too
swollen to move. The gaunt, elderly friend in a straight
black wig who had ushered Carlo in retreated to the
tiny living room.

Eula lived in public housing in the Bayview: three
cramped rooms in a complex largely inhabited by welfare recipients and crack dealers, families which formed
and dissipated, seemingly at random. The remnant of
Eula Price's own family was three framed photographs

beside her bed—solemn school photos of Payton and Rennell, plus one of a thin woman with coal black eyes who grimaced for the camera, as if she were too crazy or too dull to know that she should smile.

"That's their mother," Eula explained after a few moments of small talk. "She's still in the psychiatric ward."

Not much to say to that, Carlo thought. "I guess you couldn't keep up the house by yourself."

Eula gazed at the ceiling. "Couldn't **keep** the house, period. Went to that lawyer, like everything else."

Carlo sat beside the bed. "How did you find him?"

"He found me." She turned her head to him on the pillow, her expression mournful. "That year, seemed like trouble just kept knocking on my door."

He stood on the porch, big and gentle-seeming, wide-brimmed brown hat already held in both hands. "Mrs. Price?" he asked in a respectful tone.

Eula barely nodded; since her encounter with the towering black detective, strangers scared her.

"I'm Lawyer James," he said. "Yancey James. I heard about your grandsons' troubles, and thought maybe I could help."

Eula hesitated. For the last two sleepless days and nights, she had been sickened and confused, praying while clinging blindly to her belief in the boys' innocence, not knowing what else to do.

"May I come in?" James asked softly. "If I'm not intruding..."

Slowly, Eula nodded. Remembering her courtesies, she opened the door and graciously motioned him inside.

"Would you like some iced tea?" she asked.

"No, ma'am, thank you—I don't want to presume too much on your time."

Eula felt too numb to insist. As she directed him to the couch, he stopped to stare down at the rectangular hole in the carpet that the police had cut out and taken away.

Softly, he said, "I'm sorry for your difficulties, ma'am."

Once more, Eula could only nod.

James settled back on the opposite side of the couch, beneath her painting of Jesus, the lawyer's sloping, prosperous-looking stomach straining the vest of his brown, three-piece suit. "Do your boys have counsel, ma'am? **Experienced** counsel, I mean."

To Eula, his voice was heavy with implied concern. "There's been talk about the public defender," she ventured.

He nodded gravely, as if this were the very problem he'd anticipated. "That so often happens," he commiserated. "The defenders' office gets anyone who can't afford a proper defense. When you're drowning in cases, like those poor lawyers are, you start grinding 'em out like Spam. It's just not possible to take your client's interests to heart.

"For petty charges, maybe they can't do much harm. But in cases like this, with two lives at stake . . ."

Eula felt the specter of her grandsons' execution enter the room and sit on the couch beside him. She found herself unable to speak.

"I have an office over on Third Street," Lawyer James continued. "I know people who go to your church—like Patricia Yarnell, whose boy I personally saved from execution." He leaned toward her a little, eyes seeking trust. "All in all, I've defended sixteen cases of capital murder, with good results."

Eula fidgeted with her dress. "I just don't know what to do," she answered miserably.

Nodding his sympathy, James fell into a respectful quiet. After a time, Eula asked, "Would you be helping both of them out?"

"I'd have to see them, ma'am. But I believe we could mount a u-nited defense." James paused, seeming to reflect. "A big advantage of that is it saves you money. No point in paying for two experienced private lawyers when all you need is one."

A fresh wave of helplessness overtook her. In the silence, the lawyer fished a handkerchief out of his inside breast pocket and, head politely turned from her, sneezed softly into the white cloth. "I'm sorry, ma'am," he apologized. "Allergies."

Eula acknowledged this with a nod, her thoughts elsewhere.

"You look perplexed," he ventured quietly. "Tell me how I can help."

"Even if you can help both boys, Lawyer James, the good Lord Himself would have to pay you."

James smiled at this. "I could never presume on His bounty." His eyes perused the room and its contents. "I appreciate that this is a burden, ma'am. But Mrs. Yarnell tells me your late husband bought this house quite some time ago, when he was working in the yards. By now it's surely worth some modest amount."

A visceral fear gripped Eula's heart—the house, almost all that Joe had left her, was all she had. "Maybe something."

"You have a mortgage?"

"A small one. It's nearly paid up."

Lawyer James nodded his approval. "That's a blessing," he told her. "It would allow you to take out a second."

Eula felt herself suspended between the two young men she still loved—the incomprehensible human remnants of the scared boys she had inherited—and the house which they had appropriated: which now, she acknowledged despite a rush of shame at her selfishness, might become truly hers again. "Don't even know a bank would do that..."

"It's not a problem," James assured her. "I have a notary public who works with me. We can do the paperwork ourselves."

Eula felt the last vestiges of the life she had known slipping through her hands. But surely God would send no more than she could bear.

"I'll pray on it, Lawyer James. I surely will."

"And you should." Decorously, he dabbed at his nose. "But don't take too long, ma'am—please. In matters like this, every day is another strike against your boys."

"Allergies," Terri said to Carlo. "What you're going to find out is that 'Lawyer James' discounted the second mortgage, then sold it for cash." Glancing at her husband, she added mordantly, "I can't wait to read the trial transcript. 'Allergies' can really screw up your defense."

Smiling faintly, Chris remarked, "I keep thinking about the old white lady—the neighbor. Cross-racial identifications are the least reliable."

She nodded. "Monk and Mauriani thought of that. They ran two lineups—six-packs for each brother."

"What about Fleet?"

"Oh, they thought of **that,** too."

Flora Lewis peered through the one-way glass, flanked by Monk, Ainsworth, Mauriani, and the brothers' lawyer, Yancey James.

Mauriani, Monk noted with approval, was taking no chances. As with the first lineup, the second contained six young black men of roughly similar size. Standing beside Eddie Fleet, Rennell Price stared straight ahead.

Flora Lewis pointed a long finger toward the glass. "That's him," she said decisively, "The third man from the left, Rennell Price."

As if he had heard her, the big man in the black sweatshirt shifted his weight. Then he resumed his menacing stare toward the woman he could not see.

"You're sure?" Monk prodded.

"Absolutely."

"And that's also the man you saw forcing Thuy Sen inside the house."

"That's right."

"Okay," Monk continued. "Now I want you to look at the man standing next to him, the one in the red windbreaker. Ever seen **that** man before?"

As the woman regarded Eddie Fleet, one corner of his mouth moved fractionally, as though his presence were a macabre joke.

"Take your time, Mrs. Lewis."

Lewis squinted through her glasses. "Maybe," she allowed. "It seems like maybe I have. But so many people come to that house—all the time, at all hours."

Her tone was puzzled, as though she were disappointed in her gifts of recall. "But the one thing I **do** know," she added firmly. "I know Rennell Price when I see him. And that man in the black sweatshirt is Rennell, the man I saw with Payton and the Asian girl those two murdered. You always see them together."

Still impassive, Rennell Price stared through the glass. "Thank you," his lawyer said politely, dabbing at his nose again.

TWELVE

"Maybe prosecutors pick the defendants," Lou Mauriani remarked to Terri. "But we don't get to pick their lawyers."

Sun bathed the deck of Mauriani's retirement home, a modest A-frame in the foothills of the Sierra. His vista of rolling hillocks and pine trees and twisting roads was, Mauriani acknowledged, as different from the cramped urban neighborhood of his youth as he could afford. The crisp fall air was scented with pine needles.

"Lawyer," Terri amended. "Singular. You were clearly conscious of **that** problem."

Mauriani sipped his lunchtime glass of cabernet, blue eyes glinting with good humor. "And you, Ms. Paget, have clearly read the transcript of the prelim."

As Mauriani saw it, his biggest problem was Yancey James.

Otherwise, the prosecutor knew, the preliminary hearing should be simple. The sole obvious pitfall concerned a possible defense motion for a change of venue; in **this** courtroom, the brothers' only friend was Eula Price.

She sat to one corner, overwhelmed by the reporters crammed into the wooden benches or standing at the rear. On the other side, at Mauriani's gentle urging, Chou Sen waited with her husband, Meng, a silent portrait of suffering and incomprehension, reminding the media and the Court of the terrible reason for this hearing. And presiding was Mauriani's ex-colleague from the D.A.'s office, Municipal Court Judge John Francis Warner, a man not about to make headlines by setting these defendants loose—even if their grandmother could scrape up enough security to satisfy a bail bondsman.

Certainly there was no risk of their escape: handcuffed and dressed in the orange jumpsuits of county prisoners, Payton and Rennell sat with their ankles bound by the shackles which had hobbled their entry into Johnny Warner's domain. The sole danger to Mauriani and the judge sat between the two brothers in a three-piece suit, silently ticking like a bomb.

As soon as Yancey James entered his appearance, Mauriani stood. "Am I correct," he inquired with calculated bemusement, "that Mr. James is representing **both** defendants? If so, I suggest some inquiry is in order."

Nodding, Warner turned toward James. "The District Attorney is correct, Mr. James. Payton and Rennell may well have conflicting interests. Should they choose to testify, their accounts of critical events may differ. Or one—indeed both—may claim to be less culpable than the other.

"This creates the risk that you won't be able to adequately represent either. **Or** that one will suffer from your zealous defense of the other."

Not to mention, Mauriani thought, **the risk that the appellate court will reverse both convictions based on your conflict of interest, leaving me the problem of trying them all over again with the evidence grown cold.** But Judge Warner was doing all he could to head this off, and the anorexic-looking court reporter was taking down each precious word.

James stood with his hands clasped tightly in front of him, appearing as tense as the two brothers. But perhaps that was appropriate for a lawyer with six clients already waiting on death row. "I've considered that," he answered, a shade too assertively. "I'm confident Payton and Rennell will have the representation they deserve."

You've got that **right,** Mauriani thought. He could only hope that this glib response would not placate Johnny Warner. "The Court's obligation," Warner persisted, "is to ensure both defendants the fairest possible trial. As well as to make certain that a conviction of one or the other, should that occur, is not reversed."

James glanced about the crowded courtroom, as though absorbing that his performance would receive far more scrutiny than normal. "I fully understand that," he answered with fresh bravado. "But Payton and Rennell Price are **not** guilty, Your Honor. Their interests are identical."

"Perhaps for now," Warner responded tartly. "Sometimes interests change."

As he listened, Mauriani scrutinized both brothers. While the older one followed the proceedings with keen interest, Rennell appeared as bored as a man forced to watch an Italian art film without subtitles. "Should that happen," James answered smoothly, "we can deal with it. For now, I must remind the Court of the strong bias against interfering with a defendant's freely made choice of counsel—even in the face of a potential conflict, as set forth by the Supreme Court of California in the **Smith** and **Maxwell** cases."

Where, Mauriani wondered, had James stumbled across the law books? "Your Honor," he swiftly interjected, "for everyone's sake this case should be tried but once. I direct Mr. James to the Supreme Court case **Cuyler v. Sullivan,** wherein Justice Marshall admonished that a trial court should not only warn multiple defendants of the potential conflict but determine whether joint representation is the informed choice of each."

As he finished, Mauriani glimpsed Payton's eyes darting from him to the judge, and then to Yancey James. "Mr. James," the Court admonished, "I must inquire of your clients whether each knowingly consents to your representation of the other."

Seemingly discomfited, James glanced at the two

brothers. Firmly, Warner directed, "Will the defendants please rise."

Both did, Payton with a defiant air, Rennell only after prompting by Yancey James. The shackles made him stumble before he righted himself with palpable resentment.

"Defendant Payton Price," Warner intoned for the record, "do you understand that your interests in this case may conflict with those of your brother, Rennell Price?"

Payton stood straighter. It struck Mauriani how handsome he was, especially now that a crack-free stint in the county jail had left him sober and clear of eye. After one more glance at James, he tersely answered, "Yessir."

Turning to Rennell, Warner asked with equal solicitude, "Rennell Price, do you understand that your interests may conflict with those of your brother?"

Rennell turned—not to his lawyer but to Payton. Briefly, their eyes met, and then Rennell spoke in a monotone: "Yessir."

Such responses, Mauriani knew, were the foundation of the record he needed to make a conviction stick. But neither brother seemed to grasp the buried risks of employing Yancey James. Urgently, Mauriani glanced at Warner; the judge's eyes caught his, and then, as though prompted, Warner spoke to Payton.

"Payton Price, do you understand that, by employing Mr. James to represent you both, you assume the risk that he may not represent your individual interests as effectively as separate counsel?"

Payton hesitated, his demeanor less cool. "Yes, sir," he responded softly.

Facing Rennell, Judge Warner repeated the question. To Mauriani's surprise, the big man gazed past Warner as if he were not there.

In the silence, the prosecutor looked toward Eula Price and then Thuy Sen's mother and father. Though Mrs. Price appeared fearful, and the victim's parents stern, neither seemed to comprehend the minidrama unfolding as they watched.

"Mr. Price?" Warner prompted sharply.

Mauriani felt the sudden tension of those watching focus on Rennell. Then, leaning toward his brother, Payton murmured something. With the same grudging inexpressiveness, Rennell echoed, "Yessir," and the moment passed.

Swiftly, the judge faced Payton. "Understanding the potential for conflict, Payton, do you consent to Mr. James's representation of both Rennell and you?"

Once more, Payton glanced at Yancey James. "Yeah," the witness answered dubiously, and then corrected himself. "I mean, yessir."

Turning to Rennell, Warner repeated his inquiry, this time slowly and emphatically. Fingers poised over the stenotype machine, the court reporter waited for his answer. **It's your last chance,** Mauriani silently implored Rennell. **Dump him.**

"Yessir," Rennell repeated and resumed his look of boredom.

Frowning, the judge faced Mauriani. "That's all this Court can do, Mr. Mauriani. I can't infringe on the defendants' right to their chosen counsel."

No indeed, Mauriani thought. **All you can do is what you've done: lock them into their own folly, and hope that the cold, black letters of the transcript will read better than this looked.**

"Thank you, Your Honor," Mauriani said.

"For sure no conflict at the prelim," Terri said astringently. "Even with all the pretrial publicity, James never mentioned a change of venue. Shafting both his clients equally."

Mauriani smiled into his wineglass. "Maybe San Diego felt like a long way from home."

"Maybe," Terri countered, "San Diego felt like a long way from James's supplier."

Mauriani moved his shoulders, suggesting fatalism mingled with indifference. "Maybe so. But the recreational preferences of Rennell Price's 'chosen counsel' were outside my jurisdiction. That one falls to the State Bar."

T H I R T E E N

MAURIANI REFILLED HIS BOWL-SHAPED GLASS, THE
wine deep red beneath its sunlit surface. "Your other
problem with Yancey James," Terri pointed out, "was
that you couldn't use two lawyers to pit one brother
against the other."

"True enough. James was a dead loss all around."

"Is that why you asked for the death penalty? To
shake Rennell or Payton loose?"

Mauriani's genial expression became sober, almost
severe. "That's not enough of a reason," he answered
curtly. "Not for me."

"Then what was?"

Mauriani seemed to study the green bottle in front
of him. "The tipping point," he said at length, "was
the day the brothers Price resolved to kill again."

When Mauriani picked up the phone, Monk said
abruptly, "I've got someone you should meet, Lou."

"Who's that?"

"Name's Jamal Harrison. He's a snitch in the

Bayview—been shot three times already. Instead of feeling lucky, he's become a bitter man. Whole lot of anger in this boy, and a whole lot of cases for us. You might say he snitches out of spite."

Mauriani considered this. Snitches were notoriously self-interested and, therefore, of dubious reliability: the rule of thumb was that they had to help you make three cases stick before you'd forget whatever case you had against them. Which tended, at the least, to encourage a certain creativity.

"You can't be telling me you've found an honest man."

Monk chuckled. "Not saying **that.** I'm just saying you'd better hurry up. Jamal's got no sense of the future longer than fifteen minutes—including that his hobby is likely to get him killed. All he thinks about is that his homeboys treated him like a punk."

"So what's his deal?" Mauriani asked.

"The deal is that Jamal's been in the county jail, serving out his thirteen months for attempted rape." Monk's tone became serious. "Payton and Rennell wound up in the cell next door. Seems he knew them from the Bayview, and Payton started sharing his reminiscences. One of them concerns Eddie Fleet."

"I'm on my way," Mauriani said.

Jamal Harrison was a tubercular-looking runt so skinny that his collarbone stuck out. He wore a scraggly beard, and his darting eyes were filled with distrust.

Flanked by Monk and Ainsworth, Mauriani sat in

the interrogation room across from the erstwhile prisoner. "Tell me what you've got," Mauriani said.

Jamal fixed his narrow-eyed gaze on Mauriani, a man determined to look power in the face. Portentously, he answered, "A death sentence, maybe."

They stuck the brothers by themselves in the cell next to the one Jamal shared with some losers whose crimes weren't worth more than his—a petty burglar, a small-time dope dealer, some moron who'd been fencing cell phones. Though prisoners awaiting trial for murder got much more respect, the first appearance of the Price brothers drew hoots from the motley orange-clad gallery. "Oh, suck me," a jailhouse satirist called out in imagined ecstasy. "Can't quite fit it in your tiny little pussy."

"Pussy?" someone else chimed in. "Can't find no such thing on a baby that small."

"**Small,**" the first voice countered, "is why they were hoping they could **please** her. But there's nothin' **that** small."

As the sheriff's deputies pushed them into the empty cell, Payton kept staring straight ahead. Jamal could see him taking in what their lives would be like in a hard-core prison. Even murderers had no use for child sex killers—they were friendless, and they often wound up dead.

Jamal had no plans to talk to either one of them. At

least he'd tried to fuck a **woman,** as he reminded Charles Monk.

For days, Payton gave Jamal no sign of recognition.

He sat there, stone-faced, the only clue that he acknowledged his surroundings the utter stillness of his eyes when fresh insults issued from the cages all around them. Then Jamal could see him imagining his future, or its end. This two-hundred-foot corridor with cells smelling of urine and packed with restless, stinking prisoners, divided by race—or by sanity from the babbling crazies or those gripped by catatonia— was merely the devil's waiting room; the final step for Payton Price would be hell itself. But his brother, a torpid mass, seemed not to care. Now and then Payton would murmur stuff to Rennell, too soft for Jamal to hear. Sometimes the big man nodded.

It was only on their fourth day in jail that Payton walked over to the bars dividing the brothers from Jamal.

Softly, Payton said, "I know you, Jamal."

Even through iron bars, there was something scary about Payton Price—a deadly quiet in his speech, a stone coldness in his eyes. From the next few words, Jamal knew that Payton had a purpose.

"When you getting out?" Payton asked.

Briefly, Jamal hesitated. "Seven days," he answered.

He imagined Payton smiling.

After that, Payton turned to small talk: who
they knew in common, who was dead or in prison,
whether Jamal had bumped into someone lately
that Payton used to know, who maybe had killed
someone and gotten by with it. It struck Jamal
that Payton was reconstructing the Bayview in his
head, like some fucking scientist studying tribes in
Africa. Or maybe just some prison psychologist trying
to look into Jamal's own head. But the weirdest thing
was how soft he talked, so Jamal's cell mates could
not hear.

"Could **Rennell** hear?" Mauriani asked.

"Don't know," Jamal answered. "Didn't seem like
he much cared."

Three days before Jamal got out, Payton motioned
him to the bars. Jamal stopped three feet away. "Come
on over here," Payton demanded.

Apprehensive, Jamal did. Payton stuck his face
through the bars until it was inches from Jamal's. "You
know Eddie Fleet?" he asked.

Something in his tone made Jamal fear to answer.
"Yeah," he acknowledged. "I know him."

For once, Payton's cold black eyes seemed to give
off light. "You know why we're in this shithole?"

"Sure. That girl."

Payton grabbed the bars, eyes locking Jamal's.

"We're here," he almost whispered, "because Eddie Fleet lied to that dude Monk."

Though Payton's voice was soft, Jamal could feel the intensity of his hatred. "Lied about what?" he asked.

Payton did not answer. When he spoke again, his voice was softer yet. "No Fleet, no case. You understand what I'm sayin'?"

Silent, Jamal nodded.

"So I want 'no Fleet,' Jamal. Who you know that could make that happen?"

Reflexively Jamal felt his mind begin to work. "For what?"

"A cut of my business," Payton answered calmly. "Maybe five hundred every week. But only if Rennell and me get out."

Beneath Payton's steel veneer, Jamal could hear the depth of his despair. He glanced over his shoulder at his cell mates, idling or trying to sleep. "All that," he murmured. "Just to kill a man."

Slowly, Payton nodded. "All that, Jamal. Maybe for once it could be you."

For the next two hours, Mauriani and the cops went at Jamal hard—exactly where Payton stood, who might have seen them, who else Payton might have approached. "Let's talk about Rennell," Mauriani prodded. "How do you know **he** knew?"

This made Jamal laugh out loud. " 'Cause after I

told Payton I'd off Fleet for them, he sat back down beside Rennell and whispered in his ear. First time I ever saw Rennell Price smile."

"So where's Jamal now?" Terri asked.

"Dead." Mauriani smiled faintly. "Monk was right about him. He lasted three months past the trial."

FOURTEEN

By the time Mauriani had killed the bottle of wine, the sun of late afternoon cast a lengthening shadow across the table. Standing beside it, Mauriani pulled the cork from a second bottle as he continued his soliloquy, his power of articulation surprisingly unimpaired by his solitary consumption of the first. Then Terri remembered, from the news clips she had watched in law school, an alert and tensile man, charged with prosecuting the brothers who had killed Thuy Sen.

"And so," Mauriani went on, "Rennell Price had the distinction of being the last man sentenced to death in San Francisco County. After that, Texas went one way and San Francisco another—**they** believe executing the innocent still works as a deterrent, whereas **we've** become too precious to execute Ted Bundy. So I suppose your client was more than usually unlucky.

"But luck is a talent, as Somerset Maugham once said. Perhaps by accident, the Price brothers had committed one truly revolting crime, and then solicited another deliberate one from the soon to be late Jamal

Harrison. When Thuy Sen's father and mother said they wanted us to seek the death penalty, there wasn't much to say against it."

Mauriani paused to taste the newly poured wine, rolling it on his tongue, then spoke more softly. "When they came to my office, they brought flowers—to get on my good side, I thought, and maybe to signal me they were too impoverished for me to extract a bribe. Flowers, to propitiate the Price brothers' deaths in exchange for their daughter's. It made me think of where they'd come from—a country so murderous and venal that executions occurred at the whim of the authorities and the only conceivable way to stop them was with money." Abruptly, Mauriani switched to a sardonic undertone. "Unfortunately for the brothers, Thuy Sen's parents were Catholic, not Buddhist—after all they'd seen, executing her murderer must have seemed completely unremarkable.

"The flowers were a cluster of bright colors from a grocery or a flower shop. Holding them, I wanted to tell this little girl's parents that the brothers would never be dead enough to bring them real solace, and that our 'system of justice' would make them wait for years before they found that out. But they might have taken it as a bureaucrat's indifference."

He stopped abruptly, turning to gaze out at his vista, softened by a mistlike fog backlit by rays of sun.

"So you don't believe in the death penalty?" Terri asked.

His eyes narrowed before he spoke again; in that

moment, Terri realized that he looked more ponderous than the man she recalled. "Do I love it?" Mauriani asked rhetorically. "No—I'm not from the school of 'they're going to hell, and all I'm doing is speeding up the delivery.' But I do think there are at least **some** moral absolutes in the world, and that making a nine-year-old choke to death on semen affronts them.

"In this job, you learn all the horrible ways in which the truly guilty murder the truly innocent—like the two guys who robbed an old lady's home, kidnapped her, put her in the trunk, stopped at a corner store to buy gasoline, took her to the desert, and then burned her alive so she wouldn't be a witness. Or the handyman who raped, tortured, and sexually mutilated an eleven-year-old girl, before he decided just to watch her bleed to death to see how long it took." Pausing, Mauriani faced her. "To me, some criminals are so dangerous, and some crimes so terrible, that it's hard to envision anything short of execution as being sufficient punishment.

"That's how I wound up feeling about the murder of Thuy Sen. Perhaps I suspected that executing the Price brothers, years too late, wouldn't heal the hole in her parents' hearts." Mauriani's gaze at Terri grew pointed. "But, perhaps unlike you, I could allow myself to contemplate how Thuy had died, and still believe that I was doing good. So let me propose something which may offend your professional sensibilities—if someone forces sex on a little girl, that's not **his** tragedy. It's hers."

Once more, Terri envisioned with painful vividness what had happened to Elena. Softly, she answered, "But you don't really **know** what happened, do you. What you allowed yourself to contemplate was Thuy Sen's death as you imagined it."

"No. As Liz Shelton's autopsy showed it to be."

"That may have shown **how** she died," Terri retorted. "But not who killed her. Suppose Payton forced Thuy Sen into oral copulation but Rennell didn't. Under the law, to seek the death penalty for Rennell, you'd have to argue that he aided and abetted Payton with the intent to kill Thuy Sen. You didn't know that, and don't now."

Lazily, Mauriani shrugged. "If that were true, Rennell could have said so—or Payton could have. Neither testified. Their choice, not mine."

"Or Yancey James's choice."

"Then that was the tactical decision of their 'chosen counsel.' Tell me, would **you** have put Rennell Price on the stand?"

In truth, Terri could not be sure. "It's not just about testifying," she answered. "Like any competent lawyer in any other capital case, James could have tried to cut Rennell a deal."

"On what basis? They both pled innocent. Neither chose to share with us why we should believe that or, conversely, to tell us what really happened." With exaggerated care, Mauriani lowered himself into the seat across the table. "So let's examine all the ways in which their silence left them eligible for execution.

"Any death occurring in the commitment of a felony is chargeable as a capital crime. That leaves both brothers open to a charge of capital murder on at least five statutory grounds: kidnapping, rape, sodomy, oral copulation, and the performance of a lewd and lascivious act on a child under fourteen. In the absence of contrary evidence—like testimony from Payton or Rennell—we could let the jury pick whatever they liked." Mauriani settled back, regarding her with bleak amusement. **"That,"** he enunciated with care, "is where your client's tragedy reaches its apotheosis. You know about the **Carlos** window?"

"A little. But I've never had to deal with it."

Mauriani nodded. "Back in 1983, our highly inventive California Supreme Court—Rose Bird and her cabal of death penalty abolitionists—ruled in the **Carlos** case that a felony murder charge required the prosecution to prove intent to kill. When Thuy Sen died, **Carlos** was still the law. Needless to say," Mauriani added dryly, "oral copulation with intent to kill would have been hard for me to prove. Odds are I wouldn't have asked for the death penalty, and maybe Rennell and you would be asking for parole, instead of trying to stave off an all-too-certain execution."

As Mauriani paused to sip more wine, savoring the vagaries of fate, Terri felt him becoming more digressive; there was a flush to his forehead, and the veins in his face had begun dissecting his cheeks. "Sadly for Rennell," he pronounced, "the law, you might say, devolved. The voters sent Chief Justice Bird and her soul mates back to private practice—they were, it turned out, a bit **too** visionary. And two weeks before Thuy Sen was murdered, the new conservative majority reversed the **Carlos** rule. It was the final piece of ill luck for Payton and Rennell—they were the first defendants in a felony murder trial after **Carlos** was abolished, and they'll be the last to die at the hands of the City and County of San Francisco.

"If Rennell Price wanted to tell the jury why they shouldn't have sentenced him to death, that was up to him. But he chose not to."

"And **you** chose to seek the death penalty," Terri rejoined. "Would you have done that if Thuy Sen were the daughter of a black crack addict?"

Instantly alert, Mauriani sat straighter, regarding her with level blue eyes. "If so," he answered succinctly, "then I acted with exquisite fairness. If not, we're about to execute two men who are among the truly deserving. Either way I'll sleep tonight." He paused, as though hearing himself, then continued in a softer tone. "What you're complaining about is that, as a prosecutor, I had almost complete discretion over life and death decisions. Which was no joy to me at all.

"It's no pleasure to explain to some other victim's family the reasons—however good—that you're not seeking the death penalty for the murder of their wife or son or sister when you did so for the murder of Thuy Sen. It's not pleasant to consider what a miserable job we do of protecting children, or the fact that we're virtually guaranteeing that some of them will grow up to murder other children. Let alone to think you might be wrong—after all, you can't turn loose a dead man just because he's innocent.

"But I didn't worry about that here," Mauriani finished, "and neither did the jury." Draining his glass, he smiled without humor. "Even though the brothers came up with that sterling alibi."

FIFTEEN

FIVE DAYS BEFORE TRIAL, MAURIANI RECEIVED A LETter from Yancey James.

He read it with rising irritation. Then he placed a call to James. "What's this with the supplemental witness list?" he asked. "We're five days away from trial."

"The amenities," James rejoined in a parody of a preacher, "must give way to the in-ter-ests of justice. Tasha Bramwell's just now come forward—despite, Louis, the potential opprobrium she could face on account of your prejudicial and perverse public relations efforts to paint my clients as guilty before they're even tried. Are you now suggesting that you'll try to bar the courtroom doors to truth?"

Mauriani could imagine James lounging back in his chair, expansive with self-admiration and, perhaps, a cocaine-fueled grandiosity. "Cut the bullshit," the prosecutor said coldly. "Who the hell is Tasha Bramwell, and what 'truth' does she have to offer?"

Mauriani's annoyance elicited a soft chuckle from

Yancey James. "Time will tell, Louis. Truth will out..."

The repeated use of his given name was beginning to irk Lou Mauriani. "Damned straight it will," he shot back. "Right now. Either you give proper notice of what this mystery woman has to say, or she'll never see the inside of Judge Rotelli's courtroom."

This proposition—so plausible that even James could not dispute it—provided Mauriani with a moment's welcome silence. When James spoke again, his tone was sober and more tentative. "This young woman is close to Payton Price. She's way too concerned for his welfare to live in silence with what she knows—that she was with him and Rennell for several hours on the very afternoon that Thuy Sen disappeared."

"You **must** be joking."

"No, indeed, Louis—no, indeed. You can try to exclude her. But if you do that, you'd be condemning two innocent young men, perhaps to death."

Mauriani put down the phone and then called Charles Monk.

At eight-thirty the next morning, Monk and Ainsworth arrived at Mauriani's office, its tile floor littered with the building blocks of an impending trial—witness statements, crime lab results, mug shots, Liz Shelton's report, and autopsy photographs of Thuy

Sen. For an instant, Monk glanced at the photographs, shaking his head, and then said briskly, "Tasha Bramwell."

"Yeah." Mauriani poured himself a third cup of coffee. "Tell me all about her."

Like Eddie Fleet's girlfriend, Betty Sims, Tasha Bramwell lived in public housing in the Bayview. But the impression she made on Monk was different: more that of an office worker who aspired to be a professional—straight, processed hair; a neatly pressed skirt; clean white cotton blouse—and her apartment was as meticulous as her trimmed and painted nails. She was tall and slender, with a thin, fox-pretty face; Monk knew at once from her wary eyes that their presence made her nervous.

They sat at her kitchen table, with a vase of flowers between the two detectives and the woman. "I was with them both," Tasha insisted. "Right here. From maybe noon to almost eight o'clock."

"Was anyone else here?" Ainsworth asked.

"No. Just the three of us."

"Anyone visit—someone who might corroborate what you're telling us?"

Tasha screwed up her face in what, to Monk, seemed a pantomime of someone straining to remember. "Don't recall," she said finally. "Didn't seem important then."

"What did the three of you do?" Monk inquired. "All that time."

"Stuff. Listened to music, watched some TV—soap operas, mostly. Rennell likes those."

"That's all?"

Tasha's eyes froze and then refocused on the flowers instead of on Monk. In a wan, embarrassed voice, she answered, "Payton and me made love."

If Tasha was acting, Monk thought, she had a certain gift. Though perhaps it was lying, not sex, which discomfited her most. Evenly, he asked, "With Rennell in the room?"

"No." Her tone was sharper, defensive. "Alone, in my bedroom."

"How long were you alone?"

Tasha's eyes lowered. "I don't know. Maybe an hour or so."

"For that hour or so, where was Rennell?"

"Sitting here, I guess." She hesitated, then added, "Rennell sleeps a lot. I think maybe he was asleep on the couch when we came out."

"But you don't **know** Rennell was here."

Tasha gave a minimal shrug, as though she found the question inconsequential. "I guess not, no. But he doesn't go too many places without Payton."

Curious, Monk considered asking why. Then Ainsworth interjected, "You say they were here till eight or so. How do you remember that?"

" 'Cause I work weeknights over at the Double Rock Bar. Shift always starts at eight."

"That your only job?"

"Yeah." Tasha nodded toward a small shelf of what

appeared to be textbooks. "Days I go to City College," she amplified with a touch of pride. "I'm studying to be an accountant."

Considering her, Monk felt the habitual melancholy he experienced on returning to the Bayview, this time at the depressing fact that, even while reaching for something better, Tasha Bramwell remained entangled with a man like Payton Price. "Thuy Sen disappeared on a Tuesday," he said. "Got classes on Tuesday?"

"This semester I got three. But last semester—the Tuesday we're talking about—I only had but one. Bookkeeping."

Tasha, Monk thought, either had an excellent memory or had reviewed her prior schedule. "What time on Tuesday, Tasha?"

She smoothed her skirt, as though erasing an imagined crease. "Three o'clock."

"So you cut class?"

"Just that once." Looking up at Monk, she finished in a prideful tone. "I'm a good student—got an A in that course. Professor didn't grade us on attendance."

Monk tried to imagine this ambitious girl cutting class to hang out watching soap operas with Payton and his sluggish, sullen brother. But there was no way, for the moment, to get at this. "Do you know Eddie Fleet?" he asked abruptly.

Her lips compressed. "I know Eddie."

"What you know about him?"

"He pretended to be Payton's friend." Her voice held quiet fury. "But he's a stone liar, out for himself."

"Know why he'd lie about Payton?" Ainsworth asked.

"Jealousy. The way he used to look at me like to made my skin crawl."

"He ever hit on you?"

Her eyes flashed anger and disdain. "He knew better. He knew not to get on Payton's bad side, that I'd tell him if Eddie tried a thing. Eddie likes his women too scared to come back at him."

Monk considered her. "I guess you've been talking to him," he said more pointedly. "Payton, I mean. Records say you've been visiting County Jail."

Tasha sat straighter. "Why wouldn't I? He's my boyfriend, and he's in bad trouble for something he didn't do."

"So why didn't you just come to us, say where Payton was the day that little girl disappeared?"

For an instant, Tasha averted her head, and then she looked Monk straight in the eyes. "I hadn't put two and two together—not till Payton finally remembered where we'd been. Then it all came back to me."

"How?"

"About cutting my accounting class—'cause that's unusual for me—then seeing that girl's picture the next night on TV, working at the Double Rock." Her voice filled with defiance. "Payton would never do that with a child. I **know** him—he's gotten in trouble maybe, living down here, having to become a man before his time. But that's **all.** The rest is Eddie Fleet, using **you** to push my man aside for him."

Silent, Monk regarded her, his expression conveying muted sorrow. "You're a classy-looking young woman," he said in measured tones. "More important, you're sharp, and you've got plans. You could be someone in this world. Don't mess it up."

A spark of fear surfaced in her eyes. "How would I be doing that?"

Monk erased the sympathy from his face. "Perjury," he said flatly. "This is an important matter—to us, to the city, and to that girl's family. We're going to find the truth about it."

Tasha bit her lip, although her eyes, with an apparent effort, still met her interrogator's. "I'm telling the truth, Mr. Policeman. You just don't like hearing it."

"She's lying," Monk told Mauriani. "Payton put her up to it."

"Sure he did. But as it stands, her story gives the brothers at least a shot at acquittal, if the jury's squirrelly enough." Mauriani cocked his head. "Though I suppose there's always the chance," he added dryly, "however small, that Yancey James may not have thoroughly vetted her story. Maybe you should check her out."

"Right now," Monk answered with a smile. "Nothin' better to do."

Four days later, in the courtroom of the judge who would try **People of California v. Price,** the Honorable Angelo J. Rotelli, Mauriani moved to exclude from evidence the testimony of Tasha Bramwell.

Angie Rotelli, another former colleague, regarded Mauriani sternly. "On what grounds?"

"Surprise. Miss Bramwell was hardly unknown to the defense. And yet Mr. James disclosed her existence five days before trial. Aside from the dubious credibility this suggests, it's trial by ambush—"

"Okay, counsel," Rotelli cut in with an unimpressed manner. "I get it. Mr. James."

Slowly, James rose. "If there was any untoward delay, Your Honor, Ms. Bramwell here can account for that to this Court and the jury." His voice became solemn. "Mr. Mauriani is seeking the ultimate penalty—death. Now he wants to exclude vital evidence on a technicality. Any prejudice to the prosecutor pales in comparison to death by lethal injection."

Briskly, Rotelli nodded. "I have to concur," he told Mauriani. "Where two lives are in the balance, justice requires us to hear Ms. Bramwell out. Motion denied."

Mauriani was very careful to look somber.

Fifteen years later, he walked Teresa Peralta Paget to her car.

They had emptied the second bottle of cabernet, with Terri finally accepting a glass. The man simply wanted company, she thought, and she owed him the courtesy of not feeling set apart.

And Mauriani reacted with a courtesy of his own; dignified and solicitous, he walked her to the car, carefully repeating the directions he had already given her. When she drove away, he remained at the head of the driveway, watching.

She arrived home late, around ten-thirty, and encountered Carlo sitting in the kitchen, waiting for her as she had asked.

"Did Mrs. Price recall anything about Tasha?" she inquired.

Sitting on the stool at the kitchen counter, Carlo sipped from a steaming cup of coffee. "Some," he answered. "But more about Yancey James."

It was the last time, Eula Price remembered, that she spoke with the lawyer alone.

They sat in Eula's living room on the night before the trial began. "Tasha Bramwell," James said in forceful tones, "could become the cornerstone of our defense. But taken by herself, I can assure you, Mrs. Price, that she just won't be enough to save your boys. A death penalty case is complicated, and the prosecutor's office is bringing their full might down upon us."

"What can we do?"

"More investigation—to find all the evidence we

can, from whatever source, that this terrible crime is contrary to your grandsons' basic natures." He paused, as though reluctant, then added firmly, "We're going to need more money, Mrs. Paige. To fund our further investigation before it's too late."

Eula felt panic, a swift palpitation of her heart. "What about the money from the house?"

"Gone," he said flatly. "Investigation fees. The last dollars went into checking out Tasha Bramwell."

Tears came to Eula's eyes. "Lawyer James, I got no more money. This trouble's taken it all."

James lowered his gaze in sorrow. "Not even savings?" he asked.

Beneath the words, Eula could feel his desperation. "Just pension money," she answered, feeling her voice become husky. "We already used up all Joe left me."

Shaking his head, James reached for the familiar white handkerchief. "Then all we can do," he said mournfully, "is whatever we can. Can't do any more than that."

SIXTEEN

THE NEXT MORNING, IN THE CONFERENCE ROOM
where they sat reviewing trial transcripts, Carlo scanned
Mauriani's questioning of prospective jurors. "It reads
almost like he's helping James," Carlo remarked. "He retained two African Americans on the jury who as good
as said they thought cops target blacks."

Terri poured herself a second cup of coffee. "He was
worried about jury demographics," she answered.
"Mauriani wasn't about to risk a reversal on the
grounds of racial exclusion. But I assume the two black
jurors said they'd have no problem imposing the death
penalty."

"Yup. The judge kept bouncing people with qualms
about capital punishment."

"Not surprising. A jury with scruples isn't likely to
impose it."

Carlo frowned. "But if all the jurors were pro-
death, weren't they also likely to be pro-prosecution?"

"You'd certainly think so," Terri answered dryly.
"But Rotelli and Mauriani were only following
the law.

"A year before Rennell's trial, the U.S. Supreme Court ruled that death-qualified juries don't violate a defendant's right to an impartial jury drawn from a fair cross section of the community. That's another way the death penalty warped Rennell's trial—Mauriani got to pick a jury more likely to convict him."

"You don't suppose," Carlo suggested, "that crossed Mauriani's mind when he decided to seek the death penalty."

Terri nodded. "In a city this liberal, you can knock out a slew of jurors. But, in retrospect, he thinks any twelve people off the street would have sentenced Rennell to death."

"Because his case was that good?"

Terri put down her cup. "Partly that," she answered. "Partly James. And partly because, in Mauriani's colorful phrase, the jury found Rennell Price 'guilty of offensive smiling.' "

Mauriani first noticed Rennell during Yancey James's disastrous cross-examination of Thuy Sen's mother.

The prosecutor's decision to lead with Chou Sen was simple—of the two parents, she was the more emotive, and only she had even a limited command of English. Gently, on direct, Mauriani had led her through the tragedies that had brought the Sen family to this moment: the murder of Thuy Sen's maternal grandmother and grandfather by the Khmer Rouge;

the disappearance of Chou's brother and two sisters; the desperate flight through Vietnam of Meng and Chou—pregnant with Thuy Sen—and their three-year-old daughter, Kim; their harrowing voyage to Thailand on a boat which smuggled refugees in return for what little money the Sens had left; Thuy's birth in a refugee camp; their dream of reaching safety in America. The next minutes were spent recalling the sweetness and docility of the victim, helping the jury to see her. And then, through questions Mauriani found difficult to ask, and Chou Sen harder to answer, they evoked the two agonizing days between Thuy Sen's disappearance and the moment her parents next saw her—a bloated corpse viewed through a window—and learned how she had died.

Mauriani had an eye for swing jurors, and he had picked out three to watch—the businesslike accountant whom he guessed would become the foreman; the Latina waitress with the expressive eyes and placid manner; and the no-nonsense black day-care worker. His questioning completed, Mauriani glanced at them as he returned to the prosecution table.

The accountant, Henry Feldt, was intently watching Yancey James approach the witness. Anna Velez gazed at Meng Sen, sitting with his head bowed in mute anguish. But the day-care worker, Candace Bender, was studying the defendants.

He followed her gaze. Payton Price showed little emotion—only a narrowing of his eyes, a stiffness in the way he sat, betrayed his tension. Rennell was different. Sitting back in his chair with folded arms, he appeared either to be asleep, or to be dismissing Chou Sen and her heartache as unworthy of his attention.

As his clients' instructor in decorum, Mauriani thought, Yancey James left something to be desired. Dressing them in suit and tie would not be enough to overcome a demeanor like Rennell's—when Mauriani looked back at Candace Bender, she was staring at Rennell Price with her lips pressed tight.

James, it seemed at once, would be no help to his clients. After introducing himself to the witness, he asked bluntly, "Your daughter left school alone that day, didn't she?"

Chou Sen nodded her head in sorrow. "Yes."

Even this one-word answer seemed to drain her. In James's position, Mauriani thought, he would get her off the stand as quickly as he could, then go after the other, less sympathetic witnesses, who had actual evidence to offer. Mauriani had already accomplished his mission in leading with Chou Sen—creating sympathy while bringing Thuy Sen to life—and Clarence Darrow reincarnate could not undo the damage.

But James seemed not to know this. His only concession to this woman's tragedy was to mute his accustomed grandiloquence, as though this might disguise the offensiveness of his questions. "And why," he prodded, "was Thuy alone?"

Chou Sen clasped her hands together. "She stayed after school. For extra help from the teacher. Her sister, Kim, didn't wait."

"Did you tell Kim to wait?"

"No." Briefly Chou's eyes closed. "I thought she knew."

Could it be, Mauriani wondered in astonishment, that James would actually try to impugn the victim's family? "But when Kim came home alone," James continued, "you knew Thuy also would be walking alone. Did you go to the school?"

"No."

"Why not?"

Chou hesitated. "I eat bad fish the night before. Bad stomach."

In fact, Mauriani knew, Chou had suffered vomiting and diarrhea so debilitating that she could hardly get out of bed. He had not brought this out on direct; he had not imagined where James was going now.

Briefly, the lawyer dabbed his nose. "Bad stomach," he repeated skeptically. "Did you send Kim back to look for her?"

"No. Didn't want her to go back alone."

"Or your husband?"

Chou glanced toward Meng. "Not home."

"So you decided to let your nine-year-old daughter walk home by herself."

"Yes." Chou's voice was soft with misery. "Alone."

"How many blocks is it from school to home?"

Chou shook her head. "Don't know."

"Sixteen blocks, Mrs. Sen. Do you know what goes on in sixteen blocks in the Bayview District?"

Out of compassion for Chou Sen, Mauriani considered objecting, then decided not to disrupt her antagonist's suicide-in-progress. "What you mean?" she asked.

"Do you know that some young girls in the Bayview start trading sex for cocaine?"

Chou swallowed. "Don't know."

"You don't know? You live in the Bayview for seven years, and claim not to know of the dangers Thuy Sen might fall prey to?"

"Don't know," Chou repeated stubbornly.

James moved closer. "So you don't know," he asked with insinuating quiet, "whether Thuy decided to visit with some young men, maybe listen to music."

Mauriani experienced an emotion close to awe: James's miscalculation was attaining a grandeur all its own. The accountant, Henry Feldt, watched the lawyer with a grimness that betrayed his anger.

"Thuy not like that," her mother insisted.

Her resistance seemed to fuel James's lack of judgment; he drew himself up straighter, and his tone grew more aggressive. "How did you know, Mrs. Sen, how Thuy might react when she was on her own?"

Chou Sen looked bewildered by the question. "Thuy Sen good girl," she said plaintively.

"Even a good girl," James pressed on, "can sometimes be led astray. You just don't know who she might have fallen in with, do you? Or what distraction she might have found on any one of those sixteen blocks you let her walk alone."

Mute, Chou Sen hung her head. In her miserable

silence, Mauriani glanced at the day-care worker. To his surprise, Bender's silent fury was focused not on Yancey James but on Rennell.

He was smiling at his grandmother. Sitting in the front row, she wore a more appropriate expression—mortification at Yancey James's questions. But when Eula Price turned to him, Rennell's smile only broadened.

After James's abuse of Chou Sen, Mauriani thought, his own crisp examination of Flora Lewis was the perfect counter.

Yes, Lewis said with certainty, she had seen Rennell pull the frightened girl off the sidewalk. Yes, it was Payton who closed the door behind them. After all these years living across the street, she knew those brothers as well as she knew her own hand. And no person of feeling could ever forget Thuy Sen, stumbling as Rennell pulled her inside.

Standing to cross-examine, James got right to work. "How do you feel about blacks?" he asked.

Lewis stiffened. "Depends on the individual."

"Really? Well you sure didn't like **these** black men, did you? Long before Thuy Sen disappeared, you called the police on them."

"Only about their noise. They kept me up at night."

"So you didn't like them."

"No, I did not." Lewis paused. "I disliked them

both, and felt sorry for their grandmother. She was far more at their mercy than I was."

Eula Price, Mauriani saw, lowered her eyes. But James seemed impervious. "So maybe," he said with a note of triumph, "you **wanted** them to be the ones charged with this terrible crime. If not for your own sake, for Eula Price's."

Flora Lewis stiffened on the witness stand. "That's just not so."

"No? Then why didn't you tell your story to the police until three days later, when Inspectors Monk and Ainsworth showed up at your door?"

"I was afraid of them. Payton and Rennell, I mean."

James walked toward her, standing so close now that Mauriani, had he cared to, could have objected. "Was that your reason, Mrs. Lewis? Or did the police start asking questions about Thuy Sen, and then you saw your chance to get rid of Rennell and Payton Price—for good."

Flora Lewis half-rose from the witness chair, as though to thrust her face even closer to his. Her voice quavered with fury. "I saw Rennell Price drag that little girl inside. I saw how scared she was. And now I can't sleep for seeing that every night.

"Make something like that up? I wish I **had.** Then I wouldn't feel like a murderer for not calling the police."

James paused, taken aback. Mauriani glanced at the brothers. Payton glared at the witness with a naked hostility the prosecutor could feel. But not Rennell.

Stretching his legs in front of him, he gazed at the ceiling, a study in ostentatious boredom.

"Jesus," Carlo murmured across time. It struck Terri that for Carlo, as for her, the anger and reprisal enveloping Rennell Price fifteen years before had become a presence in the room.

"Oh," she assured her stepson, "there's so much more."

SEVENTEEN

IT WAS EDDIE FLEET, MAURIANI HAD TOLD TERRI, who brought his case to vivid life.

The first image Fleet implanted in the jurors' minds was of Rennell, materializing from the darkness outside Fleet's door. From the witness stand, he sounded haunted and subdued. "He just stood there," Fleet told Mauriani. "All he said was, 'We got need for your car.' But I knew right then this was something like I never seen before."

"Why was that?"

"It was cold out, but the sweat was runnin' off his face. More than crack, man—the dude was **scared.**"

Fleet's eyes appeared to fill with remembered panic. In the silence of the courtroom, Mauriani could sense the jury's rapt attention.

"So you both got into your car?"

"Yeah." Fleet paused to gaze at his hands, as though studying the dirt beneath his nails. "We drove down to their house," he said at length. "Payton and Rennell's. And still Rennell's not tellin' me nothin.' Just lookin' out the window, like there must be people after us, and sayin', 'This is trouble, man.'" For the first time, Fleet's eyes flickered toward the defendants, and then he added softly, "It surely was all of that."

"What happened next?"

"We got there. Then Payton opens the door." As though remembering, Fleet shook his head. "He looks so scared he's like to crazy. Then he lets me inside."

The last few words were infused with awe. Mauriani let it echo for the jury, then asked, "What did you see there?"

"Her." For an instant, the words caught in his throat. "The girl that was missing."

He stopped abruptly, as if this could forestall the events which followed. It struck Mauriani that, by craft or accident, Fleet had a gift for drawing in his listeners. In deliberate contrast, the prosecutor inquired matter-of-factly, "Where exactly did you see her?"

"On the floor." Fleet's voice combined reverence with dread. "She was dead, and drool was coming out her mouth onto the rug."

In that moment, Mauriani sensed, James's attack on Flora Lewis had turned back against him, and the jurors' disgust at his treatment of Chou Sen was transforming into hatred of his clients. Mauriani's next question might be all they needed to feel at home with that.

"Did anyone describe what happened?" he inquired.

Once more, Fleet glanced at the defendants. "Yeah," he responded quietly. "Rennell did."

For whatever reason, Mauriani thought, Fleet was stretching the drama out; perhaps there was no tragedy so terrible that it did not afford someone a moment's pleasure. "What exactly did Rennell say, Eddie?"

Fleet looked down. More softly yet, he answered, "He said she'd choked on come."

There were moments where Mauriani could feel the flow of a trial change, like a suddenly quickening stream sweeping all before it. Those words were such a moment. By the end of Fleet's narrative, when Rennell was laying Thuy Sen's body on the water, Mauriani imagined death entering the courtroom, and not just Thuy Sen's.

Before he sat, Mauriani glanced at both defendants. Payton riveted Fleet with a look of hatred so visceral and venomous that it felt like an electric current. But Rennell sat back, eyes veiled, as though Fleet's narrative did not involve him. Mauriani spotted Candace Bender in the jury box, watching the brothers with something akin to horror—not only at what she had heard, Mauriani felt certain, but at the men she saw before her now.

For the first segment of cross-examination—too long, Mauriani thought—James drew out the litany of Eddie Fleet's criminal record. By its end, the jury could have had no doubt that Fleet was a crack-dealing, girlfriend-beating, gun-trafficking sociopath and, as such, fit company for Payton and Rennell. But **not** that he was a liar.

"This tale you've told us," James said with theatrical disdain, "you made a deal with the prosecutor to tell it, right?"

Fleet merely shrugged. "No deals, man."

"No deals? Didn't they find crack cocaine in your girlfriend's apartment she said belonged to you?"

"She **said** that." The sheer pettiness of such a crime, compared with the weight of Thuy Sen's death, seemed to evoke in Fleet a flash of amusement at Yancey James. "Two lousy rocks ain't enough to make me a liar. Not about somethin' like this."

James placed both hands on his hips, softening his voice. "What about something like dumping a dead nine-year-old? The only thing we know for sure is that Thuy Sen's body was in your trunk—the whole rest of the story we've only got your word for. The jury needs to know what Mr. Mauriani promised you to tell it."

Fleet steepled his hands together. "All the cops and the D.A. told me," he answered with studied composure, "was they'd consider my cooperation if I told what happened in court. They said I'd better not be lying, and never made no deals."

James moved closer. "But you **are** lying, aren't you. You're lying about **my** clients to cover for **your** crime."

Abruptly, Fleet's expression turned defiant. "All I was doin'," he retorted, "was helpin' out my friends. Didn't want this little girl to die, don't know exactly how it happened. By the time I saw her she was already dead."

"But we've only got your word for that, don't we. Just like we've only got your word about Payton and Rennell."

Calm renewed, Fleet regarded James impassively. "Don't know about that," he answered. "Before I told the police what happened, they'd already tore up the grandmother's house for evidence.

"We're not all sittin' here just because of me. Seemed like a lot of what I told them they already knew." He paused, eyes sweeping the courtroom, and a sense of the inevitable crept into his voice. "Like that this little girl choked to death right where I saw her. Just the way Rennell told me she did."

On the stand, Charles Monk pressed the button on the tape recorder.

His own disembodied voice sounded in the courtroom. "You didn't want for her to die, did you?"

The jury seemed to tense as one. There was a long silence, and then, for the first time, the jury heard Rennell Price speak. "No."

His voice was dull and, to Lou Mauriani's practiced ear, utterly unconvincing. On the tape, Monk prodded, "You just wanted her to make you feel good."

Scrutinizing the jurors, Mauriani saw Anna Velez's eyes close. In the same emotionless monotone, Rennell's voice asked Monk, "What Payton say?"

"What does it matter?" Monk rejoined. "Was Payton the one who killed her?"

"No." Rennell answered abruptly. "No way."

"No," Monk quietly agreed. "It was you. But you didn't mean for that to happen."

Intent, Henry Feldt leaned forward in the jury box. "No," Rennell's voice said.

The damning one-word answer seemed to make Feldt freeze. "I didn't think so," Monk concurred. "You were holding her head down. When she started choking, you didn't know what to do."

There was more silence. With sudden vehemence, Rennell answered, "I didn't do that little girl."

In the courtroom, Candace Bender was staring at Rennell. Her look conveyed the disbelief which, Mauriani was sure, now pervaded the other eleven jurors. But Rennell Price only nodded to himself, smiling at the sound of his own voice.

EIGHTEEN

MAURIANI'S NEXT WITNESS WAS THE SNITCH, JAMAL Harrison.

"Why not end with him?" Carlo asked Terri. "If they took events in sequence, he'd be last."

Terri looked up from the transcript of Liz Shelton's testimony. "He was just too weird," she answered. "Mauriani wanted to finish with Shelton, the calm voice of authority. If Jamal blew up on him, Mauriani could use the medical examiner to recoup his credibility."

Carlo flipped another page, scanning it for a moment. "The way this is reading," he observed, "Mauriani didn't need to worry."

Pausing, the prosecutor reached the climax of his direct examination. "What happened," he inquired, "after you promised Payton that you'd murder Eddie Fleet?"

Twitchy, Jamal Harrison shot a glance at the defendants. Payton glared back at him with anger and contempt; calmly, Rennell finished writing on a yellow legal pad and then looked up, pen poised to take more notes. Turning to the prosecutor, Jamal said softly, "Payton didn't say nothing to me, only nodded. Then he set down next to Rennell and whispered in his ear."

"What did Rennell do?"

Jamal's restless gaze darted about the courtroom. "Just smiled, man. I guess thinking about Fleet being dead must have tickled his fancy."

To Mauriani's surprise, James did not ask Rotelli to strike the answer. Swiftly, the prosecutor followed, "But you didn't hear what Payton told him."

Shifting his weight, Jamal crossed and then recrossed his legs, as though his own skin were a prison. "All I know," he said with venomous quiet, "is what I saw—the first smile I ever saw the whole time Rennell Price was in that cell."

Satisfied, Mauriani chose to end there. "No further questions," he told Rotelli.

As he headed for the prosecution table, he shot a surreptitious glance at Rennell Price's notepad. But all he could make out was a jumble of printed words linked by arrows and, more obscure, what might have been the stick figure of a child.

James stared balefully at the witness. "You made up this whole story," he charged. "Just to curry favor with the police."

Jamal's eyes flashed. "Cops didn't do me no favors."

"Not today, Jamal. You're here doing **them** one by making out the brothers to be killers."

Sitting back, Jamal gave James a small smile of superiority, and a glint of triumph crept into his eyes. "Think so, Mr. Lawyer? Then how you think I knew Eddie Fleet was gonna be a witness for the prosecution?"

Nettled, James snapped, "I'm asking the questions here—"

"Cops and prosecutor didn't tell me," Jamal cut in. "**Payton** told me about Fleet. Those brothers were stuck in jail, and they needed Eddie dead."

Mauriani suppressed a smile. Unperturbed, Rennell kept taking notes.

Carlo flipped back several pages, then placed one finger on Mauriani's last question to Jamal. "Explain this one to me," he said to Terri. "Jamal Harrison implies that Rennell's smile meant he knew Jamal had agreed to kill Fleet, and James doesn't object. Great for the prosecution. Then Mauriani forces Jamal to admit he didn't hear what Payton whispered to Rennell."

"Read this," Terri suggested, sliding the open transcript of Elizabeth Shelton's testimony across the conference table. "Start with James's final question on cross, and then go on to Mauriani's redirect. The absence of DNA technology when Thuy Sen died didn't help. But what you're seeing is the beginning of a pattern."

"So," James thundered, "you don't know **whose** semen you found in Thuy Sen's throat."

To Mauriani, Liz Shelton remained the embodiment of professional composure, a counterpoint to James's theatrics. "No," she answered. "All I know is that the secretor, or **secretors,** of the semen were type O. The same blood type as both your clients."

"Thank you," James declaimed smoothly and, to Mauriani's surprise, sat down. Perhaps James wanted to end on a note of triumph—if only through the bewildering satisfaction conveyed by his own voice.

At once, Mauriani stood. "Dr. Shelton, I'd like to clarify the answer you just gave to Mr. James. Are you resting any part of your opinion on the blood type of the semen, or suggesting that it implicates either Rennell or Payton Price?"

At once, Shelton grasped the import of the question. "Not at all. In African Americans, roughly half the population is type O. The most I can say is that I can't exclude the brothers as possible secretors."

"So you're not suggesting that the jury should base their verdict on blood type."

"I am not. No responsible expert would."

Mauriani nodded his satisfaction. "In light of that," he continued, "and as an expert in both areas, could you summarize the medical and forensic evidence which you believe the jury **should** consider."

"Of course." As Shelton paused, turning to address them, Mauriani felt the jury's close attention. "To begin, Thuy Sen was asphyxiated by approximately five cc's of ejaculated semen which collected in her throat. At the defendants' house—along with a green thread consistent with her sweater, and a partial print from her right index finger—we found traces of semen and saliva on the carpet. We found the same thread, and the same traces, in the trunk of Fleet's car. And Thuy Sen's body washed up approximately where, according to the Coast Guard, it would have had it been dumped where Fleet claimed it was. With what appeared to be a pubic hair caught in her barrette."

In the jury box, Henry Feldt had begun nodding. "I can't tell you," Shelton concluded, "whose ejaculation caused this child's death. But the physical evidence is consistent with the testimony of Fleet and Flora Lewis.

"Thuy Sen was in the brothers' living room. Her body was in Eddie Fleet's trunk. And she choked to death on semen—just as, according to Fleet, Rennell Price said she did."

And that, Mauriani thought, was the perfect coda to his case.

As his final witness stepped down, he looked toward Thuy Sen's parents, hoping to convey at least some comfort. But they were huddled together in abject misery and did not see him.

Glancing at Eula Price, he detected tears glistening in her eyes.

A deep pity overcame him. She, too, struck Mauriani as a victim, perhaps even more alone than the Sens. Though part of her purpose in suffering this ordeal must have been to humanize the brothers, at whatever pain to her, there was no one to give her comfort— James had taken no note of her since the trial began and neither, with the exception of the ill-timed smile from Rennell, had her own grandsons.

Nor did they now. Liz Shelton's testimony seemed to have driven home to Payton how desperate were his circumstances, displacing his look of anger with a dead-eyed stare at nothing. Rennell simply scribbled on his yellow pad.

"Those questions about blood type," Carlo said now, "Mauriani was covering for the defense lawyer's screwups."

Nodding, Terri put down the felt-tipped pen she used to underline key questions. "Mauriani didn't want a verdict based on prejudicial error, or a record so bad that the verdict might be reversed for ineffective assistance of counsel. You can almost feel him wishing James were better, then deciding that the only certain answer is self-help."

"Not so certain," Carlo answered. "James's cross-examination was terrible, pretty much all the time. Like the stupid way he climbed all over Thuy Sen's mother."

Terri made a wry face. "If terrible and obnoxious were enough, our job would be a whole lot easier. At least James was awake—too awake, probably, because he was all coked up. Aside from constantly wiping his nose, grandiosity and lack of judgment are the hallmarks of a cokehead.

"But that's **our** take. The Attorney General's Office will call his tactics the aggressiveness of a dedicated advocate fighting for his clients' lives. In fact, they **did** say that, on appeal, and our state Supreme Court agreed. The Court also said the evidence was so overwhelming that nothing James did or didn't do would have changed the verdict."

"Amazing."

Terri gave him the jaded smile of a lawyer who had seen far too much of this. "Only mildly amazing," she rejoined and tossed him another transcript. "Take a look at James's defense."

NINETEEN

THE SOLE WITNESS FOR THE DEFENSE WAS TASHA Bramwell.

In Lou Mauriani's estimate, she made a good impression. Neatly dressed, well-spoken, and unusually composed, Tasha, by her relationship with Payton, suggested a man very different from the menacing crack dealer the jury saw before it. In a manner quiet but unequivocal, she told the courtroom that the brothers had been with her on the day Thuy Sen had vanished.

"So you're completely confident," James summarized, "that Payton and Rennell spent the afternoon of September twenty-seventh inside your home."

"Yessir," Tasha answered and addressed the jury with her first hint of passion. "The very next night, at work, I saw that little girl's picture on TV. I'll never forget that as long as I live. I can tell you two things—Payton would never do that, and Rennell and him **couldn't** have done it. We were together."

Rising to cross-examine, Mauriani could read the jury's puzzlement. The task before him was delicate—

though Tasha Bramwell could not account for the evidence placing Thuy Sen in the brothers' living room, her certainty must give the jurors pause, and her demeanor created sympathy. It would not do to attack her.

He stood some distance from the witness, amiable and pleasant, hands in the pockets of his suitcoat. "The afternoon of September twenty-seventh," he began, "the three of you watched TV."

"Yes, sir."

"Do you remember what programs?"

"Soap operas, mostly. I remember **Days of Our Lives** and **General Hospital**—Rennell likes those."

At the defendants' table, Mauriani noted, Rennell smiled to himself. "Did the brothers hang out with each other a lot?"

"Yes, sir. I mean they lived together."

"Would you call them inseparable?"

Bramwell seemed to turn the question over in her mind. "I'd call them close. Where Payton went, there'd usually be Rennell."

"So even though you were Payton's girl, Rennell spent time with both of you."

Bramwell nodded. "He liked being with us, and Payton didn't seem to mind. So I didn't either."

With this answer, Mauriani had created an assumption that buttressed Flora Lewis's testimony—where one brother was, so was the other. He chose not to solicit Tasha's admission that, for an hour of private lovemaking, Rennell was left alone: it did nothing for

Mauriani's case, directed at both brothers, and James had chosen not to raise it.

"Every Tuesday," Mauriani asked, "you had a book-keeping class. Correct?"

"Yessir. Tuesday, Thursday, and Friday. At three o'clock."

"But **that** Tuesday, you chose to skip it."

"Yes."

"How many classes did you skip that semester?"

"Just the one."

Approvingly, Mauriani nodded. "I guess you're pretty diligent about attendance."

"I am that," Tasha affirmed. "I want to do my best."

"But you felt comfortable cutting that one class."

"Yessir." Pausing, Bramwell smoothed her skirt, then looked back at Mauriani, adding with satisfaction, "I got an A for the semester."

Mauriani cocked his head, feigning curiosity. "On what basis did your professor grade you?"

"Mostly the exams."

"How many were there?"

For the first time, Bramwell hesitated, puzzled by the level of Mauriani's interest. "Two," she answered. "A midterm, and a final."

"And were these take-home exams? Or did Professor Lee give them to you in class?"

The name of her professor, slipped into Mauriani's question with seeming casualness, caused Bramwell to pause yet again. "In class."

"In class," Mauriani repeated. "How'd you do on the midterm?"

Now Bramwell stared at him. "An A, I think."

"A minus," Mauriani corrected genially. "But close enough." Turning, he walked over to the prosecution table and then paused, asking over his shoulder, "You don't happen to remember the date, do you?"

Suspicion formed in Bramwell's eyes. Tersely, she answered, "No."

Reaching into a file folder, Mauriani withdrew a document, three photocopied pages, stapled together at the left-hand corner. Courteously, he showed the document to Yancey James, noting the glassy look appearing in his opponent's gaze. Payton's eyes narrowed to slits; only Rennell seemed unaffected. As Mauriani completed the ritual of marking People's Exhibit 27, he spotted Henry Feldt following its progress back into Tasha Bramwell's hands.

Turning, the prosecutor walked toward Bramwell. She slid back in the witness chair, her slender body suddenly appearing frail. When he held out the document for Bramwell to take, she hesitated before accepting it. "Can you identify this document?" he asked.

Silent, she seemed fixated on one corner of the paper. "Yes."

The smile had vanished, Mauriani noted. "Is that your midterm exam?"

"Yes."

She looked stunned, almost sick. Evenly, Mauriani

said, "I draw your attention to the upper-right-hand corner of the first page. Can you tell the jury what you see."

"A date."

"Would you mind reading it aloud?"

Bramwell exhaled, a slow release of breath. "September twenty-seventh, 1987."

"September twenty-seventh," Mauriani repeated. "If Professor Lee says that this date is correct, and his grading records confirm that, do you have any concrete reason to believe that was **not** the date you took the midterm?"

Bramwell's lips parted slightly. "Just my own recollection," she answered softly. "Nothing else."

Mauriani nodded. "And if your recollection's wrong, then you **were** in class that afternoon, and couldn't have been with Payton and Rennell the afternoon when Thuy Sen disappeared."

Bramwell glanced toward Payton, as though in silent apology. "No, sir."

"In that case, you don't know **where** they were, do you? Or what they might have done?"

Briefly, Tasha's eyes closed. "No, sir. Except Payton would never do that."

With a chivalrous air, Mauriani took the document from her hands. "You care about Payton, don't you?"

"Course I do." Bramwell's voice held a renewed strength. "I love him."

"Enough to visit him in jail?"

"Yes, sir. Every day I can."

Gravely, Mauriani considered her. "During those visits, Tasha, did Payton ask you to tell this story?"

Tasha folded her arms, unable to look at anyone. Before she could form an answer, Mauriani decided that showing mercy, and even pity, would be better than forcing her to lie. Turning to Rotelli, he said, "I'll withdraw the question, Your Honor. I think we've done enough."

"**That** was the defense?" Carlo murmured.

"Yup." Terri unwrapped her tuna sandwich. "One bad alibi witness whose story James never checked out. Not much to show in exchange for Eula Price's house. Plus, Mauriani sandbagged James. His motion to exclude Bramwell was a charade. He already knew that she was lying—he intended to lose the motion, and then let James hang both his clients."

"Good, wasn't he?"

"Mauriani? The best. Shameless, too." She passed across the deli bag with "roast beef on rye" scrawled across it. "Eat your sandwich, then take a look at his final argument."

"Thuy Sen's death," Mauriani told the jury, "was the culmination of all you've heard. The witness who saw the brothers abduct her off the street. The sad traces of her last moments alive—a green thread, a fingerprint—in their living room. Semen and saliva, the residue of her anguish, on the defendants' rug and Eddie Fleet's car. The body which washed up where Fleet's testimony suggests it should have.

"What terrible luck these two must have. What an unhappy series of coincidences it is that every piece of evidence points to their guilt." Pausing, Mauriani looked into Candace Bender's eyes. "If all that's not enough," he said with muted anger, "remember the man Payton asked to murder Eddie Fleet."

Candace Bender glanced at the defendants, sitting mutely with their lawyer, and Mauriani chose this moment to stop and then nod toward Yancey James. "Mr. James," he continued, "is deeply experienced in capital cases. If a lawyer of his skills had any decent evidence casting doubt on his clients' guilt, don't you think you would have heard it? But all he had to offer was a misguided young woman who chose to tell a lie. As **if,**" Mauriani added with quiet scorn, "the lies of a single witness would expunge the shocking and disgusting acts which took this child's life."

With this tacit reminder that neither brother had testified on his own behalf, Mauriani paused to survey the courtroom. Meng Sen was still and pale; across the gulf which separated them, Chou Sen covered her face to hide the tears Eula Price did not bother to conceal. But Payton looked defiant, and Rennell's face had become an emotionless mask. Mauriani could not have offered a more chilling depiction of their indifference to the torment of Thuy Sen.

"You see her murderers before you," he told the jury. "In the name of an innocent, find them guilty."

James's final argument took seven minutes. Mauriani had offered no witness to the death, he reminded the jurors, no physical evidence to prove that his clients caused it. All the prosecutor had was an old lady who despised them, a crack dealer who admitted disposing of the body, and a jailhouse snitch trying to get in good with the police.

He never mentioned Tasha Bramwell. Less than two hours after receiving Judge Rotelli's instructions, the jurors convicted Payton and Rennell Price of the felony murder of Thuy Sen. All that remained for them was to choose between life and death.

TWENTY

BY THE TIME TERRI AND CARLO BEGAN THE FINAL volume of the trial transcript, it was past eight o'clock, and dusk was gathering outside the floor-to-ceiling windows of the conference room. Lights glimmered from the city, from the distant hills of Sausalito, and from the cars which crept like illuminated soldier ants across the shadowy bridge which linked them. They had been here since dawn; Terri's eyes felt scratchy, and the cheese had begun to congeal on the two remaining slices of pizza in the open box between them.

"In 1987," Terri explained to Carlo, "the sentencing phase of a death penalty case worked pretty much the way it does now. The prosecutor presents the so-called aggravating factors, like the callousness or brutality of the crime itself, which support a sentence of death. Then the defense offers the 'mitigating factors' which cut against it—like character or mental state of the defendant, or his miserable personal history, or that he acted under the influence of someone else, or maybe drugs or alcohol. In theory, the jury finds for death only if the factors in its favor outweigh those against. Whether to **impose** death then lies with the judge."

Terri began flipping through the transcript. "According to Mauriani," she continued, "Payton and Rennell were forced to wear prison clothes at the sentencing phase. The idea was to remind the jurors that Payton and Rennell were different from the rest of humanity. Psychologically, it might make them a little easier to kill." Finding the first page she had marked with a paper clip, Terri passed the transcript to Carlo. "But here's where you'll find the one truly special touch. It'll help you appreciate how ruthless Mauriani could be."

On the witness stand, Thuy Sen's twelve-year-old sister, Kim, looked even smaller than she was, and her thin legs in a schoolgirl's red knee socks dangled without touching the floor. Dressed in bright orange jumpsuits, the brothers watched her; Payton closely, Rennell without expression. Anna Velez, Mauriani noted, dabbed away tears of sympathy; from her mother's testimony, the jury already knew that Kim still could barely eat or sleep. But Mauriani wanted the more clinical jurors, like Henry Feldt, to see this child for themselves.

"When you think of Thuy Sen," Mauriani softly asked her, "what do you remember?"

Kim seemed to choke on the words. When at last they emerged, it was in a light, whispery voice which her perfect diction only made more affecting. "That I didn't wait for her, like I should have." She swallowed, staring at the floor. "Because of me my sister's dead . . ."

Abruptly, the child covered her face. The only other sign that she was crying was the uncontrollable trembling of frail shoulders.

Chou Sen stood, face twisted in anguish.

Struck by regret, Mauriani nodded to her. But as she came forward for her surviving daughter, leading her from the courtroom, Mauriani saw the grim set of Henry Feldt's face.

"Jesus," Carlo murmured.

"Yeah." Terri discarded the last, half-eaten slice of pizza. "Kim Sen's twenty-seven now. But wherever she is, it's a fair bet she's wearing out some psychologist."

"How did James respond?"

"Start reading where I put the second clip," Terri answered, "and prepare to be amazed."

James paused to dab at his nose. "From your verdict," he told the jury, "you've cleared the legal hurdle called reasonable doubt. But that does not mean there is **no** doubt—with no witnesses to the death, there must be at least **some** lingering doubt." Theatrically, James flung his arms open wide. "In the presence of doubt, why condemn these men to death?

"They will **die** in prison, ladies and gentlemen, a

threat to no one. You do not need to accelerate their demise."

In disbelief, Mauriani glanced at Henry Feldt. Frowning, Feldt had turned from James to his clients, studying them with the same lack of sympathy they had shown throughout the trial for Thuy Sen.

At the close of James's argument, Mauriani stood at once. "Your Honor, I ask the Court to meet in chambers with prosecution and defense counsel."

The keenness of Rotelli's glance confirmed his instant comprehension. "Very well," he said and motioned his courtroom deputy to open the door to his chambers.

They gathered inside, Mauriani and James seated in front of Angelo Rotelli's walnut desk, the court reporter set up to the side, surrounded by the trappings of a trial judge—tomes on evidence, treatises on trial practice, bound jury instructions, and green leather chairs suitable to the inner sanctum of a men's club.

Rotelli steepled his hands. "Mr. Mauriani?"

"The defense has concluded its argument for mitigation," the prosecutor began. "By my calculation, in eleven minutes. Mr. James has called no witnesses, or attempted to introduce any mitigating factors—for example, regarding the defendants' background." Pausing, Mauriani added pointedly, "On behalf of **either** client.

"In light of this, I believe it's appropriate for the Court to inquire as to the nature of counsel's preparations for the sentencing phase, and the options he considered on behalf of Rennell and Payton Price—as individuals. Including his investigation with respect to their personal histories."

James drew himself up. "Your Honor," he said in a defensive tone, "I can assure you that defense counsel has been nothing less than diligent. Mr. Mauriani is seeking privileged information—an unwarranted peek beneath the veil of my strategy. At whatever prejudice to **both** of my clients."

Turning to Mauriani, the judge raised his eyebrows. James's implication was clear—that any material he had uncovered was so damning it would grease the skids toward execution. That it was also, Mauriani suspected, a cover for James's sloth could not be helped. Mauriani had done what he could—raised the issue, and forced James to put his excuses on the record. With luck, Angelo Rotelli had helped him bury a potential claim that the brothers had ineffective assistance of counsel—at least during the sentencing phase.

"Thank you, Your Honor," Mauriani said solemnly.

Rising in rebuttal, Mauriani walked toward the jury box. "Defense counsel," he began with quiet scorn, "has argued that there is 'lingering doubt.' What about this case would leave you **any** doubt—about who killed Thuy Sen, or about the agony of this child's last moments of life, asphyxiated by an act no child should ever know about?"

For the first time, Henry Feldt nodded. "There is only one question," Mauriani told him. "What penalty does justice to Thuy Sen and her family?

"That penalty is death."

With this, Mauriani sat, a minute after he had risen.

Alone, Terri reviewed the last few pages; Carlo had skipped out for a quick cup of coffee with a new woman in his life, a medical student, almost as busy as he.

The judge, Terri found, had given the jury clear instructions on the option of life without parole. But in Terri's experience, few jurors believed that this alternative was real, and **these** jurors had probably despised the brothers as deeply as they sorrowed for the Sens.

In less than an hour their foreman, Henry Feldt, announced the verdict: death for both defendants.

The final decision was Rotelli's.

He could confirm the penalty of death or impose life without parole. In the courtroom, Mauriani watched as Rotelli, in his first capital murder trial as a judge, gravely began fulfilling a new role in a familiar play. Rotelli had become a judge by prosecuting high-profile murder cases; the question was whether he could enter a death sentence as readily as he once had sought it.

The courtroom was still: the Price brothers, James, the Sen family, and Eula Price were united in their sobriety by this final, fateful moment. With great deliberation, Rotelli began reciting the factors before him—the odious nature of the crime, the youth and innocence of the victim, the lack of remorse shown by the defendants, and their effort to cause the murder of the principal witness against them. Then he turned to the defendants. "The defense," Rotelli told them in somber tones, "has introduced no mitigating factors, and this Court is aware of none."

For an instant, the judge seemed to pause at the duty before him, then intoned for Payton Price—now as impassive as his brother—and then for Rennell the awesome words Mauriani had come to think of as, quite literally, a sentence of death.

"Rennell Price, it is the judgment of this Court, and it is hereby ordered, adjudged, and decreed, that you shall be put to death in accordance with California law within the walls of the State Prison at San Quentin.

"The defendant Rennell Price is therefore remanded to the custody of the Sheriff of San Francisco County to be delivered to the administrator of that prison, within ten days from this date, for execution of the sentence of death for the murder of Thuy Sen..."

To Mauriani's astonishment, Rennell Price stood.

For the only time, his deep voice sounded in the court-room. "I didn't do that little girl..."

Closing the transcript, Terri prepared to go home, try to get some sleep. There were fifty-four days until the date of execution.

PART TWO

THE INVESTIGATION

O N E

It was that kind of San Francisco morning when drizzle spattered through a mistlike fog which clung chill and close to the slick pavement. As Carlo drove, Terri sipped coffee from a porcelain mug, warming her cupped hands. The breath of the defroster cleared circles on the windshield of her cluttered Jeep.

Carlo turned down Pine Street toward Laurel Heights. "So tell me about Laura Finney," he said.

"Until a few weeks ago she was a senior counsel at Kenyon and Walker. She's the only lawyer who worked on Rennell's appeal from the start." Pausing, Terri sipped her coffee. "In theory, Kenyon and Walker's as different from Yancey James as you can get—six hundred lawyers from top-tier law schools, the elite of their profession, with resources to burn. More help than most would think Rennell deserved."

"You don't sound impressed."

"We'll see," Terri answered with a shrug. "What struck me about their filings was how neatly prepared they were. Perfect margins—not a typo I could find. The only thing missing was Rennell."

———

Laura Finney snatched at a stray hair which had eluded the rubber band pulling her brown curls back in a bun.

Dressed in blue jeans, she was slender and pale, her eyes unsmiling behind wire-rim glasses. In the living room of her one-story stucco bungalow a toddler girl watched **Sesame Street** while an infant boy writhed in a playpen, vainly attempting to master the art of flipping on his stomach. The circles beneath her eyes made Finney look so tired that Carlo could imagine her on the treadmill of new motherhood.

"The second baby got to be too much," she told them. "I took maternity leave one month before the Supreme Court turned down Rennell's **habeas corpus** petition. By then I was the senior lawyer on the case— the only one who had been there since Rennell's direct appeal got assigned to us, when I was just out of law school." Pausing, she added in a tone Carlo heard as bemusement. "That was fourteen years ago."

"Why so long?" he asked.

Finney shot a glance of wan amusement at Terri, sitting beside her stepson on the gray wool couch. "Bureaucracy," she told Carlo. "Inertia. Despite all the right-wing politicians bleating about tricky lawyers abusing the system to put years between our death row clients and the needle, thus extending the agony of people like Thuy Sen's parents.

"Truth is, it's the **process** that's excruciating, and all we needed to invoke it was show up." Leaning forward in her chair toward Carlo, she began ticking off its stages on her fingers. "Let's review the stations of the cross. First three were the so-called direct appeal of Rennell's conviction to the California Supreme Court. The Court hears only about twenty or so direct appeals a year. And direct appeals include only issues which are presented by the record of the trial itself. That made our direct appeal pretty close to worthless when it came to whether 'Lawyer James' greased the wheels of death for his own client."

"Why? You can see **that** much from the trial transcript."

"All you can see," Finney rejoined, "is that James was a crummy lawyer with terrible judgment. The courtrooms of America are crawling with those. What you **can't** tell is whether he's what the Sixth Amendment right to counsel supposedly guarantees: a lawyer who investigates, with at least minimal competence, all the options for sparing his client death."

"Or," Terri interjected pointedly, "whether his lawyer had a coke habit?"

The inquiry, cutting off Finney's clipped, ironic narrative, induced a look of doubt and surprise. "Why do you think that?"

"Just surmise. You interview the grandmother?"

"**I** didn't." The hint of doubt in Finney's manner became defensiveness. "A junior associate did, I think. There was a lot to do, and so a lot of us worked this case."

Carlo could read in Terri's skepticism her imaginings of some rookie lawyer, too lightly supervised, interviewing an elderly woman from the Bayview across the gap of race and age and culture—though Carlo himself had adduced from Eula Price the telling detail of James's runny nose. But then his life until age seven had given him a preternatural sense of people, and what was left unsaid.

"Who was the partner in charge?" Terri asked.

"Which year?" Finney's tone retrieved its irony. "The direct appeal took seven years by itself, and the **habeas corpus** petition—the first time we could present facts outside the record—was decided seven years after that. About halfway through, the first partner, Frank Goldmark, died of a massive coronary at a 49ers game. The next one, Leslie Keller, left to become General Counsel of an Internet start-up in return for stock options which became worthless once the company crashed and burned. I guess you could say Rennell Price was a real killer."

Terri did not smile. "After Keller left," she asked, "who took over the case?"

Finney glanced at her daughter. In a corner of the living room, the child watched a purple puppet chirp at her from the television. Turning, Finney answered, "I did. After all those years, the case was too attenuated to explain to another partner, and would have required too much learning the law for him to get a grip on. After all," she added sardonically, "we were doing this for free."

This time Terri's expression was so polite that only Carlo might read it as a mask. "I guess that's why they call it **pro bono,**" she answered, and the baby in the playpen began to whimper.

They waited in the living room while Finney took twenty minutes to breast-feed her son. "What's wrong?" Carlo asked.

Terri looked at him in surprise. Softly, she answered, "To me, it's classic—the intellectual severity, the unearned cynicism, the ability to see every irony but how badly they served Rennell. Sometimes I'm not sure what makes me crazier—smug big-firm lawyers, or privileged white women."

Carlo looked at the plastic kids' toys scattered across the carpet. "**This** is privilege?"

"To a mother." Terri's smile was sour. "She's home, isn't she? Rennell Price is about to die."

When Finney returned without the baby, she began speaking as if she'd never left. "The problem with the direct appeal was that the record was so clear.

"Mauriani played it straight. No racial bias in jury selection. No withholding of exculpatory evidence. If his witnesses gave answers which were objectionable and James failed to object, Mauriani would caution them and then rephrase the questions..."

"Why not?" Terri observed mildly. "When you're getting away with murder, why not wrap it with a bow?"

"The point is," Finney retorted, "that all the record left us was to argue that, on its face, James was so incompetent as to effectively deny Rennell Price his right to counsel. The Attorney General's Office argued that there might be strategic reasons for even his worst lapses. Though no one could guess what they were..."

"What did **James** tell you?" Carlo asked.

"Nothing," Finney responded in an arid tone. "He was in the middle of disbarment proceedings, so his lawyer advised him not to meet with us." She glanced at Terri. "All he told me on the phone was that Rennell's case was so hopeless that nothing he did, or didn't do, would have made any difference. Lest that sound too self-serving, the California Supreme Court read the record, and agreed." Pausing, she smiled thinly. "For **that** meager result, we bought Rennell Price seven more years on death row. Clever lawyering, don't you think?"

Turning from the screen, the little girl pronounced herself hungry. A look of martyred patience crossed Finney's face, and she invited Terri and Carlo to the kitchen while she made a peanut butter sandwich and cut it into bite-size squares. Placing this offering before her daughter, she said with a faint smile, "Here you are, sweetie. Quicker than you can say 'paternity leave.'"

The little girl looked up at her, uncomprehending, then slipped the first brown and white square into her mouth. "Not that I blame my husband," Finney remarked. "Our firm's got upward of three hundred male lawyers, and not one has taken the six-month leave we offer. Its mere existence is enough to make them paragons of feminism."

The bitterness beneath this observation made Carlo imagine a disenchanted and, perhaps, no longer quite attentive lawyer left by attrition to deal with a hopeless client.

"At least that's something," Terri answered. "**My** first husband was just a deadbeat." But, of course, Ricardo Arias had been so much more than that.

As they went back to the living room, Terri turned to Carlo. "Once Rennell lost his direct appeal," she explained, "the next step was **habeas corpus.** Basically, you claim that a prisoner is being imprisoned in violation of his constitutional rights, and then try to get him out by proving it.

"In Rennell's case, that enabled Kenyon and Walker to file a separate petition, also before the California Supreme Court, presenting evidence outside the record—maybe of innocence, or factors which might cut against a death sentence. As well as why James might have failed to uncover evidence of either." Of Finney, she inquired, "Who looked into Rennell's school or medical records?"

Finney settled back in her chair. "That part got assigned to another associate, I can't remember who. What comes to me is a lot of truancy, and a couple of accidents—things like falls and broken bones."

Terri studied her. "Kid stuff?" she asked softly.

"I guess so, yeah."

Carlo glanced at Terri. "What about Rennell's IQ?" he asked.

"I remember he was no genius," Finney said reluctantly. "But if you're talking about retardation, that became more critical after I left the firm. By the time the **Atkins** case came down, it was too late for us to use it—our **habeas corpus** petition had already been shot down by the State Supreme Court, the Federal District Court, and the Ninth Circuit Court of Appeals, and the U.S. Supremes had declined to review. So raising retardation falls to you."

No problem, Carlo thought. **We've got seven weeks.** It struck him that Terri's face was never more arresting than when her green-flecked brown eyes betrayed the swiftness of her thoughts. "Did you try to interview Rennell's teachers?" she asked.

"I think so. But I don't recall anything coming of it."

"What about the family?"

"Not much there. Mom killed Dad, Grandmother's literally sick and tired, and his brother, Payton, hasn't opened his mouth for a decade and a half. All we got from any of them was the grandma saying that the Rennell who came to live with her was a sweet and gentle boy. I guess that's what she had to cling to."

Terri's features suddenly lacked all expression—a sign, Carlo guessed, of how hard she was working to conceal her impatience with Laura Finney. "What about the mother?" she asked.

"We tried," Finney answered. "But the woman's crazy. Talking to her was like listening to some street person jabber to herself."

"No doubt," Terri responded. "But tell me about it, anyway."

What Laura Finney remembered was eyes like burn holes.

She sat with Athalie Price in a mental institution so grim that it could have been nothing else. The woman's processed hair was hacked off, her face gaunt, her body as stringy as beef jerky. But it was the eyes—to Finney, they spat madness.

"Fool," Athalie Price muttered with contempt. "And he thought that boy was stupid 'cause **I** was. That made **him** the stupidest of us all."

When Laura asked if she meant Rennell's father, Athalie leaned back, head against the wall, and started laughing to herself, a hiss of rage escaping from her lips. She refused to speak another word.

"All I came away with," Finney said now, "is this wasn't the Cleaver family. That much I already knew."

"What about Thuy Sen's family?" Terri asked. "Ever talk to them?"

"No." Finney's face registered palpable surprise. "What could they tell me that wouldn't add to their misery? Even before having my own daughter, I wouldn't have wanted to remind them all over again of how theirs died. Not unless it did some good."

Carlo glanced at Terri and saw nothing in her eyes about Elena. But, uncharacteristically, she seemed to have no follow-up question. "What about DNA?" he asked Finney.

"We tried every test there was. But Thuy Sen had been floating for two days before they found her. The semen samples from her mouth and throat were too degraded to show whose sperm it was." Pausing, Finney drew a breath. "To tell the truth, part of me was relieved. I was too afraid of knowing."

Terri stared at her. "Knowing what?" she quietly asked. "That Rennell was guilty, or that he might not be? Only the latter scares **me**."

Still watching Terri, Carlo wondered if this were true.

T W O

SILENT, FINNEY CONSIDERED TERRI. "TO BE HONEST,"
she said sharply, "I never felt at risk of finding out Rennell was innocent. God knows I tried."

Terri was unsurprised, except by Finney's candor.
"What did Rennell say happened?" she asked.

" 'I didn't do that little girl.' Over and over, for fifteen years. But he didn't give us any reason to believe
that."

"Didn't?" Terri countered in even tones. "Or
couldn't? Suppose he **is** retarded—that wouldn't
make him gifted at constructing an alternative. Or
suppose he wasn't there at all. He wouldn't know
what happened."

"True," Finney answered. "But Thuy Sen **was** inside their living room. We know that from the forensics, from Flora Lewis, and from Fleet."

"Then let's start with Lewis. Did you talk to her
yourself?"

Finney nodded. "Shortly before she died in her parents' home—as she made clear to us she'd always
planned on, no matter what had happened to the

neighborhood. She was as certain with us of what she'd seen that day as she was with Charles Monk."

"Maybe so," Terri responded. "But as Monk well knows, a white woman like Lewis—elderly, isolated, and frightened—might not distinguish one black man from another. She might even have wanted one of the men she saw, or **said** she saw, to be Rennell."

"Who else would Flora Lewis have seen?"

"A black man," Terri answered dryly. "That much we can count on. Did you consult any experts on the reliability of cross-racial IDs?"

"No." Finney's voice rose. "You **do** understand that, when we started, the State of California allowed only twelve thousand dollars in investigative fees, and that the federal court's allowance for expenses on **habeas corpus** was largely left to the discretion of the judge. It's not just that Kenyon and Walker didn't bill for our time for fourteen years—we pretty much carried the cost of Rennell Price's petition, however slim the prospect of success."

From Finney's perspective, Terri acknowledged, that was fair—the fees allowed the Pagets were well below their normal rates. "I appreciate the problem," she offered in a mollifying tone. "But we've only got forty-nine days and a very hard road. I need to know how many avenues are left to keep the state from killing Rennell Price. Did you talk to Eddie Fleet?"

"I tried, the last time maybe seven years ago." Something, perhaps a memory, seemed to make

Finney glance briefly at her daughter. "The nearest I got to him was Betty Sims's front door."

The Bayview, Finney acknowledged to herself, made her apprehensive—there was a sense of danger, as frightening for its randomness as for its malignity. Laura Finney suffered from the lawyer's belief in cause and effect; the idea of dying for no reason—except perhaps that she was white, or a woman, or in the wrong place when some drug dealer fired a gun—made her feel powerless and afraid, as vulnerable as if she were standing naked on a street corner. Knocking on a stranger's door in the featureless squalor of the Double Rock project, she felt pinpricks on the back of her neck.

After the second knock, a woman in a bathrobe slowly opened the door. She was perhaps in her mid-thirties, but her eyes, wide and wary, seemed older, as if no surprise in her life had ever been a good one. A girl of seven or eight leaned against her, gripping the belt of her robe as though it were a lifeline.

"I'm looking for Betty Sims," Finney told her. "Can you help me?"

The woman paused before curtly answering. "**I'm** Betty." As she did, Finney saw that her lower lip was swollen, marred by the remnants of a scab which suggested that the lip had been cut by her own tooth.

Finney extended her hand. "I'm Laura Finney," she said. "I represent Rennell Price."

Sims stared at her hand as though the gesture were Martian. When she took it, her grasp was tentative and fleeting. "Rennell's on death row," Finney continued. "You probably know that."

Sims hesitated. "What you want with me?"

The query was delivered in a muted undertone, echoing the fright Finney felt just from being there. "According to the police files," she explained, "you were a friend of Eddie Fleet's. I wanted to talk with you about him, maybe to Mr. Fleet himself."

What happened next was, to Finney, deeply disturbing: Betty Sims stiffened, looking back over her shoulder, as the girl at her side cast a silent, pleading look upward—first at Sims, then at Laura Finney. In a near whisper, Sims said, "We got nothin' to say."

Finney steeled herself to persist. "Is Eddie here?"

The girl's lips parted, as though to speak. Then Sims jerked her back and, with stricken eyes, closed the door in Finney's face.

Listening, Terri felt a frisson, the shadow of her own childhood passing through her mind. Softly, she asked Finney, "What did you make of it?"

Finney's expression was a curious mix of rueful and resigned. "That Fleet was there—or **some** guy—and whoever it was beat her. But I never set eyes on Eddie Fleet." Finney's gaze expanded to take in Carlo, sitting beside Terri with a notebook in his hand. "Whatever Fleet's peculiarities, we never found a reason to challenge Mauriani's case—Lewis, Fleet, and the forensics. The absence of DNA evidence was the clincher."

Though she had several disturbing thoughts of her own, Terri did not question this. "About the little girl with Sims," she asked. "Do you know who she was?"

"Her niece, the neighbors said—actually her cousin's daughter by some guy named Demetrius, who was serving life for murder. His name stuck in my mind."

Cordelia and Demetrius, Terri remembered from Monk's narrative, almost like Shakespeare. It was not hard to imagine the chain of events, beginning with Monk's and Larry Minnehan's appearance in her living room, that had delivered this child to Betty Sims and whatever fate they both might suffer. But she kept this melancholy reflection to herself and turned to another subject. "What about James's failure to seek a change of venue? How did that pan out?"

"We interviewed whatever jurors we could find. They said what you'd expect—that they decided on the evidence, not on pretrial publicity. More than plausible given the trial transcript." Finney paused to gather her thoughts. "In the end, we fell back on mitigation—the absence of any prior record of violence by Rennell, or of his involvement in any sex crimes. Plus the patent misery of his childhood."

Carlo looked up from his notes. "What about that in particular?"

"The misery part was obvious. Payton and Rennell saw their mother stab their father to death, and I guess it took him a while to die. Before that, the police records make pretty clear, Dad beat Mom—at least from time to time. Some of the neighbors thought he hit the brothers as well. They tended to stay away from him—they thought he was unpredictable, or maybe a little crazy."

"What did Rennell say about him?" Terri inquired.

"Not a lot—just that 'sometimes he took a belt to us.' Even that was like pulling teeth." Finney's voice held the edge of frustration. "See Rennell once, and you've pretty well experienced his full emotional range—from sullen to merely uncommunicative, with minor variations in between."

"How often **did** you see him?"

"Two or three times a year. There wasn't a lot to tell him, and he sure didn't have a lot to say to us, on any subject. Let alone the tribulations of childhood."

Two or three times a year, Terri thought, was not enough to gain any trust Rennell Price might have to offer. "Still," she said, "he did have an abusive home. How did you frame the argument?"

"The theory, more or less, was that trauma, combined with drug use, diminished his capacity to make moral judgments." Finney adjusted her glasses at the bridge. "The principal proponent of that theory was the state public defender, on behalf of Payton. We more or less piggybacked on that for Rennell—given the lack of investigative money, there was no point in duplicating their work."

At this, Carlo caught Terri's eye: she could imagine

him thinking, as she did, that Kenyon and Walker, like Yancey James, had never tried to separate Rennell's defense from that of his older brother. "Did you uncover any evidence that **James** had looked into Rennell's background? Or, for that matter, Payton's?"

"None. As near as we could tell, James's assertion to Judge Rotelli that he offered no mitigation evidence for tactical reasons—the insinuation being that background evidence would have hurt both brothers—was a cover-up for laziness. In fact, we argued in our **habeas** papers that there was no indication whatsoever that he'd done **any** work on behalf of Rennell, whether in the guilt or in the mitigation phase." Finney paused to grimace. "As with our direct appeal," she continued, "the California Supreme Court made short work of that without a hearing—a one-page order, the gist of which was that Rennell had knowingly waived any conflict arising from James's joint representation of Payton and him. And that even if James should have offered evidence of Rennell's first eighteen years of life, nothing we offered outweighed the heinous nature of Thuy Sen's death. As you can guess, that pretty much doomed our federal **habeas** petition."

At this, Terri turned to Carlo. "Since 1996," she explained, "the federal **habeas corpus** procedure is governed by a nasty piece of legislation called the Antiterrorism and Effective Death Penalty Act, inspired by the Oklahoma City bombing. Its purpose is to make it as hard as possible to overturn a state court denial of a **habeas corpus** petition. And the federal district judge in Rennell's case, Gardner Bond, pretty much views the death penalty as a form of population control."

This first mention of Judge Bond, Terri saw, ignited in Finney a spark of indignation. "We asked Bond for an evidentiary hearing," she told Carlo. "He denied it. The Ninth Circuit affirmed Bond without a hearing, and the U.S. Supreme Court turned down our petition. It was like Rennell was doomed from the time that Grandma hired Yancey James."

Which, Terri believed, was a fair summary of the truth, defective only in Laura Finney's failure to assign Kenyon and Walker its portion of responsibility. "I respect you for taking this on," Finney continued in a tone which combined rationalization with commiseration. "I wish I could see any promise in what you're doing. But the State of California wants to execute this man, and I don't see any way of stopping it."

As though hearing something in her mother's voice, the little girl came to Finney's side, silently tugging at the sleeve of her sweatshirt. Evenly, Terri asked, "In the end, how did you feel about Rennell?"

Finney paused to consider this. "Except for his one mantra," she said with some reluctance, "there was no sign that he gave a damn about Thuy Sen, or us, or anyone but maybe Payton. Almost like he was already dead."

Terri thanked Finney for her time and left with Carlo.

THREE

CHRISTOPHER PAGET SAT WITH HIS WIFE AND son. "How was your time at Kenyon and Walker?" he asked.

It was late afternoon of the following day, and a slanting sunlight grazed the waters of the bay, uncommonly serene. While Terri and Carlo had reviewed the files of Kenyon and Walker, Chris had amused Elena and Kit by taking them sailing. Now the family gathered on Chris's sailboat moored along the Marina District—Elena sprawled on her stomach reading a fashion magazine, Kit constructing an intricate fortress from Legos, and the three adults gathered around an improvised picnic. Carlo glanced at his stepmother. "According to Terri," he answered with some amusement, " 'just good enough to lose.' "

Turning to Terri, Chris raised his eyebrows. "They should stick to representing Merrill Lynch," she told him. "Assigning them Rennell's appeal was like putting the Good Housekeeping Seal of Approval on his death warrant."

"How so?"

"Because they know enough law to raise all the issues. And next to nothing about digging into a murder, or probing the lives of a dysfunctional black family in a subculture like the Bayview." Terri spread cheese on a cracker, her first nourishment since breakfast. "Laura Finney was right about this much—they made our job on a second petition as uphill as the evil geniuses who drafted AEDPA intended."

To his father, Carlo saw, this was all the explanation required: the acronym AEDPA—pronounced "edpa"—seemed to carry a totemic power. "Walk me through this," Carlo requested. "Terri mentioned it yesterday, but AEDPA's a new concept to me."

"AEDPA," his father answered promptly, "exists to keep folks like Rennell Price from delaying their own deaths. Let alone preventing them.

"The statute has two principal aims: to make state court impositions of the death penalty—no matter how biased or defective—nearly impossible to challenge; and to ensure that after the first **habeas** petition is ruled on, a second petition—even one based on new evidence of innocence—has almost no chance of staving off an execution."

"All Rennell's got left," Terri interjected, "is a second petition—under AEDPA the dregs of **habeas corpus,** bristling with restrictions." Preparing another cracker, she continued, "A claim presented in a first petition, however badly, is barred in a second—no matter how skimpy Kenyon and Walker's underlying inquiry. **Habeas** lawyers can be as lousy as they care to be."

At the corner of Carlo's vision, a seagull was creeping closer along the bow, perhaps preparing to snatch Terri's cracker in his bill. "Mind shooing him off?" he asked Kit. With far too much good cheer, Kit attempted a roar. But only when he half-rose, imitating a scarecrow, did the bird retreat.

"Impressive," Carlo assured his half brother and turned back to Terri. "Go on."

"Second, if Rennell is making an argument that the law has changed—for example, that we no longer execute the retarded—it can be based only on a Supreme Court ruling, and **then** only if the Court expressly held that it should apply to inmates who've already filed a **habeas corpus** petition. Otherwise, it's too late—the state can execute you, even if everyone who comes after you in a similar position would be saved—"

"Timing," Chris interjected dryly, "is truly all."

With this, both Terri and Chris fell silent, allowing Carlo to absorb what he had heard. He saw Terri's attention shift to Elena, still lying alone on the bow of the boat. It was a source of real guilt, he knew, that the unrelenting demands of an eleventh-hour death penalty petition all but deprived Elena of a mother. And the facts of **this** case, should Elena ever learn of them, surely deepened Terri's apprehension. A long moment later, Terri suspended her contemplation of Elena, turning back to Carlo. "Even as to innocence," she told him in a softer tone, "any new evidence must be so 'clear and convincing' that no reasonable jury would have convicted Rennell of murder. 'Reasonable doubt' is out the window—under AEDPA, the presumption of innocence has become a presumption of guilt."

"I had no idea the law of **habeas corpus** was that bad."

"No one does, except the lawyers who do this work. For the most part, the rest of America sits there, secure in our boundless fairness, believing that we coddle the condemned." Terri sipped from a can of cranberry juice. "We could find compelling evidence that Rennell is innocent," she continued, "and still end up witnessing his execution. Simply because some of the evidence was raised before, however badly. Or **could** have been raised before. Or because the trial was technically a fair one, even if the verdict was wrong. Or because the possibility of innocence is only fifty-fifty. Or maybe"—Terri picked up a cracker—"just because a three-judge panel of the Court of Appeals is in a crummy mood and won't give us leave to file a second petition under AEDPA. In which case we won't have to bother with all those other problems."

Chris and Carlo fell briefly silent. "How's Elena doing?" Chris asked.

"All right," Terri answered tiredly and then amended, "Not **quite** all right—there're some problems with her girlfriends. Thirteen's hard, even if you're not her."

"Want me to take her out for Mexican food?" Carlo asked. "We haven't done that in a while. And I've got street cred—she doesn't have to take it on faith that I used to be a teenager."

For a moment, Terri smiled, and her body, slumping slightly, seemed to relax. "That would be great," she told him. "Even if you're ducking work. You can meet us later."

"Who's 'us'?"

"Me. An experienced investigator, Johnny Moore. A Ph.D. in anthropology, Tammy Mattox—she's a mitigation specialist, and her job is putting together an entire social history of Rennell Price and his family. A psychiatric expert, Dr. Anthony Lane. All working around the clock until and unless, God forbid, the clock runs out."

Rising from his Lego fort, Kit crawled into his father's lap, his bare legs dangling above the deck. "I'm cold," he said.

Kissing the crown of Kit's head, Chris took off his windbreaker and draped it over the boy's shoulders. "We'll be going soon," Chris promised.

Such moments, Carlo reflected, summoned his earliest memories of his father. Except that Kit, his brother, looked so like Teresa Peralta. "Death cases are painful," she told Carlo. "I've learned to redefine my notions of success. So should you—because Rennell Price is very likely to die. It helps to believe two things. First, that your client is on death row because of what life dealt him, and he deserves to have that story told.

The Attorney General's aim is to ensure that story is **never** told—to the judge, or to the public. Your job is to make sure he fails."

"What's the second thing?"

"That your client deserves each day of life that you can give him. No matter what he's done, or who he seems to be."

Carlo glanced toward Elena, still reading: noting her isolation, he wondered if she somehow knew about the nature of the case and, if so, how she felt about Rennell's lawyers—her own family. Which, once again, caused him to ponder how Terri would deal with Elena while representing Rennell Price, and with what Carlo knew to be Terri's ineradicable guilt. "Doesn't seem like Rennell can help us much," he said at length.

Terri shook her head. "Neither Yancey James nor Laura Finney tried to build a relationship with him. They just took it as a given that Rennell was sullen and uncooperative, a kind of sociopath. It never seems to have occurred to them that maybe he was frightened, or confused, or just plain couldn't help them because he really doesn't know what's going on. And never did."

"That's our biggest hope," Chris opined. "Proving that Rennell's retarded. It means that he could be manipulated and confused by the police, unable to assist his own defense, unable to knowingly waive James's conflict or comprehend the trial, and prone to look unfeeling to a jury when he didn't know what was happening all around him."

Glancing at Elena, Terri stood, ready to leave—perhaps, Carlo guessed, to sublimate through action some thought too painful to express. "More than that," she told both men, "it's the gateway to explaining his entire life, and our excuse for trying to jam in all the new evidence we can find." Looking down at Carlo, she finished, "If Rennell's still alive in forty-eight days, it'll be because we succeeded. So take Elena to dinner, and then we'll get to work."

FOUR

AT EIGHT-THIRTY THAT NIGHT, THE **HABEAS CORPUS** team gathered in a booth at Terri's favorite steak house, Alfred's—from past experience, she knew them to be carnivores.

Terri sat across from Carlo. To her left was Johnny Moore, bearded and grizzled, a sixtyish former FBI agent turned investigator. On her right sat Tammy Mattox, the mitigation specialist, a Buddha-faced Alabaman with an ample belly and raucous laugh, so tenacious in her gathering of evidence that she claimed—credibly—to know the layout of every trailer park in America. On the drive over, Terri had told Carlo a story that typified Tammy's zeal: learning that the family of a death row inmate held an annual reunion deep in the hills of Arkansas, Tammy had simply shown up with a fresh-cooked ham and a basket of biscuits. When, three hours later, somebody finally asked who she was, her answer didn't much matter; by then she was family herself.

"The thing about retarded folks," Tammy told Carlo, "is people expect them to be slack-jowled and bug-eyed. Otherwise they're a real disappointment."

Sitting beside Carlo, Dr. Anthony Lane nodded his agreement. He was both a neuropsychiatrist—an expert in organic brain damage—and a specialist in retardation, and it would be his job to examine Rennell Price for impairments in mental functioning. Lane was a large black man with thick glasses, so big that Carlo would have thought of him as hulking but for the benignity of his gaze and the gentleness of his manner. "The retarded," he observed, "are as complex as the rest of us, and as varied. Assuming that Rennell is impaired, we have to make sense of what he tells us, and what he did. Even if it seems to make no sense at all."

Tammy sipped her mineral water. She did not drink the cabernet Terri had ordered for the table; years ago, when her drinking had become commensurate with the stress of her job, she had quit cold turkey. "Retarded folks," she told Carlo, "develop all sorts of strategies to keep from looking dumb. Do you know about masking?"

"No."

"Like anyone," she explained, "the retarded want to fit in. One way is to be agreeable, respond to cues the way they believe they should. A Rennell Price—if he **is** impaired—still wants to be part of the crowd, and may be smart enough to know he can't be. So he tries to cover up. Like he may have with Monk. But instead of seeing Rennell as sullen and resistant, as the cops did, consider the possibility that he was just trying to keep up, to give the answers Monk expected from him. That may be why his responses about Thuy Sen were so ambiguous."

"Except for his bottom line," Carlo said. "'I didn't do that little girl.'"

Lane touched his arm. "I'll tell you a classic story, Carlo. In a pilot program, a number of retarded people were discharged from an institution and allowed to seek work. During job interviews, the great majority tried to conceal their hospitalization by claiming that they'd been in prison. They thought that sounded better." As Carlo smiled, Lane added, "Anyhow, I find it interesting that Rennell was so adamant about his innocence. No matter how hard Monk tried."

"To be fair to Monk," Terri said, "many of the retarded can do a lot of the things anyone else can—drive, hold a job, make friends, talk sports, join the military, keep secrets, read the news, and even sound knowledgeable about one thing or another. It'd be easy for Charles Monk to meet someone like that and just write him off as 'no genius.' But what's missing is far more profound: the ability to understand and process information, to engage in logical reasoning, and to appreciate the nature of his dilemma, or respond appropriately."

"What causes all that?" Carlo asked.

Dinner arrived: chateaubriand with béarnaise sauce for Terri and Carlo; prime rib for Johnny Moore; strip steaks for Tammy Mattox and Anthony Lane. Lane hoisted his bowl-shaped glass. "Maybe **this**," he answered. "Alcohol—if Mom drinks enough while the kid's **in utero.** Or crack, or even prescription drugs pregnant women shouldn't take. There's also hereditary retardation, genetically transmitted. Sometimes you get a process of downward natural selection: inbreeding among the less gifted, which creates a smaller and smaller gene pool, so that the genetics for impaired intelligence predominates. And as the gene pool becomes more marginal, aggravating factors like fetal alcohol syndrome tend to increase—the mother's far more likely to be unaware of risks."

"Like in the Bayview," Mattox said flatly. "Part of my job is to gather up Rennell's school records, teachers' observations, medical and psychiatric records, and then interview people who knew Rennell—and Payton—from the beginning."

"Then I'll evaluate all that," Lane went on, "and meet with Rennell. That'll include testing for lesions on the brain, organic brain syndrome, head injuries, and, of course, IQ."

Carlo sat back, momentarily savoring the wine. It struck him that the warmth of their environment—red-flocked wallpaper, leather cushions, the familiar, dim-lit comfort—might represent the last relaxed moments he would enjoy in weeks. "I've read the Supreme Court opinion in **Atkins,**" he told Lane. "It bars executing the retarded without ever defining what retardation is."

"That's up to us." Lane cut a bite of steak. "There are three standard criteria. First, significantly subaverage intellectual functioning—there's no hard and fast IQ, but seventy is generally considered the cutoff point."

"**Seventy,**" Carlo repeated. "Isn't that awfully low?"

"In a word, yes," Mattox said sardonically. "But why make it easy."

"Second," Lane continued, "are significant limitations in what's called adaptive functioning, found in at least two of the areas we need to get along in life— such as communication, social skills, academic ability, use of community services, conformity to law, et cetera, et cetera, et cetera. In the case of a black kid from the Bayview, we can expect to see shortfalls like these aggravated by a chaotic and maybe abusive family, lousy social services, poor health care, poverty, low employment, and the like."

"The third criteron," Mattox finished, "is that these problems have been visible before eighteen. Otherwise, think of all the death row inmates who'll start faking retardation. Like a high school production of **One Flew over the Cuckoo's Nest.**"

Johnny Moore emitted a short laugh. "One thing you can be sure of," he told Carlo. "Give me a group of people charged with the same crime, and it's the retarded guy who's most likely to get the death penalty. Unlike our friend Eddie Fleet, he won't be smart enough to cut a deal, or navigate the system."

"I keep coming back to **seventy,**" Carlo told Lane.

"So will the Attorney General. He'll want seventy to be the absolute ceiling. And he'll play into all the lay conceptions of the retarded—they slobber, they drool, they walk stooped, they talk funny, they've got Down syndrome." Lane glanced at Moore and Mattox. "Our job's harder. Not only do we have to show how Rennell got to be who he is—his entire life—but how he coped with the cops, the trial, and the justice system..."

"Let's get back to testing," Carlo said. "What **kinds** of tests?"

"Tests that measure performance—how well and quickly the brain functions. For example, if I blindfold you, then give you blocks with various shapes—squares, triangles, and circles—I'm betting you could put the right shapes in a board with the same shapes cut out. If you're retarded, believe it or not, that may not be so easy."

Carlo tried to imagine the brooding thug of Laura Finney's description wearing a blindfold and putting shapes in a board, like a kid at a kindergartner's birthday party. Shaking his head, he said, "What if Rennell doesn't want to do it?"

Lane shrugged. "If he's retarded, he won't. I guarantee you that much."

"To me," Tammy said, looking to Lane for agreement, "showing limitations in adaptive behavior is the most important. No one spends their entire life faking being slow in school, lousy with girls, and short of walking-around sense."

"That's why Tammy will construct a social history," Terri added. "From prenatal care to parenting, relatives, peer relationships, school performance, mental health, substance abuse, bizarre behavior, problems with juvenile authorities, and well before all that—the same work-up for every member of his family. Plus all the records we can find—for sheer credibility, paper trumps everything, particularly with judges who don't trust us..."

"All the stuff no one ever bothered with." Mattox jabbed the table for emphasis. "No one who represented Rennell Price knows who this man really is. Probably no one in his life does—excepting Payton, maybe. But six weeks from now, we will.

"A social history is like a novel—rich in characters and incident. But the tragic aspects tend to be numbingly the same: mental problems in the family, parental substance abuse, prenatal risk factors, nightmare childhood." She paused, her southern drawl deepening. "Honey, you just won't believe what we're gonna find out. It's so goddam baroque some judges hate **us** for making them confront it—they don't ever want to know. Like it's their mission to kill somebody, but confronting the life of the guy they're executing will offend their sensibilities.

"And this stuff is common—it's **common.** I remember one mama telling me our client wasn't bad like her other kids—she'd never had to stick his hand over the hot stove. Like I was a mom, too, so I'd get what she meant."

Carlo put down his fork. "Which brings us to the heart of things," Terri said softly.

"Yup," Mattox said. "Abuse."

"Hard to get at sometimes," Lane observed. "If it exists, trauma like that can be painful to open up. Families guard their secrets—fiercely so, the more dysfunctional they are. And no one else may know. Society does a rotten job with at-risk kids."

Terri sipped her wine. "Rennell Price is on death row because Monk, Mauriani, and twelve jurors all believed he was a party to a child sexual abuse. Was **he** abused? Conversely, is there any evidence that he was predisposed to be an abuser?

"There's no direct evidence of guilt. No witnesses; no physical evidence of sexual contact between Rennell and Thuy Sen. What we're left with is a damning but wholly circumstantial case. Which Rennell denies."

"He's got a real investment in denial," Lane observed. "But if you're right—that he's a wobbler, borderline retarded—he might not be a very good liar. To me that lends his denial a certain credence."

Listening, Carlo felt himself being drawn into a complex world—equal parts psychodrama, mystery, and horror story. It gave him a new appreciation of the mettle, and complexity, of his young stepmother's character, complicated still further by the deep ambivalence which **this** case surely must create. "There's a lot to consider," Terri was saying. "Start with Rennell's relationship to Payton. Could Payton lead him into an act he wouldn't do on his own?"

Lane fiddled with his salad. "At eighteen, Rennell

would have been ragingly hormonal. And if he was retarded, he might have been more comfortable with children than with female peers. But he'd need a real antisocial component in his makeup for him to force a nine-year-old into oral copulation. Unless he was high on crack."

Cocking her head, Mattox looked across the table at Lane. "Isn't there a contraption called a pleathysmograph, or something—measures penile activity in response to visual cues, like naked women or little girls in tutus?"

"There is, actually. If you like that sort of thing."

"Too demeaning," Terri said firmly. "We're trying to build a relationship with this man, not turn him into a lab experiment from Krafft-Ebing." She drained her glass. "Still, I'd give a lot to know what really happened fifteen years ago."

Carlo gave her a quizzical smile. **Would you?** he wondered in silence.

But it was only as they left, and he and Terri stood in a dense fog waiting for the valet to bring their cars, that she asked, "How was dinner with Elena?"

"Good," Carlo answered, then added quietly, "I'm pretty sure she doesn't know, Terri. There's been nothing in the news, after all. Our client's sliding toward death without a ripple."

FIVE

It was on Terri's fourth visit to Rennell Price, with forty-one days before his execution, that she first took Carlo with her.

They crossed the Golden Gate Bridge to Marin County, the city behind them a mirage seen in glimpses through a low, swirling fog, the point of the Transamerica Pyramid piercing its highest wisps. On the far side of the bridge the parched, brown hills of Marin were like another country, bathed in the sun of a clear fall day. As they sped up Highway 101, Terri described Rennell's life.

"San Quentin has roughly six hundred prisoners on death row," she told Carlo. "More than anywhere in America. Rennell's in East Block, where most of them are—five rows of cages stacked in tiers. Each cell is six feet by six, with a bunk, a stainless steel toilet and sink, a maximum of six cubic feet for possessions, one small shelf, and maybe a TV with headphones to cut down the noise.

"There's a lot of shouting—conversations about sports, or people calling out chess moves, or just screaming for no reason. East Block's also where they put prisoners with things like psychosis, schizophrenia, or bipolar disorder. Which makes it worse for Rennell—most of the death row population is sort of dulled down, just resigned. But the mentals are loud—"

"Can Rennell see anyone?" Carlo interjected.

"Only the guards. The walls to each side are concrete—you can only look out the front, and that has bars which are crosshatched to keep the prisoners from pelting guards with urine or feces. They can peer in at you, of course—whether you're sitting on the toilet or just lying on your bunk. Otherwise there's just noise bouncing off concrete and metal."

"Does Rennell get out for meals?"

Terri shook her head. "They prepare the food in the main kitchen. Then guards push it over on carts, raise it on a mini-elevator to the tier—Rennell's on the fourth tier up—and slide it through a food slot built into the bars. The hot breakfast comes with a box lunch for later, a sandwich with peanut butter or mystery meat and maybe some fruit and a couple of cookies. Then there's another hot meal for dinner. After a time, the guards pick up the trays." Glancing at her watch, Terri stamped down on the gas pedal. "From the standpoint of the prison administration, cell feedings take up a lot of time and labor. But letting this crowd eat together would be worse. Especially with all the crazies."

Carlo had never thought to visualize Rennell Price's

day. Now he imagined himself stuck in a cage amidst five tiers of cages housing people he could only hear; the endless, dissociated sameness of waiting for trays to materialize through a slot, bringing much the same meals you'd had the day before. "What about showers?" he asked.

"Showers you get three times a week. But the showers are converted cells, which never seem to work that well. Best not to expect warm water." Squinting, Terri took her sunglasses off the dashboard and slid them on. "Or to smell very good. That's one of the prices of exercising daily."

"Where do they do that?"

Terri jerked down the sun visor. "Exercise? There are six exercise yards, each with a basketball hoop and a toilet, each surrounded by concrete walls and partially covered with a metal roof in case it's raining out. On a catwalk above the roof are guards with rifles—to quell riots or, in theory, to keep some prisoners from getting killed by others. San Quentin's a dangerous place—a lot of prisoners refuse to exercise for fear of getting killed by other inmates, or maybe just because the yards are crowded and there's nothing much to do..."

"Can't they segregate the worst ones?"

"Actually, they try." Turning on the right blinker, Terri glanced over her shoulder and changed lanes, exiting the highway at the sign for San Quentin State Prison. "They divide prisoners into categories," she continued. "Grade A's, the supposedly well-behaved ones, can exercise together up to five hours a day. Grade B's—psychotics and gang members and the obviously violent—don't get out much at all. And then there are the 'walk-alones,' like Rennell and Payton.

"Walk-alone is the name for at-risk inmates: snitches, or prisoners whose crimes are so low status that other prisoners think they don't deserve to live." Terri smiled faintly. "I guess they don't see the irony."

"Where do Rennell and Payton fit in?"

"Child sex criminals. From top to bottom, the hierarchy goes from rage killings—some guy catches his girlfriend with someone else—to someone convicted of killing a child in the course of sex. That's the Price brothers.

"In a way, they're lucky. Snitches can't go in the yard. But sex offenders get to exercise with their own kind, several hours a day." Turning down a two-lane road toward the prison, Terri added softly, "Rennell gets to see his older brother almost every day. So they get to go through life together, just like before."

San Quentin sprawled across an isolated finger of land. Parking in the lot below the guardhouse, Terri and Carlo got out.

She had schooled him in the rules. They both wore gray suits to differentiate themselves from the prison population—blue or denim was forbidden. They locked all their possessions in the Jeep except for a notepad, pen, their drivers' licenses, Terri's State Bar

ID, and the clear plastic bag filled with quarters, which—on Terri's instructions—Carlo carried so that they could get Rennell food from the vending machine. Then they headed for the guardhouse which screened all visiting lawyers.

"We're the privileged visitors," Terri remarked. "Nonlawyer visits are a bitch."

"How so?"

"People like Rennell's grandmother can only call a few hours every week to schedule visits. And the phones are so busy you have to keep hitting the rep dial and hope that you'll get through.

"Often, you won't. That means no visit. If you get lucky, then you go to the general visiting area and sit in a cage with your prisoner, surrounded by more cages holding other prisoners and their visitors. It's been like that ever since members of a rival gang got into a fight—what had been an open room became a zoo." Terri opened the door to the guardhouse, a one-story wooden structure that resembled a cheap trailer. "To the authorities, visitation is just another problem they'd sooner be without. So they make it as hard as possible for someone like Eula Price to even schedule a visit. But then running death row's no picnic, I suppose."

At the desk inside, a somewhat chatty guard—happy to be working outside the prison walls, Carlo assumed—waited while they filled out a visitor form before shooing them through security. Carlo stripped off his belt and shoes and watch and passed through a metal detector; retrieving them, he emerged from the building with Terri to find himself inside San Quentin State Prison.

To his right were mock Tudor homes, housing for prison staff; ahead, looming above the sprawling stucco prison, was a tower manned by guards with rifles. To the left was death row, next to a ventilator shaft jutting from the prison's roof.

Terri followed his gaze. "The gas chamber," she told him. "It's still available for occupancy. But lethal injection's now the death of choice."

"Who decides?"

"Rennell." Her tone was clipped. "A bullet in the brain seems more humane than either. But that's too up close and personal."

They passed through a second security station with a guardhouse and metal detector. Beyond that a neatly tended square of grass surrounded a marker engraved with the names of murdered prison guards. "You mentioned gangs?" Carlo said. "You'd think they'd keep a pretty tight lid on this place."

"They do. But somehow the folks inside come up with knives and makeshift weapons. And there's still an underground economy: people making 'pruno'— alcohol fermented from fruit—or getting drugs, maybe through employees gone bad. There's everything from weed to crack and black tar heroin." Stopping at an iron gate, the entry to death row, Terri added, "As for gangs, it's a veritable United Nations. You've got the Bloods, the Crips, the Skinheads, the

Aryan Brotherhood, the Mexican Mafia, and the North and South Mexicans. There's even alliances: at the moment, the North Mexicans and the Bloods are united against the South Mexicans and, of all people, the Aryans. Go figure. I guess it's a case of self-protection over principle."

"What about our guys?"

"They're just survivors." She paused. "I've never met Payton. But I hear he's spent the last fifteen years becoming a real badass—abs of steel, two hundred push-ups at a crack. He's made himself mean enough to live, and maybe for Rennell to live, too."

The gate buzzed open. Inside a cramped space a guard in a plastic booth took their visitor forms. Then they passed through a door composed of iron bars into the visiting area.

It was as Terri had described it—two parallel rows of Plexiglas booths encased in wire. One row had views of the bay through high windows; the second, which did not, included "Visitors' Booth 4." The guard opened its metal doors and locked them inside.

"Too bad," Terri remarked. "Rennell likes the view. But this way he'll focus better."

As they settled in two plastic chairs on one side of the small wooden table, Carlo prepared himself to meet his new client. "Building a relationship," he remembered Terri saying, "is the only way to pose hard questions and deal with hard subjects—like abuse. And we need to prepare Rennell to meet with Tony Lane." Then she had paused, and her green-flecked

eyes had become more distant. "We also have to prepare him to die. That's not a job for strangers."

At the entry to the row of booths, Carlo saw a large
black man with his hands shackled behind his back,
flanked by two guards in bulletproof vests. "Rennell,"
Terri said softly.

Silent, Carlo watched them approach.

Briefly, Terri touched his arm. "Just remember this:
as long as we're in this cage, and no matter what we
think, there's never a reason to doubt Rennell's innocence. Never give him one. Not in your words, or your
expression—for you to help him, he has to believe in
you. No matter what."

How, Carlo wondered, could she control her
thoughts with such discipline, or even believe she
could? Then the guard opened the cage, and Rennell
stepped inside.

The guard locked the door behind him. Rennell
stood over them, an otherworldly gaze dulling his large
brown eyes. His wrists thrust backward through a slot
in the door, as though schooled by habit. Then the
guard unsnapped the cuffs.

Rennell flinched. "Hi, Rennell," Terri said. "It's
good to see you."

In the next few moments, Carlo tried to absorb as
much about Rennell Price as his senses allowed.

The big man settled across from them with painful

deliberation, as though he had to think hard about the act of sitting. Carlo flashed on his maternal grandfather after his first stroke; Carlo Carelli had never again trusted his body, and to move his hand, or take a step, had seemed a willful act of memory. But this man's face, younger than his years, lacked all emotion—except that his gaze was so fixed on Terri that Carlo felt invisible.

"This is Carlo," she told Rennell. "My stepson. He's also a lawyer, and he's going to help us."

Smiling, Carlo held out his hand. It took Rennell a few seconds to grasp it, his grip as lifeless as his fleeting look at Carlo.

"How's your television working?" Terri asked. "Okay, I hope."

"Good."

The deep voice conveyed far less emotion than the word. "How's Hawkman doing?" she asked.

Rennell's brief glance at Carlo conveyed discomfort with his presence, perhaps distrust. "Good. Like I told you. But mostly same is same."

That much, Carlo believed. "What else have you been up to?" Terri asked.

Still Rennell did not look at Carlo. "I've started making a book," he said in an oddly stubborn tone. "Of my life."

Carlo heard this as a kind of narcissism, reminding him of an odd fact recalled by his father: that Lee Harvey Oswald's mother had once proposed to write a book entitled "A Mother's Place in History." But perhaps, Carlo amended, beneath this was a sad hope that his life mattered to anyone at all.

"What kind of book?" Terri asked.

"With pictures, for Grandma. Next time I want you to bring a camera."

The demand, both childish and peremptory, bemused Carlo further. He found nothing in Rennell's eyes to give him any clues as to whether his client suffered from a poverty of thought, feeling, or both.

"She wants to come see you," Terri said in a sympathetic voice. "But she's way too sick."

For the first time, Rennell's expression became probing. "Is she dead?"

Terri shook her head. "No," she answered softly. "Just old and sad and worried for you."

Rennell laughed softly. "Worry," he said. "Like she always done."

Carlo could not tell whether he heard disdain or merely fact. But Terri nodded her understanding. "That's because she loves you." She cocked her head, eyes expressing curiosity. "What else do you remember about her?"

"Chicken dinners."

What about the time she lost her house for you? Carlo wondered. But Terri smiled. "Did Payton like those, too?"

"Guess so."

"How's he doing, by the way?"

Rennell shrugged. "He say follow the rules and you be all right."

"Sounds like good advice, Rennell."

"Guess so." His stubborn tone returned. "Long as Payton be here, they don't give me no trouble in the yard."

At this, Carlo glanced at Terri: Payton's execution date was twenty-five days away, and his lawyers now had little hope—whatever else, no one believed Payton Price to be retarded.

"He say they going to kill him," Rennell continued softly. "Say he in a race with Grandma for the grave. Won't see him in the yard no more, he say. I got to keep my head down when he be gone."

Terri considered him. "When you were kids," she ventured, "I guess Payton looked after you."

For the first time, Rennell seemed to smile, the slightest change in his eyes, and at the corners of his mouth. "Yeah, he done that. Took me to school, maybe sometimes to the store."

"What else did he do?"

Rennell's eyes clouded. "Sometimes, if things was bad, he'd take me out to hide."

Once more, Terri cocked her head. "Hide from what?"

Rennell folded his arms.

"Your father?" Terri asked.

Rennell's shoulders hunched. "Sometimes he'd take a belt to me."

"Your daddy? Or Payton?"

Rennell shook his head. "Sometimes he'd hit me a lick, keep me in line. But mostly he'd look out for me."

Carlo saw Terri hesitate, trying to interpret this. Then she asked, "Did Payton ever get you in trouble?"

"No."

The stubborn tone had returned. Quietly, Terri prodded. "Not even about selling crack?"

Rennell looked up at her. "Payton never did nothing," he said in a stone-cold voice.

To Carlo it was as though, quite suddenly, Terri were a stranger. Sifting his impressions, Carlo tried to imagine how Rennell would seem to someone who, unlike him, did not strain to sympathize.

"I'm just trying to understand things," Terri told him. She paused, eyes silently seeking trust. "I want to bring another friend to see you, Dr. Lane. He can help me tell the judge what you're really like, and why you're innocent."

Rennell's eyes watched her closely. "Then get me some of that DNA. Man on TV told me about that."

"You ask Payton about it?"

Rennell nodded. "He say don't bother. They won't never be spending money on no gangbanger."

It was as good a rationalization as any, Carlo thought. "Sometimes it's not money," Terri said. "Sometimes DNA doesn't work. If it doesn't, what should I tell the judge?"

Rennell sat back. In a tone even wearier than before, he repeated, "I didn't do that little girl."

It was as though, Carlo thought, Rennell Price were

talking to himself. He could not begin to guess whether this was a statement of enduring truth, or all that a guilty man had ever known to say.

"I know that," Terri answered. "Is there anything else you can tell me to help the judge believe us?"

Rennell's eyes closed. Silent, he rocked in his chair, seemingly beyond words. "I'm a respectful man," he murmured at last. "I wouldn't do that to no child."

To Carlo, the statement had a rote quality, something learned very long ago. But Terri's gaze grew more intense. "Who taught you to be respectful?"

"Grandma."

Whose authority, Carlo thought, seemed to have expired long before Thuy Sen's death.

Terri leaned closer. "Did you always try to do what your grandma said?"

Rennell's eyes shut tighter. "Yes, ma'am."

Terri paused. Softly, she asked, "Is Payton a respectful man?"

For a long moment Rennell would not answer. "Payton never did nothin'," he insisted.

This seemed to be ingrained—the point Rennell would uphold, whatever the accusation. But it was Terri and Carlo's job, perhaps contrary to Rennell's most basic instinct, to separate him from Payton on pain of death. Still quietly, Terri inquired, "Did Payton say that Tasha Bramwell would help you? Or maybe Jamal Harrison?"

At last Rennell opened his eyes. "Payton didn't say nothin'," he said. "Took care of me, is all."

SIX

THE BAYVIEW DISTRICT IN LATE AFTERNOON EN-
veloped Terri in the deceptive lassitude of danger awaiting night to bloom: cleaning women returning home
to lock their doors; aimless youths playing pickup basketball or loitering on the streets; a squad car with a
shattered side window cruising down Third Street past
a clump of girls sharing a cigarette no doubt laced with
crack; a burglar alarm jangling that no one seemed to
notice. The bus in front of her belched exhaust.

Turning, Terri drove up a narrow street past what
had been Flora Lewis's house, a peeling remnant with
missing shutters. But she did not stop until she
reached the neatly tended stucco home to which Thuy
Sen had never returned.

The door was protected by a wrought-iron security
gate, for Terri a disturbing echo of death row, made
more unsettling by her hope that the Sens' desire for
Rennell Price's death might have lessened through the
years. She rang the bell.

After a moment she heard someone stirring inside, the rattling of a chain. The door cracked ajar. A small Asian woman regarded Terri through the bars with eyes more scared and stricken than the appearance of a female stranger would account for.

"Are you Chou Sen?" Terri asked.

The woman froze. When it came, her nod was barely perceptible, as though this admission stripped her of defenses. Her eyes drilled Terri's like a bird's, both penetrant and deflective.

"I'm Teresa Paget." With deep reluctance, she finished, "I represent Rennell Price."

The woman's face was so taut that the only sign of comprehension was a brief flutter of eyelids. "What you want?"

The words seemed barely to escape her throat. Briefly, Terri bowed her head in a gesture of respect. "I was hoping we could talk."

"About what?"

"The case." Terri paused. "Rennell's scheduled to be executed in forty-one days, Payton in twenty-five."

Crossing her arms, Chou Sen clasped both shoulders tightly. "They just tell us that. Years since they tell us anything. Now you."

Terri was unsurprised: over time, as memories faded and personnel changed, the District Attorney's solicitude for survivors too often lapsed into forgetfulness, no less unkind for its inadvertence. "I'm sorry to come here," Terri said. "But there'll be publicity, hearings where we try to stop the execution. I expect that people from the Attorney General's Office will ask you to attend."

The tight mask of Chou Sen's face began to crumble. "Fifteen years," she said.

Her voice was etched with incredulity. "I know," Terri answered. "I'm sorry for that, too."

"You don't know sorry." Each word held sibilant precision. "Sorry is a picture of a child who never gets older. Sorry is a father looking at his living daughter with questions she can never answer."

Terri felt the tremor of a long-ago psychic explosion, still reverberating, which this woman would feel in her bones until she died. Cautiously, she asked, "How is your daughter Kim doing now?"

Chou Sen stood straighter. **"Leave Kim be,"** she hissed at Terri. Tears in her eyes, she softly shut the door.

Alone, Terri stood on the desolate spit of land where—in Eddie Fleet's telling—Thuy Sen had begun her journey to Candlestick Point.

The druidical piles of sand were gone. But enough remained—the stunted shrubs, the tallow factory with its stench of burning animal remnants. The neglected pier was now a few worn posts sticking from the water like rotted teeth, and the old, wrecked barge was a ghost of Terri's imaginings. Across the steady current of the channel, loading cranes cast fading shadows on black water.

Walking to the dirty sand along the channel, Terri

tried to envision a large black man bearing the frail body of a child, waist-deep in the current. But she could not summon Rennell's face. Perhaps that was because of the darkness she imagined—she could not fault Fleet's description of the place itself, as chilling as the water which had borne Thuy Sen away. As chilling as Terri's own memories.

In the dark of her bedroom, Terri awoke.

Shirtless, Chris slept beside her, his face still softened from their lovemaking. But though long hours of work separated Terri from her meeting with Chou Sen and her visit to the water's edge, Terri could not stop thinking of Elena.

With a mother's intuition—or perhaps the incessant worry, she acknowledged, of a woman who believed, despite Chris's generous heart, that she alone truly loved this damaged child—Terri went to her teenage daughter's room.

The door was cracked open, the inside dark. Uncertain of her purpose, Terri opened the door, pausing at the threshold of Elena's room to hear the whisper of her breathing.

Her daughter spoke from darkness. "Why are you defending him?"

Terri felt gooseflesh on her skin. Words of answer sticking in her throat, she crossed the carpet to sit at the edge of her daughter's bed, then reached for Elena's hand.

Elena snatched it away. Jerking upright, she snapped on her bedside lamp and scrutinized her mother, steadily and fiercely, as Terri blinked at circles of yellow from the sudden flood of light.

"What do you know about him?" Terri asked.

"I went to your library," Elena answered without apology. "There were papers on your desk."

Terri felt her stomach clench. "And?"

"I read about the dead girl, and what he did to her." Elena's voice filled with fury. "How can you do this? How can you not care?"

Terri felt a moment of disbelief, the wish to turn back time, followed by a hopeless sense that no words could be adequate. "I do care," she tried. "More than you can ever know. But Rennell Price doesn't have anyone else."

"He **could** have," Elena snapped back. "Don't be such a fucking martyr. Like **you're** the only lawyer in America, and nothing's more important than you and **him.**"

The words made Terri flinch. She gazed at her daughter, trying to remember the bright-eyed child with the riot of curls and elfin face, unsullied by the knowledge of violation, of solitude and secrecy and boundaries betrayed, resurrected, again and again, in weekly visits to a child therapist. Now Elena's face and body seemed an external map of her confusion—new breasts and a woman's roundness emerging from a gangling frame, a lineless face at war with burning eyes. She would not be a classic beauty, Terri guessed, but hers would become a face hard to forget.

"There **are** other lawyers," Terri answered as calmly as she could. "But I'm good at what I do."

"That's because you don't do anything else."

This indictment, so unfair in its starkness, resonated with a years-old accusation. **How can I not have known?** Terri asked herself yet again. That Richie and she had been separated when he started on his daughter—perhaps his twisted means of revenge for Christopher Paget—would never soothe her pain.

But that guilt was hers to bear. Softly, she said, "I know I work hard, Lainie. It takes too much time from us."

This acknowledgment, with its absence of excuses, seemed to still Elena's wrath. "But why for **him**?" her daughter asked, an undertone of plaintiveness beneath the vehemence.

"Because I don't think the State should kill people, no matter what they've done, or what we think they've done." Pausing, Terri sifted the arguments Elena might accept. "There's too big a risk of innocence. And some of my clients have suffered in ways it's hard for a lot of people to understand, and harder to get over." **But not, I hope, too hard for you.**

"I read about what he did," Elena repeated flatly. "What he made **her** do."

Terri looked into her adolescent daughter's brown eyes, too reminiscent of Elena's father's. Richie had betrayed Elena, and now, in her daughter's mind, Terri had betrayed her, too. Quietly, Terri amended, "What the jury believed he did."

Elena closed her eyes. "I hate him," she said with quiet vehemence. Only when she spoke again was Terri certain that Elena was referring to her own father. "I remember it all now," the girl continued. "I still dream about it. I am so damned glad he's dead."

So am I. Though Terri's stomach wrenched at the truth of this, she could not slow the current of her thoughts. **We never have to see him. He'll never show up at your wedding with his little boy's smile, expecting the forgiveness to which he'd feel entitled. Demanding that Chris and I welcome him for your sake.**

"Forgive me," Terri said at last. "I don't know **what** Rennell Price did. That's part of why I'm helping him." After pausing, she finished. "Sometimes it's hard to explain, even to myself. Like loving you more than I can tell you but still working like I do."

Eyes hooded, Elena turned her face on the pillow. Terri reached for her hand again. Elena said nothing. But after a time, her fingers curled around her mother's, perhaps from need, perhaps from a pain too deep to express.

Terri lay on the bed beside her, and after a time, Elena slowly drifted into sleep, perhaps to face her troubled dreams. Awake, Terri faced her memory of where her daughter's dreams had come from.

It was night, and Elena had been seven then. Terri had pulled the comforter beneath her daughter's chin, placed the book they had read on the child's bedside table. Turning out the light, she kissed Elena's cheek. The girl's skin felt soft, her hair and face smelled fresh and clean. At that moment, Terri could not imagine loving another person as much as this child, the vulnerable life Terri once had carried inside her.

On the table, the elephant night-light flickered, casting light and shadow across Elena's face. The light was dying, Terri realized; tomorrow she would replace it. "I love you, Elena."

"Can you stay with me, Mommy?" The little girl's arms reached out for her. "Just for a while, okay?"

Terri smiled at the child's bargaining. How many times, she wondered, had Elena said "just a minute" or "one more time"? And how often had Terri spent the time Elena needed?

"Okay," she said and lay down on the comforter.

"Get inside the covers with me, Mommy. Please."

Terri slid beneath the covers and turned on her side. Automatically, Elena turned and curled her legs and back against her mother, waiting for Terri to put her arms around her. Terri felt an almost primal familiarity: she and Elena called this "making spoons," just as Terri's mother had, lying next to Terri when she had been so young that she now remembered little else. Lying beside Elena, Terri remembered her own father's angry voice, could still feel the rage that had driven her mother to Terri's bed, until Terri herself had not known who was giving or receiving comfort.

"I love you," Terri told Elena.

Elena burrowed closer. "I love you, too, Mommy."

Gently, Terri stroked Elena's hair until the child's breathing became deep and even, the pulse of sleep.

She herself should not fall asleep, Terri realized. She might have her lifelong dream of Ramon Peralta and cry out in fear, making Elena's own repeated nightmare that much more frightening to her. It was the adult's job to seem strong and competent, Terri told herself. At least until the child is old enough, and secure enough, to accept the doubts beneath.

Next to her, Terri felt Elena stirring and she hoped that her daughter would not dream again.

In her dream, Elena Arias was in a pitch-black room.

The little girl was alone. Her night-light was out; Elena sat up in bed, stiff and fearful, eyes adjusting to the dark. Her mother was gone and could not help her.

Someone was banging on the door.

It was the black dog; Elena was certain of this, although she had never seen him. Her mouth was dry.

The dog had never come through the door. But tonight, Elena knew, he would.

The knocking grew louder.

Elena trembled. Tears ran down her face.

She already knew what the dog wanted from her.

Desperate, Elena turned to the window, looking for escape. But it was nailed shut; even in the dark, she remembered that Grandma Rosa feared the vagrants in Dolores Park.

The door began to splinter.

Elena tried to scream. But the cry caught in her throat; suddenly she could not breathe.

He was coming.

The door burst open.

The pale light in the hallway was from candles. Shivering and silent, Elena could hear and feel the dog's breath. But still she could not see him.

Elena hugged herself, and then his shadow rose above the bed.

It was more human than dog. For an instant, Elena prayed that it was her mother, and then his face came into the light.

Standing over the bed, her father smiled down at her.

Elena woke up screaming.

In the flicker of the night-light, Terri had seen her seven-year-old daughter's eyes as black holes of terror.

"Sweetheart," she cried out, and held Elena close.

The little girl's heart pounded against Terri's chest. "It's **okay,**" Terri urged. "I'm here."

Terri could feel her own heart race. Elena's trembling arms held Terri like a vise. "It was just your nightmare," Terri said in a soothing voice. "Only the nightmare."

Elena could not seem to speak. Softly, Terri stroked the little girl's hair again, and then Elena began to cry.

Terri kissed her face. "What was it, Elena?"

The little girl kept on crying, softly, raggedly, pausing to breathe. After a time, her keening became half spasm, half hiccup, the residue of fear.

All at once, Elena was still.

Gently, Terri pulled away a little, cupping one hand at the side of Elena's face. Fearful, the child looked back at her.

"Tell me what it was," Terri said softly, "and maybe you won't feel alone."

The little girl watched her face, afraid to look away. Her mouth opened once, closed, and then opened again.

"Yes, sweetheart?"

Swallowing, Elena said softly, "Daddy was here."

"In your dream?"

Elena nodded. "I saw him."

Terri wondered what to say. "It **was** a dream, Elena. Daddy's dead now. He died in an accident."

Slowly, Elena shook her head, and then tears began again, ragged and shuddering.

"What happened?" Terri asked.

Elena clutched her mother's nightdress with both hands, voice suddenly higher. "I was **scared,** Mommy."

"Why?"

Elena's lips trembled. Half-choking, she whispered, "He was going to **hurt** the little girl."

Terri swallowed. In a calm voice, she asked, "How?"

Elena looked away. Her voice was small and shamed. "He was going to take her panties off."

"Who?"

Elena seemed to choke. And then she whispered, "Daddy."

Terri swallowed. "What else was Daddy going to do?"

"Touch her." The little girl's face twisted. "It was just their secret."

Terri stared at her. "Why is it a secret?"

"Daddy feels lonely. Sometimes he needs a girl." Elena looked into her mother's face. "To put his pee-pee in her mouth and feel better. Because you left him for Chris, and Daddy's all alone now."

Terri's sudden rage was almost blinding. "Did he do anything else to you?"

"That's all, Mommy." Elena's eyes shut, as if at what she saw on her mother's face. "But he let me light the candles for him. To make it special."

Terri pulled her close.

She did not know how long she held Elena. Terri asked her nothing more; through her grief and shock and impotent anger, she knew that she should not push her daughter. It was some time before Terri realized that she, too, was crying—silently, so that Elena could not hear her.

Perhaps, the reasoning part of Terri had felt with pitiless shame, she had always known this. Perhaps she had simply chosen not to believe it, with the same preconditioned numbness that had protected her since the day she discovered, as a child smaller than Elena, that to know her own father was to know a fear she could not endure. So that she, Ramon Peralta's daughter, was able blindly to live with a man who could do this to her own daughter.

"Elena Rosa," Terri had murmured at last. "How I wish you could have told me..."

But Elena had not, and now, six years later, the dream still overtook her, the price of sleep.

SEVEN

"Any good family story," Tammy Mattox began, "starts with Mom."

The others—Terri, Carlo, and Anthony Lane— were gathered around a conference table in the Pagets' law office, consuming coffee and bagels. "What about **this** mom?" Terri asked.

"Right out of Tennessee Williams. Near as I can make out, Mama was retarded, likely bipolar, an alcohol abuser, a battered wife, and—quite possibly—abusive to her children." Mattox took a quick swallow of coffee. "Pretty damned clear that someone was."

"How so?"

"I'll get to that. As far as 'who,' Dad's a genuine prospect—crazy as a bedbug, and quick to anger. Just because Mom's crazy, too, doesn't mean sticking a knife in him wasn't a rational decision." She glanced at Lane. "Before she killed him, Vernon Price spent a stint in a state mental hospital—long enough to be diagnosed as a paranoid schizophrenic. Grandma was probably the one safe haven these boys had ever known."

With an involuntary chill, Terri thought of the one safe haven in her childhood, her mother, so at the mercy of the sudden outbreaks of her father's drunkenness and brutality that Terri could only watch. How much worse if Rennell's only hope of safety was to wish both parents dead.

"For Rennell," Mattox continued, "not even his first trimester as a fetus was safe. Mom was hospitalized for alcohol poisoning after 'falling'—she'd drunk so much she damn near died. When she was sober enough to talk, she told the ER doc she'd tried to end her pregnancy by jumping off Grandma's porch."

Lane began taking notes. "What about prenatal care?"

"That was it—no other record of doctors' visits. To call Rennell 'unwanted' doesn't begin to cover it."

Lane nodded. "Neither does 'fetal alcohol syndrome' cover all his problems, I expect. But that may be part of Rennell's deficiencies."

"How does fetal alcohol syndrome," Carlo asked, "fit into our **habeas** petition?"

Tammy leaned forward, elbows resting on the table. "It's part of the history we tell the court—beginning with Rennell's beginning. But fetal alcohol syndrome would have burdened him to the day Thuy Sen died—"

"Among the potential outcomes," Lane interjected, "are defects in cerebral development which manifest physically: widened forehead, cleft palate, harelip. None of that shows up in Rennell. But there's also what you described—impaired coordination, the awkward movements of a Frankenstein monster..."

"Sounds right," Carlo affirmed. "But what's it got to do with Thuy Sen's death?"

"Nothing, in itself—it's just evidence of brain damage. But fetal alcohol also impairs the brain's executive function, the capacity to deliberate before you act. Cut **that** out and Rennell becomes a creature of excitation and impulse—"

"As in using a child for sex," Mattox said flatly. "But outside of what he's charged with, I'm not finding much evidence of impulsive behavior, and none at all of violence. The childhood I'm beginning to construct is more like Ferdinand the Bull's—all that was scary about Rennell was what he looked like, **not** who he really was."

"And who **was** that?" Terri asked after a moment.

"A big, clumsy kid, slow to react—same as now. Neighbors remember him staying close to Payton." She spoke to Lane again. "If I'm right about life before Grandma, Payton was the only sane person in the family. And Payton was just a kid himself, coping with a familial horror story."

"If there was abuse," Lane interposed, "then Rennell may have become deeply fearful of anything unpredictable—especially random violence. That could have made Payton a human life raft, all Rennell had to hang on to."

"That fits with Rennell the crack dealer," Tammy

said. "All people recall is him being Payton's gofer, running errands. Which makes it criminal that Yancey James presented them as one and the same, a couple of thugs."

"What about school?" Terri asked.

"I found Rennell's third-grade teacher." Briefly, Tammy flipped a spiral notepad, reviewing notes that, to Terri, looked indecipherable. "Sharon Brooks. 'Slow but sort of sweet' is how she described him—impairment of fine motor skills, difficulty in drawing and writing. So school was painful for him." Tammy glanced up at Terri. "But the reason Brooks remembers him," she finished, "is that he never wanted to leave when school was over."

For an instant, Terri thought of Thuy Sen, perhaps an hour from death, fatefully lingering after school for help with math. "Did Brooks say why?"

"She guessed there was nothing waiting for him at home—which would have been a mercy, were it true. Anyhow, he just stayed there near her desk. Eventually they developed a routine, Brooks doing her work with Rennell close by." Tammy shook her head. "If no one came for him, sometimes she'd drop him by the house. But usually Payton showed up to fetch him."

"What does she say about **their** relationship?" Lane asked.

"That Payton would be short with him, like Rennell was more a burden than a companion." Mattox glanced at the notepad. "She remembers Payton being cool and wary and sort of hostile. But with Rennell he had what she calls 'this little man's sense of responsibility.' "

Terri wondered how that might have played itself out in the lives of these two young boys, and then in the death of Thuy Sen—the black hole in Terri's knowledge—followed by Payton's desperate solicitation of Jamal Harrison to kill Eddie Fleet and, at the last, of Tasha Bramwell's alibi. "Did Brooks ever meet the parents?" she asked.

"No. The adults in Rennell's life were phantoms," she said. "But she gave me this." Reaching into an accordion folder, Mattox withdrew a piece of art paper with a child's primitive drawing: a head with a crooked mouth and shoe-button eyes, its ears sprouting sticks representing arms and legs. "It was a present—Rennell's picture of her. She kept it in a scrapbook."

Examining Rennell's gift, tendered in exchange for a teacher's desultory kindness, Terri felt immensely sad. Turning to Carlo, she asked, "Remember the drawings Kit used to send to you in law school?"

Carlo studied the picture. "Sure. Compared to this, they were Renoirs. And Kit was five or six."

"It was like that across the board." Mattox ran a finger down her notes. "In the fourth grade, the school gave Rennell a battery of tests. The results were abysmal: excessive anxiety, poor ego strength, lousy coordination, rotten academics, minimal attention span, poor reality contact, substandard intellectual development, and poor impulse control." Pausing, she frowned. "Needless to say, they found him eligible for special ed. Somehow he never got any."

"Poor impulse control," Lane repeated. "But no school-ground fights."

"No sign of them. Brooks described him as 'fundamentally passive.' The one thing kids seemed to notice about him was that he couldn't keep up."

Lane rubbed his temples. "Here's what I'd guess began happening," he ventured. "Around third grade the other kids figure out he's different. And because he can't be a member of the group anymore, they start to pull away. In reaction, he slowly begins the process of withdrawal.

"He can't play like other kids can, 'cause he can't grasp the rules." Lane looked at Carlo. "Remember learning board games with other kids? Rennell can't do that—he'll lose track of the rules, like a child too young to grasp chess. So kids just cut him out." His gaze taking in the others, Lane finished, "And so, perhaps fatefully, he becomes even more dependent on the only person who still deals with him—Payton."

"According to Rennell," Carlo noted, "Payton never did anything wrong."

Lane shrugged. "If Payton did, Carlo, what would the world be for Rennell?"

"That's pretty much what Sharon Brooks said," Tammy observed. "If Payton did something, so did Rennell. Except Payton was a blacktop shark—quick to take offense and ready to fight in a nanosecond.

Rennell wasn't. Brooks says he did all he could to stay out of fights."

"And out of trouble?" Lane asked.

"Seems like. Though trouble followed him. He was nine when Mama killed Daddy with a knife—though how that affected Rennell, and what he saw, no one quite seems to know. But Mom went to the mental hospital, and the boys went to live with Grandma—the only other consistent figure in his life."

"What did her influence seem to be?"

Mattox placed the pen to her lips. "She seems to have had **some**—she was a churchgoing woman of firm moral beliefs, which she tried to instill in the boys. She clearly loved them. But she wasn't one of those iron-willed black matriarchs people like to imagine, bent on scaring those two boys straight. Payton was eleven by the time she got him—he already lived in the streets. Rennell just followed in his wake."

"How so?" Carlo asked.

"As best he could," Tammy answered wryly. "His crack career was paltry, a stretch in juvenile hall for street dealing. That's a singular achievement—in the Bayview it's not easy to get caught. After that, Payton seems to have thought better of using his chucklehead brother as a dealer." She smiled briefly. "Must have been Payton's deep family feeling. He didn't seem to give a shit about his other human sacrifices."

Terri poured herself more coffee. "What do we know about his time in juvenile hall?"

"Not much—no behavior problems." Again, Mattox reached into the bulging folder and placed a paper in front of Terri. "All I could find of interest is this letter."

The letters were printed—as primitive, it seemed to Terri, as they were heartfelt:

DEAR Judge,

This Letter CONCERN ME and My PROBLEM I have BEEN HEAR OVER TIME. I DON'T PLAN TO BE HERE much longEST. PLEASE write a letter HEAR saying r*ennell price gRandmother need ma home.

rennell price

Reflecting on Rennell's tools, so painfully limited, Terri wondered about the circumstances which would cause him to employ them in such a plan. "Problem is," Tammy remarked, "he could actually write this. I can hear the A.G. saying that a man of such superior gifts couldn't possibly be retarded."

Terri looked up from the letter. "You think there was abuse," she prodded. "Was that in his parents' home?"

"That'll take some piecing together." Mattox fished inside the folder and produced a faded photograph. "I started here."

In the photo were two black kids: a slender, sharp-eyed boy she guessed was Payton, and a much younger but bulkier one—Rennell at something like Kit's age, six or seven. A large bandage covered a portion of his scalp.

"What happened?" Terri asked.

"Grandma didn't remember. So I checked out the admissions records at S.F. General." Mattox gave Terri a two-page Xerox. "On December twenty-third, 1976, Mama brought him to the hospital on a bus. He was seven years old, and it was twelve-thirty-five at night. Mama told the doctor he 'fell off a curb.'"

Terri gazed at the picture. "Some curb," she said softly.

"Some fall," Mattox answered. "But the doctor didn't see fit to question what a kid was doing falling off a curb at midnight. He just noted that Mom had liquor on her breath and then wrote her bullshit down like it was gospel.

"His notes also describe Rennell as crying off and on, apologizing to the nurse for being trouble. And that he was lethargic and slow to communicate..."

"A concussion would do that."

"So would retardation," Mattox answered with a smile so tight it was murderous. "But here's the best part. The doctor looked for bruises on his body like you'd find if he'd fallen on cement. There were none. All Dr. Kildare could come up with were burn marks on his buttocks."

Briefly, Terri closed her eyes. "What did the doctor say about that?"

"That the burns weren't recent, and therefore required no treatment." Mattox's voice flattened out.

"Mom told the doctor Rennell was so damned slow he'd sat on a space heater without thinking."

Terri sat back, drawing a breath. Through the floor-to-ceiling windows, the sunlight of late morning had reached the edge of the conference table: for the last three hours, she realized, Rennell Price's childhood had absorbed her too much to notice her surroundings.

"What do **you** think?" she asked Mattox.

"Something a little different." Tammy's voice held suppressed anger. "Yesterday, I reviewed the prison doctor's records from when Rennell came onto death row. Turns out the burn marks were still there. They were permanent—and symmetrical."

"Which means . . . ?"

"That Rennell Price had been tortured." Now Mattox spoke slowly, and very softly. "Someone in this child's family made him sit naked on a space heater while he screamed in pain. Keeping him there must have been the fun part."

EIGHT

FOUR DAYS LATER, WITH TWO MORE VISITS FROM TERRI intervening, Rennell Price met for the first time with Dr. Anthony Lane.

Lane and Terri sat with Rennell at a bare table in the psychiatric conference room of San Quentin Prison, a windowless, ten-by-fifteen cubicle with a chair for the inmate bolted to the floor. As a prisoner under an execution warrant, Rennell was handcuffed, his legs shackled. A burly guard with a baton stood outside.

Lane was dressed in khakis, a work shirt, and tennis shoes. He had greeted Rennell with a power shake and introduced himself in the vernacular; it was his plan, Terri knew, that a black man with a casual air would at some point put Rennell more at ease. But Rennell greeted the doctor as Lane had predicted—with wariness and near-total silence. "If he's retarded," Lane had told Terri, "he'll try to place people into categories, hoping to figure out what their deal is so he can respond appropriately." The role of intermediary fell to Terri.

Rennell slumped in a chair, his eyes fixed exclusively on her. "Tony's an expert," Terri told him. "He can help the judge understand you better."

Rennell hesitated, then slowly nodded, his face devoid of comprehension. "He's just going to talk with us," she continued easily. "Later—not today—he'll help me give you tests."

Rennell's face clouded. "They already give me tests in school."

Terri nodded in acknowledgment. "What kind of tests do you remember?"

"All kinds. Made my head hurt from too many fucking questions."

Lane chuckled appreciatively. "I hear you. We won't pile on quite as many, and we'll break it up a little."

Rennell tilted his head back, eyes fixed on the wall, as though struggling to retrieve a memory. "Mrs. Brooks said I did good," he reported in tones of doubt.

"Mrs. Brooks liked you," Terri assured Rennell. "Still does."

Slowly, his gaze returned to Terri. "You're like Mrs. Brooks," he said. "Sometimes I have dreams about you."

Startled, Terri managed a smile, trying to sort out her own confusion—it was at once the most unguarded thing Rennell had said to her and the most sexually ambiguous. "That's a nice thing to tell me," she answered. "I know Mrs. Brooks was important to you."

Rennell stared at her now, oblivious to Lane. "She

was beautiful. She said she missed me every night at home. Like I miss you in my cell."

"Tell me about that," Lane said with amiable curiosity. "Your cell."

The inquiry seemed to startle Rennell from his contemplation of Terri or, perhaps, his memories. In a recalcitrant, near-sullen tone, he asked Lane, "What about?"

Lane gave a casual shrug. "I don't know. Maybe just what it looks like."

Rennell glanced at Terri, who smiled, tilting her head in inquiry. "I try to make it like my home," he told her, "best I can. But I always keep the light on." His face darkened. "Least till the bulb blows out."

The first part of the answer Terri understood: the mentally challenged, as Lane had told her, are more likely to accept the limits of a cell, whereas Payton might rage at his confinement. But Rennell's last comment bespoke a fear that she could not define.

"What do you do during the day?" Lane inquired.

Rennell turned to him at last, considering his answer. "The same stuff. Boring."

Lane nodded in commiseration. "You've been here for a long time, Rennell. How do you think you're different than when you came?"

It was the kind of abstract question, Terri thought, which most Americans in the age of therapy—or daytime talk shows—could answer by rote. But Rennell looked wary and distrustful. Grudgingly, he answered, "I'm the same."

"Sure," Lane agreed. "But maybe you've learned different things."

Rennell seemed to grope for some response. "I know about law—the DNA stuff."

"Yeah. Tell me about that."

Rennell regarded his hands. "DNA makes you innocent," he said at length. "It's like a test."

"So sometimes tests can help you. Like the tests Terri and I want to give you."

Rennell glanced at the guard on the other side of the glass. "That's what I'm scared of. That's the problem I'm in with you—I don't know things about this test. I just try to do the best I can."

"Man can't do no more than that." Reaching into his briefcase, Lane placed Rennell's third-grade report card on the table. "Remember this? It's your report card from Mrs. Brooks."

A disaster carefully recorded in black ink, Terri thought. Gazing down at it, Rennell touched its edge with his finger, eyes widening with what seemed like wonder at the cursive name at the bottom. "Sharon Brooks," he read aloud.

That was all the meaning the report card seemed to have. "Mrs. Brooks was a good teacher," Lane said. "She knew it was hard for you to read sometimes. The tests will help us understand why."

Rennell's upper teeth dug into his lip. "I'm not sure about no tests. Might not want to take them."

Tense, Terri wondered what to say: if Rennell failed to cooperate, the defense of retardation—Rennell's last and best hope of living—would evaporate. Instinctively, she reached for his hand. "Please," she said. "If you help Dr. Lane test you, I'll be there."

Surprised, Rennell gazed down at her hand, small and delicate on top of his. Then he looked into her face with the eyes of a frightened child. "Will the test make me innocent?" he asked.

Terri's throat tightened, and her hand clasped his wrist. "I hope so," she answered and realized how much, for her own sake, she wished this could be true.

NINE

JOHNNY MOORE ARRIVED AT TERRI'S OFFICE WITHIN ten minutes of her return. "Yancey James," he told her without preface, "got disbarred six years ago. I guess Kenyon and Walker forgot to get back to him."

"Amazing." She waved him to a chair in front of her desk. "Getting disbarred is a trick," she told him. "Anything in James's record relevant to us?"

"Twelve clients on death row by the time he lost his ticket—they just kept piling up. Eventually he earned the charming sobriquet Death's Co-Counsel." Moore's blue eyes held a cynical amusement. "His defenses were so cursory they give new meaning to the concept 'speedy trial.'"

"Any sins in particular?"

"One failure after another to investigate, all rationalized as 'tactical decisions'—which tended, unsurprisingly, to shaft his clients." Moore pulled a notebook from his briefcase and put on his half-glasses. "I've got notes on his five other capital cases in 1987, the year he represented the brothers Price.

"In the Curtis Smith case, he failed to present

Smith's only meritorious defense. On behalf of Earl Prentice, he failed to challenge the eyewitness ID of his client, though he had a witness who could have. He defended Stevie Washburn by depending entirely on the investigation conducted by the lawyer for Stevie's codefendant and doing nothing on his own—"

"Like our case," Terri interjected, "except there was no codefendant to rely on. Yancey had them both."

"Indeed," Moore answered dryly. "But at least he gave them a two-day defense—a day for each client. In the Serge Dieterman case, James lost a one-day murder trial. Reason it was so short is that he didn't call the defendant and three other witnesses to testify that the defendant had withdrawn from a conspiracy to murder and, in fact, was leaving the scene when one of the others shot the victim . . ."

"It's almost comical," Terri observed. "Except for the lives at stake."

"I doubt you'll find the last one very amusing—the Calvin Coolman case." Moore glanced at his notes. "Try this, Terri. Calvin, James's client, was accused of shooting Roy Sylvester to death in the Double Rock section of the Bayview. The only person who claimed to have seen the killing was Stace Morgan, a convicted rapist and crack dealer. Stace did **not** hurry down to the police station with his story. But three weeks later the cops busted him for dealing, and he came up with his story about Calvin capping Sylvester in exchange for probation on the drug rap—"

"Eddie Fleet," Terri said flatly.

"**That's** what jumped out at me. But James never went after Stace Morgan—even though the cops had found a possible murder weapon in his apartment. Nor did James share with the jury that Morgan and poor old Calvin were rivals in the drug trade, or that the victim, Sylvester, worked for Calvin." Moore closed the notebook. "Inquiring minds might wonder why. But James refused to discuss his so-called strategy with the State Bar investigators—a matter of keeping client confidences, he said."

"Sounds familiar. In our case, James should have gone after Fleet like hell wouldn't have it. You find him yet?"

"Eddie? No. There's a trail of battered girlfriends from here to Oakland and beyond. But so far, no Eddie. If nothing else the sonofabitch is a survivor."

"Keep looking. And try Betty Sims, the girlfriend Laura Finney tried to interview. Something in Finney's story keeps tugging at me." Terri picked up her pen. "Out of the five cases you told me about, how many clients got the death penalty?"

"Four. Everyone but Calvin Coolman."

"And how many sentences were reversed because James was found constitutionally ineffective?"

"One—Calvin's. In the other four, the appellate courts said James was good enough to get his client executed."

"Why am I not surprised." Hastily Terri scribbled a note: "Carlo—read Coolman appellate case." "Eula

Price," she continued, "wanted the best counsel she could buy, and got the worst. So what was James disbarred for?"

"You'd suppose incompetence. But you know your own fraternity—shafting your clients isn't enough to get disbarred. You have to steal from them."

"James misused client funds?"

"Yup—beginning in 1986. In extenuation, he pleaded his cocaine addiction. Money went up his nose." Moore's smile was jaded and a little weary. "You've got exactly what you guessed you had—a crappy lawyer who ripped off Grandma to keep himself in coke, then blew off Rennell's defense once he'd blown her money."

"Terrific," Terri remarked. "I just love being right."

"You know the problem," Terri said.

It was past eleven at night. Naked, she lay across their bed as Chris rubbed her back and shoulders, one of the conditions of their marriage. "Sure," he answered. "Either you get James's cooperation, or he may blow up in your face."

"Not just cooperation—I need his enthusiastic testimony that his incompetence sunk Rennell's defense. Suppose we're 'lucky' enough to get an evidentiary hearing in front of Gardner Bond, and I put James on without knowing what he'll say. To pave the way for new evidence under AEDPA, I've first got to prove James was constitutionally ineffective—"

"Which waives the attorney-client privilege, of course."

"Of course." Terri turned her head on the pillow. "Mind concentrating on my neck? I've got a headache going from there all the way through my temples to my eyes."

Chris's thumbs began pressing into the base of her skull. "Thanks," she murmured. "Maybe James's excuse in the Calvin Coolman case—about not disclosing client confidences—was bullshit. But maybe it wasn't. The risk in our case is that James will testify that Rennell confessed to murder—or that James learned something from Rennell, or maybe even Payton, which points to guilt. That not only would eviscerate any claim of innocence but suggests Rennell is at least smart enough to lie in a consistent way. Lousy atmospherics for claiming he's retarded."

She heard Chris laugh softly. "No wonder you've got a headache. Does James have any friends we can locate?"

"Not really. Johnny says his associates from back then seem to have dropped away—mostly sleazebags, anyhow. But there **is** an ex-wife, and ex-wives can be useful."

"You might start there. We need to feel out his frame of mind before we go stirring up old memories. And for all you know, he's descended from coke to crack."

"Maybe. But Johnny says he's working in a law library."

"Nice to know that James could find one." Chris's thumbs increased their pressure. "How's that?"

"Fine. Eyes still hurt though."

"I'll get you a damp cloth to put over them before you go to sleep. Unless there's some other service I can perform."

Terri smiled into the pillow. "Does it require my involvement?"

"It might—depends, I suppose. So what other of your problems can I resolve?"

"DNA." Terri closed her eyes, feeling the slow release of pain flowing through her neck. "Retesting the semen may be a long shot. But there's other evidence, too—like the hair caught in Thuy Sen's barrette."

"Sure. But if the hair's not Rennell's, it doesn't prove him innocent. And what if it **is** Rennell's?"

Terri's temples still throbbed: the last vestiges of the headache, she guessed, would stubbornly survive Chris's ministrations. "At least we'll know," she answered. "What if the Attorney General already does?"

TEN

RENNELL BEGAN TO SMILE AS SOON AS HE GLIMPSED Terri.

She waited inside the plastic cubicle as the guards brought him from death row. Tentative at first, his smile broadened into a rare show of teeth as the guards locked him inside with her. Then he reached into his pocket and placed an object on the table with an expression that, despite the smile, struck Terri as imploring.

"I been wantin' to show you this," he told her.

She could not imagine what it was besides an artifact constructed of paper clips, dental floss, the handle of a toothbrush, a small piece of metal, and two plastic straws with copper wire extending from the straws. To obscure her mystification, Terri said, "It looks really complicated."

Rennell gazed down at the object as though it bore a talismanic power. "You got that right," he said with a tincture of bravado. "Took me a long, long time. I'm mechanical, for sure. Bet you can't guess what it is."

Terri continued her examination of what—however

unfathomable its purpose—was quite intricate in design. Smiling, she shook her head.

"It heats water." The forefinger of his large hand lovingly traced the two parallel copper wires. "I put these in the socket thing, and the metal part in the water. Then it gets hot."

Looking up, Terri felt herself grinning. "Amazing."

Rennell's expression changed once more, his probing look at Terri combining pride with uncertainty. "Pretty smart, huh."

"Yeah," she answered softly. "Pretty smart."

His smile vanished. "When those tests the doctor talking about?"

Suddenly she could feel his worry as strongly as heat passing through his copper wires—a fear she shared, though she could never let him know this. "Pretty soon now," she answered, gazing down at his invention. "I can't wait for you to show this to Dr. Lane."

They talked for another hour. Their conversation drifted with Rennell's shifting attention, sometimes foundering—Terri now suspected—on the shoals of fears too deep for Rennell to acknowledge, a stifling admixture of retardation and repression. But Terri knew that such fear could lead to a more palpable form of numbing—the need to dull consciousness until one's surroundings, and one's actions, seemed part of a dream state occupied by some other, more indifferent Rennell Price.

"I guess sometimes you smoked crack," Terri ventured. "To feel better."

Rennell's eyelids lowered. "Long time ago," he said in a dull, distant voice. "With Payton."

Terri restrained herself from asking about Thuy Sen. "When you smoked crack, Rennell, did you ever drink alcohol, too?"

Rennell's face darkened, and he could not look at her—if **this** was difficult, Terri thought with some despair, how might they ever talk about his parents? Then, to her surprise, he mumbled, "I drank beer 'fore I even know about no crack."

The softness of his voice did not conceal a tremor. With equal quiet, Terri asked, "When did you start drinking beer?"

For a long time, Rennell was silent, and then the lid of one half-closed eye fluttered. "Daddy," he mumbled. "It was my daddy."

After this, he barely spoke at all. He would not, or could not, tell Terri what he meant.

Chatting amiably, Carlo Paget and his father sat drinking beer and half-watching the Giants play their last day game of the summer on a sunstruck afternoon at Pacific Bell Park. Closing his eyes, Carlo tilted his head back toward the sun. "Baseball in San Francisco shouldn't be played on a day like this," he said lazily. "Weather's way too nice."

Chris smiled at this. Carlo and he had watched

baseball together for almost two decades, and the memories of Giants games were part of the warp and woof of their shared history, even—or perhaps especially—their mutual determination to endure the misery of night games once played at Candlestick Park, enveloped by the chill dampness of the bay. A phrase passed from one to the other—perhaps as simple as "remember the night"—would evoke for Kit's benefit, and their own amusement, the memory of the Dodgers' right-hander who disappeared in an impenetrable fog enveloping the pitcher's mound, from which his pitches emerged like bullets fired from ambush. Other images were, quite literally, warmer: the day game when the Pirates catcher Tony Pena decided to toss a baseball to the eight-year-old Carlo instead of to a gaggle of rude and clamoring adults; the sudden arrival of Barry Bonds, which the fifteen-year-old Carlo had insisted—in the face of his father's skepticism— would change San Francisco Giants baseball as they knew it; the other bone-chilling night when Bonds had changed the quality of Christopher Paget's life by hitting an eleventh-inning home run to put his teammates, and Carlo's shivering father, out of their collective misery.

Carlo had been fifteen then. Now he was twenty-five, and his father had acquired a brace of tickets in anticipation of Carlo's return to the city. And so, for these few hours, he had resolved to bail Carlo out of their office and, he hoped, out of his increasingly grim preoccupation with the impending execution of Rennell Price. But the game through eight innings was scoreless and, for the most part, lacking in incident, save for a couple of double plays and a base-running blunder by the Giants which had left Carlo muttering darkly about brainlock. Then he gazed into the bottom of his empty cup of beer and began relating Terri's account of this morning's interview with Rennell, and the way his stepmother's questions had suddenly hit a wall.

"It could be that he's just inarticulate," Chris observed. "Or maybe it's something too awful to articulate. As terrible as it is, we're left hoping to find out the latter—and that it'll matter."

"Shouldn't it?"

"**Atkins** gives us a shot," Chris answered in an undertone too soft for others to hear. Leaning back, he cast an eye upon the sunlit field and restive fans around them. "But lately I find myself looking at Kit and wondering how I would feel about anyone who did to him what Rennell Price is supposed to have done to Thuy Sen. And what kind of man would Kit become if he suffered as a child like Rennell may have? Considering either question makes me sick. Though not as sick as wondering about what Terri must feel about this case, but can never let herself say."

Pensive, Carlo touched the bridge of his nose, a characteristic gesture Chris first had noticed when his older son had been the age Kit was now. "So how did you decide you were against the death penalty?"

Chris gazed out toward left field, with its giant

baseball mitt rising above the stands, the palm trees jutting from behind them toward an electric blue sky. "When I was eight or nine," he answered finally, "and I heard there was a thing called the death chamber, I had a kid's visceral sense that it wasn't right. But I was twenty-one when Sirhan Sirhan shot Bobby Kennedy, and I felt like I could have pulled the switch on that sonofabitch myself, for murdering our future." Turning to Carlo, his father smiled briefly. "Marrying your somewhat determined stepmother required me to sort death out for good. In the end, what clinched it for me was the real fear of executing the innocent, and the absolute conviction we've done that already."

"Think we'll ever prove that?"

"Sure. Maybe starting with Texas, if the state doesn't cover up its crime to spare the rest of our delicate sensibilities. I only hope it'll make a difference." Chris's tone became sardonic. "A lot of people figure it won't happen to folks like them—white, well-educated, privileged—so why does it matter? At the very least, they rationalize, someone charged with a capital crime probably did **something**, so we're merely weeding out a few social undesirables."

Carlo nodded. "The people who most people never see."

"Uh-huh. When it comes to capital punishment, America suffers from a massive failure of empathy and imagination." Chris's face was somber now. "A sentence of death cuts fault lines through the lives of everyone involved: not just Rennell and Payton Price, but their grandmother; the father, mother, and sister of Thuy Sen; and Yancey James. Perhaps even Eddie Fleet, and whatever lives he may have touched since he dimed out his two friends. The death sentence becomes a life sentence for those it doesn't kill."

Saying this, Chris Paget fully confronted his subconscious fear: Carlo, like Terri, might devote his life to this. This was selfish, he acknowledged, but not entirely—he did not want his son to take on a career that hard, or to develop all the defenses he would need to endure it. He did not want the death penalty to claim Carlo Paget.

Suddenly, Carlo smiled at him—the easy, charming grin Chris had known since Carlo was seven—and turned his eyes toward home plate. "You'd better pay attention, Dad. Bonds is up, and something might actually happen here. Another piece of family lore."

ELEVEN

SAN QUENTIN PRISON ALLOWED PSYCHOLOGICAL TEST-ing Mondays, Tuesdays, and Wednesdays between eight-thirty and two, and on Thursdays or Fridays for another three hours beginning at eleven in the morning. Even if the testing consumed the maximum five and a half hours, the prison authorities allowed no food in the psychiatric conference room—not for Rennell, Lane, or Terri. Though she disliked the inhumanity of forcing Rennell to go five hours without food, a condition which made Terri herself irritable, this was one test she badly needed him to fail.

Among the problems of retardation, Lane had confirmed, is that it affects attention—the ability to sustain it, and to choose among competing stimuli the one which is most important. A second area for testing was the ability to absorb and remember information. Another lay in the visual and perceptual function—whether Rennell could see a triangle and then copy it. Yet another was basic reading, spelling, and arithmetic. For the first three and a half hours, Terri observed what she had expected: that Rennell was easily distracted;

that his memory was short-lived and erratic; that shapes translated poorly from his eye to his hand, triangles becoming cubes and squares morphing into rectangles; and that Rennell's scholastic skills remained roughly those of the third grader taught by Sharon Brooks. Yet Rennell tried so hard that Terri found it heartbreaking to watch. By the time he began the IQ test, it was past noon. The big man froze, a vacant-eyed replica of himself, with his pencil suspended over the paper as though fearing further shame.

And still he tried.

Now he glanced sideways at Terri, as though fearful of her judgment or, perhaps, imploring her to stop. Tiredly, Rennell said, "You're really workin' my mind today."

She forced herself to smile and stay quiet. "You're doing good," Tony Lane assured him. "Just stick with it awhile longer, and this stuff will all be over."

Rennell closed his eyes, sucking stale air into his lungs. Outside, one guard with a baton took the place of another, this one looking bored and disdainful, as though watching a dumb show performed by a murderer attempting to cheat justice.

Rennell resumed the test, pencil stabbing at the paper.

At a little past one-thirty, Lane placed a wooden board in front of Rennell—a replica of the child's game Elena and Kit had played in preschool, which challenged them to fit wooden pieces into the hollow shapes presented by the board. Rennell stared at it, suspicion warring with embarrassment.

"I seen this before. In school."

Lane smiled. "But I do this one a little different— it's for adults."

Rennell's shoulders sagged. "How's that?"

"Before you put the shapes in, I'll be covering your eyes with a blindfold."

For the first time, Rennell's tone bespoke resistance. "What's **that** for?"

"It's just part of the rules. Helps us know what you remember."

Staring at the board, Rennell shook his head from side to side. "At that trial, I didn't have no blindfold."

Silent, Terri watched, worried Rennell was on the edge of exhaustion, so fearful of looking stupid that he would refuse to go on. "True enough," Lane answered. "But they didn't test you at the trial. This will help us explain you to the judge. How you think and all."

"This game's got nothin' to do with me being inno- cent." Rennell's tone of voice became implacable. "I don't want no blindfold, man. Damn straight I don't."

Terri realized that fatigue and hunger had slowed her thoughts and dulled her instincts. "This is the last part," she interjected with quiet urgency. "We need it to try and save your life."

Once more Rennell shook his head. "I didn't **do** that little girl. Don't want no blindfold—just tell that judge I didn't do her."

"Please trust me about this, Rennell. I'd never ask if this test wasn't good for you..."

He stared at her, as though straining to hear Terri through his need to resist. Terri looked into his eyes. "Please," she repeated. "It won't take long at all."

The distance seeping into his gaze began to frighten her—it was as though he were reverting to the stranger who first had confronted her with the wall of his seeming indifference. "Why don't we take a minute," she suggested. "Try and relax."

Turning from her, Rennell folded his hands in front of him and stared mutely at the wooden board. Terri let the second hand on the schoolroom clock above the guard's head trace its circle twice, then nodded at Lane.

"Look at the pieces," he said encouragingly. "Just try to remember where a piece fits on the board. Then we can start."

Rennell did not acknowledge him. Terri couldn't tell whether he was struggling to absorb the instructions or had receded to some other place or time.

"I'll put the blindfold on now," she told him. "Okay, Rennell?"

When he did not answer, Lane handed her the black swatch of cloth. Standing behind Rennell, she paused, one hand resting lightly on his shoulder. Then she folded the cloth once and placed it over his eyes, tying it behind his head.

"Okay, brother Rennell," Lane said in his most companionable voice. "You can start with any piece you want."

Slowly, Rennell groped for the piece nearest him, a star.

"Good," Lane said.

Rennell's hand began twitching. "Can't," he whispered.

"You're doing fine."

Rennell hesitated, shoulders bracing with the effort. A tremor ran through his body.

"It's okay." This time it was Terri who spoke. "It'll be okay."

Abruptly, Rennell's mouth clamped shut, the part of his face she could see screwed tight. He folded his arms as though to fight off cold.

"Rennell . . ."

From beneath the blindfold, a single tear trickled down his face.

Abruptly, Terri stood, removing the blindfold. Rennell hunched forward, head pressed against his drawn-up knees. A cry of anguish ripped from deep inside his chest.

Terri hugged him from behind, face pressed against the top of his head, watching Lane's narrow-eyed scrutiny of the sobbing man before him.

"It's okay," Terri whispered, trying to breathe with him. She could feel his body trembling in her grasp.

Emerging from the prison, Terri felt diminished. Her only hope was that what she'd wrung from Rennell Price had some meaning larger than the fatigue and hunger of a man beaten down and then betrayed by a lawyer too intent on her goals to see him.

"I don't know what that was about," Lane had told her. "Maybe we never will. But it felt like more than a sugar deficit. The man was scared."

"Maybe scared of looking stupid," Terri answered. "Or maybe of what he thought I was doing."

For a moment, Terri thought of her childhood, her own nightmares and fear of darkness and then, unavoidably, their recurrence in Elena, and the terrible reasons for that. But all she could do was keep on going. So she drove downtown to Macy's, where Yancey James's ex-wife, Diana, worked behind a cosmetics counter.

Though quite striking, Diana James used too much of her own product for Terri's taste, and the spiky eyelashes made her enormous black eyes too prominent in a face so long and thin. But an edgy humor flashed through the makeup when Terri explained herself. "Oh, Lord," James said. "Another one of poor Yancey's condemned. They find their way to his door like swallows coming back to Capistrano."

"My swallow's got twenty-nine days," Terri said. "And his next stop won't be Capistrano. I was hoping we could talk."

Diana rolled her eyes, her expression hovering between exasperation and hard-earned resignation. "I'm a sucker for nostalgia. I mean, why would merely **living** with the man ever have been enough." She glanced at her watch. "Tell you what, counselor, my break's in twenty minutes. Chance to get us some fresh air."

Terri sat with Diana James on a wooden bench in Union Square, watching the pigeons strut by with their chests stuck out while peering about for food.

James eyed them with amused disdain. "Like Yancey before the fall," she said. "Posing like wild, all the time trying to figure out how to get through the next twenty-four hours. Excepting pigeons don't lie."

Terri managed a smile. "Nostalgia," she remarked, "isn't what it used to be."

"Not for this girl." James gave Terri a look of shrewd appraisal. "I guess you want to talk with him, and you're needing my supposed expertise. Or intervention."

"That **was** the idea," Terri acknowledged. "Especially the intervention part."

A corner of James's mouth twisted up. "You're Rennell Price's lawyer, right? So hard to keep them straight. As I recall things, Yancey didn't much like Rennell's last pack of lawyers when they came sniffing around." Pausing, James stretched out her syllables in an orotund mimicry of her ex-husband. " 'Acc-u-sa-tory,' he called them. 'Con-de-scending.' Poor bastard was scared to death of losing everything like he was losing me, so naturally he inflated himself with bluster like it was helium. Or," she finished with sudden bitterness, "white powder. By the time I left him, he wasn't anything but coke and pretense. Nobody home no more."

Terri studied her with genuine curiosity. "Did you have kids?"

"No, thank God." The eyelids lowered. "I say that, but now I've got no kids, too far south of forty. Yancey's the only child I'll ever have."

"I guess you still see him."

"If that's what you call propping somebody up." Diana James sighed, her voice combining weariness with a certain measured sympathy. "Yancey's got a long, hard road. One of the steps to recovery, they say, is apologizing to those you've wronged. He can't even remember all the people he owes apologies, and the ones he **can** remember make for a very long list. Sort of makes the road to Calvary look like the hundred-yard dash." Her tone sharpened. "One thing I **do** remember is your client made some poor Asian child choke to death on his own dick. Compared to that, lethal injection seems like a cakewalk. But maybe there's no exceptions on the path to true repentance."

The abrupt mutation of James's attitude made Terri fearful she would not help. "My client has a story," Terri answered. "No one ever told it. We're still discovering what it is."

"We all got stories, counselor. And nobody **ever** tells them. There's no reality TV show wanting mine."

Terri paused a moment. In a neutral tone, she

asked, "Do you think Yancey will talk to me about Rennell?"

James briefly closed her eyes. "Only if you let him apologize enough." Her voice softened, a muted apology of her own. "I'll call him for you, all right? Don't want to stand in the way of my baby growing up."

TWELVE

Entering the psychiatric interview room with Anthony Lane, Terri studied Rennell with apprehension, fearful that she had destroyed his trust. But when she gave him the sheaf of Hawkman comics she had brought as a present, the smile of gratitude spreading across his face caused her to reach for his manacled hands.

"I love your smile," she told him and realized that she meant it.

A hint of bashful pleasure crept into his eyes. "Grandma always say that. She tole me I had a happy disposition."

"I think you do, Rennell. Where'd you get that, I wonder."

"Payton." The reflexive answer was followed by a sudden remembrance of their circumstances, causing Rennell's smile to vanish, his voice to soften. "But now they're gonna kill him."

"Let's not think about that now," Lane suggested gently. "Your smile got me thinking about when Payton was little, and you were just a knee baby. What were things like then?"

Rennell studied his handcuffs. "Long time ago, man. Don't remember much about that, excepting Payton always took care of me."

"How'd he do that?"

The question caused Rennell's eyes and mouth to tighten in concentration, or perhaps, Terri suspected, in fear. "When I got scared."

Lane glanced at Terri. In a tone of amiable sympathy, he said, "When I was a kid, the dark used to scare me. What used to scare you?"

Rennell's expression seemed to close. "Maybe when I got in trouble at school. Not learnin' stuff and all, like you said."

The answer was so plainly deflective that it sparked a new keenness in Lane's eyes, though his smile remained in place. "Ever get scared when you were just at home?"

Rennell flipped open a Hawkman comic with his thumb, staring at its images. "I got scared, yeah."

"When you got scared, what'd you do?"

Rennell kept gazing at the bright-colored pages. Lane waited for some moments before prodding, "Rennell?"

The big man's eyes closed, and Terri saw that it was not the comics which had captured his mind. "Sometimes Payton took me to the bush."

"Tell me about the bush."

"We be hiding out there." Rennell's voice slowed, as though speaking a memory as it came to him. "It was in the park, all thick and tangled up, with places where we hid. Seems like we're stayin' there for a long time."

"What did you do?"

"Just hidin'. Sometimes Payton tell me stories."

Lane smiled again. "What kind of stories?"

" 'Bout what he'd be doin', when he growed up. Like havin' a big house with guard dogs all around it. He tole me I could live with him."

"Bet that sounded good."

"Yeah." Terri heard a complex mix of warmth and fear and melancholy seep into Rennell's words. "When we was kids, it sounded real good."

"Sure. I get the part about hiding," Lane ventured. "Sometimes when we're little kids, our daddies get mad at us."

In the silence which followed, Terri and Lane watched Rennell settle into an expressionless torpor. "Yeah," Rennell finally allowed. "Sometimes he get mad."

"Tell about a time your daddy gets mad."

Rennell's shoulders twitched—a shrug, Terri thought, or perhaps a flinch. "Gets mad a lot."

"How can you tell he's mad?"

"When his eyes get bigger."

"What happens when you see his eyes get bigger?"

Rennell raised his hands to his face, rubbing both eyes with his thumbs. "He does bad things to me."

Terri felt herself tense. But Lane maintained the same manner of empathic curiosity. "What things are those?"

"Things." Rennell kept rubbing, and his next words had a strangled quality. "He hurts me."

"Yeah," Lane answered. "I'm sorry he hurt you."

Rennell's body shuddered, as though he was receding into his moments of darkest fear. Softly, Lane asked, "What does he do to you, Rennell?"

Rennell shook his head. No more words came out.

Lane considered him and then, glancing at Terri, briefly frowned. After a moment, he asked Rennell, "What did you do to be safe?"

Slowly, Rennell let his fingers slip from his face. "Find Payton," he answered. "Sometimes he takes me to the bush."

Lane, Terri saw, had begun studying Rennell's hands. "Tell me about your mom," he said.

Rennell's eyes remained closed. "She didn't want me."

"How do you know that?"

Rennell inhaled, inward pain filling his voice. "She always tole me that."

"Why'd she say that?"

Rennell's silence was followed by a shrug of resignation. " 'Cause I did stupid things, I guess. Just acted stupid without knowin' I was."

Terri could feel him sliding into a depression. "When you were a kid," she asked as a diversion, "what did you want to be?"

Rennell's eyes remained closed. "Maybe a pilot, or a superhero. Like Hawkman. Just fly over everything, where it's safe."

The poignancy of his last phrase made Terri pause. "What were the best things that ever happened to you?"

"Don't know." Rennell's voice softened. "Maybe when Payton took me to the store. Or maybe," he amended, "when he sat with me in the cafeteria at school. Sometimes no one else ever sits with me."

Lane, Terri saw, was still gazing at Rennell's hands. "I guess that made you feel bad," he said. "What else made you feel bad?"

Rennell's head bent forward slightly. "When it rained."

"Why don't you like rain?"

"Can't go outside then."

"Why'd you want to go outside?"

Pausing, Rennell seemed to swallow. "Daddy. Rain was like it was at night."

"And you didn't like night, I guess."

Rennell shook his head.

"Why not?"

" 'Cause I'm afraid. Don't want to go to sleep."

"Why?"

Lightly, Rennell touched the side of his face. "Sometimes I wake up crying."

"Is that what you were afraid of—crying?"

Silent, Rennell rested his forehead in the chain between his hands.

"Rennell?"

"Sometimes I'd hear Daddy, my mama screaming." His eyes shut tighter. "Head hurts so much it's like it's going to explode. Least it keeps me awake."

"What did your daddy do to Mama?"

Rennell shook his head, a stubborn gesture of refusal. Gently, Lane took Rennell's hands from beneath his face and laid them on the table, tracing a scar on Rennell's left wrist that Terri had not noticed. Voice still quiet, Lane asked, "When did you try to hurt yourself, Rennell?"

Once more, Rennell shook his head. No words came out.

"Okay," Lane said softly. "Okay. We'll just take a rest for a little while, and then maybe you can help me out with something."

Rennell's eyes slowly opened.

"Okay." Lane's fingers intertwined with Rennell's. "Stay with me, son."

Waiting, Terri felt the gooseflesh on her skin, a hollowness in the pit of her stomach. "I want you to remember something for us," Lane told Rennell. "Something hard. Because it's important."

Rennell's eyes screwed up again. "Your mama stabbed your daddy," Lane said, "when you were nine years old. Terri and I need for you to tell us what you saw."

Rennell raised his face as though to gaze at the ceiling, save that his eyes remained closed. "Blood," he answered finally and then, with his next few broken words, summoned an image which pierced Terri's heart.

Vernon Price lay on the carpet, eyes wild with shock and fright and hatred, white T-shirt shining with his blood pumping from his chest. Rennell could not speak or move.

"Want my blood?" Price shrieked at the boy. "Then you come here, you stupid pussy."

Fear made Rennell's feet move closer to his father. With a spasm of rage, his father grabbed his wrists, drawing Rennell's face close to his. His ragged breath smelled like blood and whiskey.

"**She** did this, you son of a whore." Price placed his palm to his pulsing wound, then slowly wiped his blood across the boy's face and eyes. "Only blood of mine you'll ever get."

A stream of red came gushing from his mouth.

That was all Rennell would say.

When they were done, Terri stood with Anthony Lane in the parking lot. "It's way too hard on him," she said. "And there's too damned much I know we're missing."

Lane nodded. "Wish we could talk to Payton. Before they shut him up for good."

"I've tried. His lawyers say no."

Lane considered this. "It may seem pointless," he said with resignation, "but Tammy needs to take another run at Mama."

THIRTEEN

"WE TRIED WITH THE SEMEN," DR. DAVID LEVY TOLD
Terri. "No soap. It's way too degraded to yield DNA."

Terri did not know whether to feel disappointment
or relief. Telephone in hand, she began to pace, gazing
out her office window as Alcatraz began merging in
the dusk with the dark waters of the bay. "What about
the hairs?" she asked.

"The so-called Asian-type hairs from the brothers'
carpet turn out to be Thuy Sen's—no surprise there."
The criminalist's tone turned dry. "As for the hairs
from her barrette, it's a classic case of 'good news, bad
news.' Which do you want first?"

"The good news," Terri answered promptly. "I
could use a little."

"It's not Rennell's. The DNA doesn't match
with his."

Terri felt her own slow release of breath. "And
the bad?"

"The DNA's so similar to his that the hair must
have come from a very close relative. I guess we can
rule out Grandma."

"Payton," Terri said softly.

"Pretty much has to be," Levy agreed. "I guess that's not so helpful. But I suppose it still leaves open the question of Rennell."

Terri thanked him and got off. She did not raise the other question David Levy could not answer: what Yancey James might know about Payton and, she feared, Rennell.

It was past seven at night when Tammy Mattox appeared in Terri's conference room, perusing its table strewn with records from Rennell's past—what Tammy called the bones of the dinosaur. The mitigation specialist looked weary; she plopped herself in a chair and sat flat-footed, the folds beneath her chin compressing as she bowed her head.

"Well," she said, as much to herself as Terri, "**that** was a long day."

"Rennell's mother?"

Tammy nodded. "My new friend Athalie Price. Mama's still in an asylum. Even if she weren't pretty much bughouse, you have to circle around her defenses a good while." Tammy emitted a sigh of fatigue. "And you never know what may come out. Does she hate Rennell and want him dead? Does she know something no one else does? But you can't just come out and **ask** that—you have to try and divine it. For a woman with a low IQ, our Athalie's a devious one."

Tammy, Terri realized, felt the need to tell her story.

Settling back in her chair, she inquired. "What's she like?"

"Which second? Girl's got moods like mercury." Eyeing Terri, Tammy gave her a slow smile. "You had a long day, too, I imagine. So I'll spare you the gibberish and cut to the lucid moments. You don't have my boundless patience."

After an hour, Athalie Price flashed Tammy a sudden, startling grin. "You **still** here?" she asked.

Tammy smiled. "Sure," she drawled. "Got nowhere to go, and nothing to do."

Athalie's smile vanished. "Like me, I guess. Nowhere to go. Been like that ever since I met Vernon, and then Payton got born."

"Was Vernon your first man?"

"You mean," Athalie inquired with mild incredulity, "did he teach me sex?"

"Someone had to, right?"

"Someone did. Not Vernon, though—my granddaddy." Athalie's tone sounded matter-of-fact. "Used to give me a quarter for stand-up sex, sliding up and down his thing. Vernon just gave me Payton. That and a beating or six."

Tammy poured herself more coffee. "Near as I can make out," she said to Terri, "Vernon was physically **and** sexually abusive—got hard for Athalie to tell the difference between a beating and a fucking. All as random as the payoff from a slot machine."

"Did she give a reason for staying?"

"Does a woman that damaged need one?" Tammy asked. "Sometimes the most powerful weapon an abuser has is sheer unpredictability—you never know when you're going to get it. And in the amazing world of human hope, it sometimes takes damned little to keep a woman coming back for more.

"Athalie's just smart enough to know she's not right—not just disturbed but probably retarded. Whereas Vernon was crazy **and** controlling." Tammy's tone was grim. "And smart enough to know exactly what he had—a woman he could torment till the day he died."

"What about Payton and Rennell?"

"The kids were just a sidelight." Tammy placed the cup in front of her. "But with Rennell, if you believe his mama, Vernon started early."

"Rennell?" Athalie repeated with the same sardonic smile. "Vernon didn't even bother waiting for that boy to be born."

"How do you mean?"

Athalie touched her face. "Didn't just hit me in the head no more. Used to kick me in the stomach."

"You mean when you were pregnant."

"Uh-huh. Said he didn't want this baby to get born." The words were tinged with a brittle triumph

Tammy could not fathom. "But he got born, didn't he. He got made, and he got born."

"What happened to him after that?"

Athalie did not acknowledge the question. She lay her head back in the worn chair, eyes losing their focus, a deranged woman in a bare, green room in a mental institution, yet suddenly a thousand miles away.

"She'd come and go," Tammy said. "Like she was in a trance, then wake up and see I was still there, and start talking again like nothing had happened. Mostly this Delphic kind of disconnected nonsense, with nuggets of sense."

Terri scribbled a note to herself, "Prenatal trauma— organic brain damage?" "Still," she said, "a developing fetus is vulnerable to the same abuse his mother gets— a uterine wall is not much more of a barrier to trauma than it is to alcohol."

"Sure. But try putting Athalie Price on the witness stand. All I can do is claim to have understood her— for whatever a judge may think it's worth."

"What did she tell you about Rennell?"

"Disjointed phrases, mainly." Tammy flipped open her notebook. "I made some notes in the parking lot. The words she used were 'sad,' 'slow,' 'clumsy,' 'picked on.' Said he 'couldn't tie his shoes' and 'always took the blame.' String them all together, and it paints a picture. But that's seven and a half hours' worth."

"What about the abuse?"

Tammy put down her notes. "Athalie's fine with killing her husband," she answered. "But some things make her feel ashamed."

The subject of abuse to Rennell, it seemed to Tammy, caused his mother to shut down. Her eyes were blank, and it was hard to know how much she still remembered.

"Back then," Tammy offered, "we didn't know how to protect our babies. Remember the time Rennell fell off the curb and you took him to the hospital? You were trying to protect him then, weren't you?"

Athalie shrugged—whether out of indifference or avoidance, Tammy could not tell. Softly, she asked, "Was that Vernon's doing, Athalie?"

Athalie did not answer. "Sometimes," Tammy continued, "things happen to us when we're kids, and we promise ourselves we'll never let them happen to our kids. But sometimes they do anyway. Maybe it was like that being Rennell's mama."

Athalie said nothing. The only sign that she had heard Tammy's voice was that she turned away.

"Those burn marks on Rennell's backside," Tammy said, "did Vernon do that?"

Athalie froze. Studying her silent profile, Tammy briefly thought that tears might have caused her eyes to blink.

"After he got born," Athalie murmured, "boy always cried at night. Pissed Vernon off so bad he spanked him, and Rennell just a baby in diapers."

"What did you do?"

"Put beer in his bottle. Made him sleep better."

"That was how she protected him," Tammy said. "Feeding Budweiser to an infant. Not very good for the cerebrum, I wouldn't think."

Terri made a note. "But nothing about abuse beyond the crib."

"Nothing." Tammy gave an ironic smile. "When I tried to push her, something else came out. You could say it's the difference between Payton and Rennell."

How, Tammy wondered, could she get Athalie Price to tell her what she needed?

The woman before her had receded into the silence of the insane, so profound that her essence seemed to have vanished. The husk who remained, face turned toward the wall, was preternaturally still. "Were you afraid," Tammy inquired gently, "that Rennell might turn out to be like Vernon?"

At first, Athalie did not seem to hear. Then, to Tammy's astonishment, the woman slowly shook her head.

"Because Rennell was different?" she asked.

" 'Cause his daddy was different." Athalie Price turned to her, a tight smile of anger lighting her eyes.

"I got my revenge on Vernon Price. Rennell's daddy was a boy from down the street—real slow, but real sweet. Just like Rennell."

Listening, Terri felt a psychic shiver.

Only blood of mine you'll ever get.

"She wouldn't give me a name," Tammy concluded. "But if you believe her, Rennell's father was someone else. Maybe retarded himself."

"We need to try and find him." Terri rubbed her temples. "Athalie thought Vernon didn't know. But for sure he suspected, and Rennell became his scapegoat."

"If you ask me," Tammy answered, "he still is."

FOURTEEN

EARLY MORNING FOUND THE SAME CONFERENCE ROOM occupied by Anthony Lane, Tammy Mattox, Johnny Moore, Carlo Paget, and Teresa Peralta Paget, the last running on three hours' sleep.

"So," Terri asked Lane bluntly, "is our guy retarded?"

Lane rested both elbows on the table. "The state will say no. I need to do more work, but my tentative answer is yes. The biggest problem we've got is Rennell's IQ."

"Which is . . ."

"Seventy-two, according to our test. Seventy's the standard, of course. With a standard deviation of five points either way, Rennell's IQ falls within a range of sixty-seven to seventy-seven—"

"Seventy-two," Carlo interjected, "is dismal."

"Maybe to you," Lane answered. "But we're dealing with a death row population whose IQ, on average, is in the eighties."

Carlo shook his head in disbelief. "Are you telling me the State of California's going to execute Rennell Price for being two points too smart?"

"Not necessarily. Remember that IQ is only one of

three indicators. The second is age of onset—there it's clear Rennell had problems from early childhood. As for the last, adaptive functioning, he's got problems in basic life skills all across the board. Which is why Payton looked after him: Rennell's brain just doesn't work right."

"What about organic brain damage?" Tammy asked. "Mama drank all during pregnancy, and then put beer in his bottle."

Lane turned to her; in this meeting, Carlo began to notice, his voice and manner were more deliberate, the judicious aura of an expert crafting an opinion on which a life might depend. "Let's start with fetal alcohol syndrome. That's one of the common causes of retardation. And it can affect a couple of capacities: intellectual functioning, where Rennell has real problems, and impulse control." Lane paused to adjust his glasses. "Problems with impulse control could make Rennell more likely to force a nine-year-old girl into giving him oral sex. He could go from idea to execution in a matter of seconds."

Carlo thought of Flora Lewis's testimony that it was Rennell, not Payton, who had pulled Thuy Sen inside. "Does Rennell seem like that to you—impulsive?"

"Not particularly," Lane answered. "He strikes me as depressed—the headaches, the fear of sleeping, phobias about rain and darkness, feelings of worthlessness. Not to mention that very troubling scar on his wrist. He's more like a person who had the joy beat out of him."

"Still," Moore observed, "once you throw in smoking crack, even a slug can have an impulsive moment." Glancing at Tammy, he added, "We've still got no evidence that he ever had sex with anyone, right?"

"Not so much as a hand job."

"That's helpful," Lane told Terri. "But it's a problem that Rennell looks normal, except maybe for impaired coordination..."

"That could be fetal alcohol."

"Sure. But a judge may see just another sullen murderer, with what the A.G.'s folks will portray as superior lineage: Vernon Price may have been crazy but not dumb. Even Mom's IQ—at least from the hospital records—checks in at seventy-eight..."

"So all I've got to do," Tammy said dryly, "is find his supposed real dad, the nameless slow but sweet one, and blood-test him for paternity."

Lane smiled. "That would help, yeah."

A moment passed in silence, the others sifting their thoughts and drinking coffee. "Another problem," Moore said to Terri, "is this pubic hair of Payton's."

"That's Payton's problem," Terri answered. "There's still no physical evidence directly linking Rennell to a sex act with Thuy Sen."

Moore stroked his grizzled beard. "But if I'm the A.G., my version goes like this: Payton told Rennell to pull Thuy Sen off the street, then hold her head while she goes down on Payton. Even if Rennell's got no sexual interest in a nine-year-old, his brother does. The semen belongs to Payton. But Rennell's still guilty of felony murder—"

"But not fit to be executed," Carlo objected. "Isn't a mitigating factor against the death penalty that Rennell acted under the domination and control of Payton? He's retarded, for Godsakes—Payton ran him his whole life."

"That," Terri answered, "would be the argument." She sat back, her gaze taking in her team. "I still wish we knew what really happened. Whatever it is, I'd work with it."

Moore frowned. "I'm not so sure, Terri. This may be one case where ignorance is as close to bliss as we'll ever get—"

The telephone rang.

Terri stood, her expression of annoyance quickly switching to curiosity. "I told Julie to hold my calls, unless it's the President or the Easter bunny."

"Maybe," Moore suggested helpfully, "it's Rennell's real father, calling in from Yale. Where he's chairman of the Physics Department."

With a wan smile, Terri walked over to the far end of the conference room and picked up the phone. "Teresa Paget."

Carlo watched her expression change to one of taut attention, so complete that she barely seemed to breathe. "When?" she asked and then, a moment later, said simply, "I'll be there."

As the others watched, she slowly put down the phone, taking a moment to acknowledge their presence.

"You'll never guess," she told them. "That was Payton's lawyer. Before he dies, Payton wants to see me."

FIFTEEN

From the moment that Terri stepped into the plastic cubicle where he waited with his lawyer, Payton Price surprised her.

The first jolt was his appearance. She still thought of him as the twenty-two-year-old crack dealer in the mug shot, with a smooth, hard handsomeness and the cold, indifferent stare meant to signal his lethality. But fifteen years had passed. The man sitting across from her had a premature touch of gray in his close-cropped hair and creases of age in a thin face lit by eyes bright with intelligence, its harsh angles leavened by a full mouth, turned up slightly at one end to signal amusement at their circumstances. The other thing that struck Terri was Payton's stillness. Compared with his lawyer, Paul Rubin—a lean, bespectacled, thirtyish public defender twitching with repressed energy—Payton seemed an oasis of calm, facing his last ten days of life with the fatalism of someone who has moved beyond hope.

"So," Payton said to Terri, "you're Rennell's lawyer. Talks about you all the time."

The curiosity in Payton's tone was matched by his expression. But for their surroundings, he could have been meeting his kid brother's first girlfriend, brought home for a family dinner. "We've spent a lot of time together," Terri answered.

"So he tells me. You're the first one he ever gave a damn about, or thinks gave a damn about him." A brief smile showed a flash of gold-capped teeth. "Keeps runnin' on about how beautiful you are. Course he's been in here a good while now, and he never had much luck with women."

The last remark, too wryly delivered to be slighting, was darkened by its tacit reference—which Terri thought intended—to the murder of Thuy Sen, reinforcing her queasy near-certainty that this man was guilty of a loathsome crime into which, perhaps, he had led Rennell. As he sat beside his client, Rubin's eyes darted between Payton and Terri. It was all too apparent the lawyer did not want her here.

She decided to start slowly. "Fifteen years," she said. "How have you two gotten by?"

"Day at a time—one push-up or sit-up at a time, five hundred of each, each and every day." His mouth twisted in a brief, bitter smile. "Helps to have a purpose. One of mine was to keep Rennell and me from gettin' buttfucked. This life could have been hard on him."

The sardonic acknowledgment of his responsibility for Rennell suggested, to Terri, more self-awareness than she had expected. "Still," she said, "you spend a lot of the day alone."

He gave a measured shrug, a slight movement of the head. "You learn to organize your time, make prison serve you as best you can. I read a lot of history—African mostly. Try to write a little poetry." His tone took on the pride of the self-educated. "Keep up with the world, like what's happenin' in the Middle East. Don't think a pack of white folks in Washington ever gonna be able to fix **that**. I mean, we **invented** fucking Osama-been-missin', and this guy Saddam, and **then** when they don't turn out like they're supposed to, we have to kill 'em. Think we'd of learned by now."

The pithiness of this assessment made Terri laugh with surprise. Then her amusement was overshadowed by the sad realization that fifteen years on death row had produced a more thoughtful man than selling crack in the Bayview ever could have—assuming the unlikely, that Payton Price would have lived that long. But the end result would be the same, his premature death.

He seemed to read her thoughts. "Well," he said evenly, "you didn't come to hear my views on ge-o-politics. You're hopin' to keep Rennell from joinin' me in Paradise."

Terri nodded. "I thought one of you was enough."

For the first time, Payton averted his eyes, gazing down at the table. "Rennell says you been askin' about when we was kids. Think any of that shit matters?"

"It should." Acutely conscious of Paul Rubin's presence, Terri decided to avoid, until the end, the circumstances of Thuy Sen's death. "Rennell's slow," she continued. "That much we know for sure. But we don't know all we need to about how his family affected him."

Payton glanced up. "What?" he inquired in mock amazement. "You mean our Mama hasn't straightened all that out?"

Terri said nothing.

Again Payton gazed at the table. "Weren't no Disneyland," he said in a quieter tone. "I'll say that much for it."

"How did you get through it?"

His fleeting smile suggested weary tolerance of a question which, while both gratuitous and stupid, managed to evoke pain. "Bein' Vernon Price's kid teach a man to lower his expectations. But Rennell had it worse—that's what you're here for, right?"

"Uh-huh."

" 'Slow' don't **begin** to cover that boy. He was slow crawlin', slow standin' up, slow walkin'. Our daddy treated him like some dog you'd kick for havin' half a brain." Payton looked up at her, unsmiling now, voice toneless. "When he was two, maybe three, Daddy would feed Rennell beer so his head flopped to the side. Then he'd sit him down on the porch and spin him in circles till he tumbled off the edge and started crying. Made our daddy laugh like he was crazy."

The last laconic phrase was pregnant with horror: at

six or seven, Payton Price had realized that his father was insane, his brother helpless. "Is that when you started hiding him?" she asked.

Another fleeting smile. "He told you about that?"

"He kept talking about the bush."

"He liked it there. But there was nothin' I could do to hide that boy enough—he was just so stupid. When my mama was passed out, and Daddy gone, sometime I'd have to find their money and go to the store for food, then get back to the house, all without gettin' rolled. No way to do that and take Rennell. So I'd tie him to the bedpost so he wouldn't try and follow me and get hisself run over." Payton folded his hands in front of him. "I could see why Daddy wanted to cuff him. Couldn't do a thing with him—too stupid even to keep hisself away from old Vernon. He'd just take it and take it and take it, like that was how his life was s'posed to be."

Listening, Terri felt a frisson of pity: for the older brother, riven by compassion, anger, and contempt, and more piercingly, for Rennell. The scapegoat, he must surely have grown to believe himself deserving of the most arbitrary abuse, and been both mystified and pathetically grateful for Payton's every protective act. "Did your mother try to protect him?" she asked.

Payton stared at his hands. "She'd cuff him, too. He was so pitiful he just brought more trouble down on her—Daddy always pissed at her for givin' him such a stupid child." Payton's voice grew harsh with memory. "All I had to do was look at either one of them, and I could see trouble comin'. Rennell didn't have no clue. So I was stuck with him."

Terri cocked her head. "Why did you bother?"

Payton looked up at her with a bleak smile which never reached his eyes. "Ever wake up at night to hear a child screaming 'cause his daddy's stripped him naked and made him sit on a radiator so hot it's spittin' steam and water? That's a sound you don't want to hear but once."

Paul Rubin's eyes closed briefly, reflecting the nausea Terri felt. Softly, she asked, "Is that why Rennell couldn't sleep?"

Payton nodded. "Way too scared to sleep. No way out for him at all—neighbors were scared of Daddy, their kids don't want nothin' to do with Rennell. Only place it's safe is on the streets, and even there you gotta get by, get food, and keep Rennell out of trouble. I figured it out for both of us."

"Dealing crack?"

Payton shook his head. "Rennell wasn't no good there, either. Too slow to be muscle—got hisself beat up on. The one time I let him deal he wound up with a stretch in juvenile hall. Come out a whole different person."

"How so?"

Payton sat back, eyes veiled as though remembering. "At our grandma's we each had our own room. But when Rennell come back he wanted to sleep with me. 'Cept he couldn't sleep—he'd pace up and down half the night, and when I'd make him lay on the bed he'd do it in his street clothes, holdin' his pocketknife and layin' on his back. First all he told me was 'You don't never sleep facedown in lockup.'"

For Terri, the last detail held a premonition. "And later?"

"He finally wore hisself out so bad he fell asleep. I could feel him twistin' up the sheets. Then he started screamin' 'Stop' over and over, sweat streamin' down his face, both hands gripping his jeans by the belt loops." Payton looked up at Terri, voice softer. "He didn't have to tell me nothin' then."

"Did he ever tell you?"

"Never made him. Just made him sleep alone. Boy couldn't sleep without no nightmares."

For an instant, silent, Terri flashed on Elena. Absently, Rubin removed his glasses and began to wipe them. "Always the same nightmare?" Terri asked.

"No." Payton sounded tired now. "Sometimes about Mama and Daddy."

"What exactly?"

Payton seemed to slump, his air of laconic composure slipping away. "Daddy used to tie her naked to a door handle and whip her with a belt. Made us watch that. Then he'd fuck her in the booty till she couldn't cry no more. Watchin' made Rennell cry, too. Still cryin' about it when he's eighteen." Briefly, Payton shrugged. "Maybe now, for all I know. Don't sleep with him no more."

Terri sat back, quiet for a moment. Payton looked up at her. "No more questions, counselor? Spent enough time at the zoo?"

"Not yet," she answered with some effort. "I've been reading the police reports from when your mother stabbed your father. All they tell me is that she did, not what happened before."

Payton's eyes narrowed slightly. "That's 'cause I never told 'em," he said at length. "You really want to know?"

"Yes."

"Our daddy made Mama suck Rennell's dick."

Startled, Terri shuddered: in one sentence, Payton had cast her worst imaginings of Rennell and Thuy Sen, and what psychology might underlie it—as well as the potental reason for Rennell's stubborn refusal to admit the act itself—in a horrific new light. "After all Daddy did," Payton added conversationally, "a nine-year-old's dick seems like a small thing to kill him over. But I guess Mama had her standards."

Terri gazed at him, face cradled in one hand, her stomach feeling raw and empty. Rubin slumped in his chair.

Softly, Terri asked, "What happened with Thuy Sen?"

Twitching to life, Rubin clamped a hand on Payton's wrist. "He can't answer that," the lawyer snapped at Terri.

Payton faced him. "You don't **know** the answer," he

said. "Gonna die, man—no help for that at all. Might as well tell someone."

Rubin shook his head. "Whatever you tell Ms. Paget won't be confidential. You could be admitting to a capital crime."

"Yeah," Payton answered tersely. "I got that. The crime I'm gonna die for. I just learnt the word for that: re-dun-dant."

Without awaiting a response, Payton turned to Terri. "Happened just like they said—girl choked to death on come. Only thing they got wrong was 'bout Rennell." Payton paused, his smile tinged with an ironic melancholy. "He's scared of the dark—afternoon was the only time Rennell could sleep. Poor sucker slept right through that girl dyin'."

S I X T E E N

Taut, Terri stared across the table at Payton Price. "Let me get this right," she said softly. "You're telling me that Rennell wasn't involved in Thuy Sen's death."

Payton smiled. "I talk too fast for you to hear?"

"Then Flora Lewis couldn't have seen him."

The sardonic glint lingered in Payton's eyes. "It's like I say, all white people **see** alike. But that black cop Monk should have asked hisself how Eddie Fleet knew so much. Almost like Eddie was there."

Terri sat back. "Of course," she said. "Because he was."

They're high on crack, Payton and Eddie, sitting on Grandma's porch. Payton's keeping time in his head to some hip-hop music. When the girl comes by, Payton doesn't notice her. But then he can hardly see.

Eddie's staring at the street. "Wonder if she'd like to party."

After a time, Payton tracks his gaze to this slender

Asian child passing their house with eyes glued to the sidewalk. The idea makes so little sense Payton says nothing at all. Still keeping time, he shuts his eyes.

"Who she gonna tell, man?" he hears Eddie mumble.

It seems like crack's turning Eddie's sex drive inside out. Before Payton can focus, Eddie's calling out to her. Then the porch starts creaking with Eddie's footsteps like it's Payton's own pulse beating.

Paul Rubin studied his client, eyes narrow. "The man Lewis saw with her," Terri said. "That was Eddie Fleet."

Payton looked away. "Eddie was wearin' a big hooded sweatshirt, like Rennell wore mostly. So that dried up old bitch thinks she saw Rennell goin' after some nine-year-old." His voice held a quiet bitterness. "What **she** know about that poor fool, 'ceptin' what she saw every time she be peekin' at us out the window—somebody big and black and scary enough to do every kind of de-prav-ity."

Terri felt an anger of her own. "**Someone** did," she said. "Just not Rennell."

Her tone doused the edge in Payton's voice. "Someone did," he echoed softly.

At least it's Eddie that forces the kid to her knees.

Her eyes are closed like those of some China doll, but she's makin' these scared little noises and her body's shakin'. "Come on," Eddie says, all excited sounding, "I'll watch her do you first."

Payton's still in the zone. After a while he unzips his pants and moves toward them. But when Eddie forces her down on him, Payton feels her tears on his skin.

Shuddering, he pulls away.

It's like some fucked-up dream. Payton sees the TV's still on. He pulls up his pants and begins to watch the colored images, like what's going on behind him isn't happening.

"Keep goin', bitch," Eddie's voice says, and then Payton hears a moaning coming from Eddie's throat, another sound like coughing. On the TV there's a car chase, highway patrol after some bank robber, and then the wail of police sirens starts drowning out Eddie's cries of pleasure.

Terri felt nauseous, her skin cold.

Payton's voice was dull. " 'Mother fuck,' I hear Eddie sayin'. He wasn't excited no more." His shoulders slumped, and he continued with an air of shame. "Dumping the body went just like Eddie said in court. 'Cept it was just us two. Or us three—guess seeing that dead girl on the floor made her real."

They're standing in the dark, stink of tallow up their noses, Fleet with the girl's body in his arms.

Across the water, the shadows of the loading cranes are like giant insects in some horror flick.

Payton's come all the way down now, cold wind biting into his face. "**You** do it," he says to Eddie. "You got all the good out of her."

Eddie doesn't argue. Standing in the sand, Payton watches him step slowly into waist-deep water, staggering in the current, side to side like fucking King Kong. Payton starts wishing the tide would sweep them both away—Eddie doesn't know how to swim.

Instead he rights himself, then just lets her go. All Payton knows is he'll always remember the girl bobbing in the water, hair swirling as she disappears from sight.

Just like Eddie told them at the trial.

Later, Eddie drops him off.

Payton walks into Grandma's living room, half-expecting to see that girl lying on the carpet, face turned sideways with her mouth still open. But all that's there is Rennell, lying on the couch so sluggish in his baggy clothes he's looking more like a pile of laundry than a person. Except he looks glad to see Payton, like always.

"Hey, bro'," he says in that slow way of his, trying to sound cool. "What's up?"

"Nothin'," Payton answers and flips the TV back on as if things are still the same. Then he feels his hands start shaking.

———

"Rennell never had no clue." Payton paused, his voice plangent with self-disgust. "But then he never figured I'd fuck around with no little girl. Don't know why that happened—only time I did."

"But then they'd locked you up," Terri answered coolly. "Did Eddie 'fuck around' with little girls, too?"

Still Payton averted his eyes. "Far as I know, just that one time. But it's not the kind of thing he'd go braggin' about."

"What about Rennell?"

"Rennell?" A faint smile reappeared, directed at the table. "I don't think he had sex with a woman his whole damned life, young or old. 'Ceptin' Mama when he was nine."

Terri sat back. "Let's skip Mom and Dad. You're the one who helped Eddie Fleet put your own brother on death row."

Payton gazed up at her, impassive. "Things got all screwed up. I didn't know that old white lady would be lookin' out the window, and mix up Rennell with Eddie. The plan was for Eddie and me to shut up."

The night of the day Payton sees Eddie come out of the interrogation room with Monk and the other cop, Payton meets him at the Double Rock Inn.

A few nobodies are hanging off the bar. Payton and Eddie are sitting in a dark corner drinking malt liquor, voices too quiet for the others to hear. Payton stares into his face. "You don't know nothin'," he orders. "Let the cops start fuckin' with us, we **both** go down. You don't want to be on trial for no dead little girl even if they're what you like best. If I ever feel you even **thinkin'** about any more talks with Monk, last thought you'll ever have."

Fleet looks antsy. "What **Rennell** know?"

"Nothin'," Payton snaps. "Think I'm the kind of fool tell secrets to a fool? Like it or not, **this** fucking secret belongs to you and me."

"I was right about that," Payton said to Terri. "I was more the kind of fool let Eddie set me up." He shook his head in anger and disgust. "Couldn't say nothin' against Eddie without implicatin' myself, and Rennell couldn't say or do nothin' to help. That's what Eddie figured out before me."

Pen clasped in her hand, Terri stared at her client's brother. "So you decided to help yourself. Starting with the brilliant idea of asking Jamal Harrison to cap Eddie."

Payton shrugged. "County jail was short of talent. Weren't nobody better in the next cell."

"What did Rennell know about Jamal?"

"Nothin', like always. When Jamal saw me whisperin' to Rennell, all I was tellin' him was everything was cool." Payton's voice was soft with irony. "Rennell smiled 'cause he believed me."

Dismayed, Terri rubbed her temples. "Same with Tasha Bramwell's alibi?"

"For all Rennell remembers, maybe it's true. Near as I can make out, his days sort of run together."

The full dimensions of Rennell's potential innocence, Terri realized, were hard for her to grasp. "Does anyone else know what you've just told me?"

"Just Eddie." Payton looked somber. He paused and then asked softly, "Do you know what ever happened to her? Tasha, I mean."

Surprised, Terri heard the regret in his voice, a sense of loss that involved more than his own death. "No," she answered, "I don't know anything about Tasha."

Payton closed his eyes. "She just disappeared, 'bout a week after we was convicted. Don't blame her, really, the shit I did, even things she never found out about. Just wish I knew..."

His voice trailed off. In a tone devoid of sentiment, Terri redirected his attention to Eddie Fleet. "Do you think **Fleet** told anyone what you two did?"

After a moment, Payton shrugged. "Why would he do that?"

"Why would **you** do that?" Terri stood, palms resting on the table as she stared down at Payton Price. "You're the smart brother, after all. So you let a judge and jury sentence Rennell to death for a sex crime committed by you and the principal prosecution witness. Then you watched him sit here for fifteen years, waiting to die, and said nothing. All to save your own ass."

Expressionless, Payton met her eyes. "Maybe so, counselor. But you tell me this—if I'm inside, and he's on the streets, how's Rennell gonna survive?" The mirthless smile returned. "Least here I could keep an eye on him."

Terri drew a breath. "But now you've found religion. At last."

Payton gave her a long, cool look. "You're a caring person, Ms. Teresa. You know Rennell can't stay here no more. Remember what they did to his ass in juvenile hall?" His voice softened. "Next place I'm goin', don't want that sucker taggin' after me. Maybe **you** can see to him now."

Terri sat down again. "Thank you," she said succinctly. "Too bad for 'all our sakes' it's probably too damned late. You've out-waited your credibility."

She watched the comprehension in his eyes turn to apprehension. " 'Cause now I've got nothing to lose?"

"Worse," she answered. "Now you've got something to gain—time. That's the other problem with waiting until they're ready to kill Rennell. They're planning to kill you first."

SEVENTEEN

AT ELEVEN THAT NIGHT, AS ELENA AND KIT SLEPT UP-
stairs, the adult Pagets—Terri, Carlo, and Chris—met
with Anthony Lane and Tammy Mattox around the
Pagets' kitchen table. The conversation was tense and
muted. Only Johnny Moore was absent; he was already
searching for Eddie Fleet's ex-girlfriend, Betty Sims.
Only Terri knew, behind her façade of detachment,
how much she needed Rennell to be innocent for her
own sake, and for Elena's. And only Terri knew how
much she wanted to tell Elena what she had learned, before her own complex set of boundaries—that it was
wrong to further immerse Elena in the case, false to intimate that Terri's continuing involvement rested on
Rennell's innocence—made her withhold Payton
Price's confession from the member of her family who,
for her own reasons, might have cared the most.

" 'I didn't do that little girl,' " Tammy murmured
aloud.

"Could just be the truth," Lane told her. "Rennell's
got a low capacity for lying, I think. And Monk
couldn't draw him into a confession."

"Course not, the A.G.'s gonna say. Even a dummy's too smart to hang himself."

"Maybe so. But I think Rennell's asexual, or pretty close to it. Being retarded may have held him back."

"There's at least one problem with that," Terri cautioned. "Payton's story about their father forcing Mom to go down on Rennell. It's a paradigm for what happened with Thuy Sen: the A.G.'s shrink could argue that the family normalized pedophilia—it seems to have done that for Payton, after all. A shrink could also say that a retarded man is more likely to feel comfortable with children than to feel shame about having sex with them."

Tammy nodded. "Grandma's important here. Doesn't Rennell claim she taught him to be 'a respectful man'?"

"True," Terri answered. "But how persuasive that is depends on who else Rennell identified with most. Maybe it's Eula. But there's Payton, who abused Thuy Sen, then lied to the cops about it. Then there's Mom. Does Rennell identify with her, the victim—or Dad, the abuser? And given what he saw as a child, where would Rennell learn the difference between sex and sexual violence?" Pausing, Terri looked at Lane. "Unless," she inquired softly, "the sex act his father forced on him would cause him to identify with someone as helpless as Thuy Sen?"

"That's possible," Lane agreed. "In Rennell's own childhood, sex probably meant dominance and aggression. But there's no evidence that experience made him into a child predator."

Carlo touched the bridge of his nose. "What about being gang-raped at juvenile hall?" he asked Lane. "What might that do to him?"

"Nothing good." Lane's voice was tinged with melancholy. "I'd guess that was what caused Rennell to slash his wrist. I think he tried to end his own misery—the sleeplessness, his constant fear of darkness and violation. Which no doubt goes back to his father sitting him naked on a space heater."

Carlo puffed his cheeks. "Unbelievable."

Though she cast an ironic glance around the gleaming modern kitchen, Tammy's voice was kind. "Welcome to the 'other America.'"

"There's another thing," Chris said evenly. "Maybe there's no evidence that Rennell's a pedophile. But child victims tend not to report abuse, and a chaotic environment like the Bayview makes underreporting more likely. Plus sexual predators tend to act alone."

"Except with Thuy Sen," Terri countered. "So everything you just said about Rennell applies to Eddie Fleet."

Tammy nodded. "We know Fleet beat up Betty Sims. And we're pretty sure Rennell's not violent. Ask me to 'pick the pervert,' and I'm going with Eddie."

"The problem's Payton," Chris rejoined. "He's admitted to abusing Thuy Sen; the only question left is who helped him. It's pretty easy to imagine Rennell falling in with whatever Payton wanted from her."

"That cuts both ways," Lane observed. "It's an argument that Rennell might have helped Payton molest a child. But it also cuts against sentencing Rennell to death: Yancey James never developed the degree to which Payton directed Rennell's whole life."

Nodding, Chris turned to Terri. "When are you seeing James?" he asked.

"Tomorrow afternoon. We can only hope he chooses to help."

Chris faced Tony Lane again. "What might have been the impact on Rennell of watching his mother knife his father? Not to mention the father's dying act of sadism—'Want my blood,' and all of that?"

"It's Gothic." Lane shook his head in bemusement. "But the answer is I don't know. Still, Rennell was only nine when he went to Eula Price. That gave her a little time to mold him before Payton took over."

"What about our claim that he's retarded? Can the A.G. find some psychiatrist to testify that retardation limits Rennell's empathy for someone like Thuy Sen?"

"Probably. But I don't believe that. There's a difference between intellectual and emotional capacity— even a retarded person like Rennell could have learned love from his grandmother and, in an odd way, from Payton. So it's possible for Rennell to feel much the same sensitivities as you or I. Just like it's possible for a decent man to emerge from a nightmare child-hood—"

"But that's also the A.G.'s argument," Chris objected. "That Rennell had choices, so his environment shouldn't make a difference when it comes to meting out the death penalty."

"**We've** got no choice," Terri said flatly. "If Rennell's guilty, we have two arguments—he's retarded, and therefore **can't** be executed, or he was dominated by Payton, and therefore **shouldn't** be executed. So let's turn to whether he might actually be innocent."

"Starting with how he got convicted," Tammy suggested, "and all the assumptions that got him there. First, they both lived with Grandma, so it was easy for Lewis to assume she saw Rennell."

"Second," Terri interjected sardonically, "they're black. Therefore they're guilty. They're already guilty of being crack dealers in the Bayview, so the police are quicker to assume the worst than if some white lady had pointed the finger at, say, Carlo." She paused, surveying the others. "But what's missing is critical—any physical evidence tying Rennell to Thuy Sen's death."

"And after she died," Carlo added quickly, "everything that made the brothers look guilty was Payton's doing—soliciting Jamal Harrison, and Tasha Bramwell's stupid alibi. So without Flora Lewis and Eddie Fleet, the case against Rennell rests on nothing. And Payton just turned their testimony upside down."

Chris shook his head. "You've just named the problem with that," he told Carlo. "In two words—'Payton' and 'just.' As in 'at the eleventh hour.'"

"If you're the A.G.," Terri concurred, "Payton's not only an admitted murderer, but he lied to Monk about being one. Now he's lying about Fleet to save Rennell—and to screw an innocent man for putting both of them on death row. If that's not motive enough,

Payton knows I'll try to keep him alive as long as it takes to bail out his brother. As long as there's life, there's hope."

"So the A.G. figures Payton's gaming you," Tammy finished, "knowing you'll game the system for him, trying to save Rennell."

Carlo turned to Terri. "This is surreal. With Payton's testimony, no jury would find Rennell guilty beyond a reasonable doubt."

"But we don't have a jury," she reminded him. "Or the presumption of innocence. We've got AEDPA, which presumes the jury was right fifteen years ago, Yancey James or no. Now **we** have to prove Rennell's innocent. Payton's not enough."

"But do you believe him?" Carlo persisted.

Terri paused. "Yeah, I believe him. I guess you had to be there. But to me his story makes sense."

Tammy leaned forward, both elbows resting on the table. "We have to package innocence with retardation, folks—Rennell was convicted 'cause he didn't remember he was sleeping, couldn't figure out what was happening with Eddie Fleet, couldn't tell James was selling him down the river, and couldn't keep Payton from digging both their graves."

"The last also helps with mitigation," Carlo added. "The idea that Payton may have led him into the crime."

"Of course," Tammy answered tiredly. "But there's a conflict between 'only my brother did it,' and 'my brother made me do it.' The A.G. will exploit that—"

"No help for it," Terri said. "The problem's proving 'only my brother did it.' We can't make Lewis retract her testimony—she's dead. We can't DNA the semen—it's degraded. The pubic hair's Payton's, not Fleet's." Terri sat back. "We need to find Eddie Fleet, and then we need to nail him. Johnny's looking for every scrap of evidence that suggests it's Fleet who choked Thuy Sen—other acts of pedophilia, inconsistent statements to the cops. Everything beyond what's also obvious about Payton, only in reverse: that pointing the finger at Rennell kept Eddie Fleet off death row."

Restless, Carlo stood. "There's Laura Finney's story about Fleet's girlfriend and her child. It sounded like he scared them both."

"Johnny's looking for them," Terri told him. "On Rennell's behalf, we should hope that Finney sensed something more than Sims's fear of another beating. Though I wouldn't wish the other possibility on any child."

Carlo fell quiet, as did the rest. In their silence, Terri again felt how intensely she wanted Rennell Price to be innocent. It was a weakness, surely.

Quietly, Chris asked, "When are you telling Rennell about Payton?"

For Terri, the question was shadowed by another: Why can't you tell Elena? "Tomorrow morning," she answered.

EIGHTEEN

ALONE IN THE KITCHEN, TERRI SIPPED HER THIRD glass of red Bordeaux, contemplating the filigreed label of a half-empty bottle too expensive to be drunk as she was drinking it, to find escape.

Chris was upstairs, asleep, as were Kit and, she could only hope, Elena, for once lost in a dreamless slumber. But for Elena and, Terri knew, herself, escape was momentary and memory never far from the surface. And now, Terri's memories were roiled by Payton's confession, his wrenching evocation of the childhood which had formed Rennell, the man she had vowed to save.

Feeling the glow of wine, Terri slowly closed her eyes, and remembered.

She was fourteen; Terri could no longer hide beneath the covers or inside the closet. And now her mother's cries have drawn her from her bedroom.

Terri creeps down the stairs. Unsure of what will happen, afraid of what she will see. Knowing only that, this time, she must stop him.

The first thing she sees is her mother's face.

In the dim light of a single lamp, it is beautiful and ravaged, and drained of hope. Her mouth has begun to swell.

Her father, Ramon Peralta, steps into the light.

His hand is raised. Terri's mother, Rosa, backs to the wall. Her eyes glisten with tears. By now Terri knows that the tears will never fall; it is Rosa's pride that she endures this without crying. But she cannot stifle the sounds when he hits her, cries from deep within her soul.

"Whore," Ramon says softly.

Helpless, Rosa shakes her head. Her shoulders graze the wall behind her.

"I saw you look at him," Ramon prods. His accusation is sibilant, precise; Terri can imagine his whiskey breath in her mother's face. Ramon comes closer.

Watching, Terri freezes.

She stands there, trembling, ashamed of her own cowardice. No one sees her; there is still time to turn away.

Her father's hand flashes through the light.

Terri flinches. Hears the crack of his palm on Rosa's cheekbone, the short cry she seems to bite off, the heavy sound of his breathing. In the pit of her stomach, Terri understands; her mother's cries draw him on for more. Rosa's lip is bleeding now.

"No!" Terri cries out.

Tears have sprung to her eyes; she is not sure she has spoken aloud. And then, slowly, her father turns.

Seeing Terri, his face fills with astonishment and rage, but still she cannot look away.

"You **like** this," she tells her father. "You think it makes you strong. But we hate you—"

"Teresa, **don't**!"

Her mother steps from the wall. "This is **our** business—"

"**We** live here too." Without thinking, Terri steps between her parents. "Don't **ever** hit her," she tells her father. "Ever again. Or we'll hate you for the rest of your life."

Ramon's face darkens. "You little bitch. You're just like **her**."

Terri points at her chest. "I'm **me**. **I'm** saying this."

His hand flies back to hit her.

"**No**." Her mother has clutched Terri's shoulders, pulling her away from him. Her father reaches out and jerks Terri by the arm.

Blinding pain shoots through Terri's shoulder. She feels him twist her arm behind her back, push her face-down on the sofa. Terri wills herself to make no sound at all.

"What," her father asks softly, "would you like me to do now?"

Terri cannot be certain whether he asks this of Rosa or of Terri herself. Can sense only that her mother has draped both arms around her father's neck.

"Let her go, Ramon." Rosa's voice is gentle now. "You were right. I shouldn't have looked at him that way."

Terri twists her head to see. But she can only see her mother carefully watching Ramon as she whispers, "I'll make it up to you. Please, let her go."

In her anguish, Terri senses her father turning to Rosa, sees the look on her mother's face. The look of a woman who has met the man she was fated for. Lips parted, eyes resolute, accepting her destiny.

With a sharp jerk, Ramon Peralta releases his daughter's arm.

"Go," Rosa tells her. "Go to bed, Teresa."

Standing, Terri turns to her mother. Her legs are unsteady, but Rosa does not reach for her. She leans against her husband now, one arm around his waist. Two parents confronting their child.

"Go," Rosa repeats softly. "Please."

Terri turns, walking toward the stairs. Knowing that, in some strange way, her father has accepted Rosa as a substitute for Terri. Her arm aches, and her face burns with shame. She does not know for whom.

At the top of the darkened stairway, Terri stops. She cannot, somehow, return to her room.

She stands there. It is as if, from a distance, she is standing guard over Rosa.

From the living room below, a soft cry.

Terri cannot help herself. The second cry, a deeper moan, draws her back toward the living room.

At the foot of the stairs, Terri stops.

Two profiles in the yellow light, her mother and her father.

Her father wears only a shirt. Her mother is bent over the couch, facedown, as Terri was. Her dress is raised around her waist; her panties lie ripped on the floor. As Ramon Peralta drives himself into her from behind, again and again, she cries out for him with each thrust.

Terri cannot look away. Her mother's face, turned to the light, is an unfeeling mask. Only her lips move, to make the cries.

And then Rosa sees her.

Her eyes open wider, looking into her daughter's face with a depth of pain and anguish that Terri has never seen before. She stops making the sounds. Silently pleading with her daughter, her lips form the word "Go."

In Rosa's silence, Ramon Peralta thrusts harder.

"Go," her mother's lips repeat, and then, still looking at Terri, she makes the soft cry of pleasure her husband wants.

Terri turns and slowly climbs the stairs, footsteps soft so that her father will not hear. Her eyes fill with tears...

Tonight, twenty-five years later, Terri opened her eyes and saw the Pagets' gleaming kitchen. She had escaped, and now she owed Rennell Price, whose trauma she understood in a way that Chris and Carlo could not, all that she had to give.

She had escaped her own childhood, and yet she had not escaped. The past had reached out for her, and taken Elena.

Exhausted from her sleepless night, Terri finished telling Rennell of Payton's confession. "He says the second man was Eddie," she concluded. "And that no one knows but them."

Rennell said nothing. Terri studied his face for evidence of Payton's betrayal—at once fearful of the pain she had inflicted and hoping for some sign of his innocence.

At last he swallowed, a twitch of the throat muscles. "For sure they're gonna kill him now."

"What do you mean, Rennell?"

Rennell blinked, his voice thick with grief. "Payton's trying to take care of me, and now they're gonna kill him for it."

Perhaps the depth of Payton's wrong was too enormous for him to grasp. "He's not dying for you," she answered. "He's dying because he's guilty of Thuy Sen's murder. He doesn't want **you** to die for what he did."

Rennell's hand covered hers. "Save him," he whispered. "Please."

Briefly, Terri closed her eyes. But are you innocent? she wanted to ask. When she opened her eyes again, tears were running down his face. "I can't," she told him. "There's only you to save now."

NINETEEN

TERRI SAT WITH YANCEY JAMES ON A PARK BENCH across from City Hall, its golden dome glistening in the sunlight of a crisp fall afternoon. In the carefully tended park in front of them, homeless men and women, some with shopping carts, patrolled the walkways which crisscrossed the grass. James observed them with what, to Terri, seemed empathy and self-recognition.

"So easy to fall," he murmured, "so hard to get back up. Folks don't often appreciate how little separates them from us."

To Terri, James's manner and appearance had come as a surprise. The man Eula Price and Lou Mauriani had described to her was fleshy and bombastic, with a voice which wafted multisyllabic phrases with the resonance of a church organ. But this Yancey James was quiet and reflective, with the hollowed-out look of a man who had lost weight too quickly, perhaps because of illness. His neck was a loose crepe of skin, his face smoother but close to gaunt. The life in his eyes had vanished.

Terri herself was wary—fearful that James might know some fact that exploded Payton's confession, or pointed to Rennell's guilt; concerned that her need to establish James's incompetence might keep him from talking. "About the Price case," she began, "I wasn't there. I just need to know what you know, for better or worse. And how the case looked to you."

This elicited the wisp of a smile, which briefly touched his eyes. "You don't have to be so kindly, Ms. Paget. The A.G.'s folks already been sniffin' around, sayin' how you gonna be bad-mouthing me in court— them hopin' I'd tell them how great I'd done for Rennell Price." His voice was weary. "Everybody's tiptoein' up to me like I'm mentally ill, like if they say somethin' mean—or even truthful—I might go postal. Or maybe just break down weepin'."

Terri smiled. "Then I'll skip the niceties. If you want to tell me how you screwed up this case, it's okay by me. You're Rennell's last chance of living."

James gave a rueful shake of the head. "Odds are it's the only chance I'll ever give him. Just wish I could remember more—fifteen years was a long time ago, even without a wicked cross-addiction to Jack Daniel's and cocaine." He turned to the park again, gaze distant, speaking softly. "Know what it's like to be sober, and disbarred? It's like wakin' up in your car in your own garage, but the windshield's busted so bad you can't see out and the hood's all bent out of shape. And all you can do is sit there and wonder how it happened and why you're still alive, 'cause you can't remember drivin' home."

"What **do** you remember?"

James's eyes narrowed. "The grandmother," he said at length, "when I told her the boys were in trouble, and I needed more money to investigate. The fear in her eyes gave me a moment of remorse. Maybe even two."

Terri watched his profile; he seemed to study the park less from interest than from the wish not to look at her. "**Did** you investigate?" she asked.

"Me? At no time. I hired another cokehead, a so-called investigator named Rufus Cross, who kicked back half his fees to me. Don't imagine he did squat, either." He paused, an ironic resignation seeping into his voice. "You're welcome to look at my files."

For whatever good they would be, Terri thought. "What do you remember about Rennell?"

"Nothing much. Never said nothin', really. Just looked right through me. I remember thinkin', Here he is charged with chokin' a nine-year-old on his own come, and he don't give a damn."

The image of Rennell at eighteen, inexorably headed toward a fate he was too impaired to see, hit Terri hard. "Did you consider that he might be re-tarded?"

"Retarded?" James spoke the word with bemuse-ment and, it seemed, a touch of self-reproach. "He acted like a guilty man stickin' to his big brother's story, and waitin' for Payton to find him a way out. Maybe if I'd ever met with him alone..."

In an even tone, Terri said, "A 'way out' like asking a snitch to kill Eddie Fleet?"

"That's right. Hard to feel like that reflected well on either one of them."

"What about Eddie? Ever take a hard look at him?"

James seemed to study a homeless man at the center of the park, painstakingly folding a raveled blanket to stuff it in the garbage bag he used to carry his possessions. "What I remember," he said vaguely, "is tryin' to figure out his deal with the cops. Never found out that it was anything more than what all of them said it was—he'd testify, and Mauriani would consider that before charging him as an accessory."

"What about Fleet's story itself—that Rennell helped to dispose of the body. Didn't you wonder about that?"

"No," James said flatly.

Something new in his manner gave Terri pause. With some reluctance, she asked, "Why was that?"

James's eyes were suddenly harder. "This part, I **do** remember. Always will. No amount of drugs or whiskey could make a man forget."

Even through the glass in the county jail, Payton Price scared him some—the look in his eyes was implacable, that of a killer. "They're sayin' you hired a hit man," James repeated. "Jamal Harrison."

Payton's mouth curled in contempt. "Fleet's the whole case, or pretty damn near. You sayin' you'd miss him?" He paused, then added a perfunctory denial. "Jamal's a snitch, like Fleet. That makes him a liar."

"Maybe so. But him sayin' you wanted him to whack Eddie Fleet gives Eddie credibility." James leaned closer to the glass, speaking in an undertone. "This case is smellin' like death to me, son."

Payton met his eyes. "Then I better figure out where else we was."

James felt tired and flat: the coke was wearing off. "What are you tellin' me, Payton?"

Payton seemed never to blink; even through the glass James found this frightening. "Whatever you need to hear," Payton said.

"Like what?"

Payton angled his head, as though searching for an answer. "Like we was with my girlfriend, man. No way we killed that little girl."

His monotone bore no effort to persuade. "Payton," James said with new urgency, "I'm not puttin' on no perjured testimony. No good for either one of us."

Payton leaned closer, forehead nearly touching the glass. "Don't give me that jive," he hissed. "You look here at me, and listen hard. We was with my girlfriend, Tasha. You don't put her up there, we gonna die, and **you** gonna wind up floatin' in the bay like that little girl did." Payton looked him up and down, voice soft again. "Current like that, fat man like you float all the way to Oakland."

Softly, James said, "I hear you."

"Jesus," Carlo said.

"I know." Terri gazed out the window of the Waterfront Restaurant at the gray, white-capped current flowing under the Bay Bridge. "James assumed Payton was a liar. And that 'I didn't do that little girl' was just Rennell's pitiful excuse for an alibi. The fact that Rennell couldn't help, or even remember where he was, was just more proof of guilt—allowing James to rationalize pocketing the money from Grandma and blowing it on cocaine. All without doing any work."

"Pathetic," Carlo agreed. "But good for us."

Terri nodded. "Rennell never got his own defense, in either the guilt or the sentencing phase. James never even met with him alone. And the reason fits in neatly with mental retardation—Rennell's total reliance on Payton." She paused to spear a piece of sashimi. "So let's take stock of where AEDPA leaves us on the guilt phase."

"First," Carlo said promptly, "we need a constitutional error at trial. In this case, ineffective assistance of counsel, at least partly due to the conflict of representing both brothers. In short, that better lawyering might well have gotten Rennell acquitted."

Terri finished her meal. "The A.G. will say that

nothing James did or didn't do made any difference. So under AEDPA, Rennell got a constitutionally fair trial. The fact that a jury might not have convicted him if Payton had said what he told me is irrelevant."

Carlo shook his head in wonder. "So where does that leave us?"

"Looking for Eddie Fleet," Terri answered briskly. "If we can dirty him now, maybe someone could have in 1987."

TWENTY

RETURNING FROM INTERVIEWING ANNA VELEZ, a former juror, Terri sat with Chris and Carlo in Chris's office. "I told her about Payton," Terri said. "But when I asked if it would have changed her mind fifteen years ago, all she promised was to read Payton's deposition and get back to me."

"It's a start," Chris observed. "If you can get Velez to help, we'll add her statement to his clemency petition."

"When **is** the clemency hearing?" Carlo asked.

"Six days—unless we can get the execution set aside," Terri told him. "We'll have to prepare a supplemental filing, and I'll need you to help me draft it."

"No problem. But don't we need more on Eddie?"

"It would certainly be nice," Chris agreed. "Most of all, we need to preserve Payton's testimony." Glancing at Terri, he asked, "When's the last day we can go to court?"

"Two days from now. Wait any longer to find Eddie, and Payton's dead."

"Clemency," Carlo said, "means mercy. Even if we

don't have enough proof to satisfy AEDPA, if the governor has doubts—"

"**This** governor," Chris cut in, "has no doubts. Clemency is bad politics; executions are good politics. He'll call self-interest 'closure' for Thuy Sen's family."

It was true, Terri thought: Thuy Sen's parents might hold the power of life and death over Rennell Price. "For better or worse," she said, "I've got to try her parents again."

Chou Sen stared at Terri through the iron bars which guarded the door of their home. She seemed to stand lightly, as if ready to take flight.

"Payton will die," Terri concluded. "But now that we know Rennell's retarded, and what happened in his childhood, should he die, too?"

Chou Sen seemed to stiffen. "My little girl not die from a sickness," she answered in a soft, clear voice. "Not die from a ray-gime, like the Khmer Rouge, which killed so many in our family. Died because two men wanted sex.

"One named Rennell. For fifteen years my daughter dead, and he's still living. Breathing and eating and not feeling the pain of her parents." She blinked, fighting to control her emotions. "Not feeling the shame of her sister. Time for this to be over."

For an instant, Terri desperately wanted to tell her of Payton's confession. But to do so, she was certain, would be to tell the Attorney General's Office.

"If Rennell dies," Terri asked, "do you really think things will be better?"

Briefly Chou's eyes shut. "Maybe some man can do that to a child of yours, and then you can come back and tell me."

Terri could find no words. In her silence, Chou Sen drew herself up. "I ask you, no come back no more. You bring death to our house."

The door closed between them.

Driving away, Terri remembered to check her cell phone for messages.

The fifth message, in Johnny Moore's voice, began conversationally. "If you're Eddie Fleet, and a scammer with a prior record, your credit rating's no good. So you change your name to Howard Flood."

Behind the wheel, Terri tensed, reminding herself to watch the traffic light hanging over Third Avenue. From the cell phone, Moore chuckled softly in her ear. "Fucker's right here in Oakland, still up to no good. Want his phone number, or you want to just leave him...?"

"Quit screwing with me," Terri said aloud, then began laughing at the note of triumph in his message, perhaps out of sheer relief.

"If you really do want his number," Moore's voice continued, "it's 510-555-6777. All those sevens make it lucky, I guess."

Terri pulled over in front of a soul food restaurant, snatched a legal pad from her briefcase, and wrote the number down. For minutes, she idly watched the pedestrian traffic—a few men returning from work outside the neighborhood, a gaggle of girls smoking something and going nowhere fast. Then, at last, she punched out the numerals on her cell phone.

Phone pressed to her ear, she listened intently, as if she could force Fleet to answer by sheer effort of will.

"**Go,**" a man's cool voice answered.

Startled, Terri blurted. "Eddie Fleet?"

There was a long silence. "Eddie Fleet? He be dead. Who wants him?"

"Teresa Paget. I'm a lawyer for Rennell Price." She paused, then added flatly, "Rennell's about to be executed."

"Yeah? Well this be Howard Flood." The voice took on the lilt of quiet laughter. "Rennell **who,** you say?"

"Rennell Price," Terri answered. "And you used to be Eddie Fleet."

The man hesitated. "What you want, lady?"

"To talk to who you used to be." She amended her tone to be respectful, close to precatory. "We're working on a clemency petition, trying to persuade the Governor that Rennell shouldn't die along with Payton. I was hoping you could help us."

"Yeah?" The smooth voice took on an edge. "And why might that be? Sucker killed a child."

"Maybe so. But we think Rennell might be retarded. They don't execute those folks anymore."

The voice laughed softly. "Retarded? No way. Rennell Price was Alfred fucking Einstein."

Keep him talking, Terri urged herself. "Maybe you can tell me about him."

"Like when he invented the nu-cu-lar bomb, and all?"

"Sure. Unless you'd like to share it with a judge."

Fleet was silent. Beneath this, Terri imagined the calculations of a clever man—would it be better to talk with her, and could he avoid trouble if he did not?

"It's Eddie Fleet you're wantin', right?"

"Right."

Fleet laughed again, more quietly. "Might come with a price tag," he told her. "But maybe I could arrange a séance."

TWENTY-ONE

EDDIE FLEET HAD TOLD TERRI TO MEET HIM AT THE Double Rock Bar.

It was the scene—according to Payton—of their last meeting before Fleet's betrayal. If that was true, Terri found it an unsettling choice, as though Eddie Fleet were indifferent to the demons of his own past. Pushing open the swinging double door, Terri entered a dim-lit world which must have changed little in fifteen years: laminated tables, a long bar facing three neon beer signs, the whiff of smoke too fresh for attribution—despite the city's smoking ban—to the stale smell of old cigarettes absorbed by older leather.

Two men leaned on the bar—one, turning, gave Terri the cool once-over reserved for a strange woman or, perhaps, anybody not black. Then she spotted a lone man at a corner table, his appraisal seeming more amused and openly sexual. Approaching, she felt his smile as a form of muted aggression.

"Eddie Fleet?" she asked.

Gold teeth flashed. His eyes, unusual in their slightly Asian cast, held the insinuating power of a less than wholesome man from whom an attractive woman needs a favor. "Howard Flood," he amended. "Mr. Ed-ward Fleet's rep-re-sentative. Mr. Fleet's, how they say, re-clusive."

Terri sat across from him. He seemed tall—roughly Rennell's height, though not as bulky—and his face was thinner, its calculation animated by a cleverness wholly lacking in Rennell. But then Fleet had outrun the dire prospects of his youth: in his late thirties he was neither dead nor in prison. What had compelled him to meet her, Terri suspected, was a well-honed instinct for survival.

He nodded toward the beer in front of him. "Have a drink, lady? Make this more of a social occasion."

"Budweiser's fine."

Fleet stood, confirming Terri's estimate of his height. He wore a tight black T-shirt which displayed his muscles and the tattoos on both arms, and moved with what Terri supposed was meant to be a swaying, calypso rhythm. Suddenly she imagined Fleet in a bulky sweatshirt sauntering toward Thuy Sen, and conjured the man Flora Lewis thought was Rennell Price, mistaking Fleet's swagger for the lurching gait of impaired coordination. Startled, Terri imagined Fleet—as Payton had described him—at the moment Thuy Sen died.

She kept her face expressionless. Returning with a chipped glass, Fleet poured beer for her with exaggerated delicacy. Raising his own glass, he offered in satirically pious tones, "To Rennell Price, and our Lord Jesus's promise of e-ternal life."

Terri stared. "I'm not in the eternal life business, Eddie. That's why I'm here."

Fleet emitted a terse chuckle, eyes still bright as he took a long sip of beer, gazing at her over the rim. Slowly placing down his glass, he said, "What you want from me? At least that I want to give you."

"Anything you can tell me about Rennell. Maybe just what he was like."

Fleet grinned. "The boy stood out, that's for sure. Want to know the **first** thing I remember about him, from when we was kids?"

"Sure."

"Sucker couldn't play hide-and-seek." The memory produced a laugh. "Should have heard him try to count to twenty. If Payton hadn't helped him, he'd **still** be It, standin' there with his eyes closed, stuck on 'twelve.' " Fleet's full lips formed a sour smile. "You got one thing right. Rennell's dumb as a rock."

Dumb enough to be framed for murder, Terri thought. To her, Fleet's manner betrayed a man lethally Darwinian—taught from childhood to seek out, and exploit, the weakness of whomever he encountered. "Ever say that to the police?" she said.

A corner of Fleet's mouth flickered upward. "They never asked. Guess they figured e-jac-u-lation don't require no college degree."

"No," Terri said agreeably. "All it takes is interest. Did Rennell have any?"

Fleet's eyes glinted. "Maybe in little girls. No way he could handle a woman. You know how it is. Women got more in the way of requirements, and need more in the way of managing."

Like a few blows to the face? Terri wanted to ask. Instead, she inquired mildly, "Do you really think Rennell was sexually interested in children?"

Fleet shrugged. "Liked **this** one, didn't he?"

"I don't know that. If you've got some reason to believe that it was Rennell who choked Thuy Sen, I'd like to hear it."

The look Fleet gave her was cooler. "When I saw her on the floor," he said coldly, "**somebody's** come was dribbling out the corner of her mouth. Didn't seem like the occasion to ask whose."

"Did you ever find out?"

Eyes distant, Fleet took another swallow of beer. "Let me paint you a picture, lady. When I come on the scene, that girl was already dead—nothin' I could do to save her. Payton was crashing hard, sweat pourin' off him like he was a sponge and somebody be squeezin' him. And you're expectin' me to be conductin' interviews?"

Terri took a sip of beer. "How did Rennell act?"

Fleet studied the table. "Like he'd gone to some other planet. Maybe had his brain taken over by aliens."

"And he was like that when he came to your door."

"Yeah." Fleet seemed to think, then swiftly added, "Maybe a little more jittery, like I told the cops."

Terri angled her head. "I guess Payton didn't rely on Rennell much, at least when it came to dealing crack."

Behind his newly impassive mask, Fleet seemed to watch her, wondering what lay behind this unexpected question. "Too stupid," he answered. "Boy get himself busted."

"So why didn't Payton come for you himself, instead of sending Rennell?"

"Payton was too screwed up, maybe. Or maybe he didn't trust Rennell with her alone."

"Are you saying Rennell liked **dead** children, Eddie?"

Fleet shrugged. "Maybe Payton was worried—leave Rennell alone, and he'd do somethin' stupid. Maybe tell Grandma, and then **she'd** call the cops."

Then why didn't he just call you? Terri thought. But Fleet was no fool, then or now—the image of Rennell arriving at his door made him sound more culpable, his brother's partner in a terrible crime. "Why'd **you** tell the cops?" she asked.

Fleet's eyes widened in satiric amazement. "What planet are **you** on? Cops are puttin' pressure on us all. Maybe Payton's not gonna crack, but guy like Monk could think rings around Rennell. If **he** confesses, I'm on my way to prison just for helpin' dump her body." His voice took an edge. "No time for sentiment. That's why I'm sittin' here, enjoyin' your society, and those boys about to die."

Terri appraised him. Fleet's story, while plausible enough, could be a fun-house mirror of the truth: if Payton had confessed, choosing to save Rennell, then it was Fleet who might wind up on death row. And so Fleet had chosen to frame the retarded brother, and dared Payton to choose between keeping silent and contradicting Fleet at the cost of his own life.

"So what did Monk offer you?" she asked.

"Just what I told their fool lawyer at the trial—consideration for cooperation, long as I told the truth. Nothin' more than that."

"Did you have anything against either Payton or Rennell?"

Eddie's smile was brief and chilly. "Not until they tried to get me capped."

"Think that was Rennell's idea?"

"Nothin' was ever Rennell's idea. Spent his whole damned life waitin' to have one. You can bet it was Payton that dreamed up my de-mise."

In that moment, Terri felt Rennell—and she—were caught in a continuing war between Payton and Fleet. But whether Fleet was trying to save himself or Payton was lying to exact revenge before dying, she didn't know. For now, desperate as she was, she could only try to exploit Fleet's animus toward Payton by inducing him to help Rennell at the margins.

"You knew them both," she said, "pretty much all your life. If you had to guess, which brother strangled Thuy Sen?"

Fleet seemed to ponder the question and, perhaps, the advantage of answering. Then a fresh thought appeared to hit him so hard that he flinched, his eyes narrowing in distrust. "What about this DNA stuff?" His tone, though soft, was wary. "Can't they test the come now, figure out **whose** it was?"

It was **you,** Terri thought. For an instant, all the time she had, Terri weighed the merits of keeping him in doubt. But the advantage would be temporary, the risk too great—inducing silence, or even flight. "No DNA available," she answered. "Thuy Sen was in the bay too long."

Light crept back into Fleet's eyes. "Then I'd guess Payton," he answered flatly. "Don't think Rennell's brain could send signals all the way to his thing. Or figure out a nine-year-old's mouth might work better than her pussy."

But you could, Terri thought. "Think so?"

"Yeah." Fleet smiled slightly. "Rennell's way too stupid to teach a child no tricks. Even ones that want to learn."

Terri felt the pinpricks on her skin. Fleet had let his mask slip, exposing the narcissism and perversion beneath the veneer of a survivor. Some men, Terri knew too well, could want both a woman and her child.

Softly, she said, "I think you can help me, Eddie."

Fleet had begun studying her mouth. "How might that be?"

"I'd like you to execute a declaration—saying that

Rennell was slow, and that he depended on Payton for everything. Maybe that you never knew Rennell to be sexually involved with women of any age."

Once more, Fleet seemed to weigh his choices. "Maybe," he allowed. "Them executin' that fool won't do nothin' much for me. Let Payton pay the piper."

Of course, Terri thought. **Payton's the brother who knows what happened, the one that you need dead.** "Can I draft a declaration and bring it to you?"

"Why don't you bring it to my place?" Smiling, Fleet gently placed his fingers on her wrist. "You can read it aloud, just you and me. Sort of an oral presentation."

TWENTY-TWO

THE NEXT MORNING, WITH FOUR DAYS REMAINing before Payton Price was scheduled to die by lethal injection, Terri applied with Payton's lawyer, Paul Rubin, for a stay of execution from the same federal district judge who had denied Rennell's prior habeas petition.

She, Carlo, and Chris had worked until three o'clock that morning, assembling the legal papers which outlined Payton's confession and her meeting with Eddie Fleet. The risk of filing was clear: that exposing Payton's accusation of Fleet would, if Fleet learned of it, end any chance of entrapping him. But there was no more time. So at 10:00 A.M., her nerves jangled with coffee, Terri found herself in the chambers of Judge Gardner W. Bond, as crisp and imperious as the pin-striped suit and starched white shirt which were his uniform, his peremptory gaze trained on those who gathered around his conference table—Bond's supplicants, Terri, Rubin, and the Assistant California Attorney General Laurence D. Pell—as well as the impassive female court reporter he had summoned to record his rulings.

With his gold wire-rim glasses, neatly clipped, graying brown mustache, and an erect posture which made him seem to tower while sitting, Gardner Bond often seemed to Terri less a person than a series of poses intended to convey his pride of place, the conviction that a well-ordered world was best run by men whose stringent sense of law was unleavened by sentiment and sloppiness of thought. But Judge Bond's sense of law—just as subjective as Terri knew her own to be— had been tempered on the forge of the Federalist Society, whose conservative philosophy held the death penalty to be redemptive of good moral order. At least the knowledge that Payton Price would die—perhaps quite soon—made Bond's behavior less peremptory than was his norm. Of course, Terri thought unkindly, the judge knew himself to be in good hands: those of death's bureaucrat, Larry Pell.

Pell was African American, a former college quarterback with keen eyes, a pleasant but somewhat guarded expression, and a gift for swaddling executions in what Terri considered sanitizing legalisms, making lethal injection sound like the resolution of a boundary dispute. Aside from a healthy professional respect for his skill in preserving executions, what Terri felt for Larry Pell was less dislike than bemusement: she could not understand how a black man could devote his professional life to making cosseted white males like Gardner Bond even more comfortable in their assumptions. But then life was full of such quandaries, not the least of which, in Terri's mind, was the pervasive and quite persuasive rumor that Gardner Bond, steward of the right-wing moral order, was a closeted homosexual.

"Your Honor," Pell told him calmly, "Payton Price can't get a stay of execution on his own merits. So he's piggybacked on his brother, Rennell, to save himself by claiming, incredibly, that he's been keeping Rennell on death row all these years in order to save himself. The sole consistent theme is 'whatever it takes to cheat death.' "

Gardner Bond turned to Terri, fingers steepled in front of him. "What's so compelling now, Ms. Paget, that the Court should be constrained to keep Payton Price alive?"

"The fact that he **will** die," Terri said flatly. "Either in four days or whenever his brother's second **habeas corpus** petition is resolved." Swiftly, she glanced at Rubin. "As Mr. Rubin can tell you, Payton Price has directed him not to pursue any further avenues to avoid execution—"

"As if his confession hadn't foreclosed them," Bond interjected.

"Then it's hardly a 'convenience,' is it?" Terri angled her head toward Pell. "Even from the State's point of view, what interest is greater—executing Payton Price as swiftly as possible, or ensuring that it doesn't execute an innocent man? Mr. Pell's argument comes perilously close to asking this Court to bury Payton Price so that the State of California can bury its mistake."

" 'As swiftly as possible'?" Pell echoed in an incredulous tone. "Fifteen years—during which Payton Price could have spoken out any time he wished? What of the State of California's interest in justice? What of Thuy Sen's family—**awaiting** justice? We'll be happy to let Ms. Paget depose Payton Price before he dies. It should be enough for her purposes to let his words live after him."

Pell's argument, Terri thought, was more raw than normal. "Words aren't enough," she answered. "It's important for a court to judge Payton's demeanor—the conviction of his testimony, the persuasiveness with which he answers the State's questions. That can only be captured by seeing and hearing a living witness."

Bond pressed his steepled fingers to his lips, a gesture of contemplation which Terri thought both stagy and overfastidious. "Would you consider a videotaped deposition, Mr. Pell?"

"We're opposed to that," Pell answered crisply. "A transcript will preserve what is said. A videotape serves only the kind of media public relations campaign which all too often pervades these cases—the desperate attempt to influence the legal process by extralegal means."

Fatigue frayed Terri's temper. "I want a living witness for this Court, not for the media. What's desperate is for the State to execute **both** Payton and Rennell

Price in a way that keeps us from ever knowing that they'd executed an innocent man. After all, we wouldn't want the citizens of California to lose faith in our system of justice—"

"That's uncalled for," Pell said swiftly.

"Then so is your indecent haste to execute the only witness to my client's innocence." As Bond held up a hand in warning, Terri paused, her next words clear and calm. "My point, Your Honor, is that Payton confessed six days ago. Our inquiry is just beginning—including into Eddie Fleet, the potential second murderer, upon whose very dubious testimony the State's case depends. This Court should see Payton, Fleet, and any other witness for itself before determining Rennell's guilt or innocence."

"This is not a trial," Pell rejoined. "Five courts have, effectively, found Rennell Price guilty: the trial court, the California Supreme Court, this Court, the Federal Court of Appeals, and the U.S. Supreme Court. He had his trial fifteen years ago."

The reporter's fingers tapped swiftly now.

"He should have another," Terri shot back, "if new evidence suggests that verdict was wrong. In the meanwhile, this Court can allow Payton Price to take a polygraph—"

"They're not admissible as evidence," the judge remonstrated. "You're well aware of that."

The opacity of Bond's expression made Terri more anxious yet. "True, Your Honor. But it may be indicative of Payton's veracity and, therefore, whether his life should be preserved until his brother's petition is re-solved."

Bond raised a dubious eyebrow in Pell's direction, inviting a response. With the serenity of a man who sensed himself winning, Pell replied, "Any sociopath can pass a polygraph. That's why they're not admissible in court. Payton Price should not be permitted to use this discredited tool as a 'life preserver'—"

"He's going to **die,**" Paul Rubin burst out in anger. "Do you understand that, Larry? Do you really think they'll abolish the death penalty before you can kill him off?"

"That's enough," Bond snapped. "Next time you would care to be heard, Mr. Rubin, ask first. You might also stop to consider what you wish to say, and to whom you wish to say it. This is a court of law, not a school yard."

Of course, Terri thought to herself. At whatever cost, the decorum of death must be preserved. But Rubin's outburst had not helped her position. "Your Honor," she tried again, "the State of California wishes to execute Rennell Price. His guilt or innocence is what's important here—not 'sanitizing' the process by eliminating such unseemly spectacles as polygraphs and videotapes. Let alone, Lord help us, a living witness to his innocence. The State's priorities are skewed."

Bond sat back, surveying the lawyers, his expression closed to further argument. "The interests of the parties," he admonished Terri, "are for this Court to balance. Including those of the victim's parents, who have no voice but Mr. Pell, and who would only suffer more from needless publicity and unwarranted delay. And your argument, Ms. Paget, prematurely assumes that your client's **next** petition will, under the AEDPA statute, prove meritorious enough to be heard at all. Let alone granted.

"Mr. Pell is **not** attempting to suppress Payton Price's testimony. By order of this Court, you'll have his deposition—two days from now." He turned to Pell. "And four days from now, by order of its Supreme Court, the State of California may carry out his sentence."

"Thank you, Your Honor," Pell said swiftly, the rote obeisance of an advocate. Terri could not bring herself to emulate the courtesy.

Afterward, Terri, Rubin, and Pell left Bond's chambers together, silent until they reached the long tiled corridor outside his courtroom. For a moment the only sounds were the click of Terri's heels and the deeper echoes of the two men's hard-soled shoes. "Tell me," she asked Pell, "have you ever witnessed an execution?"

He looked at her sideways, curious. "Why should it matter?"

"It just seems funny to me," Terri said. "Like a football coach skipping the postgame celebration."

Pell's slight smile was defensive. "I don't have to

see it to believe in it. Have **you** ever watched a client die?"

"No."

"Then isn't that like a doctor abandoning her patient because the operation failed?"

"No," Terri answered. "It's like a lawyer who's still trying to stop the process you've chosen **not** to see. I guess it helps your side 'believe' if death remains invisible. So why not put yourself to the test?"

TWENTY-THREE

LESS THAN AN HOUR LATER, TERRI AND CHARLES MONK sat in a windowless interrogation room at the Robbery and Homicide Division. "I flunked retirement," he told her matter-of-factly. "Back here part-time, doing special investigations. Chumps who gave me the golf clubs at my farewell party are wanting a refund."

Terri gave him a perfunctory smile. "Got time to excavate the past?"

"Whose past?"

"Eddie Fleet. The guy who asphyxiated Thuy Sen while Rennell Price was fast asleep."

Monk dealt with surprise, Terri realized, by summoning a total absence of expression. But his eyes betrayed his swiftness of thought. "If Rennell was sleeping, and Fleet still says he wasn't there, that makes Payton your witness."

"Think about it," Terri urged. "You **had** no witnesses to the murder. So Flora Lewis could mistake Fleet for Rennell, and Fleet could lie to you about him."

"That'd be a pretty nasty coincidence, counselor. I

never told Fleet about Lewis. Their stories jibed without any help from me."

Terri felt a surge of desperation. "I **have** a witness," she retorted. "One of the men who killed her. You can't ignore what Payton says."

Monk appraised her, his expression softening a bit. "But the A.G.'s Office can," he said. "Death row confessions are nothing new to them. You'd better tell me exactly where things stand."

Eyes still fixed on his, Terri summarized her theory as succinctly as she could. "Rennell never knew what happened," she concluded. "He still doesn't. I'm sure Fleet does. I'm almost as sure that if you kick over enough rocks, you'll find a pedophile who likes forcing children into oral sex, and is going to keep on doing it until somebody stops him. And maybe, if we're lucky, he told somebody sometime how clever he was to frame Rennell."

"You've got investigators. Why me?"

Terri paused, then chose total candor. "Because we're striking out. Because there's ten days left for me to save Rennell. And because you've got as big a stake in that as I do." She softened her voice. "Maybe bigger. Whatever happens, I'll have done my best to save an innocent man. But if I'm right, his death—and the next child Fleet forces into sex—will be the dark side of your storied career."

Monk shook his head in demurral. "I went where the evidence took me. I'm not the prosecutor, or the judge, or his lawyer, or the jury that convicted him."

"They were all standing on your work," Terri

replied. "Fleet's story saved his ass; Payton's story seals his execution. Why are you so sure that Fleet didn't play you?"

For the first time Monk looked away from her, eyes narrow in thought. "Rennell's retarded," she continued. "He was too impaired to **have** a story, and Fleet knew it. That put him one jump ahead of you."

"Matter of fact," Monk quietly remarked, "this room is where he fingered the brothers." His smile was almost imperceptible, a ghost of deeper reflections. "What exactly you want me to do?"

"To use all your street contacts—check out Eddie Fleet, a.k.a. Howard Flood. If you find something that troubles you, tell Larry Pell. Soon."

Wincing, Monk stretched his legs in front of him, reminding Terri of his chronically painful knee. "Have to tell Pell first," he responded. "It's his case now, not mine. But I'll try and see what I can do."

"Thanks, Charles," Terri said simply.

"Last time I ever see him," Rennell told Terri. "Tole me in the yard warden gonna lock us down now..."

He stopped, choking on his words. Tears ran down the broad planes of his face, so riven with grief that he did not seem to notice them. His next words came in a near-whisper. "Says not to leave my cell no more. Not till you get me out."

Miserable, Terri took his hand. Rennell's lips fluttered. "Says I can't go with him," he mumbled.

Terri's chest felt tight. "To heaven?"

Eyes shut, Rennell slowly shook his head. "The death chamber."

Helpless, Terri tried to answer as though this were a commonplace. "They don't let other inmates watch. It's the rules."

Rennell wiped his eyes with the back of his curled hand. "Grandma can't come either. Too sick, Payton says."

This was true. But only Terri knew that Payton had not given his permission for Eula Price to attend. He did not wish her to see him die, or bear witness to his shame.

Fumbling in the pocket of his denim shirt, Rennell withdrew a piece of paper, then carefully unfolded it on the table before her. "I drew this for him."

Heartsick, Terri stared at two stick figures, one larger and one smaller, drawn in orange Magic Marker. The larger figure seemed to be reaching down to catch the other's hand.

"It's beautiful."

"Want you to give it to him," Rennell said softly. "At the death chamber, so he'll have it."

She could not tell him that a pane of glass would separate Payton from those who came to watch him die. "I don't think I can be there, Rennell."

Rennell looked up at her, his eyes pleading. "He's my brother—always lookin' out for me. Don't want him to be alone."

The realization of what he was asking crept over her. Terri's mouth felt dry. "What does Payton say?"

"Up to you. Is it okay?"

The enormity of this request, Terri saw, was well beyond his ken. She had given Rennell comfort, and so could comfort Payton as well. The Teresa Paget of Rennell's imaginings slept soundly.

"It's okay," she assured him.

Christopher Paget gazed down at the drawing his wife had placed on his ink pad.

"Jesus," he murmured and slowly shook his head. "It captures this whole tragedy—far better than I can do in a hundred pages of legal argument. I'm just so sorry, sweetheart."

Terri mustered a wan smile. "I know you are. Save Rennell, I thought, and I could keep my innocence intact. But there's no innocence quite like his."

Chris glanced toward the marked-up pile of papers beside Rennell's drawing. "I'm a half hour from being finished. Then I'll run these to Sacramento, and ask the Governor's office for a reprieve. Bond notwithstanding, the State ought not execute Rennell's only witness before we can make our case."

"Do you think you've got a prayer?"

"An agnostic's prayer," Chris quietly allowed. "You're the Catholic, however lapsed. Maybe you can resurrect your rosary and pray that God will whisper in our Governor's ear. As opposed to his pollsters' here on earth."

Tiredly, Terri sat. "I don't want Payton to die,

Chris. I'm not ready to watch that. Not when Rennell is with me night and day."

Chris's look of compassion carried a hint of his own solitude. "I know," he answered.

Terri went to her office and hit buttons on her cell phone until she found the number she had recorded for Eddie Fleet. She pressed one more button, then heard his telephone ringing.

"Go," Fleet answered tersely.

Terri hesitated. "This is Terri Paget. I've got a declaration to go over with you."

"That's sure nice, Terri Paget." His silken voice was suffused with anger. "Only problem is the A.G. called me first. Seems like you tryin' to trade me for Rennell."

"That's not right—"

"You take me for a fool?" His tone became quiet, poisonous. "You can still come on over. But now you got to get down on your knees and suck my dick till I'm done. See if you're woman enough to live through what I got stored up just for you." Fleet emitted a harsh laugh. "That's what this case is all about, right? 'Cept your mouth is bigger."

For a terrible instant—born, Terri understood at once, of a mother's primal instinct to protect—she feared this man not for herself but for Elena. Then the line went dead.

TWENTY-FOUR

FOR TERRI, THE NEXT TWO DAYS WERE A BLUR OF AC-
tion through which she tried to save her client by preserving the life of his brother.

Rennell and Payton were in lockdown with the entire population of death row—no visitors, no exercise,
no doctor visits save for medical emergencies. East
Block would be particularly quiet, its pall deepened by
the knowledge that one among them would soon die,
to be followed, quite likely, by another lockdown and
another execution. Even the crazies were muted.

The only break in this routine was Payton's deposition. Shackled, he sat at a wooden table in the psychiatric conference room, responding first to Terri's
questions, then to Larry Pell's, with a precision and
composure which astonished her. It was as though he
wished to perform the last meaningful act of his life, the
only one in which he retained volition, by employing all
the resources he had acquired since receiving his sentence of death. With conviction and persuasiveness, he
spelled out for the lawyers and a court reporter that Eddie Fleet was the murderer of Thuy Sen. For Terri, his

story, terrible in itself, was made more tragic by the fact that—unless the Governor granted a reprieve—no one else would ever see or hear Payton tell it.

This sense was only deepened by the fierce dignity of Payton's response to Pell's cross-examination. "No," he answered, biting off each word. "I didn't lie. Don't want to die with a lie on my lips. Don't want Rennell to die for me." He paused, face twisted with emotion, and then he spoke more softly, looking directly at Larry Pell as if daring him to hear. "You about to kill my brother, who done nothin' to that girl. All that poor sucker ever did was love me, and what he got for it is **this.** Only thing I can give him now is truth."

Tears welled in his eyes. But he would not look away from Pell until, at last, Pell decided he had no more questions.

After this, Payton's only words were for Terri. With a weary smile, he murmured, "Guess I'll be seeing you." Then the guards took him away.

The press conference which followed preceded Terri's call to Thuy Sen's family.

In a hotel meeting room crowded with reporters, she distributed Payton's deposition, transcribed overnight by a team of stenographers. Then she spoke to the cameras. Though she would always find this surreal, Terri had learned to imagine her audience behind the blank lens of a mini-camera.

"Payton Price's confession," she told them, "exonerates Rennell Price for the murder of Thuy Sen. And it places responsibility for this horrible act squarely where it belongs—on Eddie Fleet, whose perjured testimony has brought Rennell within eleven days of execution.

"Therefore, we have asked Governor Darrow to delay Payton's execution until—**if** we're granted the hearing Rennell deserves—Payton can be heard in open court..."

This would yield headlines, Terri knew, be the lead story on newscasts across California and, therefore, put pressure on the Governor and, once she filed Rennell's second **habeas** petition, on Gardner Bond. The price could be Bond's enmity.

As to Thuy Sen's family, she was uncertain of their reaction until, for the first time, she found herself speaking to her father. "Rennell's innocent," she said simply. "He shouldn't die for what Eddie Fleet did to your daughter. All we're asking is that you support our petition to the Governor, so that the right man can be punished."

"Payton Price die," Meng Sen interjected coldly. "Attorney General say you already got his testimony."

"He **will** die..."

"**Tomorrow.**" The spat-out word was followed by a pause. "Tomorrow," the man repeated quietly. "I watch him."

The phone clicked off.

On the morning of Payton's scheduled execution, Terri began drafting Rennell's **habeas corpus** petition while Chris, a prisoner in his office, awaited a telephone call from Governor Craig Darrow.

Shortly before 11:00 A.M., Carlo cracked open Terri's door. "Darrow's on the line," he said urgently. "Dad's talking to him now."

Swiftly, Terri followed Carlo to Chris's office. Through the squawk box, the Governor was speaking in the careful tones of a diplomat. "I understand your concern, Chris. But my job is to see that our laws are carried out, including those with respect to capital punishment—"

"We're not asking for a commutation, Craig. Just a delay."

Terri and Carlo stood by Chris's chair. "Fifteen years," the Governor said in mild reproof, "seems like delay enough. The Attorney General advises me that her family wishes this execution to go forward. Where the man's admitted his guilt of a terrible crime, and you've preserved his eleventh-hour testimony, I'm inclined to agree."

Anxious, Terri turned from the squawk box to her husband, willing him to give the answer **she** would give. "You were a trial lawyer," Chris told Darrow. "You know the difference between a typed page and the words of a living witness."

"I do," Darrow replied with measured sympathy. "But, in itself, it's not enough for me to act. There are other interests at stake..."

"Can we talk about this?" Terri whispered sharply.

Chris glanced up at her. "Could you hold, Craig?" he asked. "Just for a moment. I need a word with co-counsel."

Quickly, he stabbed the mute button. "What is it?"

"Dammit," Terri burst out. "He's not just the only real witness, he's the only **living** witness. Flora Lewis wasn't even there, and now she's dead."

"So's Payton," Chris said evenly. "Darrow's not changing his mind on this."

Carlo looked from his father to his stepmother.

"You raised money for this creep," she shot back. "You at least can push him some."

Anger glinted in Chris's clear blue eyes. "Back off, Terri. The day I push him it'll be for Rennell. If your **habeas** petition fails, Darrow's all we've got. I'm not using up my chits for Payton Price."

Terri stared at him. "The Governor's waiting," Chris said with perilous calm. "What do you want me to tell him?"

Silent, Terri turned away.

She heard Chris switch the speaker back on. "We understand," he told the Governor. "Thanks so much for your time. We hope you'll keep all this in mind—particularly about Eddie Fleet—should we bring you a clemency petition on behalf of Rennell Price..."

Terri glanced at her watch. In thirteen hours, Payton Price would die by lethal injection.

TWENTY-FIVE

THAT EVENING, THE PAGET FAMILY ATE LATER than usual, about seven-thirty, and the conversation was quieter, although Carlo, their frequent guest, tried to focus on Elena and Kit. But Carlo, too, was somber. Only Kit seemed unaffected; Elena, knowing her mother's plans for that evening, had lapsed into a silence Terri found ambiguous. Terri ate little, declining Chris's offer to open a bottle of Brunello di Montalcino, a favorite from their Italian honeymoon. In the midst of their dinner, softly lit by candles whose flicker refracted on the crystal facets of their chandelier, it struck Terri that by the unvarying protocol of San Quentin, Payton Price was being offered his last meal. She put down her fork.

"I'll read to Kit tonight," she told her husband. "I haven't in a while."

In the event, this ritual of parenthood, usually Chris's domain, soothed her for a time. The current book was from the Lemony Snicket series, and Terri's rendering of its skewed humor was satisfactory enough that she was intermittently rewarded with the laughter in Kit's dark eyes, the play of humor around his mouth, which reminded her of Chris and yet was wonderfully Kit's own. Finishing, she kissed his forehead and repeated a prayer with him, as her own mother had with her, then went down the hall to Elena's room.

Terri's knock on her door was tentative, a mother's request for admission into the moody realm of a thirteen-year-old girl. But Elena's expression was opaque. "Are you really going out there?" she inquired.

Nodding, Terri sat on the edge of her bed. "No choice. Rennell asked me to."

"Too bad," Elena answered. "But I guess you'd do anything for **Rennell,** wouldn't you. No matter what it does to us."

Terri composed herself. "I know you hate my work. But no one matters as much as you."

The child-woman in the Winnie-the-Pooh T-shirt gave an indifferent shrug. "I don't **understand** your work," she said in an accusatory voice. "And no one matters as much as **it** does. Rennell Price deserves to die, and it will just kill you when he does."

Though this cutting remark was, at bottom, about something more, Terri had little will to surface that tonight. "It will," she answered finally. "But not nearly as much as what happened to you."

The look on her own face must be miserable, Terri realized; as Elena studied her mother, her expression changed. "Then why," she asked, "do you spend more time on **him** than me?"

The accusation pierced Terri's heart. As with Kit,

Terri kissed her forehead. "I'm sorry about tonight," she tried. "I'm sorry about everything."

Elena gazed at her, tears welling, and then she turned away.

Chris was in the kitchen, listening to Carlo describe his new girlfriend. Of Terri, Chris inquired, "Did Kit induce you to read the entire series?"

"I was counting Elena's moods."

Chris gave her the long, somewhat veiled look he reserved for efforts to gauge her own moods. "Let me drive you, Terri. Carlo's volunteered to watch the kids."

"No," she said sharply, then saw the brief flicker of worry on Carlo's face, the residue of the child who feared conflict. In a more temperate tone, she added, "Really, this is mine to do. I honestly don't want either of you holding my hand."

She went to their bedroom to change. Reflecting on which of her suits was most suitable for an execution, she chose gray over black.

When she returned, Carlo was gone and Chris was sipping brandy. He looked up at her, openly concerned.

"I'm really not punishing you for the Governor," she said.

"I didn't think you were."

She walked over to him, resting a hand on his chair. "I don't know how this is going to be for me. It just feels like I'll do better alone."

Standing, Chris gave her a tentative hug. Then she went to the garage and backed her car out into what, even without the chill and drizzle, would have seemed a miserable night. Even the vigil outside the gates of San Quentin, deprived of candlelight, seemed dispirited and ill-attended. For a brief moment, in the cool breath of night, Terri felt the presence of Eddie Fleet.

At eleven-thirty, thirty-one minutes before Payton Price was to die, Terri was admitted to the viewing room.

The guard directed her to the far side of the chamber, reserved for the friends or family of the prisoner about to be executed. No one else stood with her. Several reporters and the warden separated her from Thuy Sen's family, huddled close together on the other side. Silent, they stared through the windows of the execution chamber.

The chamber itself was much as Terri had envisioned—an octagon roughly eight feet in diameter, with a padded table beside a cardiac monitor and a machine for intravenous injection. But for the straps, Terri thought, the table was eerily like the hospital bed in an intensive care unit, a site dedicated to preserving life. The large oval door at the rear of the chamber, through which Payton Price would enter, seemed to hypnotize those awaiting him.

With that thought, the strangeness of this setting hit Terri hard—the raised platform for the witnesses, the five windows of the chamber, their blinds raised to permit those assembled to view the state-sanctioned death of another human. "He'll probably be pretty subdued," an older lawyer had predicted to her. "The 'People's' victims don't tend to be kickers or screamers, or even very defiant. A decade or two on death row breeds a certain level of acceptance."

Terri drew a breath.

Desperate for distraction, she began a surreptitious study of Thuy Sen's family. Only Chou Sen was familiar. Her husband, Meng, was a small, well-knit man with jet-black hair and a seamed face which betrayed his age and, perhaps, years of grief. Stoic, his wife stood between him and the young woman whom Terri thought of as the second victim, Kim Sen.

She was slight, with straight black hair cut shoulder length and a look of keen intelligence accented by gold wire-rim glasses, suggesting the graduate student that she was. Though they stood close to each other, the Sens neither spoke nor touched. To Terri, they seemed bereft, a family smaller than it should have been. Only when Kim Sen flinched did Terri's gaze return to the execution chamber.

Its door had opened. Through it shuffled Payton Price, shackled, dressed in the stiff new denim work shirt and trousers issued for the occasion.

He stood straighter, mustering what dignity he could, and then paused to register each face on the other side of the glass, lingering on the three Asians whose suffering he had caused, as if to assess the changes fifteen years had wrought. Only when his gaze met Terri's did he nod, a brief acknowledgment that she, the surrogate for friends or family, had kept her word to Rennell. Forcing herself to smile, she took out Rennell's drawing from the pocket of her suit, holding it up for him to see.

Payton stared at it, then slowly shook his head. The faintest of smiles did not conceal the sorrow in his glistening eyes.

He looked down, composing himself. Then the guards escorted him to the center of the execution chamber. Terri could hear his shackles clink through the sound system linking him to those who watched.

Payton seemed to reach within himself. When at last he faced the Sens, Kim raised a black-and-white photograph of the solemn Asian child she had left to walk home alone.

Briefly, Payton shut his eyes. When he spoke it was to Kim. "I'm sorry—not 'cause I'm gonna die, but for what I done to all of you. If watching me die makes any difference to you, then maybe there's some good in this. But they got no reason to kill Rennell." His voice quavered. "Rennell's innocent. It was Eddie Fleet that choked her. I know, 'cause I was part of it." His gaze moved from Thuy Sen's sister to her mother, and finally to her father. "Killin' my brother," he finished softly, "be one more murder. No good can come to you from that."

Meng Sen stiffened, a posture of anger and rejection. Kim raised Thuy Sen's photograph between Payton and her own face.

Payton's eyes dulled. Slowly, he faced Terri. "Tell my brother I didn't feel no pain." His voice was tired and husky, a near-whisper. "Tell him I'm sorry for leavin', and for what I done to put him here."

Turning to one of the guards, he nodded toward the table.

In silence, they moved him there. Payton sat, then lay on his side, rolling himself onto the table. The guards strapped him in, face upward. He no longer looked around him.

Slowly, the warden nodded.

A prison technician entered the chamber. He approached Payton, face as devoid of expression as was the warden's, and connected two IVs into the tubes already inserted in the flesh of his left forearm. Terri forced herself to watch.

"You may carry out the death warrant," the warden intoned.

Through the plastic tubes, Terri knew, would flow fifty cc's of potassium chloride. As the doctor stood beside him, Payton closed his eyes.

Minutes seemed to pass. Neither Payton nor those who watched him made a sound. **Please,** Terri thought, **let it be done.**

Abruptly, Payton's mouth opened, expelling a deep, guttural exhalation which preceded a final gasp for air. His body convulsed, as though from an electric shock, followed by shudders. Terri felt Rennell's drawing crumple in her fist.

At last the shuddering subsided. As Terri turned to her, Kim Sen, tears streaming from her eyes, held out Thuy Sen's photograph as if Payton still could see.

PART THREE

THE CIRCUIT

ONE

ON THE DAY AFTER THE EXECUTION OF PAYTON PRICE, Caroline Clark Masters, Chief Justice of the United States Supreme Court, and her onetime mentor, Judge Blair Montgomery of the United States Court of Appeals for the Ninth Circuit, decided to follow their leisurely and discursive lunch at the Old Angler's Inn outside Washington with a walk along the shallow river which ran beside it.

It was a crisp day in early November, suitable for a stroll along the well-worn path which meandered amidst the rocks and gravel, and the echo of water rushing blended with the bright orange woods around them to make Caroline feel, for a blessed afternoon, far removed from the cloistered intensity of the ideologically riven Court over which—however uneasily—she presided. But her slow pace reflected less a desire to escape than her knowledge that Blair Montgomery, while still spare and bright-eyed, was frailer and more halting than the last time she had seen him.

At fifty-three, Caroline was a fitness fanatic, and her height and leanness accented the attributes which made other hikers notice her at once: an erect posture, a casual grace of movement, and striking features—a long, aquiline nose; wide-set brown eyes; a high forehead; and still-glossy black hair, which began with a widow's peak. She looked and sounded like what she was, the daughter of a patrician New England family, save for a touch of the exotic—emphatic gestures, olive skin, a somewhat sardonic smile—which suggested her mother, a French Jewish beauty whose parents had died in the Holocaust.

Beside her, Blair Montgomery was shorter and smaller, a white-haired miniature of his younger self. The casual observer would not have seen him as did the judicial conservatives: a liberal bomb thrower whose passion for civil liberties, reproductive choice, and the separation of church and state was as unrelenting as his loathing of the death penalty, and whose closeness to the new Chief Justice was yet more proof—if any was needed—that her appointment by President Kerry Kilcannon was a triumph for secular humanism over the forces of faith and judicial restraint. It was a suspicion shared, to Caroline's regret, by several members of her own Court. This was deepened by their hostility to the intermediate court on which both Caroline and Montgomery once had served, the Ninth Circuit, which heard appeals from federal district courts in nine western states, most notably California: twenty-eight active judges, a combustible mixture of conservatives, moderates, and liberals, combined in random three-judge panels to issue rulings which—depending on the panel—were considered by conservatives to enshrine a lawless disregard for precedent and common sense.

"The work of the Supreme Court," Caroline's conservative predecessor, Roger Bannon, had once remarked, "is to interpret what the law is, and explain to the Ninth Circuit what the law is not." Fortunately for Caroline, this aphorism had found much wider currency than her own prior remark to Judge Montgomery that the transition from her contentious Senate confirmation hearing to the cloistered quiet of the Supreme Court had been like "going from a circus to a monastery—except that some of the monks are vicious."

"Is your working environment any better these days?" Montgomery asked now.

Caroline paused to afford him a rest, hands shoved in the pockets of her slacks, surveying the swift rush of water over rocks as she contemplated her answer. "Superficially," she said. "This last term didn't have quite as many contentious cases—except from **your** circuit, of course." She turned to him. "I see you had an execution yesterday."

"Yes. But there was nothing for our Court to do—this man Price told his lawyers to take him off life support. What he left us is more problematic: a last-minute confession claiming that the next one scheduled to die, his brother, is innocent. The evidence is ambiguous."

"Spare me ambiguity," Caroline said dryly. "In the

death penalty, even the cut-and-dried can turn into a morass. At least in our Court."

Montgomery began walking again, eyes on the path before them. "A morass?" His tone became bitter. "More like an abattoir. In his nearly twenty-five years as Chief Justice, Roger Bannon never once voted to overturn a death sentence. But what truly distinguished him was a driving lack of curiosity as to whether any of these defendants were, in fact, innocent."

Caroline smiled. "Oh, Roger Bannon may have been 'curious,' in the abstract," she answered. "He just didn't think guilt or innocence was any of his business. Or yours."

Montgomery gave her a keen look. "After the first decade or two of executions, I ceased to believe that Bannon cared about anything I recognize as justice. No defense counsel was too incompetent, no racial disparity too glaring, no condemned too young or too retarded, no judge or jury too biased. As for the small matter of innocence, Bannon labored mightily to erect a Byzantine morass of arbitrary legal barriers between federal judges and deciding what, to me, is the most basic question we should address: whether we kill some people for no reason but their misfortune and our own ineradicable imperfections."

What she was hearing, Caroline knew, was a lifetime of frustration and moral passion, based on a single, diamond-hard belief: that the death penalty was tainted by human failings too profound to cure, and that imposing it was an act of arrogance which diminished our humanity. For Blair Montgomery, no Ted Bundy or Timothy McVeigh would ever compensate for the execution of the innocent.

"Blair," she said gently, "you've earned the right to feel as you do. But the death penalty is the law, and I promised Congress to uphold it. All I can do is try to make it fairer."

"Impossible." Her old friend's tone brooked no doubt. "Your problem is about far more than AEDPA. It's about Justice Anthony Fini, and his desire to control the Court."

"Don't be condescending, Blair. I fully appreciate that Tony Fini and I occupy different moral universes, and that he sees himself as Chief Justice Bannon's heir. But I put together the majority which barred executing the retarded—"

"Provoking the nastiest dissent from Fini I've read in years." Montgomery's tone mixed admonition with concern. "You haven't had a death penalty case which directly confronts what AEDPA does to narrow death penalty appeals, and sanction executions, no matter what the facts. You can bet Fini is looking for one. Knowing how his mind works, he'll use it to try to place his stamp on death penalty jurisprudence, and stake his claim to leadership of the Court."

"And how might he do that?"

"He'll fight for an unequivocal ruling that, under AEDPA, guilt or innocence no longer matters as long as—by Fini's extremely elastic standards—the defendant's trial was 'fair.'" Montgomery stood, as though made restless by his own words. "That it's the role of the state courts to determine guilt, and the role of the Supreme Court to assure finality—that a state court sentence of death, if 'fairly' imposed, is carried out. You may have no illusions, Caroline. But unlike you or me, state court judges are elected. In a number of states, the right wing has defeated state supreme court judges who reverse death sentences, no matter how justified. So state supreme courts don't reverse them anymore. Look at California—"

"California," Caroline objected, "makes my point about judges who follow their own beliefs, and not the law. Until the mid-1980s, Rose Bird and her colleagues on the Court practiced abolition by judicial fiat, reversing death sentence after death sentence on grounds so flimsy that they gave death penalty proponents all they needed to defeat them at the polls. It was worse than stupid—it was intellectually dishonest—"

"Perhaps so. But what replaced them was a California Supreme Court afraid to reverse death sentences no matter how egregious the case. Which means **my** Court has to review with extreme care everything they do—"

"Setting off a vicious cycle," Caroline interposed. "Your Court began reversing the California Supreme Court, and then the Bannon Court began reversing your reversals. That's where Tony Fini cut his teeth on death penalty cases—on you."

They started walking again, though Montgomery's gaze, while nominally directed at the meandering path before them, was distant and troubled. "You missed the worst one," he said at length. "An execution that happened while you were tied up in your confirmation hearings. It was my most terrible experience as a judge, and one which undermined any notion that the death penalty isn't poison for us all."

Side by side, he and Caroline picked their way across a rock-strewn stretch of growth, the spill of water serving as background to his narrative. "The victim," he continued, "was stabbed to death in her apartment. There was substantial reason to believe that she was killed by her ex-husband, the roommate of the man about to be executed for the murder. But the District Attorney chose to prosecute both men, in separate trials, based on two conflicting theories.

"The first theory was that the ex-husband had recruited the condemned to help murder the ex-wife. That culminated in the ex-husband's imprisonment for life. The prosecution's second theory, based on jailhouse snitches of dubious honesty, was that the condemned was the sole murderer and that his motive was to cover up his rape of the victim. **This** time the defendant was sentenced to death." Montgomery's tone, though quiet, was laden with anger. "Both theories could not be true. Indeed, the two conflicting prosecutions were so blatantly unethical that seven former prosecutors spoke out on behalf of the condemned man. None of which prevented the California Supreme Court from upholding both convictions, and affirming the man's sentence of death."

"What was their reasoning?"

"They gave none." Montgomery shook his head in remembered disbelief. "Both opinions were one-pagers.

"But that was only the beginning. A federal district judge reversed the condemned man's conviction, ruling that his spectacularly inept lawyer had, by failing to contest the prosecution's dubious evidence, denied him effective assistance of counsel. Three of my conservative colleagues reversed **that.** So the man's new lawyers filed a petition for rehearing to be ruled upon by the Ninth Circuit as a whole."

"Which, I assume, was granted."

"Not quite. As you know, a vote for a rehearing requires, as a first step, that one of us suggest it be re-heard in such a fashion." Montgomery's speech became weary, drained of all vigor. "Through an administrative error by a law clerk, none of us—including me—did so in the time required by our circuit's rules.

"I requested my three conservative colleagues to grant an extension. Shockingly, they refused. But our Chief Judge ordered the extension granted. A week before the defendant was to die, eleven judges voted seven to four to reverse the conviction and set aside the condemned man's execution.

"The California Attorney General petitioned the

Bannon Court for review." Montgomery paused, breathing more heavily. "The sole ground for review, the United States Supreme Court decided, was **not** whether the man had received a fair trial but whether our Court had the authority to act—"

"Just because you'd violated your own internal rules?"

Montgomery stopped walking. He stood, appearing stooped and old, looking not at Caroline but at the patch of earth beside her. "It never occurred to me that a procedural error, committed **not** by a defendant's lawyer but by our own Court, would condemn a man to death. And I'll never forget Justice Fini's opinion for the majority." Montgomery looked up at her. "I can give you the last two sentences verbatim. 'A mishandled law clerk transaction in one judge's chambers constitutes the slightest of grounds for setting aside the deep-rooted policy in favor of the finality of justice. And it would be the rarest of cases where the negligent delay of that single judge in expressing his views is sufficient grounds to frustrate the interests of a state of some thirty-four million persons in enforcing a final judgment in its favor.'

"**I** was the judge, Caroline. The man died eight days later."

In that moment, Caroline understood the weight Montgomery carried, and the passion of his warnings. "It's the world we live in," he continued. "Clemency's become a joke. State supreme court judges are frightened or indifferent. The Ninth Circuit is a target. And

Tony Fini and his allies are armed with a law that safe-guards unfair convictions, and guarantees that innocent people will be executed.

"That's the world you preside over, Caroline. Counting his own, Tony Fini's got four votes out of nine for any interpretation of AEDPA he desires. All he needs is the right case, and a single vote, and the Masters Court will turn its back on judicial murder for at least another generation, and perhaps for good."

Caroline faced him. "All I can tell you," she said finally, "is that I don't intend to preside over a Court which sanctions the execution of the innocent."

Montgomery laughed softly. "You already do," he answered. "The only question is how many, and who they'll turn out to be."

TWO

Two DAYS AFTER PAYTON'S DEATH, TERRI AND CARLO prepared a habeas corpus petition for the California Supreme Court, asking the Court to set aside Rennell's death sentence because he was retarded, and to order a new trial on the question of guilt.

Sitting at the conference table, Terri reviewed their final draft. "They'll turn us down, of course. But we're required by AEDPA to 'exhaust' Rennell's state court remedies before we can go to federal court."

"What's the point?" Carlo asked.

"In Rennell's case? None. But Pell won't agree to let us skip that step, and the federal courts won't consider our petition until the California Supreme Court denies it."

"Even this close to his date of execution?"

Terri shrugged. "Maybe **that's** the point," she answered and resumed her review of Rennell's petition.

To Carlo, her new flatness of affect and laconic manner had begun with her return from Payton's execution. Terri spoke little about that night, deflecting questions about what she had seen or felt. She seemed to prefer—or, perhaps, need—to lose herself in their mission of saving Rennell Price.

The thought spurred her stepson to ask a related but, he hoped, safer question. "Was Rennell any better this morning?"

Terri remained silent, seeming to scrutinize the page before her, and Carlo was uncertain that she had heard him. At last she looked up from the petition. "He barely speaks. It's like his soul has left his body.

"After they killed Payton, Rennell tore up his cell—his first violent behavior in fifteen years. Once they'd subdued him, it was as though he went into a coma—he won't shower, or eat. Just lies in his bed." She paused, adding softly, "For all his life, Payton was all he had, in the Bayview or prison. I think Rennell can't comprehend a life without his brother. He's in a depression too deep for me to imagine."

"Doesn't the prison provide mental health care?"

"Sometimes. But even that's a mess. As his lawyer, I have to worry about the State using a psychiatrist to undermine Rennell's claim of retardation. As far as Pell is concerned, treatment might raise whether Rennell's mentally competent to be executed. Although they can—and sometimes do—give an inmate psychotropic drugs to make him fully aware that he's being killed."

The last comment, delivered factually and without the outrage Carlo would have expected, made him wonder if she, too, was depressed—both from what she had seen and from sheer exhaustion. After a moment, he asked bluntly, "Are **you** okay, Terri?"

She mustered a faint smile. "I'm just not feeling very festive. But nothing like Rennell." Her smile vanished. "Even if Pell and I could work it out, Rennell refuses to talk with a prison psychologist. I think Payton's death feels too enormous to get over, or even put into words.

"From his perspective, I understand. But it scares me. The next worst thing to being executed is being dead inside."

With that, she returned to her work.

Carlo went out for sandwiches. When he returned, Terri was standing in a corner with the telephone pressed to her ear, a stricken expression frozen on a face far paler than Carlo had ever seen it.

"I'll be right out," Terri said swiftly and hung up.

She folded her arms, hugging herself as though to ward off cold. "Rennell tried to hang himself."

"How?" Carlo asked and then realized how stupid the question must sound to her.

But Terri did not seem to notice. "A bedsheet," she answered. "It's all he's got left."

After they brought him to her, Rennell slumped, staring at the table—though whether from shame or indifference or complete dissociation Terri could not tell. A purple bruise smudged his throat.

"What were you trying to do, Rennell?"

He did not answer, or even look up. In her own sadness, Terri heard her question as a futile inquiry into what was, at bottom, a rational response to a fathomless loss, which would be followed—unless she could succeed—by fourteen more days of misery before Rennell met Payton's fate.

She took his hand, holding it in silent commiseration.

Still he did not look at her. But she felt his hand begin to grasp hers, the slightest increase of pressure. In a husky near-whisper, he said, "Payton's gone. Never gonna be with me no more."

"He's in heaven, Rennell. He still loves you, and cares about you. Just like I do."

His eyes tightened to fight back tears. "That's why he's dead."

At once, Terri understood what she had not fully grasped before: that what made the devastation of Payton's death unbearable was not only loss but guilt. Rennell would never comprehend the depth of Payton's betrayal.

"Payton wants you to live," she told him. "He asked me to help you, and help take care of you."

For the first time Rennell looked up at her, as though struggling to believe this. With painful vividness, Terri imagined the retarded boy standing by the desk of his third-grade teacher, then his only solace besides Payton.

"Please don't hurt yourself, Rennell. For my sake."

Hearing her own words, Terri felt the full weight of her responsibility, far greater now than just a lawyer's. "I'll come see you every day," she promised, "no matter what. Until you don't have to live here anymore."

Rennell began to sob, clasping the hand of his lawyer, his last protector.

THREE

READING THE OPINION OF THE CALIFORNIA SUPREME Court in response to Rennell's petition, Terri experienced the jolt familiar to death penalty lawyers. Even though she had tried to steel herself against disappointment, the cold reality of the judicial approval of a death warrant, set forth in typed print on a single page, made her feel queasy.

"One sentence," Carlo said from over her shoulder. "A man's life, and all these issues, and they blow it off with 'each claim is denied on the merits.'"

A few words of legal shorthand, Terri thought, a concise staccato that did not reveal the Court's reasoning or suggest the seriousness of its decision. Only the swiftness of its issuance bespoke the fact that Rennell's execution was days away.

Contemptuously, Chris tossed the page toward a corner of the room. "At least our clemency petition is in."

Terri gazed out the window of the conference room. Through a dense fog, rain spattered on the glass, droplets zigzagging down the ten-foot panes. "Okay," she said emphatically. "They've given us what we needed to file in federal court—today. All we have to do is fill in the part of our brief reserved for their considered wisdom."

"**That** shouldn't take long," Carlo said.

Within two hours all that remained was to photocopy their revised **habeas corpus** petition and their application to the Ninth Circuit Court of Appeals for permission to file the petition before Judge Gardner Bond of the United States District Court. The most important part of which—and all that stood between Rennell Price and lethal injection—was his plea for a stay of execution.

This knowledge, Terri supposed, accounted for Carlo's unwonted silence. "I can't believe it's down to this," he finally said. "That if the same Ninth Circuit panel which turned down Rennell's first petition refuses to let us file this one, it's over. No recourse—no petition for rehearing **or** to the U.S. Supreme Court."

"That's because AEDPA bars them," Terri answered. "Another of its unique efficiencies, intended solely to end matters: if the same three judges turn Rennell down again, they can't be reviewed by anyone. Their word is literally final."

"Do we have a chance with them?"

"One judge is hopeless, I think—Viet Nhu. He's young, brilliant, a hard-line conservative, and a potential Republican appointment to the Supreme Court.

He's also a former clerk for Justice Fini." Terri sipped her coffee. "Fini got him a key job in the Criminal Division of the Justice Department when he was barely thirty. That pretty much tells you where he stands on the death penalty."

"What about the other two?"

"Iffy. Judge Sanders is a moderate. If he thinks we've made a reasonable showing that we might succeed on the merits, he may not be comfortable consigning Rennell to death without **some** type of proceeding before Judge Bond. Especially on retardation, which wasn't before them last time around." Terri paused, rubbing her temples. "A lot may depend on the third member of the panel."

"Who is?"

"Dead." As her legal assistant rushed into the room with a stack of pleadings, Terri picked up her pen. "Judge Olinger died of a heart attack three days after ruling on Rennell's last **habeas** petition. Too bad— both in itself and because he was another middle-of-the-roader who might have been persuadable this time."

"So we don't know who the third judge will be."

"No. And won't until the day they rule." Swiftly, Terri signed her name to the original pleading to be filed with the Court, feeling, as she did, the weight these papers carried, Rennell's last chance at life. "Believe it or not, whether Rennell lives or dies this Friday will be settled by computer. That's how they pick the final judge."

Carlo shook his head, silent again.

FOUR

ON THE MORNING OF THE HEARING WHICH WOULD determine whether Rennell Price died in three days' time, Terri, Carlo, and Chris gathered around a speakerphone in the Pagets' conference room. Across the table were Laurence Pell and his cocounsel, Janice Terrell, a cool, angular blonde in her early thirties whom Terri had come to think of as death's understudy.

All five lawyers gazed at the speakerphone, waiting for the three-judge panel of the Ninth Circuit Court of Appeals—hastily assembled in their own conference room in Pasadena—to announce themselves. There was no time for a formal hearing. But the prospect of pleading with disembodied voices struck Terri as the judicial equivalent of imploring three Wizards of Oz, hidden behind the screen of the squawk box. Perhaps they found the distance prophylactic, she thought sardonically—a safe execution, where no one saw Rennell, or even the faces of his lawyers. She still did not know who would replace Judge Olinger.

"Good morning." The voice abruptly issuing from

the box was rough with age. "Are the lawyers for the parties there?"

Swiftly, Terri glanced at Chris and Carlo. The man speaking was clearly older than either Judge Nhu or Judge Sanders. Eyes narrowing, Larry Pell stared at the box.

"We are," he answered.

"This is Judge Blair Montgomery," the aged voice responded. "With me are Judges Harry Sanders and Viet Nhu. As fate and random selection would have it, I've replaced Judge Olinger as the presiding member of the panel."

Pell shot Janice Terrell a look of concern. "We've read your papers," Montgomery continued, "as well as the ruling of the California Supreme Court. The first issue we'd like to hear about is mental retardation. In light of the United States Supreme Court's recent decision in **Atkins,** barring execution of the retarded, why should this man die on Friday?"

"The answer is that he shouldn't," Terri said swiftly. "If shown, mental retardation now bars his execution. The California legislature has adopted no definition for retardation. The California Supreme Court offers none."

Pell began furiously scribbling notes. "At most," Terri continued, "the Court seems to accept that an IQ of seventy-two—despite a standard deviation of plus or minus five—means that Rennell Price is fit to execute. If so, the Court is measuring retardation as though Rennell were taking the college boards—by applying an arbitrary numerical standard of seventy

IQ points, which ignores all the evidence of his life-long inability to learn or cope on his own.'"

Pell shook his head. "Mr. Price's IQ is above seventy. Under AEDPA, state court rulings are presumptively correct, and the petitioner must rebut this presumption by clear and convincing evidence." Pell leaned toward the box, as if to speak past Montgomery to Judges Nhu and Sanders. "Plainly, the Court did not find the evidence convincing. AEDPA does not allow **this** Court to second-guess them."

"Indeed." The Asian-accented voice, sibilant and precise, was Judge Nhu's. "But does **Atkins** even apply to Mr. Price? For a **new** ruling such as **Atkins** to be retroactive—that is, applicable to defendants on **habeas corpus,** like Mr. Price—the Supreme Court must expressly say so in the ruling itself. **Atkins** contains no such statement. Why then, Mr. Pell, should this Court even allow Mr. Price to raise it?"

Though pleased, Pell seemed as startled as Terri. "Because in the **Penry** case," she interjected, "the Supreme Court said that **if** the Court later barred executing the retarded—as they did subsequently in **Atkins**—that ruling **would** be retroactive..."

"True enough." Montgomery's tone was deceptively benign. "Perhaps, Mr. Pell, you can explain to Judge Nhu—and certainly to me—why the Supreme Court didn't mean what it said in **Penry,** and therefore why this Court should allow the State to execute Mr. Price without a more thorough review of his intellectual capacities."

Pell hesitated, caught between the chance of victory offered him by Judge Nhu and the risk of antagonizing Montgomery with an argument that, but for Nhu's encouragement, he would never have dared to make. On either side of her, Terri saw Chris and Carlo looking anxiously toward Pell.

"The Supreme Court," Pell ventured at last, "cannot be deemed guilty of an oversight. Judge Nhu is correct—their silence in **Atkins** speaks for itself."

"I might sleep a little better," Montgomery observed dryly, "if they'd spoken about **Penry.** Or if the California Supreme Court had so much as mentioned it in the single sentence they devoted to condemning Rennell Price. But let's move to another matter— whether Mr. Price's new evidence creates a serious doubt that he's guilty of anything but being slow."

"Let's do that," Nhu amended sharply, "with respect to what AEDPA demands of **you,** Ms. Paget. First, whether your claim of innocence is based on facts which **none** of Mr. Price's prior counsel—in the exercise of due diligence—could have discovered before."

"That's simple," Terri answered. "That Payton Price remained silent for fifteen years is not the fault of Mr. James, or of Kenyon and Walker—"

"Precisely." Nhu's tone bespoke the triumph of a didactic law professor curbing a bumptious student. "When you concede that Yancey James did not have the benefit of Payton's death row confession, how can you claim that your client was convicted because Mr. James, to use the vernacular, 'blew it'?"

"We're getting dangerously close," Montgomery interjected with veiled sarcasm, "to actually considering the facts—including whether the State is about to execute an innocent dupe. But perhaps the People can protect us from such a painful exercise. For example, Mr. Pell, might Mr. James—short of extracting a confession from Payton—have honored Rennell Price's claim of innocence by investigating Mr. Fleet, whose implication of both brothers may have spared him from taking Rennell's place in this somewhat baleful proceeding?"

Carlo, Terri saw, was smiling grimly at the table. But though Blair Montgomery's participation had to be viewed as a stroke of luck, the dynamic of this hearing—a battle between Montgomery and Nhu, with the opposing lawyers as their surrogates—was made even more unpredictable by the silence of Judge Sanders.

"The requirements of AEDPA," Pell responded, "are not a technicality but the will of Congress. If Yancey James could not have discovered Payton Price's confession, Rennell Price cannot show that James was inadequate, and therefore fails **that** requirement of AEDPA. Conversely, if Rennell now complains that James should have questioned Fleet's credibility, that is not 'new evidence' at all, and therefore should have been presented earlier. Because Rennell Price fails both tests under AEDPA, this Court cannot consider his claim of innocence."

"Let's get to that," Montgomery said crisply. "Assuming, Ms. Paget, that you **do** satisfy the prerequisites outlined by Mr. Pell, why does Payton's confession entitle your client to go free? Or, at least, to receive a new trial?"

"And while you answer **that,**" Judge Nhu cut in, "perhaps you can explain why that confession is 'clear and convincing' evidence of his brother's innocence."

Terri knew that her next few words might mean Rennell's life or death. "Your Honors," she began, "there is no direct evidence of Rennell Price's guilt. In fact, the only admitted witness to Thuy Sen's death, Payton Price, claims that Rennell was sleeping." She paused, slowing her speech for emphasis. "The key witness against Rennell was Eddie Fleet, who admitted disposing of the body. We know that he escaped prosecution by fingering Rennell Price. We **believe**—and there is nothing to refute us—that Fleet could testify in such persuasive detail because **he** was the actual murderer.

"Under this circuit's holding in **Carriger v. Stewart,** Rennell Price is **not** required to affirmatively prove his innocence but simply to present sufficient evidence of innocence to 'undermine confidence in the outcome of the trial'—"

"**Or,**" Nhu interrupted, "put another way, that Mr. James's supposed failures 'probably resulted in the conviction of one who is actually innocent.' Does Ms.

Paget's new evidence suggest that probability, Mr. Pell?"

"The eleventh-hour accusation," Pell asked rhetorically, "of an admitted murderer of a child, made against a witness he **also** tried to have murdered? Of course not. This is a last-ditch effort to have the State of California do to Eddie Fleet what Payton Price couldn't do himself—exact jailhouse revenge. The very kind of abuse AEDPA is meant to stop." Pell sat back, palms on the table, speaking with renewed confidence. "Fifteen years ago, the Superior Court of California held an utterly fair trial, after which twelve jurors condemned Rennell Price to death. Three times since—on direct appeal, on a prior petition, and now on **this** petition—the California Supreme Court has upheld that judgment. It is time to end this matter, today."

"So soon?" Blair Montgomery asked. "**Carriger** rested on a standard enunciated by the U.S. Supreme Court: whether, given the new evidence, 'it is more likely than not that no reasonable juror would have found the defendant guilty beyond a reasonable doubt.' On the evidence before us today—which Ms. Paget fairly described—could you, as a juror, convict Mr. Price in good conscience?"

The question, stunning in its directness, caught Pell short. He glanced at Janice Terrell, who bit her lip. "The California Supreme Court," Pell ventured, "decided as a question of fact that the 'new' evidence of innocence was insufficient."

"I know all about AEDPA," Montgomery snapped.

"I know all about the California Supreme Court. I even took the ten seconds or so required to read its opinion—in its entirety. So please answer my question."

Pell shrugged, a silent gesture of helplessness. "I can't put myself in the place of a juror," he answered. "My answer is appropriate under AEDPA—this Court cannot say that the California Supreme Court's refusal to believe Payton Price's confession is in error, and therefore **should not** overrule it—"

"If it doesn't," Terri cut in, "then even this cursory opinion is beyond review. So it is well to ask on what basis this Court should 'defer' to the California Supreme Court.

"Its hearing on the facts? There was none.

"The reasoning of its opinion? There is none.

"Its record in death penalty cases?" Terri's voice became quietly scathing. "There, at last, we have something to go on.

"The State Supreme Court reverses less than ten percent of all death penalty convictions. Of the other ninety percent, the federal courts—including this Court—have reversed almost two-thirds, the highest reversal rate for any state supreme court in the country."

Terri looked at Pell directly. "The State of California has, again and again, hidden behind the shield of AEDPA. 'We're entitled to a presumption of correctness,' the State tells us. 'So please don't look too hard at the facts. After all, **we** don't.' "

Though Pell's calm demeanor was unchanged, he seemed to grip his pen more tightly. Terri turned to address the plastic box. "Fifteen years ago, an old woman—now deceased—saw two black men across the street, and thought one of them was Rennell Price. Without explanation or the inconvenience of a hearing, the California Supreme Court dismissed—in a single sentence—compelling evidence that she was wrong. That single sentence is entitled to the precise amount of 'deference' it deserves, and nothing more."

For the first time, no immediate questions issued from the squawk box. "Mr. Pell," Judge Montgomery said at last, "if this Court concludes that Mr. James's defects did not affect the outcome of the trial, are you saying that—under AEDPA—we are barred from considering whether Rennell Price is innocent?"

Briefly, Pell hesitated. "Yes," he answered without apology. "Under AEDPA, there is no right to a new determination of guilt or innocence as long as the original trial was fair. This one was."

"No exceptions?"

"If there **is** one," Pell said dubiously, "it would require evidence so compelling as to make clear beyond all doubt that the petitioner is innocent. That's not this case."

"Thank you," Montgomery said dryly. "That's admirably straightforward."

"So it is," Judge Nhu said in a more approving tone. "Let me ask the Attorney General to respond briefly to Rennell Price's somewhat contradictory assertion that—if he **did** help cause Thuy Sen's death—an abusive childhood made him so dependent on Payton that it cuts against imposing the death penalty."

"This is nothing new," Pell answered. "All the evidence cited by Ms. Paget was available in 1987. Even if Mr. James failed to present it, Kenyon and Walker presented some of it and could have presented more. AEDPA says enough is enough."

"And so it is," Montgomery said brusquely. "We can rely on the papers before us on that issue, and on the other claims raised by Mr. Price. Before we conclude, is there anything else anyone cares to say?"

For all Terri could tell, Judge Sanders had slept through the entire hearing. Nonetheless, she framed her final words for him. "Simply this. If this panel denies permission to file, Rennell Price will die on Friday.

"He'll die even though we've made a substantial showing that he's retarded.

"He'll die even though there's substantial new evidence that he's innocent.

"He'll die without any court ever giving him a hearing on those claims." Terri drew herself up. "That, Your Honors, is the nearest thing to a summary execution I can imagine. It substitutes finality for justice. Its only 'virtue' is to remove one more human being from the system which, at bottom, exists to **protect** him, not to erase him."

"Mr. Pell?" Montgomery asked.

Pell glanced at his notes. "According to the United

States Supreme Court, in the words of Justice Fini, granting a stay of execution on a second **habeas corpus** petition is 'particularly egregious' unless there are 'substantial grounds' on which such relief should be granted. The California Supreme Court has already found that this petition fails.

"AEDPA exists to keep federal courts from being bogged down in endless death penalty litigation—however heartfelt." He leaned forward. "This case is no different. Fifteen years ago, a nine-year-old girl was murdered. Fifteen years is time enough for justice. For her, and for her family."

"The application is submitted," Judge Montgomery pronounced. "We expect to rule within the hour, by telephone."

The squawk box went dead.

An awkward silence descended on the room. "Well," Terri said at length, "we've got an hour to kill."

The others shifted, discomfited. "How're your kids?" Pell asked of Terri and Chris, flashing a brief smile at Carlo. "I mean the ones who haven't gone bad yet."

Let's start with Elena, Terri thought to herself, who hates me for what I've been doing here. "Oh, they're fine," she said. "And yours?"

"Good. Julie's seven and in ballet school, and so serious I can't smile at her recitals, even when the kids make me want to laugh out loud." Amiably, he turned to Carlo. "How do you like the practice of law?"

"Depends on the day." Carlo glanced at his watch, then at the squawk box. "Can't say I've laughed in a while."

Janice Terrell raised her eyebrows, as though noting a display of bad manners. Silently, Terri blessed her stepson for casting a pall on the chitchat through which lawyers pretended to rise above their differences.

The telephone rang.

Terri hit the button on the speakerphone. "Teresa Paget."

"This is Judge Montgomery. Are both sides there?"

"Yes," Terri answered in a tight voice. "We are."

"Very well." Montgomery paused, his tone soft and grave. "We've reached our decision."

Briefly, Terri closed her eyes. "By a vote of two to one," Montgomery continued, "Judge Viet Nhu dissenting, this Court stays the execution of Rennell Price and grants his counsel permission to file a petition for **habeas corpus**—on **all** issues—before United States District Judge Gardner Bond."

Carlo bent forward, hands covering his face. But Terri kept herself from showing any emotion. Pell, too, remained impassive, making notations on his legal pad.

"A written order will follow," Montgomery finished. "Thank you, all."

The phone clicked off.

"The Ninth Circuit's done it again," Terri heard Janice Terrell murmur in disgust.

Scraping up his papers, Pell mustered a fatalistic smile. "Congratulations, 'all,' " he said across the table. "See you in court, as they say."

It was not until the next morning—two days before what would have been his date of execution—that Terri was able to see Rennell.

She gazed into his eyes, encouraging him to take heart. "Your execution's been put off," she told him. "At least for now. The judges heard what Payton said. Payton saved you, Rennell, just like he wanted to."

Rennell's eyes widened. With painful slowness, he struggled to comprehend. In a tentative voice, he asked, "You mean I can leave here?"

Heartsick, Terri shook her head. "Not yet. What it means is that you should take care of yourself, do what Payton asked." She took his hand, speaking softly. "The important thing is that no one's going to take you from here on Friday. You're safe from that, okay?"

The first light seemed to seep through his depression and with it, Terri hoped, renewed appreciation of the chance to live. "What they gonna do to me?"

"Keep you here, for now." Terri forced herself to sound confident. "I'm going to see another judge, tomorrow morning. I'll do my best to make him understand who you really are."

FIVE

GARDNER BOND SAT AT THE HEAD OF HIS CONFER-
ence table, for once in shirtsleeves, as though prepared
to grapple with a distasteful task. On one side of him,
Terri and Carlo sat, facing Larry Pell and Janice Terrell
on the other. "The Ninth Circuit has permitted you to
file," he told Terri. "But how we resolve your petition
remains a matter for this Court.

"You've moved for discovery, and to be allowed to
present evidence at a hearing with live witnesses. Let's
talk about discovery first. Tell me what you want."

"To be able to put the circumstances of Rennell
Price's life, and of his conviction, before this Court."
Terri nodded toward Pell. "In terms of documents, we
request the D.A.'s files regarding Eddie Fleet—"

"That's fine," Bond said in a clipped manner. "Who
do you wish to depose?"

"The players in Rennell's conviction." Terri ticked
them off on her fingers. "Charles Monk, Lou Mauriani, Dr. Elizabeth Shelton, and—critically—Eddie
Fleet."

Bond turned to Pell. "Mr. Pell?"

"We'll scrape up whatever we have on Eddie Fleet. But there's no automatic right to **any** depositions, and no need to depose Monk, Mauriani, or Shelton. As for Fleet, he's beyond our control . . ."

"Not quite," Terri snapped. "You told him about Payton's accusation, which prevented me from talking to him any further. That's a **de facto** cover-up, with you protecting Fleet at Rennell's expense."

"That's nonsense," Pell told Bond briskly. "Payton Price made certain accusations. On behalf of the State, I was required to ask Fleet if they were true. He denied them. Whether he kept talking to Ms. Paget was wholly up to him." Turning to Terri, he added, "You have the transcript of Fleet's original testimony. That should be enough."

"For what?" Terri said to Bond. "Fleet's the only key witness against Rennell who's still alive. We're convinced that he's the murderer, which also makes him a flight risk. There's no way to resolve this petition fairly without his testimony."

Bond considered her and also, Terri guessed, the publicity which would ensue if he were perceived to shelter a man guilty of Thuy Sen's murder. "I'll give you Fleet," he said curtly. "As to the others, your motion for discovery is denied—this proceeding is supposed to be fair, not endless.

"This is beginning to sound like a second trial. Instead of a proceeding to determine whether Mr. Price **deserves** a second trial."

"We agree," Pell put in hastily. "The original prosecution team knows nothing about guilt or innocence beyond what Inspector Monk and Dr. Shelton testified to at trial. Nor does Mr. James, who can testify by affidavit." Briefly, Pell glanced at a note passed to him by Janice Terrell. "That leaves Mr. Fleet. Where the Court has already ordered his deposition, there's no need to call him live..."

"**No** live witnesses?" Carlo whispered in Terri's ear. "What kind of kangaroo court would **that** be?"

"Your Honor," she protested, "the Attorney General is trying to reduce any hearing to an argument between lawyers over fifteen-year-old evidence, rather than the live testimony of witnesses regarding **new** evidence—"

"Which comes down," Bond admonished, "to the deposition of Payton Price, already granted you by order of this Court. With respect to the man he accuses, Eddie Fleet, I'll reserve my ruling until after you depose him."

Terri felt a rising desperation. "As to **that,** Your Honor, we continue to search for evidence that Mr. Fleet—in addition to being physically abusive—has a sexual interest in children. Which would suggest that he, not Rennell, was involved in the murder of Thuy Sen—"

"Do you have any such witness?"

"Not at this time—"

"Then that's all speculation, isn't it?" Examining his cuff links, Bond asked, "Do you have anything to offer which is real?"

"Yes, Your Honor. The testimony of three of the jurors who sentenced Rennell Price to death. They would not have voted for the death sentence if Payton had testified against Eddie Fleet—"

"Based on what?" Pell interjected with what seemed to be genuine scorn. "We can't replicate the trial, or assess the state of mind of jurors who—fifteen years later—may be moved by a murderer's imminent death to forget why he deserves it."

"Go no further," Bond cut in. "Their testimony is inadmissible, and Ms. Paget knows it. Or should."

With great effort, Terri maintained her surface equanimity. "Your Honor," she said in a respectful tone, "the question is whether, on the evidence we now have, a reasonable juror would have voted to convict—"

"Which determination," Bond interrupted, "will be made by this Court. We've told you what evidence we'll hear on the matter of guilt or innocence. Give us your wish list with respect to presenting the state of Mr. Price's mental functioning."

To her side, Terri saw Carlo staring at the table in an effort to conceal his frustration. Across the table, Janice Terrell watched him, the first hint of a smile surfacing in her cornflower blue eyes. But Terri spoke as though Bond's adverse ruling had never occurred. "We have at least two key witnesses, Your Honor. The first is a social historian, Dr. Tammy Mattox, who will reconstruct Rennell's life history."

"Is that necessary, counselor? You have the records."

"We agree," Pell said promptly. "We'll stipulate to

the admission of all records concerning Mr. Price, whether from school, doctors, or his incarceration in juvenile hall. We're also amenable to affidavits from Rennell's third-grade teacher, and even from Dr. Mattox herself." His tone became dismissive, that of someone granting a favor. "Even though what she has to say is hearsay, entirely derived from other people and sources."

Bond nodded. "That seems fair enough."

"It's wholly insufficient," Terri countered. "Dr. Mattox interviewed Rennell Price's mother, who is paranoid schizophrenic, and his grandmother, who's bedridden—"

"Concerning what?" Bond asked with muted incredulity. "What exactly does the resident of a mental institution—or, for that matter, a sick and elderly woman who never testified at trial—have to offer us?"

"Evidence regarding Rennell Price's childhood and adolescence," Terri answered. "Including his mental capacity—"

"According to a lunatic?" Bond shot back. "Let's hope you have someone more edifying than **that.**"

"To see Rennell's mother," Terri said firmly, "is to be edified. Including, if she's willing to share it, the true identity of Rennell's father."

Bond raised his eyebrows. "Who might **he** be?"

"A boy from the neighborhood who she describes as 'slow.' But she won't give his name, and we haven't been able to track him down."

"Ms. Paget," Bond remonstrated, "I cannot imagine listening to an insane woman testify regarding her liaison with a nameless, and perhaps apocryphal, boyfriend. Spare me, please—except by affidavit."

Leaning forward, Terri tried to keep the anger she felt from showing in her eyes. "Rennell Price," she said, "grew up in the Bayview, the presumed son of a psychotic and abusive father and a deeply troubled mother. His environment was brutal and chaotic. The witnesses to his life will be found not among the friends and acquaintances of those sitting at this table but among people who are—and whom we like to keep—invisible to us. Either we can bring them here or we can have an expert like Dr. Mattox integrate what they told her.

"What Mr. Pell wants is to reduce this case to a jumble of paper, a dry record to which he can apply the 'presumptions' of AEDPA and the presumptive wisdom of the California Supreme Court. It's a way of sanitizing Rennell's death without ever looking at his life. We believe that the most critical evidence of Rennell Price's retardation can be found not in tests but in his life. Which can be knit together only through the narrative of an expert . . ."

"Is your Dr. Mattox a psychiatrist or psychologist?"

"No. She's a Ph.D. in anthropology, which enables her to interpret the impact of Rennell's family and environment—"

"But not his mental condition, I would think."

"What she has to say," Terri parried, "bears on his mental condition. We also have Dr. Anthony Lane, both a psychiatrist and a neuropsychologist, who examined Rennell extensively and whom we wish to call as an expert witness."

"Then isn't he enough?" Turning to Pell, Bond inquired wryly, "What say **you,** Mr. Pell?"

"That the Court's reservations about Dr. Mattox are well taken, and that it can hear Dr. Lane by means of affidavit. And that the Court is correct in observing that this hearing is not a second trial." Briefly, Pell paused, listening as Janice Terrell murmured a few brief words. "We do, however, request leave to conduct our own mental examination of Rennell Price, so that Dr. Lane's affidavit is not the only evidence before the Court. In particular, we'd like to administer a second IQ test."

"Which won't be accurate," Terri protested. "It's called the 'practice effect.' Even the retarded do better with repeated testing."

Pell leaned forward, offering her a sardonic smile before he turned to Bond. "Which is no doubt why Ms. Paget seems to have given her client every test of mental functioning known to man. So that when our tests prove him not to be retarded, she can claim it's the result of her personal Head Start program."

Though Terri could not acknowledge it, the accusation was true. "Since when is thoroughness merely a ploy?" she objected. "The State's prison clinicians are hardly objective—they're notorious for cookie-cutter findings."

This, as Pell well knew, was also true. " 'Sauce for the goose,' " he quoted easily to Bond.

"Agreed. You may have your examination of Mr. Price."

"May we be present?" Terri asked quickly.

"Why?" Pell shot back. "**We** weren't." Facing Bond, he said, "To make Ms. Paget more comfortable, we'll record our examination on videotape, and make it available to her and to the Court."

Larry Pell, Terri conceded, was even more clever than she had thought: in a videotape, Rennell Price would appear to be a dull but normal man, unremarkable in appearance, plodding through his tests— sullen, perhaps, but not retarded. "So ordered," Bond said quickly. "Anything else, Ms. Paget?"

"Yes. The Court should permit us to call Dr. Lane as a witness, and to cross-examine whomever Mr. Pell selects to administer the tests."

"Very well." The judge's tone became faintly arid. "Judge Montgomery has expressed his preference for a hearing, and we must take cognizance of that."

This gratuitous remark, with its intimation of distaste for Blair Montgomery, unsettled Terri further. "In that case," Pell interposed, "we'd like the chance to cross-examine Rennell Price himself. Nothing can be more pertinent to retardation than for this Court to see him."

Startled, Terri shot back, "He's **retarded,** Larry. That's the whole point."

With veiled amusement, Bond remonstrated. "There are also Fifth Amendment considerations, Mr. Pell. Retarded or not, the Court cannot force Mr. Price to incriminate himself." Once more he turned to Terri. "I'll leave it to your discretion, Ms. Paget, as to whether Mr. Price will testify. Either to confirm his innocence or to exemplify his mental retardation."

Bond's tone, insinuating and faintly accusatory, drove home to Terri that Pell had trapped her in a painful choice: to call Rennell Price, or to leave the implication in this judge's mind that her petition was a sham. "Thank you, Your Honor. We'll advise the Court of our decision."

"All right then." Folding his hands, Bond surveyed each lawyer. "Rennell Price was sentenced fifteen years ago, and this Court has no desire to attenuate that sorry record. Therefore, the parties will complete their discovery within five days, and the hearing will commence in seven. Anything else?"

Startled, Terri considered whether to protest, then decided that, in light of her next request, further straining Bond's patience was ill-advised. "Yes, Your Honor. It concerns the standard of proof under which this Court will determine whether Rennell Price is retarded and, therefore, quite possibly, whether he lives or dies.

"The Supreme Court did not bar executing the retarded until **after** the federal courts denied Mr. Price's first **habeas corpus** petition. The fact that we must raise it on a second petition, for the first time, should not facilitate his execution—"

"I don't understand your point."

Terri stared directly at Larry Pell. "At the Ninth Circuit hearing, Judge Nhu suggested that **Atkins** was **not** retroactive, and therefore that Rennell Price could not avoid execution by demonstrating mental retardation. Mr. Pell agreed, albeit tentatively." She softened her voice. "Executing Rennell Price because **Atkins** came down three days after the Supreme Court denied his first petition is something out of Kafka. **Atkins** is a new case. On the issue of retardation, Rennell Price deserves a fresh start, as he would have at a new trial."

"Mr. Pell?" the Court inquired.

Pell glanced at Janice Terrell. "We'll have to take it under advisement," Pell temporized.

"In that case," Terri said promptly, "we ask the Court to rule that **Atkins** applies, and that we are required only to prove retardation by the preponderance of the evidence." Facing Bond, she spoke firmly and emphatically. "Denying Rennell Price the benefit of **Atkins** cannot be called justice. This Court has choices."

"Then we'll make them," Bond answered crisply. "But not until after the hearing. We'll rule on **Atkins** when we rule on Mr. Price's petition."

Once again, Terri felt herself caught between Pell and Bond, under pressure—as Pell surely intended—to demonstrate retardation by calling Rennell as a witness. But there was no more Terri could do. With a feeling of foreboding, she uttered the formulaic "Thank you, Your Honor," and the first hearing before Gardner Bond was at an end.

SIX

BRIGHT-EYED, EDDIE FLEET STARED AT TERRI, HIS smile slowly widening to expose the gold in his teeth.

Meeting Fleet's eyes, Terri tried to calm her nerves. It was nine-thirty, and the sunlight through her law firm's conference room window cast a sheen across the cherry table. Beside Fleet sat Brian Hall, a gray-haired public defender with a curt manner and a cynical air. To Terri's right, at the end of the conference table, an elderly court reporter with his sleeves rolled up waited to transcribe the questions and answers. Carlo sat at Terri's left, between her and the representatives of the State, Laurence Pell and Janice Terrell.

Turning to the reporter, Terri nodded.

The man raised his right hand, inviting Fleet to emulate him. The breadth of Fleet's smile diminished to a play of lips.

"Do you solemnly swear," the reporter intoned, "to tell the truth, the whole truth, and nothing but the truth?"

"Yeah, sure."

"Please state your name for the record," Terri said.

"Eddie Fleet."

"What is your occupation?"

The twitch of a smile reappeared. "Handyman."

At once, Terri decided to bypass further background questions. In the same businesslike tone, she inquired, "Do you know a woman named Betty Sims?"

The smile vanished abruptly. Though Fleet did not move, a tensile alertness seemed to seize his body. "**Knew** her," he corrected.

"In what way did you know Betty Sims?"

Fleet glanced toward his lawyer. "She was my girl-friend."

"When was the last time you saw her?"

"Long time ago," Fleet answered with a shrug. "Don't remember exactly."

"Maybe I can jog your memory," Terri said. "Did Betty Sims have a daughter?"

Fleet's eyes narrowed. "Yeah."

"What was the daughter's name?"

"Can't remember."

"Was it Lacy?"

As Fleet hesitated, Terri watched him try to calculate how she knew this. "Yeah," he allowed. "Guess that's right. Been a long time since I seen her, too."

"How long?"

Hall placed a cautionary hand on Fleet's wrist. "What's the relevance of this?" he interjected.

Terri kept staring at Fleet. "Bear with me for an-other couple of questions. Unless you think Mr. Fleet's knowledge of Lacy Sims is somehow incriminating."

"No," Hall snapped. "Just irrelevant."

"Not your call. When you last saw Lacy Sims, Mr. Fleet, how old was she?"

Down the table, two heads—Pell's and Terrell's—leaned forward for a better view. Slowly, Hall pulled back his hand. With a shrug of calculated boredom, Fleet answered, "Maybe twelve."

"Thank you," Terri said amiably. "Ever put your penis in Lacy's mouth?"

Almost imperceptibly, Fleet's shoulders twitched. His eyes on Terri's were like burn holes. "What the hell is **this**?" Hall demanded.

"A question." Barely pausing, Terri asked of Fleet, "Do you need it read back to you, or do you still have it in mind?"

Fleet glared at her. Once again, Terri imagined him wondering if she had found Betty or her daughter—or both. Without looking at the reporter, Terri requested, "Please read back the pending question."

At the corner of her vision, the reporter held up his steno tape to read it, repeating in a monotone, " 'Ever put your penis in Lacy's mouth?' "

Larry Pell put down his pen. Briefly, Fleet looked in Pell's direction, a decision forming in his eyes. "Why'd I do that?" he demanded.

"So if Betty and Lacy say you forced Lacy to give you oral sex, they'd be lying?"

It was a bluff. But—instead of answering—Fleet began turning toward Hall, then stopped himself. Beneath his hesitance, Terri was suddenly sure, lay a poisonous fear. "That would be two witnesses against one," she prodded. "Care to ask your lawyer about perjury?"

"You can skip the commentary," Hall instructed Terri, and he took Fleet by the arm, turning him away from the conference table and Terri. In profile, Hall's lips moved, and then Fleet murmured an answer.

"Let the record reflect," Terri directed the reporter, "that the witness is consulting with counsel."

Fleet spun on Terri. "Anything that bitch says," he hissed across the table, "is gettin' back at me."

"Which 'bitch'?" Terri inquired softly. "Lacy, or her mother?"

A look of entrapment stole into Fleet's eyes; in that moment, Terri felt a flash of guilt, the visceral sense that she had placed another woman and her daughter at risk. "Betty," Fleet answered. "Who you think I meant?"

"Because you beat her?"

Fleet paused again. "Just cuffed her now and then, for mouthin' off. Weren't nothin'..."

"Ever hit her on the face?"

Fleet leaned back in his chair. Terri watched him consider his choices and then decide, quite visibly, that domestic violence was both a distraction and a defense. "Sometimes," he allowed. "Maybe a black eye or two."

"Thank you for your candor. Did you ever force Lacy Sims to give you oral sex?"

"Asked and answered," Hall snapped.

"Actually, he **never** answered that question. You both just hoped I hadn't noticed." Terri kept her voice quiet and even. "So let me ask the question one more time: Did you force Betty Sims's daughter Lacy to put your penis in her mouth?"

Hall clasped Fleet's wrist. "This is **not** relevant," he insisted.

Terri looked at Hall directly. "Your client's a pedophile. To say that's 'relevant' is an understatement. He's got two choices, and not answering isn't one of them."

Hall seemed to bristle and then, more slowly, to gauge the dilemma of a client he barely knew. "I'm going to discuss this with Mr. Fleet," he said brusquely. "Outside."

Fleet remained frozen, staring at Terri with naked hatred. "Come on," Hall told him.

Fleet slowly rose, gazing down at Terri. **Yeah,** she thought, with a loathing all her own, **that's how you like it—standing up.** And then she realized the molten force which lay beneath her lawyer's coldness—for her, Eddie Fleet was her husband Richie, except that she would destroy him this time before he wounded another child. But all she let Fleet see was the smile on her lips.

Hall led Fleet outside. Through the glass windows of the conference room, Terri watched them: Hall's mouth, moving quickly, seemed to speak with increasing vehemence. A head taller than his lawyer, Fleet bent to hear him. Inside the conference room, no one spoke.

At last, Hall stopped speaking. Scowling, Fleet gazed down at him, then nodded. Ignoring the expectant gazes of those waiting, Fleet, then his lawyer, reclaimed their seats across from Terri.

"Mr. Fleet," Hall announced, "objects to this irrelevant harping on domestic disputes and other ancillary matters. Therefore, he's forced to invoke his Fifth Amendment right not to answer the pending question."

"The purpose of the Fifth Amendment," Terri answered calmly, "is not to avoid questions simply because a witness doesn't like them." Turning to Fleet, she said, "I asked if you ever forced Lacy Sims to take your penis in her mouth. Are you invoking the Fifth Amendment because your answer might tend to incriminate you?"

Fleet folded his arms. "I invoke the Fifth Amendment."

Terri tilted her head in a pose of curiosity. "Have you **ever** forced a minor child to take your penis in her mouth?"

At the end of the table, Larry Pell shifted in his chair, fully appreciating, Terri felt sure, the nature of her trap for Eddie Fleet, and for him. Fleet's lip, curling to expose his upper teeth, lent a feral aspect to his eyes.

"I invoke the Fifth Amendment," he repeated.

"Have you ever put your penis in the mouth of a minor Asian female?"

Fleet's voice rose. "I invoke the Fifth Amendment."

Eyes still fixed on Fleet, Terri drew a photograph from the manila folder between them. Calmly, she slid it down the table to the court reporter. "I ask that this photograph be marked as Fleet exhibit number one."

Pale, the reporter gazed down at the exhibit, then made a notation in its margin.

He slid it back to Terri. Silent, she handed the photograph to Carlo. Turning to Janice Terrell, he placed it in her hands, eyes locking hers until she looked down at what he had given her. "Thank you," Carlo said politely. "Please pass it on."

Pell took the exhibit from Terrell's hands. After a perfunctory glance, he passed it back to Carlo.

Carlo placed it in front of Fleet. "This is for you, I think."

Expression frozen, Fleet studied the autopsy photo of Thuy Sen. With clinical detachment, Terri inquired, "Did you ever force **this** minor Asian female to put your penis in her mouth?"

Holding up his hand, Hall leaned awkwardly between Terri and the witness. "For the record," he interjected, "Mr. Fleet will invoke the Fifth Amendment in response to any further questions." Gathering himself up, he mustered a show of indignation. "Your strategy's transparent—to present Mr. Fleet as the guilty party and to expose him to charges of perjury. No matter how irrelevant to the matter at hand—"

"The matter at hand," Terri interrupted, "is the murder of this child. That was the subject of Mr. Fleet's trial testimony fifteen years ago, on which basis my client stands to die.

"So let's be clear, counselor. We're going to be here for however long it takes for me to read aloud every answer he gave, to every question Lou Mauriani asked him about the murder of Thuy Sen, and then to ask him if the answer's true. By my count, that's roughly sixty-seven chances to invoke the Fifth Amendment. Is that what Mr. Fleet intends to do?"

Hall folded his arms. "On my advice, yes."

Terri turned to Pell. "Any suggestions, Mr. Pell?"

"No."

"Then I've got one: grant Mr. Fleet immunity from prosecution—for both perjury and the murder of Thuy Sen—based on any answer he gives in this proceeding." Terri allowed disdain to seep into her voice. "That would satisfy all of our needs—Mr. Fleet's continuing need to escape prosecution for the murder of Thuy Sen, Rennell Price's need not to be executed for Mr. Fleet's crime, and **your** need to learn the truth. Which is the reason, I recall, you gave me for informing Mr. Fleet of Payton Price's confession."

With apparent effort, Pell remained inscrutable, marshaling the careful phrasing which, Terri knew, he had composed to evade entrapment. "Whether to grant immunity," he said in his most professional manner, "is a question of policy, based on a number of very complicated factors, to be decided at the highest levels of the Attorney General's Office. It's not within my authority to immunize Mr. Fleet in the middle of his deposition."

"Too bad," Terri answered. "I guess we're in for a long day. But please get back to me before the next time we see Judge Bond."

Across the table, Eddie Fleet watched her, malevolence filling his eyes.

"Why don't you take a break?" she said to him. "**Your** 'oral presentation' has just begun."

"Pell's expression was a study," Carlo told his father that evening. "But Fleet's made me afraid for Terri. He hates her as much as she hates him."

With an expression of worry, Chris sat back, the State's response to Rennell's postponed clemency petition spread across his desk. "She got what she wanted," he answered at length. "Maybe the A.G. will grant immunity—"

"Don't count on it." Terri stood in the doorway, causing Carlo to wonder how much she had heard. "It's a matter of 'policy,' " she continued. "If they start immunizing snitches to help petitioners on **habeas corpus,** just think how long these cases might go on. There'd be no end to them." Turning to Chris, she asked, "So, do I put Rennell on?"

Chris rubbed the back of his head. "Depends on what Pell does about Fleet, I think. Or Bond—"

The telephone rang. Picking it up, Chris listened

for a moment, then pushed the speaker button. Tammy Mattox's smoke and whiskey drawl filled the office. "When you gonna see Rennell?" she asked without preface.

"Tomorrow," Terri answered. "Why?"

"Grandma's dead. After all this time, I think Payton dying was all she could take." Tammy's voice softened. "Rennell's got no family now but crazy Mama. Know you got a full plate, Terri, but someone needs to tell him."

SEVEN

RENNELL'S EXPRESSION BARELY CHANGED. FROM THE distance in his eyes, Terri sensed him retreating within himself, perhaps from yet more pain and loss. She tried to guess at his emotions—or even whether, after Payton, he had much emotion left.

"She always stay in her room," he mumbled. "That where she die?"

Eula Price had lost the house over fourteen years ago, to the poisonous confluence of Thuy Sen's murder and Yancey James's coke-addicted greed. And yet the external world must remain, in Rennell's limited imaginings, that which he had left. "Yes," Terri answered, "in her room."

He bowed his head. "That's where she hide. Like she be scared."

Had Eula Price not felt like a prisoner, it struck Terri, Thuy Sen might not have died. But this was only one of the many mischances which worked variations on Rennell's fate, ordained by family, the Bayview, and Rennell's inability to cope with either. "She was just tired," Terri said. "She got old, and started wearing out."

Rennell did not raise his head. "Started once that cop came for us—the black dude. At that trial, I kep' tryin' to smile at her. She just kep' shakin' her head. Like we been bad to her so long she don't know how to smile back."

A deeper sadness overcame Terri, both at what Rennell remembered and at how little he understood it: Eula Price had surely known how he appeared to others and done her best to warn him. "She was afraid for you," Terri said. "That's all it was."

Rennell said nothing. Terri sat back, gazing down the row of cubicles at other prisoners in conference with their lawyers. For a curious moment it reminded her of confession, condemned men seeking absolution in plastic booths from priests disguised in suits.

"How she die?" Rennell asked.

"In her sleep. She just slipped out of life to heaven, without feeling any pain."

He looked up at her. "Like Payton?"

Terri winced inside. **Much better,** she thought. **She never knew it was her time, and she didn't die twitching and gasping for breath.** "Like Payton," she answered.

"There was no way to talk about the hearing," Terri said, "or whether he might testify. But we have to decide whether we put him on."

Her listeners—Chris, Carlo, Anthony Lane, and Tammy Mattox—sat around the conference table with soft drinks and sandwiches on paper plates. They all looked tired.

"High risk," Chris answered. "But maybe high reward."

"How so?"

"If Bond finds that we haven't shown sufficient proof of retardation, or innocence—it will be fatal." Chris allowed himself a quick, sharp taste of Diet Coke. "One way to change the balance is to **show** Bond—and the media—a retarded man, and then ask how the Court can affirm his sentence of death."

Lane shook his head. "Rennell doesn't get that he's retarded. So he doesn't know how he's supposed to act, any more than Bond will know how to interpret what he sees. Too many people expect a drooling moron, or someone who looks like he's got Down syndrome. Bond may see Rennell as an actor in our morality play, trying to fake his way off death row. And if we coach Rennell to the point where he can cope with Larry Pell, and make a case for his innocence, we may have made him smart enough to kill—"

"If he's not at the hearing," Carlo objected, "he's an abstraction fought over by lawyers and mental health experts—ours, and theirs." His tone became angry. "How the hell can you have a hearing about whether Rennell lives or dies without Rennell?"

"Because he looks **normal**," Lane retorted. "I remember one sensitive pair of lawyers who gave their arguably retarded client a suit and glasses and law books to 'read' at the defense table, all so he could feel as smart as they were. In **that** case, he probably was. They got him executed."

"Aren't we forgetting Rennell?" Tammy asked. "We've all been all caught up on how he might look at a hearing, or what he might say, but not about how he might **feel.**

"He'll get to hear us tell Bond what a nightmare his childhood was, how Payton screwed him over, and how his last fifteen years were all about him being too stupid to defend himself in a courtroom. All while he's **sitting** in a courtroom—"

"He's going to **die,**" Chris snapped. "Think how bad he'll feel then. If we hurt his feelings and he lives, we can try to fix that later. But we can't fix a dead man."

"Who's already tried to kill himself," Tammy answered. "The way I understand this, Terri's managed to keep him going. You want to fuck that up, Chris?"

"No," Chris said evenly. "But I'd rather gamble on Rennell helping us out now, and us being able to help him later, than on Bond's compassion for a putatively retarded man he's never seen—as described by lawyers he'll never trust."

Lane's forehead knit, a sign of his annoyance. "You're missing something," he remonstrated. "**This** time around, Rennell will know a court can kill him. Because of Payton. Can you imagine how scared he'll be once Pell starts asking questions? Especially once I've told him how unfit he is to cope with that.

"You haven't seen this man. I have. I don't want to devastate him in order to 'save' him."

"Then he doesn't have to be there for **your** testimony. Only for his—"

"If I don't destroy him," Lane shot back, "Pell will on cross-examination—"

"How?" Chris retorted. "By making him look retarded? Unless we win, Rennell's terminal. I find it odd to be discussing his quality of life, like we're some kind of hospice."

In the tense silence that followed, Terri felt torn between Lane's concern about scarring Rennell further and the ruthless logic of her husband, founded in a compassion that the others, except for Carlo, might not see. "We've got a lot to do," she said. "I'm visiting Rennell after his grandma's funeral. Then we can decide."

Eula Price's funeral was beautiful, the church filled with mourners, the casket covered in flowers. When the choir sang "Amazing Grace," Terri could feel Eula's soul nestling with the angels.

That was what Terri told him. None of it was so, save for the flowers, the Pagets' gift. But the business of the angels made Rennell's eyes glisten.

"She was a good woman," Terri said. "And she loved you." The truth, at last.

Rennell closed his eyes. Silent, Terri studied the book of string and cardboard he had brought to her. Its pages were bright-colored cards sent him by Eula Price, Scotch-taped to rough drawing paper, and the letters "DNA" were scribbled in crayon on the cover.

"What's this book?" she asked.

It took Rennell a moment to refocus. "It's about me being innocent, like my grandma knew I was. I want you to show it to those people."

"Which people?"

"Them that come to give me those tests. Tired of tests."

Terri tilted her head. "Know what **our** tests were about, Rennell?"

He grasped one curled hand with the other. **"I'm not dumb,"** he said with sudden anger. "I was just a fuck-off, like Payton said. Didn't care about no schoolin'."

Terri had never heard this before. For a moment it startled her, and then she saw that, in Rennell's mind, it made him like anyone else he knew—just another street kid who made bad choices. "What makes you say that?"

"Don't want to see those people from the State no more." Rennell's face was a mask of rage. "Don't want them comin' at me. Don't want nobody fucking with me. Even you."

With the jolt of a connection made, Terri remembered the story which made his aversion to hurting the powerless—including Thuy Sen—more plausible. "When you were in juvenile hall," she ventured, "people did something terrible to you. Things that made you even more afraid to sleep at night. Can you tell me about that?"

Rennell shut his eyes again. The skin around his knuckles, clenched tightly together, seemed paler. "Nothin' happened."

"It's okay to talk," she assured him. "Payton told me about it."

Rennell's eyes flew open. "Don't want no more tests. Don't want no more people comin' after me. Had too much of that."

Terri touched his wrist, waiting for him to calm. "I'll try," she promised. "That's all I can do."

EIGHT

ON THE MORNING RENNELL'S HEARING BEGAN, demonstrators slowed the Pagets' progress to the entrance of the Federal Building. Near the glass doors, a clump of anti–death penalty protesters—including a prominent actor and a Pulitzer Prize–winning poet—faced a smaller but vehement group beneath a sign which read justice for victims. One of its members, a graying woman whose plump face might have seemed pleasant but for its anger, stepped in front of Terri.

"I've seen you on TV," she said in accusation. "How can you be so sick and twisted?"

Chris took Terri's arm, signaling his intention, if he must, to shoulder the woman aside. But Terri would not move. Calmly, she said, "If I'm 'sick and twisted,' so are Nelson Mandela, Martin Luther King, and the Pope. And every Western democracy but us—"

"Then send all our murderers to France," a man called out, "if **they're** so morally superior. Lawyers like you are the reason animals like him can force children to have sex."

"Let's go," Carlo murmured. This time Terri did not resist.

Gazing down from the bench, Judge Bond, dressed in his crisp black robe, spoke so that his voice would carry to the reporters who filled his airy but Spartan courtroom. That and his manner, slightly preening, reminded Terri of the grand inquisitor in a venerable Italian opera.

"The first phase of this hearing," Bond declared, "will focus on whether Rennell Price is mentally retarded and therefore immune from execution. As well as whether—assuming this argument is not foreclosed by AEDPA—mitigating evidence omitted at his original trial militates against imposition of the death penalty.

"I'm limiting each side to a single witness." The judge curtly nodded in Terri's direction. "Unless, Ms. Paget, you've decided to call Mr. Price himself."

"As of now," Terri answered, "we're relying on our expert."

With that, she stood, preparing to place the burden of explaining Rennell Price on the shoulders of Dr. Anthony Lane.

Facing Terri from the witness stand, Anthony Lane, a double-breasted suit swaddling his bulky frame, looked far more professorial than the casual black man who had first met with Rennell Price. Part of Terri found this disconcerting—it reminded her of the gulf between the rawness of Rennell's life as he had lived it and its translation by a psychiatrist in a sterile courtroom light-years from the Bayview.

As they had planned, Lane tried to bridge the gap, framing the facts for Bond as plainly as he could. "Rennell Price," he said succinctly, "was cursed from birth. Or, more precisely, from the moment of conception.

"His mother was intoxicated during pregnancy, blacking out from poisonous levels of alcohol in her first trimester. His nominal father—whose psychosis rendered him a sadist—gave Rennell beer so he could watch his two-year-old fall off the porch. Then his mother put **more** beer in his baby bottle so that Vernon Price wouldn't beat her because the child cried.

"When Rennell was seven, Athalie Price took him to the hospital with a head injury, a concussion, clearly inflicted in his home—"

"Which," Bond interjected, "if true, is tragic. But many children get concussions, Doctor—by accident or design. We can't hold them less accountable as adults."

"Perhaps," Lane answered in a respectful tone. "But not many suffer from organic brain damage, caused by fetal alcohol syndrome and aggravated by deliberate blows to the head. In my opinion—based on testing and on his performance from early childhood—Rennell Price does."

"Are these alleged organic problems," Bond inquired, "the cause of his supposed retardation?"

"No," Lane answered crisply. "The damage inflicted by his family was their own special, and quite separate, environmental contribution. But Rennell would have been retarded if he'd been raised in Mister Rogers' Neighborhood—instead of in the Bayview, by a psychotic father and a retarded, alcoholic, paranoid schizophrenic mother—"

"Then do you also infer," Bond asked sharply, "that Payton—on whose deposition so much of your petition rests—was retarded?"

"No, Your Honor. But we think they had different biological fathers. According to their mother, Rennell's father was a 'sweet, slow boy down the street.' She may be mistaken, but she's probably too impaired to make it up.

"It seems that Vernon Price believed that, too— which may be why he despised Rennell." As though recalling that his other audience was the media, Lane raised his voice, infusing it with irony. "Unlike Payton, Rennell derived no benefit from Vernon Price's intellect. Instead, he bore the weight of Vernon's psychosis."

Pell, Terri noticed, had begun to regard Tony Lane with the raptness reserved for a dangerous expert. Behind her, she felt an absence of whispering or stirring, heard a silence so deep that she imagined a reporter flipping the page of a notebook.

"What form did that take?" she asked.

Lane folded his hands, gazing past her at those watching. "Rennell suffers from a sleep disorder: chronic nightmares, broken slumber, fear of falling asleep in darkness. We believe that started because the sounds of his father beating or raping his mother kept Rennell up at night—his bedroom was next to theirs. But no doubt his sleeplessness worsened at the age of four, when his father sat him naked on a white-hot space heater."

One of Bond's law clerks, listening from the jury box, began fumbling absently with the knot of his tie. Bond himself squinted, as though the light in his courtroom had become too bright. But whether this was in sympathy or aversion, Terri could not tell. "What other events," she asked Lane, "may have contributed to Rennell's sleep disorder?"

Lane turned to Bond again, pitching his voice to sound more confiding. "According to Payton's deposition, Vernon Price would rape Athalie in front of the boys, sometimes penetrating her anus or vagina with a broomstick. The only restraint on Vernon's behavior was that the kids were not participants.

"All that changed on the day when Vernon forced Athalie to take the child's penis in her mouth." Lane's tone remained even, allowing the words to carry their own weight. "Once she finished, Vernon lapsed into an alcoholic stupor. That was when Athalie went to the kitchen, got a butcher knife, and stabbed him in the heart."

Bond's pursed mouth formed a small **o**. Terri could

428

guess his thoughts: **So this is where Rennell Price learned to force oral sex on children.** "In your view," she inquired, "how did being forced into a sex act with his mother affect Rennell Price?"

Lane seemed to gather himself. "To begin, I believe that Rennell's reaction to witnessing his father's murder—and being an unwilling party to the sex act which caused it—triggered a form of post-traumatic stress disorder, not dissimilar to that of soldiers who've suffered a horrific experience in combat. **Except** that Rennell was seven, not twenty, and the trauma Rennell wished to repress was that of a child forced into oral sex. From which, in his own experience, a terrible death resulted." Lane slowly shook his head. "Forget conscience, Your Honor, or the normal sexual taboos. In my opinion, for Rennell Price to force oral sex on a nine-year-old girl would have been a self-inflicted wound too difficult to bear. Long before Rennell was raped himself."

With these words, Lane had veered sharply into guilt or innocence—just as Terri had designed—while creating sympathy for Rennell. Bond hesitated, seemingly torn between annoyance at this detour and interest in what Lane had to say.

"What **about** retardation?" the judge finally demanded. "That's supposed to be the focus of your testimony."

"I'm coming to retardation," Lane promised. "But that's not what makes Rennell Price a tragic figure. It's everything else about him.

"Rennell was genetically predisposed to retardation, substance addiction, and mental difficulties. He was completely unwanted from birth, and suffered chronic neglect, physical illnesses, and extreme abuse since infancy. By early childhood, he was mentally, socially, and emotionally impaired. His history shows severe learning problems, mental retardation, organic deficits, and trauma. He was raised in poverty, in a chaotic environment that lacked supervision, guidance, or any positive role models. He was failed by his home, school, and community, all of which deprived him of a basic foundation for healthy development." Lane paused, his face and manner filled with a sad conviction. "Rennell Price, Your Honor, is the worst case of neglect and abuse I've ever seen."

Bond regarded him, fingertips steepled together. "Perhaps so, Dr. Lane. But I hear any number of **habeas corpus** petitions, and I can't recall one where the petitioner's childhood was not portrayed as a horror story."

Lane held the judge's gaze. "Perhaps so," he answered quietly. "But Rennell Price's childhood is the perfect storm."

After a moment, Bond's expression became inscrutable. "All right," he said. "We'll recess for ten minutes," he said. "Then perhaps you'd care to address **why** we would find this man retarded. Which, rather than guilt or innocence, is the proper purview of your profession."

The courtroom stirred, tension released in a Babel

of voices and shifting bodies. Terri turned to her husband and murmured, "How do you feel about calling Rennell now?"

With cool eyes, Chris watched Gardner Bond as he retreated from the bench. "Ask me later," he said.

NINE

"A score of seventy," Anthony Lane advised the judge, "is not an absolute ceiling on retardation. And seventy-two is not a passing grade—"

Bond held up a hand. "How **do** we impose a standard, Dr. Lane?"

"By looking at whether retardation was clear from childhood, and the degree to which it affected Rennell's capacity to act in daily life." Lane's voice was cool. "Which, as we know, is a long, sad story—a devil's brew of heredity, brain trauma, and abuse. The only question is whether a number justifies ignoring all that."

Stepping closer to the witness stand, Terri interposed a question of her own. "The Supreme Court's opinion in **Atkins,** Dr. Lane, emphasized the difficulties of a retarded man in coping with the legal system. Can you describe how retardation landed Rennell Price on death row?"

Lane settled back, hands folded in his lap, assuming a more academic tone. "I'd describe it as a series of misperceptions and disconnects, beginning with Rennell's first interrogation and ending when the jury and judge sentenced him to death.

"Inspector Monk saw a sullen crack dealer unable to conceal his own sense of guilt. What Monk actually faced was a frightened boy of extremely low intellect, searching for answers which would please the police—"

"Didn't Rennell," Bond interrupted, "admit seeing Thuy Sen at a store?"

"Maybe he did," Lane answered with a shrug. "Maybe he was just guessing. The real mystery is why he didn't confess to killing her.

"All too often, retarded people make false confessions to ingratiate themselves, or simply to put an end to repeated questioning. No matter how many times Monk asked him, Rennell came back to 'I didn't do that little girl.' But he couldn't make the police believe him."

"Perhaps," Bond retorted, "because he couldn't account for his whereabouts."

Though the judge's comment was delivered as a counterthrust, Lane nodded in amiable agreement. "Precisely. Monk imagined seeing a child molester without an alibi. What he really saw was someone without any capacity to remember, or any specific sense of time or place—let alone of where he was the day Thuy Sen disappeared.

"Payton says Rennell was asleep. In an even deeper sense than that, he was—**each** day and **every** day. For

Rennell, one day was like any other, an indeterminate moment spent in a darkened room."

The somber description made Gardner Bond pause. "What about Jamal Harrison?" Terri interposed. "His story to the police helped persuade Assistant D.A. Mauriani to seek the death penalty."

"It's the same phenomenon. Harrison believed Rennell smiled because Payton had just told him Jamal would take care of Eddie Fleet. But Payton says it was simply because he'd promised Rennell that things would be okay." Lane's tone softened. "As always, Rennell believed him. Which is why we're all here."

"Did Rennell's retardation affect his relationship to Yancey James?" Terri asked.

"Yes," Lane answered gravely. "At the preliminary hearing, Judge Warner asked Payton, then Rennell, whether they'd agree to waive James's conflict of interest in representing them both. When Rennell's turn came to answer, Warner heard the answer yes. But what he **really** heard was a retarded teenager taking cues from his older brother. In terms of Rennell's comprehension, the judge could have been speaking in Bulgarian.

"As for James, once Payton had tacitly confessed his guilt, James assumed that Rennell must also be guilty. To James, Rennell's insistence that he 'didn't do that little girl' was merely a failure of imagination—for which Payton compensated by inveigling Tasha Bramwell to lie for both of them." Lane's smile was etched with irony. "The only 'true' part of her story was that Rennell slept through the afternoon Thuy Sen died. Which, given his deficits in memory, surely came as news to Rennell. But all the jury saw was an inept lawyer offering a pathetic alibi to cover up for two degenerates."

To Terri, Lane's measured account of Rennell's fate, accumulating step by step, seemed to have sobered those who watched. The courtroom felt preternaturally quiet. "How do you relate retardation," Terri asked, "to the question of whether Rennell was innocent and wrongly convicted?"

"To me, they're intimately related. Knowing that he was innocent, if Rennell were a man of functional intellect he would have known that Eddie Fleet was framing him and, in all likelihood, favored his lawyer with some conclusions about why. A man of functional intellect might even have challenged Payton about what happened." Sitting back, Lane seemed to imagine Rennell at trial. "Rennell just sat there. With respect to Eddie Fleet, he was truly innocent."

"Unless Rennell knew himself to be guilty," Bond objected.

This, Terri knew, was the opening Tony Lane had been waiting for. "In my view," Lane replied, "retardation only made him **look** guilty. Aside from the compelling psychological reasons I gave you for believing that he'd never molest a child, there's not the slightest evidence in his life that Rennell would ever do so."

Larry Pell leapt up at once. "Your Honor," he interrupted, "we've been more than tolerant of Dr. Lane's digressions from his area of expertise. But Rennell Price's guilt or innocence is a question for this Court, not for a mental health professional who has no personal knowledge of **what** happened on the day Thuy Sen was killed. We object to any further speculation."

With an air of agreement, Bond swiveled his chair toward Terri. "Mr. Pell," she answered, "objects to a great deal. He objects to our calling Eddie Fleet. He objects to our calling Dr. Tammy Mattox to testify to Rennell Price's personal history." Turning on Pell, she asked, "You **do** still object, don't you?"

"Yes."

"In which case," she said to Bond, "I'd like Dr. Lane to set forth the reasons that the accusation of murdering Thuy Sen is in conflict with Rennell's entire life."

Trapped by the presence of the media, Bond gave a grudging nod. "Go ahead."

Quickly, Terri asked Lane, "What factors in Rennell's past suggest that he is **not** disposed to the crime for which he was sentenced to death?"

"It's more an absence of any factors suggesting that he is." Pausing, Lane summoned the list that he and Terri had rehearsed. "Unlike Eddie Fleet—who has a rich legal history of physically abusing women—Rennell has no such history. Unlike Eddie Fleet, Rennell has no history of violence whatsoever. Either before his imprisonment or after. Unlike what we believe is true about Eddie Fleet, Rennell Price has no history of sexual misconduct—"

"Including with children?"

"Yes," Lane said firmly. "In fact, we can find no evidence that Rennell Price ever had sexual relations—consensual or forcible—with anyone. In this sense, as well, it seems that Rennell is innocent."

Pell folded his arms, a portrait of frustration. "As I comprehend it," Lane continued, "the purpose of this proceeding is to determine whether we can—or should—execute Rennell Price on the basis of the legal system's understanding of him fifteen years ago." Turning to Pell, he finished softly, "Our obligation is to understand him now. You're correct, Mr. Pell, that I wasn't present at the murder of Thuy Sen. But based on **my** understanding of him, neither was Rennell. And even if he were 'present,' in a more profound sense he wasn't. To execute him would be a crime."

"Thank you," Terri said and sat, satisfied that she and Anthony Lane had accomplished everything they could.

TEN

WHEN THE HEARING RESUMED THE NEXT MORNING, Thuy Sen's father, mother, and sister—at the request, Terri was certain, of Larry Pell—were seated in the front row with Ellen Sutter, a prominent advocate of victims' rights whose four-year-old son had been murdered by a pedophile. Bond's persistent glances toward Sutter and the Sens made Terri uneasy.

She forced herself to concentrate on Pell. Standing a respectful distance from Anthony Lane, Pell inquired, "How many times, Dr. Lane, have you testified with respect to the mental condition of a man charged with—or convicted of—a crime which carried the penalty of death?"

Lane squinted at the ceiling, seeming to conduct a mental count. "Upwards of thirty."

"In how many of those cases did you testify for the prosecution?"

"None."

"Is there a reason?"

Lane regarded him with a neutral look, neither hostile nor ingratiating. "Too many prosecutors view the mental condition of a defendant simply as an impediment to execution. That's not my orientation."

"How **would** you define your orientation?"

"To form my opinions as objectively as possible."

In the front row, Terri saw Meng Sen fold his arms, signaling his disapproval. Sitting between her husband and her daughter, Chou Sen clasped Kim's hand. But Thuy Sen's sister looked waxen and far away. "Is it objective," Pell demanded, "never to testify for the State?"

"That's not the issue, Mr. Pell. It's objective to refuse to testify for a defendant whose mental condition—in my professional opinion—does not support his claims. Which I've done."

"In how many cases?"

"Ten, at least."

Pell paused, seeming to make his own mathematical calculation. "In other words, Dr. Lane, in roughly three-quarters of the cases brought to you by defense lawyers, you believed that the defendant was mentally unfit to execute."

Lane curled one hand in the fingers of another. "That sounds about right," he answered. "But the death row population is far more troubled than the average run of citizens. And the lawyers I've worked with know better than to bring me a bogus claim."

"But what **makes** a bogus claim," Pell countered, "is subjective. Do you have a moral position on the death penalty?"

Bond glanced at Terri, expecting an objection. But

she did not move or change expression. "Yes," Lane answered. "I'm opposed to it."

"In **all** cases?"

"Yes."

"Even with respect to serial killers?"

"Yes."

Pell skipped a beat. "Or child molesters?"

"Yes." Lane leaned forward. "I don't believe that we, as humans, are equipped to understand, or to judge, why people commit crimes that society rightly considers despicable. Or, in any given case, **if** they did. Therefore, I'm uneasy with capital punishment, especially when one alternative is life without parole in a maximum-security prison. But these are my **personal** beliefs.

"What you're asking by insinuation is whether those beliefs affect my testimony in this case." Pausing, Lane said emphatically. "They do **not**. Capital punishment is the law. I have an obligation to this Court—and every court—to testify within the legal standards which govern whether we execute a chosen individual. When I took the oath yesterday, I left my personal opinions behind."

"Good answer," Carlo murmured. But in Terri's judgment, Larry Pell had done precisely what he intended—to drain Lane's depiction of Rennell of its force, and to bring its credibility into question. She found Bond's silence worrisome.

"All right," Pell said to Lane abruptly, "you assert that Rennell Price has an IQ of seventy-two, while ad-

mitting that the accepted professional measure of retardation is seventy—at the **high** end. Is it also true
that Rennell's IQ could actually be seventy-seven?"

"Or sixty-seven. The standard range of error is plus
or minus five." Lane glanced at the judge. "As I said,
IQ is a social measure rather than merely a numerical
one. You have to look at Rennell's adaptive skills and
state of functioning."

"What level of adaptive skills does it take to force a
child into oral copulation?"

With the same air of equanimity, Lane answered,
"Performance skills are irrelevant to sex crimes. A re-
tarded man may be as capable of pedophilia as Eddie
Fleet. I don't quite grasp the import of your question."

Pell crossed his arms. "Then let me try this, Doctor.
You say that Rennell's IQ is a 'social measure.' Isn't it
quite possible that Rennell's allegedly low adaptive skills
are a result of the substandard schooling, chaotic family
life, abuse, truancy, and all the other **social** barriers you
described for Ms. Paget?"

"They all contribute."

"And all of these factors **also** affect thousands of en-
vironmentally challenged criminals with IQs well over
seventy, correct?"

Lane hesitated. "Of course. But—"

"So can't we set these factors aside?" Pell interrupted.
"At least as a gauge of retardation—or, for that matter,
moral responsibility. Let's return to Rennell's IQ.
Would it surprise you to learn that our expert psychologist scored it at seventy-eight?"

"Not at all," Lane answered with unruffled authority. "To me, that says three important things. First, that Rennell was as cooperative as I found him to be. Second, that he was not malingering for the sake of scoring low. And third, that like anyone with **any** capacity to learn, practice made him better." Lane's tone became sardonic. "Six points better, to be precise. But those defendants who are 'mongoloids,' or who visibly drool, don't end up on death row. That's reserved for the more gifted of our retarded population."

Unfazed, Pell stepped closer. "You also believe that Rennell suffered from fetal alcohol syndrome. Isn't that difficult to diagnose?"

"It can be."

"Is it also difficult to measure its impact on intelligence?"

"With precision, yes—"

"So we keep returning to that damnable number," Pell cut in with a fleeting smile. "But let's change the subject to Rennell's role in the crime for which the jury found him guilty."

Terri stood at once. "Objection," she called out. "Mr. Pell is asking Dr. Lane to assume the truth of facts which are very much in doubt—asserted fifteen years ago by a self-serving witness, Eddie Fleet. Who now refuses to repeat them."

"Facts," Pell corrected for Bond's benefit, "found true by a jury, confirmed three times by the California Supreme Court, and therefore entitled to a presumption of correctness under AEDPA. We can't pretend these facts don't exist, Your Honor. And even if we could, I'm entitled to ask an expert witness to assume certain facts for the purpose of eliciting his professional opinion."

Bond folded his hands. "Mr. Pell is well within his rights," he told Terri. "The witness may assume, for the purposes of answering, that the facts to which Mr. Fleet testified at trial are true."

Terri searched for a retort. "Then I hope Mr. Pell will give Mr. Fleet limited immunity, and allow this court to hear his testimony. That way we won't have to 'assume' his dubious credibility."

"You'll have time to argue that," Bond answered with a wave of the hand. "Go ahead, Mr. Pell."

Pell turned on Lane. "Are you familiar with Mr. Fleet's trial testimony?"

"Of course."

"Assume for the moment all that's true." Pell placed his hands on his hips, projecting an attitude of skepticism. "Would you **still** contend, Dr. Lane, that this series of deliberate actions by Rennell Price—starting with fetching Fleet and ending with Mr. Price disposing of Thuy Sen's body—betrays a 'failure of adaptive skills'?"

"That's difficult to say," Lane responded after a moment. "Even assuming that any of that happened, a great deal would depend on whether Rennell was acting under Payton's directions—"

"According to Fleet," Pell interrupted, "they were acting as co-equals."

"Then it would be the only time." Lane rested both arms on the witness chair. "That's one of many reasons I don't believe it."

"You can't make the rules here," Pell said sharply. "Assuming the truth of these facts—as did the jury— do they undermine the assertion that Rennell Price is retarded?"

Caught in Pell's construct, Lane paused. "Taken out of their context, and taken as gospel, they might. **If** the larger context weren't Rennell's lifetime incapacities."

"Let's look at that," Pell persisted. "At the trial, Rennell listened to Tasha Bramwell lie to exculpate him and Payton. You suggest that it's another sign of retardation. Couldn't it also be the behavior of a man who knew perfectly well that he was guilty, and that Bramwell was his last chance of getting off?"

"**If** Rennell weren't retarded."

Pell shook his head in a theatrical show of wonder. "Assuming the truth of Mr. Fleet's account, was it 'retarded' for Rennell to insist to Inspector Monk that he didn't force Thuy Sen to give him oral sex? Or was it the rational response of a guilty man who knew that confession meant conviction and, perhaps, death?"

Terri saw Kim Sen, seated in the first row, staring fixedly at Tony Lane.

"Even assuming the 'truth' of Mr. Fleet's statements," Lane answered, "that's impossible to know."

"Really? I thought you suggested that Rennell's mother was too retarded to fabricate a lie about his parentage."

Lane hesitated. "I believe that, yes."

"And that a frequent hallmark of retardation is false confessions."

"That's also true."

"And yet you also implied that Rennell's insistence on his innocence was **evidence** of his innocence. Couldn't it—just as plausibly—be evidence of a man smart enough to lie?"

Bond scrutinized Lane's demeanor with a jeweler's eye. "This entire exercise," Lane protested, "has become untethered from reality. In my considered opinion, Rennell Price not only is too retarded to lie well but didn't truly comprehend the circumstances of his interrogation. Your questions wholly ignore the Rennell Price who exists in real life."

"And who, in your view, suffers from a 'failure of adaptive skills.' Yet you cited his record in prison as evidence of nonviolence."

"True."

Pell smiled. "But many death row inmates exhibit exemplary behavior. Isn't all this more evidence of Rennell's superior adaptive skills?"

"No. Although it does refute your argument that he's antisocial." Beneath the firmness of Lane's voice lay anger at Pell's studied incomprehension. "Outside of the exercise yard, death row was the first secure environment Rennell Price had ever known. You'd go mad there, Mr. Pell. So would I. But for Rennell, solitary confinement in a six-by-six cell became an opportunity to sleep without fear. That he was pathetically grateful for this refuge is a measure of his tragedy, and his impairment..."

"Yes," Terri whispered in approval. "It's true."

But her husband was watching Gardner Bond. "That's why you need Rennell to testify," he said.

ELEVEN

THE EXPERT PSYCHOLOGIST FOR THE STATE OF CALI-
fornia, Dr. Davis Kuhl, was a slender, dark-haired man
in his early forties, with watchful, dark eyes, a prominent nose, and a dispassionate manner which lent
weight to his opinions. "My conclusion," he told Larry
Pell from the witness stand, "is that the evidence does
not support a finding that Rennell Price is mentally retarded."

Terri watched him, pen poised over her legal pad.
"In reaching that conclusion," Pell asked, "what meth-
ods did you employ?"

Kuhl placed his hands together, fingertips touching.
"Extensive testing, obviously. But the essence of my
approach is what I call forensic behavioral analysis: to
re-create the defendant's behavior in his normal life
and—minute by minute—in the commitment of the
crime."

"Assumes guilt," Terri scribbled. "Opinion depends
on Fleet—"

"There's a somewhat tired joke," Kuhl continued,
"about how to tell if defendants are lying. The punch

line is 'Because their lips are moving.'" Absently, he began rubbing his fingertips together. "I don't accept that, of course. But their actions can be far more telling than anything they say—or, for this case, anything that Payton Price said when he had nothing more to lose."

"Or Fleet," Carlo whispered to Terri. "When he had everything to gain."

"Kuhl's very selective," she answered dryly.

With a satisfied expression, Pell inquired, "I'd like you to begin with your examination of Rennell Price. What conclusions did you reach with respect to fetal alcohol syndrome or organic brain damage?"

Kuhl shook his head. "Fetal alcohol syndrome tends to affect impulse control, and I found no sign of impulsivity in my dealings with Rennell. Or in his life history as set forth by his own lawyers." Kuhl faced the defense table, as though to underscore his evenhandedness. "Claims of fetal alcohol syndrome and organic brain damage have become commonplace among petitioners in **habeas corpus** cases. Chaotic and abusive backgrounds, such as those existing in Rennell's family of origin, lend a superficial plausibility to such a claim. But the clearest manifestations of fetal alcohol syndrome are physical features—like a high palate or abnormal eye placement—wholly absent in this man, whose appearance is quite normal. Nor do the MRI and CAT scans we administered reveal any trauma to the brain."

Kuhl's mien of academic neutrality, Terri perceived,

was well-chosen for an expert whose role was to preserve the State's right of execution. With a look of approval, Gardner Bond had taken out a fountain pen, making notes of his own.

Pell, too, seemed pleased. "As I understand it, you also find Rennell Price's numeric IQ to be well above the standard for retardation."

"Seventy-eight, to be precise." Giving Terri a deferential nod, he added, "But whether you believe his IQ is seventy-two or seventy-eight, **neither** score supports his claim to be retarded. Indeed, taken together, they contradict that claim." Cocking his head toward Bond, Kuhl adopted the manner of an expert clearing up confusion. "Dr. Lane himself noted that the improvement in IQ score evinces Rennell Price's ability to learn. Add the fact that he also says—correctly—that IQ is affected by deficits in education, and Rennell's actual intelligence may be higher than either score suggests."

"What about the relationship," Bond inquired, "between Mr. Price's alleged retardation and the reputed acts of abuse he suffered as a child, and in juvenile hall?"

"In my opinion there is no relationship. I also note that the specific assertions of abuse rest almost entirely on the deposition of Payton Price, whose credibility may be suspect..."

"What about the burn marks on Rennell's buttocks?" Chris murmured in disgust.

"Nonetheless," Kuhl continued, "let's take Payton's

word as gospel. Abuse may affect a defendant's psychological makeup—even, perhaps, his sanity. But I find no evidence that the alleged abuse affected Rennell's IQ. And no one argues he's legally insane—Rennell Price clearly knows the difference between right and wrong." Kuhl's tone softened, evincing regret for his obligations as a truth teller. "Any abuse merits our sympathy as fellow humans, but it doesn't equate with mental retardation."

Bond nodded in agreement. As though emboldened, Kuhl added, "There's another thing I'd like to say, as a psychologist who studies the retarded. I accept that the Supreme Court ruled in **Atkins** that, in itself, retardation militates against the death penalty. But I have some qualms about that kind of generalization.

"In my experience, the majority of retarded people have too much empathy to contemplate a horrible crime against another person. Other retarded people may lack any empathy, or any ability to grasp the finality of murder. So I think we should be leery of making categorical judgments about the retarded, or of assuming that they're less responsible than you or me."

"**Not** the point," Terri scribbled angrily, adding, "Risk of wrongfully convicting the innocent," and then, hastily, "Doesn't understand legal system," before looking up at Kuhl with fresh intensity. Beneath his air of helpfulness, she thought, lurked the cynicism and coldness of a mercenary who had found his niche. As if to refute her, Kuhl concluded, "If I may venture an opinion, asking experts to testify that a defendant is retarded in order to spare him execution is damaging to both disciplines—psychology and law. It turns psychologists into judges, if not into God. It tempts experts to place defendants into simplistic boxes—retarded or not retarded—in order to determine their fates. Ultimately, it's corrupting.'"

Terri stood. "Your Honor," she told Judge Bond, "I move to strike that entire speech. With a touching air of melancholy, Dr. Kuhl has just informed us that the United States Supreme Court didn't know what it was doing in **Atkins** and invites this Court to nullify its ruling. It's Dr. Kuhl who has crossed the line, with a colossal arrogance dressed up as humility. All to ensure the execution of a man who is **not** like 'you or me.'

"I remind Dr. Kuhl that one purpose of **Atkins**—among many—is to keep us from executing the innocent. And that, far from being God, Dr. Kuhl's not **even** a judge." Pausing, she finished in a pointed tone, "Judges, after all, are sworn to uphold the law."

Bond's eyes narrowed in irritation. But while no doubt he, too, disliked the **Atkins** decision, Terri had invited the media to see him as he must not be seen—the judge who allowed a partisan expert to question the Supreme Court, and the law which governed whether Rennell Price might live. "This Court," he told her sternly, "is completely capable of defining the proper boundaries of expert testimony, and of setting aside any gratuitous remarks." Facing Kuhl, he added with more dispassion, "Nonetheless, any critique of **Atkins** risks blurring the question you're addressing—

whether, under **Atkins,** Rennell Price is mentally retarded. Please confine yourself to that."

Terri sat again, doubting her decision to intervene.
"No choice," Chris whispered in reassurance. "This
undertaker was hijacking Bond's courtroom. At least
you broke his rhythm."

"All right," Pell continued with the imperturbable
manner of one too confident to be diverted. "I'll ask
you to focus on Mr. Price. I believe you videotaped
your examination at San Quentin State Prison."

Kuhl's eyes flickered toward Terri. "That's correct."

"Perhaps you can show us a portion of that tape,
and give us your opinion on what it means."

Stepping off the witness stand, Kuhl stood next to
a television screen, pressing a button. For a moment
numbers flashed against a black background, five
counting down to one, and then Rennell Price's face
appeared in close-up.

To an untutored eye, Terri thought, his round face
would look normal, though somewhat lacking in expression. Perhaps only she could read the fear in his
eyes, his hope of not appearing stupid.

From off camera, Kuhl's voice was calm and encouraging. "I'm going to ask you to remember three
words, okay?"

Rennell hesitated, eyes focused on the speaker.
"Okay."

"Ap-ple," Kuhl articulated each syllable. "Ta-ble.
Mo-ney. Got that? 'Apple,' 'table,' 'money.' "

"Okay."

At the corner of the screen, a digital clock appeared, counting down five minutes. "All right," Kuhl's voice said. "I'd like you to work this puzzle for me."

The immobile stare Rennell gave Kuhl could be read as recalcitrance or, in Terri's experience, a reluctance to appear foolish. Then Rennell gazed slowly downward and, with the animation of an automaton—or the disdain of a truant—began moving pieces of a puzzle the screen did not show. Little about him seemed sympathetic or engaging.

In the silent courtroom, Kuhl and his audience watched the clock tick down. "The puzzle is a simple one," Kuhl explained to Bond. "It involved putting the figures of ten animals into spaces with corresponding shapes. He did this, as you will see, in less than two minutes..."

"Or in Kit's case," Carlo murmured, "sixty seconds. Kuhl makes it sound like Rennell just passed the bar." After a pause, he added, "What's grotesque is that if he passes, he gets to die."

"What's the animal at the bottom?" Kuhl was asking Rennell.

Rennell hesitated. "Zebra."

"And at the top?"

"Lion." Rennell's voice filled with contempt—or pride. "Not stupid, man."

The clock kept ticking down. "You know your animals," Kuhl's calm voice said. "Did you ever go to the zoo?"

Expressionless, Rennell shook his head.

"Then how did you know a zebra?"

Rennell shrugged. "Readin' books."

"From cartoons," Terri told Carlo. "Except for Hawkman comics, Rennell avoids books like the plague." In despair, she saw the clock tick down to zero, watching as Rennell resisted acknowledging his incapacity.

"How come your grades weren't better?" Kuhl asked.

Rennell shrugged again. "Just fuckin' off. Stopped tryin', is all."

The digital clock read "0:00."

"Remember the words I gave you?"

"Yeah." Rennell pursed his lips. " 'Apple,' " he repeated slowly. " 'Table.' " Briefly, his eyes seemed to roll back in his head, then to re-focus. " 'Money.' "

As the screen went blank, Kuhl turned to face the judge. "When Rennell Price cares to, Your Honor, he has a functioning memory. He is by no means bright. But I think his own words account for a good portion of his academic failures: like many of his peers, he stopped trying."

"What other evidence do you have for that?" Pell asked.

"Interviews with the prison guards." Before continuing, Kuhl returned to the witness stand. "In their observation, Rennell can count money, write and address cards to his grandmother, and answer questions in a coherent manner. One guard reports seeing Rennell reading a sports magazine."

He was looking at the pictures, Terri thought. But she could do nothing; against her will, a version of Rennell Price had materialized in the courtroom, and it was not the one she knew.

"Do still other factors," Pell pursued, "support your opinion that Rennell Price is not retarded?"

"The crime itself." Kuhl began rubbing his fingertips again. "You've already reviewed the facts established at the trial with Dr. Lane. Taken together, they suggest a course of action which was rational, purposeful, and aware..."

And a total fiction, Terri thought.

"As well as," Kuhl continued, "evincing a fully functional awareness of the need to hide Thuy Sen's body, and the consequences of getting caught."

Frozen, the Sen family watched and listened, a triptych of grief and loss, pleading with their eyes for Gardner Bond to exact a final measure of justice. "Payton and Rennell Price," Kuhl concluded, "both knew what they had done. That's why they recruited Eddie Fleet. That's why Rennell Price dumped that child's corpse. And that's why—with utter rationality—Rennell denied his own involvement. These are **not** the acts of a man too dull to cope."

"Thank you," Pell said briskly. "That's all I've got for you."

TWELVE

BASED ON HER EXPERIENCE, TERRI TENDED TO DIVIDE expert witnesses into three categories—professionals, who formed their opinions with care; ideologues, who testified according to their beliefs about the death penalty; and whores, who said anything for money. She saw Davis Kuhl as a curious combination—committed enough to be an ideologue, flexible enough in his advocacy to qualify as a whore. Her challenge was to reveal both tendencies so plainly that Bond could not dismiss them.

Rising to cross-examine, she asked without preface, "Do you have your own practice, Dr. Kuhl?"

Kuhl summoned a look of sincere interest. "If you're asking whether I see patients privately, the answer is no."

"In other words, every person you examine is either a defendant or a prisoner."

"Yes."

Terri rested a hand on the defense table. "Have you ever testified on **behalf** of a defendant, or a prisoner?"

"No."

"Of the over five hundred prisoners on death row at San Quentin Prison, how many have you met—either during the original trial or through a **habeas corpus** proceeding?"

Kuhl steepled his fingers. "I'd say between fifty and sixty."

"In what context?"

"Primarily to determine whether they were legally insane, or mentally retarded."

"And, in your opinion, how many of those you examined for insanity were, in fact, insane?"

"None."

"How many instances of mental retardation did you find?"

"None."

Still not moving, Terri smiled. "So finding Rennell Price retarded would have spoiled an otherwise perfect record?"

At the prosecution table, Larry Pell stirred, seeming to search for an objection. Kuhl glanced toward him, then answered. "That's not how I view it, Ms. Paget. In the case of Rennell Price, I could not, as a forensic psychologist, conclude that he was mentally retarded."

"As a 'forensic psychologist,' do you deal with any potentially retarded people outside the legal system?"

"No."

Terri cocked her head. "What is the professionally accepted measure for an average IQ?"

Kuhl began rubbing his fingertips together. "One hundred is the usual measure."

"Are you aware that the average IQ among death row inmates at San Quentin falls in the mid-eighties?"

Kuhl paused. "I've read that. I can't verify it."

"Really? So you have no opinion as to whether the average IQ on death row is different from that of the population as a whole?"

Kuhl placed his steepled fingers to his chin. "It may well be."

"But, presumably, you've never met a single death row inmate you'd consider to be mentally retarded?"

"Not in the cases where I've been asked to evaluate that question."

"How many of those cases have you had?"

"Roughly twenty."

Terri flashed a grin. "I guess the A.G.'s Office gives you the quick learners." Among the onlookers, someone laughed. Before Bond, plainly annoyed, could crack his gavel, Terri asked, "Outside testifying as an expert witness, what work have you done in the area of mental retardation?"

"Professional reading. Quite extensive, in fact."

"Have you personally performed any research or written any articles?"

"No."

Terri rested her hands on her hips. "In short, Dr. Kuhl, your entire professional experience with mental retardation lies in finding roughly twenty death row inmates **not** retarded."

Kuhl shifted his lean frame. "**After** performing an

examination to establish the proper basis for my opinion."

"To 'establish a proper basis' for your opinion that Rennell Price is not retarded, how much time did you spend with him?"

"About two hours."

" 'Hours,' did you say? Not 'days'?"

"I said hours." A first trace of exasperation entered Kuhl's voice. "In a case like this, one doesn't have days. And if we tested Rennell Price for days on end, you'd complain we were overtaxing him."

Terri ignored this. "Two hours," she repeated. "How many hours did it take you to form your professional opinion?"

Kuhl's restless fingers rubbed together more rapidly. "Approximately nine."

"How did you spend the extra seven hours?"

"Reading, mostly: Eddie Fleet's trial testimony, and Payton Price's deposition. Also, I interpreted Rennell's test scores."

Terri gazed at him with curiosity. "Did you interview anyone who knew Rennell?"

Kuhl rested his hands in his lap. "The prison guard I mentioned."

"The one who reported that he saw Rennell 'reading' a copy of **Sports Illustrated**?"

"Yes."

"According to the school records you reviewed, what was Rennell's reading level?"

"In the seventh grade, I believe they estimated it to be roughly at the third-grade level—"

"After which," Terri cut in, "didn't his teacher recommend remedial education—specifically to help him read?"

"I believe so."

"Did he ever receive any?"

Though Terri's voice had never changed, Kuhl had begun regarding her with wary eyes, which, even more frequently, darted toward Larry Pell. "There's no record of that."

"Did your testing give you any reason to believe that Rennell Price was able to read and comprehend the contents of **Sports Illustrated**?"

Kuhl frowned. "Certainly, at that reading level, Rennell could pick out words."

"Did you," Terri inquired mildly, "at least ask the guard if the magazine was right side up?"

"Objection," Pell called out. "The tone and substance of the question are sheer harassment."

Before Bond could issue the reprimand his expression told her was coming, Terri said respectfully, "I'll withdraw the question, Your Honor, and make my point another way." Turning back to Kuhl, she asked, "Do you know where Rennell got the magazine?"

"No."

"According to Rennell, the guard gave it to him. In all of his time on death row, is there any record of Rennell ordering books from the prison library?"

"I don't know."

"For the record, Dr. Kuhl, there is none. So why did you offer this vignette about **Sports Illustrated** as evidence that Rennell Price is not retarded?"

Kuhl shook his head. "It was ancillary—"

"It was careless," Terri snapped. "So you're not suggesting to the Court that Rennell's close encounter with **Sports Illustrated** in any way bears on whether this Court should uphold his death sentence."

"Of course not."

"Good." Terri's voice was cool now. "You also mentioned that the evidence of Rennell Price's abuse rests 'almost entirely' on Payton's deposition. Do you remember the passage about Vernon Price forcing Rennell to sit naked on a space heater?"

"Yes."

"Do you have any information regarding the accuracy of this account?"

"No."

"Then you're not aware that the records of the physical exam given Rennell upon his arrival at San Quentin revealed symmetrical burn marks on his buttocks?"

"I am not."

Terri folded her arms. "Did Mr. Pell ask you to form any opinions regarding whether Rennell was abused, or concerning the degree of his reliance on Payton?"

"No."

"So your observation that there was no real evi-

dence of abuse outside of Payton's testimony was just a
bonus you decided to throw in?"

Kuhl folded his arms. "What I said, Ms. Paget, is
that I don't believe that abuse relates to mental retardation."

"Really? So, in your opinion, even the most severe
abuse won't make a retarded person even more prone
to fright, or confusion?"

"I wasn't asked to form an opinion on that."

"Were you asked to consider whether abuse might
contribute to the potential sleep disorder described in
Payton's deposition?"

"No."

"So you have no insight to offer us on Rennell's
sleep patterns, or the likelihood he was fast asleep on
the day that Thuy Sen died."

"No."

"No," Terri repeated coldly. "This morning, you offered us a critique of **Atkins.** One of the reasons the
Supreme Court gave in **Atkins** for barring the execution
of the mentally retarded was that retarded people have a
harder time comprehending the legal system. In **this**
case, the case of Rennell Price, an allegedly retarded man
about to be executed, did you try to determine whether
he was capable of understanding—and waiving—his
lawyer's conflict of interest in also representing Payton?"

"No, Ms. Paget. The Attorney General's Office
didn't ask me to address that."

Returning to the defendants' table, Terri glanced at
a piece of paper. "Having met Rennell Price, do you—

as a professional—honestly believe that he got it when Judge Warner asked, 'Do you understand that, by employing Mr. James to represent you both, you assume the risk that he may not represent your individual interests as effectively as separate counsel?' "

Kuhl shook his head. "I need to know more, Ms. Paget. For example, how well did the lawyer explain to Rennell his choices—"

"He didn't," Terri snapped. "Assuming **that** fact, how would you evaluate Rennell's ability to comprehend the judge's admonition?"

"That's beyond the scope of my opinion."

"Isn't everything? Yet you also offered Rennell's orderly existence in prison as evidence of his adaptive skills. Precisely what skills does that existence require?"

"Conformity to rules, among other things."

"What rules are there, Dr. Kuhl? 'Stay in your cell' . . . ?"

"All right," Bond interjected. "If you have a question to ask the witness, ask it with respect."

Not so easy, Terri wanted to say. But Kuhl was shaken now, and she did not wish to give him time. "All right," she said. "Can retarded people take showers?"

"Of course."

"Can they eat meals put through the meal slot?"

"Of course."

"Can they go to the bathroom unassisted?"

"Yes."

"Can they go **where** they're told **when** they're told?"

"Yes."

"Impressive," Terri said coolly. "Isn't it true that the simplified existence of an inmate in solitary confinement presents far fewer challenges or surprises to the retarded than does the outside world?"

Kuhl regarded her with a closed expression. "It presents fewer variables..."

In the quiet of the courtroom, someone laughed again. Bond crisply banged his gavel. "You showed us a videotape," Terri said mildly, "in which Rennell attributed his academic failures to not trying. What role did this self-evaluation play in your opinion that Rennell is not retarded?"

Kuhl frowned again. "My primary reliance was testing, and his adaptive skills. My only point was that Rennell Price provided an alternative explanation for his poor performance—"

"Pretty dumb, wasn't it? I mean, here's the prisoner who may well die unless this Court finds him retarded, and he keeps on insisting that he's **not.**"

"It struck me as a matter of pride, Ms. Paget. Rennell Price did not want to be taken for something which he doesn't believe he is."

Terri gave him a dubious smile. "Isn't it true, Dr. Kuhl, that retarded people often resist acknowledging their limitations?"

"They can."

Terri skipped a beat. "How do you know?"

Kuhl looked puzzled. "I don't understand..."

"I mean, have you actually ever **met** a retarded person?"

Bond—she saw from his swift glance at the witness—perceived where Terri was going. But the witness did not seem to. "I still don't understand."

"Let's break it down. You've never met one on death row, correct?"

Kuhl's shoulders twitched. "That's not what I said..."

"What you said, Doctor, is that none of the inmates you've examined for retardation were, in your opinion, retarded. Is that correct?"

"Yes."

"And you never met a retarded person in your practice, because you have no practice—correct?"

Kuhl hesitated. "Correct."

"How long has it been since you became a psychologist?"

"Seventeen years."

"And in all those years, you never met a single retarded person?"

"I've certainly encountered them in life..."

"On the street, but not on death row?" Terri summoned a tone of mock bewilderment. "How did you know they were retarded?"

"It was obvious...," Kuhl began, and then his voice trailed off. "What I mean is, their conduct, combined with their appearance, clearly suggested retardation."

"But you didn't actually test them."

"Of course not."

"Well, based on your **reading** about retarded people, can you always determine by observation whether someone is retarded?"

"Of course not. That's why we have a regime of testing."

"And in **your** regime of testing, you've never found anyone you tested to be mentally retarded."

"Asked and answered," Pell called out.

"Point made," Bond told her with a look of annoyance. "Move on."

Kuhl looked toward the judge. "If I may say one thing, Your Honor. During my medical education, I encountered a number of persons—often in public mental facilities—who had been found to be retarded."

"But not by you," Terri said. "Correct?"

Turning, the witness summoned an expression which, Terri supposed, was meant to be long-suffering. "Not by me, counselor. But I was able to observe them."

"Did all of their eyes bug out?" Holding up a hand, she said, "Forgive me, Your Honor. I'll move on."

"Please do."

"This morning, Dr. Kuhl, you said there was no evidence that Rennell Price suffered from fetal alcohol syndrome or organic brain damage. Is it possible to have either, or both, while having a 'normal' appearance?"

"That's possible, yes."

"And that a CAT scan won't necessarily reveal either?"

"That's true."

"And that the so-called practice effect could have improved Rennell's scores on the tests you gave him to evaluate his IQ?"

"That's also true." Kuhl's voice held a trace of exasperation. "Which is why I emphasize forensic behavioral analysis, re-creating a defendant's actions in his normal life."

"Let's break that down. You'll concede that Rennell's 'normal life' on death row does **not** refute the assertion that he's retarded?"

"Not in itself, no..."

"Isn't it also true that—based on your nine-hour review—you are aware of nothing which makes his academic failure more likely to be willful than a sign of retardation?"

"Other than his own admission."

" 'Other than his own admission,' " Terri repeated softly. "I guess that leaves us with all those deliberate things he did in the commitment of this crime. Of course, if Payton Price were telling the truth, those things never happened, did they?"

"If Payton were telling the truth," the witness rejoined, "Rennell's innocent, retarded or no. But that's not what the jury found."

"True. In forming your opinion, Dr. Kuhl, did Mr. Pell give you any instructions regarding how to view the testimony of Eddie Fleet?"

"I was instructed to assume its truth."

Though questioning the witness, Terri directed her

gaze at Bond. "In other words, your 'forensic behavioral analysis' rests primarily on the testimony of Mr. Fleet."

"In some measure, yes."

"Aren't you at least curious about whether he's telling the truth?"

"Of course. But trying to second-guess the 'truth' of facts established at the trial is beyond the scope of my assignment and—frankly—the proper purview of an expert in psychology."

"I see. Were you also asked to assume by implication that Payton Price was lying?"

"I suppose so."

"Wouldn't you like to see and hear Payton Price tell his story?"

Kuhl gave her a trapped, impatient look. "Payton Price is dead."

Terri glanced at Bond again. "Oh, I know. That leaves Eddie Fleet, doesn't it? Are you aware that since Mr. Pell sought your opinion and told you to rely on Fleet's testimony, Mr. Fleet has invoked the Fifth Amendment?"

"I am."

"How does that affect your reliance on Mr. Fleet in asserting that Rennell Price is not retarded?"

Kuhl glanced at Larry Pell. "My instructions are the same."

"Doesn't that bother you, Dr. Kuhl? Maybe just a little? After all, if the Court accepts your opinion, Rennell Price may well die."

"Objection," Pell said in a disdainful monotone. "Argumentative."

"Argumentative?" Terri echoed. "Forgive me, Dr. Kuhl. Let me ask the question another way. Would you now, knowing that Mr. Fleet has taken the Fifth, prefer to see and hear him before standing on your opinion?"

From Pell's expression, he saw, perhaps too late, where Terri had taken his witness. Defensively, Kuhl answered. "That's not my decision."

"No," Terri answered, looking toward Gardner Bond. "It's Mr. Pell's."

THIRTEEN

WHEN TERRI HAD FINISHED WITH DAVIS KUHL, LARRY Pell stood at once.

"I realize," he told Judge Bond, "that the Court has heard all the witnesses it cares to with respect to Rennell Price's state of mental functioning." Here Pell darted a look at Terri. "Absent," he added pointedly, "Mr. Price himself. But I wanted to address why the State did not feel the need to ask Dr. Kuhl to opine on the 'new' issue raised by Ms. Paget: whether Rennell's purported dependence on his brother, Payton, mitigates against a sentence of death for **his** role in the murder of Thuy Sen."

Bond nodded curtly. "Go ahead."

Pell rested one hand on the prosecution table, the other on his hip, a portrait of confidence. "Set aside that this argument conflicts with the assertion that Mr. Price is innocent. Set aside that Dr. Lane's testimony is another exercise in the dark autobiographical style so common to **habeas corpus** cases, wherein a murderer's hard childhood is offered to mitigate the murder of a child." Pell's voice became mordant. "Set aside that many abused children do not commit crimes; that the 'new' evidence of **Rennell Price's** childhood emerged at the eleventh hour; or that none of the supposed horrors—new or old—cited by Dr. Lane outweigh the horror of the crime itself.

"We simply rely on the law: because this 'new' evidence in mitigation supports an old argument, it is barred by AEDPA. This Court should not—and, I respectfully submit—**cannot** entertain it—"

"According to Ms. Paget," the judge rejoined, "the 'new' evidence is, indeed, new. Because Payton Price alone controlled whether he chose to speak."

"Is Rennell Price mute?" Pell countered. "Nothing in the last fifteen years barred **him** from discussing his own childhood . . ."

"He's **retarded**," Carlo whispered in disgust.

"Where was his grandmother?" Pell went on. "Where were his lawyers, the respected firm of Kenyon and Walker? Right **here**—in **this** Court." Pell drew himself to his full height, hands clasped in front of him. "For new evidence to be accepted on a second petition, there are two predicates: that **original** counsel must have failed to offer it because he was 'ineffective'; and that **subsequent** counsel could not have offered it because—despite their exercise of due diligence—they could not find it. Neither is true. The question of mitigation is closed."

Bond assumed an attitude of gravity. "You anticipate me," he said after a moment. "This Court will not accept any further argument in mitigation of the death penalty."

Terri felt her stomach clench. Beneath the table, Chris's fingers briefly grazed her wrist. "But Ms. Paget's more pertinent issue," Bond told Pell, "is with whether your office—or this Court—can compel Eddie Fleet to testify through a grant of 'use immunity,' barring the state from using such testimony against him in connection with the murder of Thuy Sen."

At this mention of his daughter's name, Meng Sen leaned forward in the front row. "Your Honor," Pell said in a dispassionate manner, "after due consideration, the Attorney General's Office does not believe that attempting to compel Mr. Fleet to testify again—when he already did so at the trial—serves the interests of justice.

"It **is** true that, in his deposition, Mr. Fleet declined to repeat that testimony..."

"And ran like a thief," Carlo murmured. "Or a child molester..."

"But little wonder." Pell gestured toward Terri with an outstretched hand, his gaze still focused on the judge. "Defense counsel has made it clear that its entire case regarding innocence rests on the assertion—despite the eyewitness testimony of Flora Lewis—that Eddie Fleet, not Rennell Price, was the second murderer. Including the insinuation, offered without any factual corroboration, that Mr. Fleet is a pedophile.

"What mischief," Pell added with disdain. "Slander

has no standard of proof, and murder—the crime of which petitioner's counsel accuses Eddie Fleet—has no statute of limitations. So little wonder, indeed, that Mr. Fleet has concluded it will do him no good to brave the desperate tactics of dedicated counsel who, one way or the other, want this Court to rescue their client from death.

"Fifteen years ago, a jury determined the truth, and delivered justice. This Court cannot improve on it."

The judge angled his gaze toward Terri. "I imagine you have another viewpoint, Ms. Paget."

Terri rose, pausing to channel her indignation. "I have another 'truth,' " she answered. "The jury did not hear—as Mr. Pell has—the accusation of Eddie Fleet by Payton Price. The jury did not see—as Mr. Pell has—Mr. Fleet invoking the Fifth Amendment when asked whether he had ever forced a child into oral copulation. And Mr. Pell has done his level best to ensure that this Court neither sees nor hears **either** of those men.

"Payton Price is dead—as Mr. Pell so urgently requested. Eddie Fleet is **not** dead. Fifteen years ago, the State—in the person of Lou Mauriani—offered Eddie Fleet a deal for his testimony against Payton and Rennell. Now the State, in the person of Mr. Pell, protects Fleet from appearing before this Court. By incentivizing Mr. Fleet to say that Rennell Price was guilty of a crime, the State allowed Mr. Fleet, quite literally, to get away with murder." Terri's voice filled with scorn. "This Court should not allow Mr. Fleet to do it twice.

The death of Thuy Sen was tragic. The execution of Rennell Price, when the State knows there is such doubt, is tantamount to a cover-up. This Court should order the Attorney General's Office to immunize Eddie Fleet, and then drag Fleet into the light."

Pell stood. "May I comment, Your Honor?"

"Briefly."

"We've reviewed the record with Mr. Mauriani. He granted no immunity to Eddie Fleet—merely promised to consider Fleet's cooperation once the trial was done. We also conclude, upon thorough review, that the original prosecution was well-founded. There **was** no immunity, and there **is** no distortion of truth."

"If Mr. Pell were so confident of the 'truth,' " Terri rejoined, "he would not object to immunizing Mr. Fleet."

"What Mr. Pell is saying," Bond responded, "is that there were no 'terms' but only the proffer of consideration. In prudence, this Court cannot intrude on the good faith judgment of the Attorney General's Office. Therefore, we will not compel Mr. Fleet to appear before us." Bond's tone, though mild, concealed another trap. "Please be assured that the Court will consider every inference—including whatever can be drawn from the circumstances of Mr. Fleet's original testimony—as well as any testimony you offer us from Mr. Price himself.

"Tomorrow morning we turn to the alleged new evidence of innocence. Unlike with Mr. Fleet, Ms. Paget, you do control the presence of Rennell Price." After pausing, the judge concluded firmly, "It's time for you to decide. Either call the petitioner as a witness or make your showing without him."

It was midnight, and Terri sat with Chris at their kitchen table. The high from her cross-examination of Davis Kuhl seemed to have occurred in some other life, perhaps to another lawyer.

"I can't do it," Terri said. "I think Pell could destroy Rennell. I think Bond could use some foolish thing he said—like 'I was just a fuck-off'—to send him to the death chamber." Pausing, she watched her husband's expression. "On retardation, I pretty much eviscerated Davis Kuhl. On innocence, no jury would convict Rennell with the evidence we have today—"

"That's not the point, Terri, and you know it." In the harsh light of the kitchen, Chris's face, lean and weathered, held a melancholy certainty. "The only way to keep this judge from dissolving the stay of execution is to show Rennell Price to the world. That's the place Bond put you when he allowed the State to conceal Eddie Fleet."

Terri thought of Rennell as she had seen him that afternoon, listening to her account of the day's proceedings as though Bond's courtroom were a foreign country he feared to visit. "Been in court," he had said softly. "Don't never want to go again." The tremor in his voice had conveyed far more than words.

"Even if Bond turns us down," Terri told Chris,

"there's a fair chance Blair Montgomery's panel will agree to hear the case."

"Maybe so. But spin out with me what happens next.

"If Rennell wins before Bond, and then the Ninth Circuit agrees, even if Pell succeeds in getting the U.S. Supreme Court to review it, you're still in okay shape. At least you and the Ninth Circuit are **both** relying on the opinion of a very conservative district judge. But if a Ninth Circuit panel reverses Bond, and Pell takes it to the Supreme Court, you've got an entirely different dynamic—"

"I know," Terri said tiredly. "The Supreme Court will see a rogue panel from a rogue circuit, headed by a liberal judge, flouting the law as interpreted by a right-thinking conservative like Gardner Bond."

"You've got Justice Fini," Chris said flatly. "And you don't want this case ever to cross his mind."

Exhausted, Terri tried to imagine the gravitational pull between a retarded black man and a brilliant Supreme Court justice she hoped would never become aware of Rennell's existence. "Too far ahead," she finally answered. "All I can try to do is what's best to do tomorrow."

FOURTEEN

"WHAT'S YOUR PLEASURE," GARDNER BOND INQUIRED of Terri, "with respect to Rennell Price?"

Standing at the defense table, Terri hesitated—not because of last-minute indecision but because her decision felt so fateful. "We've determined not to call him as a witness, for all the reasons cited in **Atkins**—that he's prone to confusion, won't understand what he's asked, and doesn't know what happened the day that Thuy Sen died—"

"Wait a minute," Bond interrupted. "If Mr. Price wants to tell us that, he can. But don't withhold his testimony, then testify on his behalf."

"That wasn't my intention," Terri said simply.

"Good." Bond nodded her toward the podium which faced his bench. "On the question of Mr. Price's supposed innocence, you have asked us either to exonerate him, requiring his release from prison, or—at the least—to order a new trial. We've already reviewed Payton Price's deposition and the declarations of the others you wanted to call as witnesses. We're prepared to hear your argument, and that of Mr. Pell, and then rule."

Terri walked to the podium and rested her hands on its burnished wood. Bond had reduced the question of Rennell's fate to this—a half-hour argument between lawyers about a terrible event, fifteen years past, to which the actual witnesses were absent, or dead. Even the lawyers were new.

"At the moment Payton broke his silence," Terri began, "one thing was clear at once—that, on the record before this Court, the State of California should not be allowed to execute his brother—"

"You're assuming Payton's credibility," Bond interjected. "Why should this Court agree?"

"Normally," Terri conceded, "eleventh-hour confessions should be viewed with skepticism. But Payton's makes too much sense for that.

"First, it's consistent with the physical evidence. There's no forensic evidence whatsoever of Rennell's involvement in the crime itself—"

"What about Rennell's fingerprints, Ms. Paget? They were found in Fleet's car."

"But not in the trunk, Your Honor, where Fleet placed Thuy Sen's body. Payton Price confirmed what common sense suggests—because Fleet functioned as his driver, both brothers were frequent passengers in his Cadillac. Rennell's fingerprints are proof of nothing—"

"And Payton Price had nothing to lose by saying whatever he pleased."

"Perhaps," Terri answered softly. "But fifteen years ago, when Eddie Fleet testified against Rennell, Fleet had everything to gain: his freedom, and his life—despite a crime in which, even by his own self-serving admission, he was involved. And today, when Fleet has everything to lose, he refuses to repeat the testimony which sent Rennell to the death chamber.

"Today, the sole witness to the murder, Payton Price, testifies in the black and white of his deposition that Eddie Fleet killed Thuy Sen in an act of pedophilia. And that the State, by cutting a deal with Fleet then, and protecting him now, has become his accomplice in a second murder—"

"You go too far," Bond remonstrated. "What about Flora Lewis?"

"At seventy-two years old, she was looking at two men from over ninety feet away—too far to make out faces. So she 'saw' what she expected to see, Payton Price with Rennell, instead of what Payton swore she really saw: a man in a bulky sweatshirt who's the same height as Rennell, Eddie Fleet—"

Holding up his hand for silence, Bond riffled some legal pleadings in front of him. "According to the record, the police put Eddie Fleet in the same lineup with Rennell Price. Flora Lewis still picked out Rennell."

Terri nodded. "In support of our petition, we submitted school photographs of Rennell and Eddie Fleet, showing that their general features were quite similar. We've also submitted the declaration of Dr. Libby Holt, an expert on cross-racial identification, whom we've offered to call as a witness—so that the Court can see her, and Mr. Pell may cross-examine her. Dr. Holt makes two points: that eyewitness identifications are frequently driven by emotions and the witnesses' need for certainty. And that cross-racial identifications—especially those of blacks by whites—are particularly unreliable—"

"Even in a lineup?"

"Of course Flora Lewis 'identified' Rennell. She knew him." Terri paused, attempting to drain the exasperation from her voice. "At ninety feet, it's doubtful she could make out faces. All the lineup proved is that Flora Lewis could identify her neighbor, Rennell Price, from a distance of ten feet.

"Rennell's death sentence resulted from a tragic combination of Fleet's lies, Payton's self-serving silence, an old lady's mistake, and the incompetence of a lawyer who neither knew nor cared that Rennell Price is retarded—"

"**If** he is," Bond countered. "We can't assume Mr. Price's retardation for purposes of determining whether you've offered persuasive proof of innocence."

"But we know a lot," Terri countered. "As Yancey James spelled out in his declaration—and as he would tell this Court if asked—he believed Rennell guilty because Payton tacitly admitted that he, Payton, was guilty. James never developed a separate defense for Rennell, refused to believe Rennell's protestation of innocence, never investigated Eddie Fleet, and never raised the possibility that Fleet, not Rennell, was guilty—"

"Why would he?" Bond inquired sharply. "Payton Price was busy insisting that James put on the perjured testimony of Tasha Bramwell. As you point out, Payton Price didn't offer his alternative vision of the truth, admitting guilt and naming Fleet, until roughly three weeks ago. So why should we blame James's failure to attack Fleet on his supposed ineffectiveness—as required under AEDPA?"

Terri gathered her thoughts. "Mr. James's inaction offers no insight into what a competent lawyer would have done. In effect, Rennell Price had no lawyer—James didn't hear his claim of innocence, let alone try to corroborate it. This Court should not bless a death penalty imposed on a man for whom nothing was said or done—"

"Even one who waived Mr. James's supposed conflict?"

"Rennell Price is retarded, Your Honor. He couldn't comprehend the question asked him by Judge Warner."

"So your expert claims. But this Court has not heard from your client on that question, or any other."

Terri drew a breath. "With respect, Your Honor, Yancey James admits that he did nothing for Rennell. We've spelled out Rennell's intellectual deficiencies. We've set out the weakness in the State's evidence of guilt, and offered substantial new evidence of his innocence." She paused again, trying to subdue her impatience and anxiety, as well as to buttress her argument with precedent this judge might accept. "In **Rios v.**

Rocha, the Ninth Circuit held that the weakness of the prosecution case is an important measure of whether a lawyer's failings resulted in a wrongful conviction. And the Ninth Circuit has previously found James constitutionally ineffective in **People v. Coolman**—"

"And rejected such a claim in four others of James's cases. I don't assume that makes him competent here. So don't ask me to assume the opposite because of **Coolman.**" Pausing, Bond glanced at the papers spread in front of him. "Let me quote you the one presumption that AEDPA requires me to make: 'The factual findings of state courts are presumed to be correct, and the applicant shall have the burden of rebutting the presumption of correctness by clear and convincing evidence.'

"Ten days ago, the California Supreme Court found that your evidence of retardation, and your new evidence of innocence, did not justify vacating your client's death sentence. Why should this Court not defer to that finding as AEDPA directs?"

"Because it could have been written on a postcard," Terri answered promptly. "Because the opinion contained no findings, only conclusions. Because it gave this Court no basis for those conclusions. Because, in short, the California Supreme Court tells us that Rennell Price must die without condescending to tell us why—"

"Very well," Bond said coldly. "You've made your argument clear. It's time to hear from Mr. Pell."

FIFTEEN

LARRY PELL ADOPTED THE CALM BUT DISMISSIVE MAN-
ner of a lawyer confronting a frivolous claim. "This petition," he began, "is Payton Price's last laugh, an
eleventh-hour attempt to avenge himself on Eddie
Fleet.

"There is not one scrap of evidence behind his incredible story. Flora Lewis contradicts it. The forensics
do not support it. And AEDPA requires this Court to
reject it. Indeed," he added in a tone of comfortable
confidence, "the Court's questions to Ms. Paget almost
obviate the need for any argument from me.

"So I'll briefly state my case by answering those
questions.

"First, because Yancey James did not have the dubious benefit of Payton Price's story, his failure to offer it
was not a failure of effective lawyering." Pell jabbed the
podium for emphasis. "Right there, Your Honor, this
petition must fail. Because there is no constitutional
defect in the trial—in this case, ineffective assistance of
counsel—as required by AEDPA before this Court can
even consider Payton's dubious 'confession.' "

Bond listened serenely, showing no desire to interrupt. "Second," Pell told him, "and quite obviously, Payton's story is not the 'clear and convincing' evidence of innocence demanded by AEDPA before the Court can grant Rennell's petition."

"Third, the California Supreme Court has given Rennell Price three separate hearings. AEDPA does not require that Court to invest yet more time in rejecting his latest petition with the fulsomeness required to satisfy his counsel."

The wisp of a smile played at one corner of Bond's mouth.

"As for retardation," Pell continued, "it is a wholly separate issue from that of innocence. But its shortfall is the same: the evidence offered to support it is hardly sufficient to show that the California Supreme Court's decision was unreasonable. Which is why that Court should be sustained on this ground, too."

Pell stood back, hands spread on the rostrum. "AEDPA exists to bring finality to those for whom, like the family of Thuy Sen, this process must surely seem unending." Briefly, he swiveled his body toward the Sens, watching tautly from their seats in front of the assembled media. "Fifteen years after her death, their child deserves justice. That is the purpose of AEDPA. I respectfully submit that it is this Court's purpose to fulfill it."

With the ease of an athlete not required to break a sweat, Pell glided back to his chair. Quickly, Terri stood. "May I be heard in rebuttal, Your Honor?"

Even as she spoke, she saw the strain in her voice reflected in the impatience with which Bond snapped his neck to look at her. But a man's life was at stake: after the briefest hesitation, Bond said in an uninviting tone, "If you think it can illuminate what's already been said."

"Rennell Price is retarded," Terri insisted. "His entire life tells us that, and tells us why. And retardation is not separate from the question of innocence—it explains why a man whom the evidence now suggests is innocent has come within two days of execution.

"It explains why Rennell Price was his brother's shadow; why he could not help himself at trial; why the jury thought him a callous accomplice to Payton's every act, before and after the murder; and why he was convicted for a crime in which Eddie Fleet—even then—was far more obviously complicit than was Rennell." Terri's voice rose in anger. "Now Rennell is ensnared in a Byzantine, procedure-ridden legal system which allows the State to smugly claim that who Rennell Price is, and what they cannot prove he did, no longer matters at all."

Beneath Bond's silent stare she felt the deeper silence of the courtroom. "The last laugh," she continued, "doesn't belong to Payton Price. It belongs to the State, which insisted on Payton's execution, and now insists that a dead man is unworthy of belief, while inviting this Court to ignore the inconvenient fact that his brother may well be innocent. You don't need to think about innocence, they say, because you can 'presume' that the California Supreme Court has done the thinking for you.

"So let's be very clear about what Mr. Pell is really asking this Court to do." Terri turned to Pell. "There is no way—no way at all—that if Mr. Pell brought this case today, a jury would convict Rennell, let alone require his death.

"Eddie Fleet won't repeat his story. Payton Price refutes it. The State won't make Fleet tell it. There's no evidence to support it—"

"Because Flora Lewis is dead," Bond interrupted. "That's why a jury verdict rendered a year after the crime should not be endlessly relitigated until memories fade and witnesses die. At some point, we're entitled to presume that a jury verdict is reliable absent a compelling reason to doubt it."

"But this verdict?" Terri asked. "I wonder if even Flora Lewis would be so certain now. But I'm certain of this much—a case based on Flora Lewis alone would not convict Rennell. And that's all the State has left." Terri forced herself to finish calmly yet emphatically. "This Court cannot condemn Rennell Price to death without saying more than Congress ever intended in passing AEDPA, or the Constitution has ever allowed—that on the eve of execution, concepts like truth, or innocence, or justice have become irrelevant to the taking of this man's life.

"Thank you, Your Honor."

Walking back to the defense table, Terri felt the stone-faced stare of Thuy Sen's father.

"That was good," Chris told her softly, and she heard beneath his words the judgment, and the sympathy, of a man who loved her, and a lawyer who was certain that she had lost.

From the bench, Gardner Bond surveyed the parties, the media, and last of all, the Sens. "This Court," he announced, "is prepared to rule."

Looking down, the judge began reading, and Terri realized, with deep foreboding, that Bond had written his opinion the night before. "With respect to the issue of mental retardation," he began, "the question is not whether Rennell Price is of below average intelligence. Rather, even assuming that **Atkins** applies to Mr. Price's petition, the question, under AEDPA, is whether petitioner has shown that the Supreme Court of California's rejection of his claim 'was contrary to, or involved an unreasonable application of, clearly established federal law.'

"Clearly, he has not."

Blank-faced, Carlo had begun to take notes. Bond's judicial drone seemed to reach Terri from some great distance.

"With respect to innocence," the judge pronounced, "the evidence does not show a constitutional error at trial. And even were this Court to find that Mr. James's performance denied Rennell Price the effective assistance of counsel, Payton Price's last-minute confession does not warrant overturning the verdict rendered by the jury."

Pausing, Bond addressed Terri in a tone of mild reproof. "Fifteen years later, the question before this Court is not whether it believes Rennell Price guilty beyond a reasonable doubt. That decision belonged to the original jury. This Court cannot disturb it—or the decision of this state's highest court—unless it has compelling evidence that the verdict was unjust. We do not.

"Therefore, we rule as follows:

"Rennell Price's petition is denied.

"His petition to appeal this ruling is denied." Pausing, Bond finished crisply. "The stay of execution is dissolved. The State of California may now carry out the death warrant."

"Bastard," Carlo murmured.

Bond's gavel cracked. "All rise," his deputy called out, and Bond left the bench, the courtroom buzz at this release from silence sounding mournful and subdued.

Terri picked up her briefcase. "Save it for the Ninth Circuit," she told Carlo. "There's three days until the execution, and we've got work to do."

That night, after a hasty dinner with Elena, Terri returned to the office to continue preparing the papers Rennell would need for the Ninth Circuit and, she still hoped, to save his life. She worked intently, in silence. Only after an hour or so did the telephone ring. "Teresa Paget," she answered swiftly.

"Been watchin' the news," the deep voice began.

"Seems like that judge gone and fucked you in the ass. Got to thinkin' it might feel pretty good."

Terri stood, jolted upright by a current of fear. "I owe you," the voice continued softly. "But maybe you'd like it better in the mouth. Or maybe you got a kid, and I could make you watch."

Laughing softly, Eddie Fleet hung up.

Hand pressed to her mouth, Terri felt herself trembling. Fighting for self-control, she stabbed the ID button, staring at its screen. But all that appeared were the words "private caller."

Scared and angry, Terri collected herself, then called her husband.

"I'm coming to get you," Chris said.

"You don't need to—"

"No arguments, Terri—we're working together, at home. Let's just say I'm doing it for me."

And for Elena, Terri thought. She did not argue further.

Waiting for Chris, she tracked down Charles Monk at home.

She had interrupted his dinner. Nonetheless, and with considerable patience, he heard her out.

"Could have been him," he said. "Could have been some prankster pretending to be him. Your accusation's been all over the news. A more cynical man than me might say you made this up to help your own case, or get us on Fleet's case."

Disheartened, Terri realized this was true. "It was him," she insisted.

"If it was," Monk answered calmly, "he's too smart to get caught at it, and you've got no evidence at all. But we can send someone to roust him, if you want that."

Terri weighed the benefits of his offer. "Can you watch our house?" she said, and then felt foolish.

"On the basis of this? Not twenty-four/seven." Monk paused, his voice acknowledging her worry and, perhaps, his own misgivings about Fleet. "Like I said, Fleet's smart. It would take a stupid black man to start haunting a house in Pacific Heights, menacing rich white folks. Scared black folks would be more his thing."

Perhaps that was right, the reasoning part of Terri thought. But then Monk was not Elena's mother, and knew nothing about her, or the guilt and fears Terri could not express. "I just want my daughter safe," she said.

"How would he even know you have one? But my offer stands—say the word, and we'll go see him. At least it might keep him off the phone."

But maybe I can trap him, Terri thought, and then found herself caught in the crosscurrents of lawyer and mother, and confused by what was best to do for her daughter, and for Rennell.

"I'll think about it," she said simply. Then she thanked him and got off.

SIXTEEN

AT 2:00 A.M., HUDDLED IN THEIR LIBRARY NEAR Elena's bedroom, the adult Pagets cobbled together Rennell Price's petition to the Ninth Circuit Court of Appeals, seeking a stay of execution and permission to appeal the decision of Judge Bond which condemned Rennell to death. Strewn before them on the conference table were drafts of legal arguments on all potential issues.

"We have to show the 'substantial denial of a constitutional right,'" Chris argued. "If it were up to me, I'd focus exclusively on innocence and retardation. The other marginal issues we crammed into our papers before Bond will only dissipate their impact."

Still haunted by the telephone call, Terri rubbed her temples. "We should use it all. We've got Montgomery, so we've got at least one sympathetic ear. Throwing away **any** ground which could save Rennell could be throwing away his life."

"Throwing in the kitchen sink," Chris answered tartly, "is too easy. We'll look desperate instead of credible." He waved his hand at the papers. "What do we really **believe** in here?"

"Everything," Terri snapped. "I don't have a favorite reason Rennell Price ought to live. We can't let this ridiculous statute keep us from making every argument we can. Don't you think there's a constitutional problem if a statute, like AEDPA, can be used to justify executing Rennell for a crime it appears he didn't commit?"

"Are you asking me how I want the world to be? Or what I think this statute says?" Chris glanced at Carlo. "If it looks like we got the Ninth Circuit to turn AEDPA inside out, the Supreme Court will jump all over this case."

"And Rennell will still be alive," Terri answered coolly. "That's a problem I can live with." She paused, speaking with quiet force. "You've never even met Rennell. He's only an abstraction to you. I'm not going to face him tomorrow without having done everything we can to keep the State from killing him."

Softly, Chris asked, "Isn't that the problem, Terri? This isn't about how you feel . . ."

Stung, Terri was momentarily speechless. "Not fair," Carlo said to his father. "I've met Rennell, too. Does caring about him disqualify **me** from having an opinion?"

"Not unless it keeps you from functioning as a lawyer."

"As a **lawyer,** Dad, I think there's a more than decent constitutional argument that AEDPA can't be applied to render innocence irrelevant. Call me sentimental, but I'm with Terri on this."

Chris studied his son in silence, and then—despite the hour and the emotion of the evening—Terri detected a faint hint of amusement in his eyes, perhaps commingled with pride. "I guess that makes it two to one," he answered, "in favor of the kitchen sink." Turning to Terri, he said calmly, "About Fleet, Terri, we'll hire a security firm. This case is hard enough."

"We lost," Terri told Rennell. "The judge just didn't believe me."

He stared at the table, lips moving wordlessly. It was as though he were seeing something too awesome and enormous to articulate.

Terri took his hand. "There's still a chance, Rennell. There are three more judges who have power over this judge. If they don't think he did right, they can change it."

Rennell did not seem to hear. "They be comin' for me soon," he said softly. "Like Payton. Lock this whole place down till I be dead."

Terri felt a tremor pass through her, a brief flashback to Payton's death. She did not know whether it was fair, or cruel, to plead with Rennell to maintain hope, or to imbue him, despite his loss of Payton and their grandmother, with the wish to keep on living. We're so close, she wanted to say. If we can make our case for innocence, you can just walk out of here.

And then what? her conscience asked her. And her heart responded, **I'll help you find a new life, one better than you had.**

"Whatever happens," Terri promised, "I'll be with you."

It was a good thing she liked her office, Callista Hill reflected for perhaps the hundredth time, casting a weary eye at the eighteen-foot ceiling and the elegant brass chandelier. If you clerked for Chief Justice Caroline Clark Masters, you worked fourteen-hour days Monday through Saturday, easing off to half that most Sundays. The dirty clothes hamper in one corner of Callista's bedroom was filling up again; she hadn't eaten a civilized dinner in three weeks; and her sex life felt like the waste of a formerly terrific body suffering from too little exercise of any kind. But she would not trade her year with the brilliant woman who was Chief Justice for any job on earth.

Of Chief Justice Masters's four clerks, Callista knew that she stood out—not only as an African American with the look and carriage of a runway model but for her swiftness of speech and thought, along with an arid and somewhat lacerating wit most like Caroline Masters's own. Though brisk and businesslike, the Chief Justice found amusement in the foibles of law and personality that permeated the Court and, on occasion, would let this slip out in her comments when she and Callista were alone. Callista's mother, Janie, a divorced English teacher at an inner-city school in Philadelphia, had treated her gifted only child as the intelligent being she was, encouraging her freedom of thought and action, and had been rewarded with a loyal daughter who was also a good companion. Caroline Masters, Callista sometimes thought, was Janie Hill transformed into a WASP aristocrat but ironically deprived of Janie's freedom to express her sometimes caustic opinions. "The death penalty," Janie had once told Callista, "is like a war film or a monster movie. The black man always gets it first."

With a profound lack of anticipation, Callista sipped her third cup of coffee and reached into her in-box for the death list.

This was her least favorite aspect of the job: once a week, the Court's death penalty clerk circulated to the justices a photocopied sheet listing every execution pending in the United States, noting their status. In addition to her other responsibilities, Caroline Masters was the Circuit Justice for the most contentious Federal Court of Appeals in America, the Ninth Circuit, and it was Callista's business to maintain a watch list of cases which might land on the Chief's desk in the form of a last-minute request for a stay of execution. This week, Callista saw, the prisoner named Rennell Price had made it to the top of the list. From the description of its status, by next week Rennell Price might no longer be listed, and the absence of his name would give Callista goose bumps.

She picked up the telephone and called Caroline Masters's secretary.

"Okay," the Chief Justice requested, "tell me about this one."

They sat in Caroline's front office, graced with the same high ceilings and chandeliers, as well as group photos of the Court from various terms. "Man's on the bubble," Callista said flatly. "The district court judge dissolved the stay, and Price's lawyers have gone to the Ninth Circuit panel looking for a certificate of appealability. Only way they can come here for a stay of execution is if Price gets the COA, but then loses the appeal."

"What are the issues?"

"Any issue you can imagine, some of them pretty inventive. The one that jumps out at me is that AEDPA allows a claim of freestanding innocence."

The Chief raised her eyebrows. "You mean the idea we're still empowered to notice things like an innocent man being wrongly convicted? **That** could get some of my colleagues pretty excited. I assume his lawyers also try to couple this claim of innocence with a constitutional defect in the trial."

"Uh-huh. The usual ineffective assistance of counsel claim."

Caroline Masters stood, arching her back to relieve the tightness which came from too much sitting.

"Usual," she amended, "and often legitimate. I'd bet that behind at least half of the names on your death list lurks a terrible lawyer. It's the single biggest reason people get executed. Aside from the fact that—we can only hope—the condemned actually committed the murder in question." The Chief Justice stopped herself abruptly, as though feeling she had said too much. "Who's on the panel?"

"Judges Montgomery, Nhu, and Sanders."

The Chief Justice allowed herself a faint, ambiguous smile. "That should be an adventure."

"What do you want me to do?"

"Nothing yet—if the COA's not granted, you'd be wasting your time."

"And if it is?"

"Then one of two things happens. If Price loses, he's on my doorstep within twenty-four hours, asking for a stay while we consider his petition. If Price wins, the State of California will try to persuade us that the Ninth Circuit has distorted the law so grievously we're obliged to correct its errors." Caroline sat down again, no longer looking amused. "Either way, it may be fairly unpleasant. If he loses, I'll need a memo from you immediately, recommending whether or not I should grant a stay and vote to hear his case. And if you think I should grant a stay, the memo needs to be good enough to persuade four other justices to extend my stay rather than dissolve it."

A certain grimness of tone put Callista on edge. "Will it really be that difficult? The real worry would be **not** granting a stay until we can have time to look at the merits."

The Chief Justice shook her head. "Stays of execution can occasion a particular bitterness. While it takes only four of us to decide to hear a case, it takes five to grant a stay. Which creates the not-so-theoretical possibility that our Court would vote to grant a hearing to a dead man."

"What about judicial courtesy, if four of you feel that strongly?"

Caroline's smile was sour. "A good question. A few years ago, Justice Powell would step in, voting for a stay to ensure that the petitioner didn't die—at least prematurely. But we have no Lewis Powells now. Justice Fini's a stickler for the rules, and he believes that our internal rules shouldn't permit a minority of us to stave off executions. His viewpoint seems to have spread. Capital punishment," she finished wryly, "has been the death of courtesy."

Late that night, Terri sat in the Pagets' upstairs library, outlining on four-by-six note cards the argument upon which Rennell Price's life depended. When it came to the simple concept of innocence—whether the State could insist on executing Rennell despite the indisputable possibility that Eddie Fleet was guilty of Thuy Sen's death—Terri could not quite find the phrase she wanted. Note cards with words scratched out lay on the desk in front of her.

Staring at the latest card, Terri felt a tingle in the back of her neck, the slow awareness of the presence of another. Turning, she saw Elena in the doorway.

Her daughter, whom Terri had thought was sleeping, studied her as if she were a stranger. The clinical coolness in Elena's eyes cut through Terri like a knife.

"I thought you were asleep," Terri managed to say.

"How would you know?" the girl inquired coldly. "You didn't come to my room."

"It was late, Elena. I didn't want to wake you."

Elena ignored this. Walking to the desk, she picked up a note card with Terri's futile scratchings, scanning it with narrow eyes.

"I'm writing out my argument," Terri said. "If we don't win tomorrow, a man's going to die."

"No," Elena answered tersely. "A creep is going to die."

Terri expelled a breath. "You don't know him."

"I knew my father," Elena answered. "If you weren't my mother, would you have been **his** lawyer? Or maybe you would be anyhow."

Terri felt too heartsick to respond. Silently, she shook her head, less in answer than in a vain wish to banish all she felt. "You can't even look at me," she heard Elena say, and then realized that she was staring at her note cards through a film of dampness.

At length, she gazed up at her daughter. "I don't understand what your father did to you," she said softly. "I don't want to. But I understand what happened to this man, and I don't think it's right for us to kill him."

Elena folded her arms. "You think that about everyone. That's all your life's about."

What my life is about, Terri wanted to say, is too complicated for you to know. And so is Rennell Price's. But she could not explain her own childhood, the painful duality of wishing her father dead and yet knowing how defenseless a child could be against the damage inflicted by those who, themselves, had once been damaged children.

"Elena," she said quietly, "I don't think we can ever know enough about someone to execute him. I don't think we're that wise, or that fair. I don't even think we're wise enough to keep from killing innocent men.

"This man could be innocent. **I** think he is, that another man was the one who killed Thuy Sen. How can I know that and not do everything in my power to save him?"

Elena's eyelids fluttered. "Because maybe he did it, Mama. Maybe he'll do it again."

Once more, Terri thought of Eddie Fleet. She stood by instinct, reaching out to embrace her daughter. "Don't touch me," the girl said fiercely and fled the room.

SEVENTEEN

SIX HOURS LATER, ON THE MORNING THAT THEY would seek leave from the Ninth Circuit to file Rennell's appeal, Chris and Terri sat with Carlo at their sun-splashed breakfast table. They were tired and subdued—by this afternoon, if the Ninth Circuit turned them down, Rennell's legal battle would be over. And still their internal disagreements lingered.

Sipping coffee, Chris gazed at Terri across the table. "We've agreed to argue everything, I know. But how we sequence our request to be heard is still important. Unless we win on the narrowest, least-controversial issues, we may have extended Rennell's life without saving it."

Meticulously, Terri spread strawberry jam across her toast, making sure to cover every corner. "What's your suggestion?"

"**Atkins** is a new case, and no one—not the California courts, not the legislature—has set out any standards for defining what retardation is. That's our best argument, I think. It's like Rennell Price lost the lottery."

"But all retardation buys him," Carlo interposed, "is a lifetime in prison. Innocence is his ticket out."

"True. But spelling out who Rennell is should create some sympathy, even if the Court doesn't buy that he's retarded. Then we segue into innocence having implanted the idea of a guy who couldn't defend himself and begin to hammer home that he had a lawyer who didn't defend him either. That's the perfect setup for arguing that Rennell's conviction is a frame job, with Rennell the perfect dupe for Eddie Fleet." Again Chris looked at Terri, speaking more softly. "You don't want to win on freestanding innocence—that's like a red flag for the Supreme Court, begging for a reversal. When you make your pitch on **that,** remind the panel that it doesn't need to go there **if** it fits this within AEDPA by finding Yancey James incompetent. Blair Montgomery needs to take Judge Sanders with him, and Sanders is a prudent man."

Terri considered this. "Reading judges," she remarked to Carlo, "is about as much of a science as reading the entrails of a goat. But I think Chris is right about this one—we need to make it as easy for Sanders as we can. As long as we try everything to keep Rennell alive."

Carlo glanced at his father, who still contemplated Terri with a look of faint misgiving. "If we can help it," he said finally, "I don't ever want to see the inside of the United States Supreme Court. Unless, of course, we've lost."

At one o'clock, Terri, Chris, and Carlo faced Larry Pell and Janice Terrell across a conference table in the

State Office Building in San Francisco, a speaker box between them. From the beginning, Judge Sanders, silent during the first emergency proceeding, dominated this one.

"Tell me about **Atkins,**" he demanded of Terri. "What's the essence of your argument on retardation?"

She glanced at Chris. "That Rennell Price **is** retarded," she answered. "Most important, that neither the State Supreme Court nor Judge Bond gave us any idea of why they ruled otherwise, or what their standards for determining retardation are. The State can't execute this man in a vacuum—"

"All right," Sanders interjected brusquely. "Mr. Pell?"

Pell gathered his thoughts. "Mr. Price's lawyer proposed standards," Pell argued, "as did we. Two courts were unpersuaded that he met them—"

"Based on what?" Judge Montgomery interjected dryly. "Are you suggesting that our proper role is divination? Or did those courts owe us—and more important, Mr. Price—some elucidation of their reasoning prior to his execution?"

Behind the fingers curled to his lips, Chris smiled faintly. With unusual bluntness, Pell answered, "What the California Supreme Court owed Mr. Price is due consideration of his claims, followed by a ruling. AEDPA requires that the federal courts respect that ruling absent a clear showing of error, which Judge Bond did. This Court should do the same—"

"What about innocence?" Sanders cut in. "In his papers, Mr. Price says quite plainly that—regardless of whether his counsel was ineffective—he's entitled to a new trial, or even his freedom, based on his brother's confession. Is that the law?"

"Absolutely not," Pell replied with real vehemence. "Under AEDPA, it is not this Court's role to conduct a second trial but to determine whether the original trial was fair. And it was."

"What say you to that, Ms. Paget?"

Terri read the warning in Chris's eyes. "Are we deciding, Your Honor, whether a fifteen-year-old trial was good enough to justify the wrong results—in which case, it's permissible to execute a man who now appears to be innocent? Or is it this Court's duty, when faced with compelling new evidence of a condemned man's innocence, to consider whether it is still appropriate to execute him—"

"What about AEDPA?" Sanders interjected sharply. "It's very clear that its wording sets forth a precondition to considering new evidence of innocence—that the original trial denied Mr. Price a constitutional right, such as the effective assistance of counsel."

"Let me pose a hypothetical," Terri replied. "Suppose this Court was absolutely certain that new evidence showed Rennell Price to be innocent but that Mr. Pell insisted the Court ignore that evidence **unless** Mr. James's deficiencies kept Rennell's innocence from coming to light at the original trial. I do not believe that AEDPA can—or should—be read to require execution of the innocent—"

"That's not this case," Sanders retorted. "Your client's innocence is hardly certain."

"Then the difference is only a matter of degree. The evidence of Rennell Price's innocence is at least as compelling as the evidence of his guilt." Terri paused, to emphasize her final point. "But the evidence of Mr. James's ineffectiveness—beginning with his own admission—is also compelling. So this Court need not resolve the vexing question of freestanding innocence."

Her invisible audience fell momentarily silent. "It is a vexing question," Sanders concurred in more contemplative tone. "Your petition raises a number of them. Please give us a moment to confer."

Terri's hopeful glance toward Chris was met by a reflective and, she thought, somewhat worried frown. Across from her, Larry Pell's expression was opaque, Janice Terrell's dubious.

"All right." This time the disembodied voice was Judge Montgomery's. "All of us wish to make very clear that we have not prejudged the merits. But we unanimously conclude that this appeal raises issues which meet our standard for review: 'debatable among jurists of reason.' Which all of us like to think we are.

"Therefore, we are staying the execution of Rennell Price, and granting permission to appeal all claims." Montgomery's voice became peremptory. "Petitioner will file his brief tomorrow; the State will respond by the close of business two days after; we'll hear oral argument two days after that. A written order will follow."

In sheer relief, Terri glanced at Chris. But his expression showed no elation. At once she grasped his reason: the suspicion that Viet Nhu, a judicial gamesman of the first order, was giving his more liberal colleagues enough rope to hang themselves and, with it, Rennell Price—if not soon then in the far less hospitable environs of the United States Supreme Court. But that was tomorrow's problem.

"Thank you," Terri told the panel.

Returning home, Terri found Elena waiting in the living room with her arms folded, a hostile expression on her face.

"There's a strange man in my bedroom," she said with an edge Terri found hard to define.

Startled, Terri stared at her daughter and then— hearing the echo of pointed sarcasm—realized who Elena meant.

"It's someone from the security firm," Terri said.

"I know. He's putting in a camera so I can push a button and see who's at the front door. I can't wait to show my friends the present my mom gave me. They already think this case is really cool."

Terri studied her. "Sit down," she said.

Elena stared at her, resistant, and then read something in her mother's face. With a show of reluctance, she sat down beside Terri in the matching overstuffed chair.

"A few nights ago," Terri began, "I got a phone call,

I think from someone in the Price case. He made some threats—"

"Like what?"

"Just threats—he wasn't specific." Terri's voice softened. "Then he asked if I had kids. It's probably nothing. But that's why we hired a security firm and why you've got a video receiver in your room."

Elena's shoulders hunched; perhaps it was an illusion caused by the overstuffed chair, but to Terri, her daughter suddenly seemed smaller and more vulnerable. "Who is he?" Elena asked.

Terri hesitated and then, though torn, chose to speak the truth. "The second man, Elena—the one I think caused Thuy Sen's death."

Elena blanched, and then outrage overcame her fear, propelling her from the chair. "So now you're afraid he'll do that to me. There's no place I'm safe from what you do, is there? Not even my own room." Tears filled her eyes. "Maybe this time I'll die, and then **he** can be your client."

Terri stood.

"Don't **touch** me," her daughter screamed. "I just want to be alone."

Turning, Elena ran from the room.

EIGHTEEN

ON SUNDAY AFTERNOON, WHILE THE NINTH CIRCUIT heard oral argument in the case of Rennell Price, Carlo Paget worked in his cramped office, drafting a petition to the U.S. Supreme Court to be filed if Judges Montgomery, Nhu, and Sanders affirmed Rennell's sentence of death. The argument had commenced at one o'clock; every fifteen minutes or so, Carlo would glance at the digital clock on his desk and imagine the course of the arguments presented by his father and Larry Pell.

"Why is Dad doing the hearing?" he had asked Terri with genuine puzzlement.

"Watching is going to be hard for me," she had acknowledged. "But he knows the law backward and forward, and he's the best I've ever seen at oral argument on appeal. And who better to argue on behalf of a retarded black man than a white establishment lawyer who doesn't come off like an antideath fanatic?"

This was said without apparent rancor. But it impressed Carlo, once again, with the complexity of the partnership—personal and professional—between his father, on the surface the prototype of a WASP, and the younger Latina to whom little had come easily and whose passions were fueled, despite her current access to privilege, by an outsider's sensibility. He imagined her now as she watched Rennell's fate being determined by others, her anxiety intensified by her inability to speak, and hoped for both Terri's and his father's sakes that Chris's argument was flawless.

At five minutes past two, Carlo glanced at the clock again and realized the argument was now over.

He willed himself to keep writing, undistracted. He was revising the introduction when Terri rushed through his door. "How's it going?" she asked hurriedly.

The question implied to Carlo that his work would be needed. "Close to final," he answered tersely. "Where's Dad?"

"He went home to check on Elena and Kit. I'm all the help you've got."

Carlo sat back. "How'd it go?"

"If you're going to ask who won, I don't know. But by seven o'clock, we will. The Court's promised to fax their opinion." She picked up a section of his brief, preparing to read it. "In the meanwhile, we can kill some time by working..."

Shortly after five o'clock, as Terri and Carlo revised the draft of their Supreme Court petition, Chris arrived.

"How are the kids?" Terri asked.

Chris unknotted his tie. "Kit's fine," he said tiredly. "Elena's not so fine but won't say why. My guess is that she disapproves of our afternoon activities. I'm wondering if you shouldn't go home and let Carlo and me finish up here."

Terri felt trapped between her duties as a mother and her responsibilities as a lawyer for a man who aroused such loathing in her daughter—both for his supposed crime and for the way it had consumed Terri's life. "I can't leave before seven," she answered. "And only if we've won."

Chris shook his head. "Climb down off the cross," he said gently. "Let me take your place for a while."

He looked tired, Terri realized, and she then thought of how he had been the night before, too fretful about his argument to sleep, a different man from the collected and self-assured advocate she had witnessed in court. "I like it up here," she answered. "Take your son to dinner. If you're back by seven, we can sort out what we have to do."

Bright and airy, the North Beach restaurant had begun filling up with families who, like Chris and Carlo, had come for generations to banter with the same waiters and eat an early dinner on a Sunday afternoon. Chris contemplated the chill martini which Manfred, their waiter, had known to bring without a word.

He savored a first sip and put it down again. "I'm

fried," he confessed to Carlo. "This job wears me out more than it used to. The price of getting older, I guess."

It was a rare admission, his son reflected, especially from this man who appeared to have aged little in the eighteen years since Carlo, at seven, had come to live with him. Then it struck Carlo that what burdened his father was the knowledge, born of hard experience, that failure meant not only the certain death of another human being but the quiet suffering of his own wife.

"Terri says you were magnificent," Carlo assured him dryly.

Chris did not smile. "I did all I could," he answered. "Maybe too much. If we lose, Rennell Price will die. But if we win because the Ninth Circuit bought the wrong argument, the Supreme Court may require that he die anyhow—just later rather than sooner. That may be what I did in arguing freestanding innocence.

"You'd think it a simple proposition: that even if Rennell Price's original trial was 'fair,' if new evidence proving him innocent emerges at **any** time before his execution, then he should go free. That's all 'freestanding innocence' means. But under the law, merely being innocent may not be enough."

Carlo took his first swallow of beer. "Tell me about it," he requested.

All of them—the lawyers, the media, the three judges of the Ninth Circuit, and Thuy Sen's family—

were assembled in the grandeur of Courtroom One, a lavish mélange of carved Corinthian columns, plaster cupids and flowers, and stained-glass windows filtering a golden light which augmented the intended sense of awe. In Terri's mind, this opulence, an expression of Gilded Age extravagance, was a curious setting in which to determine whether Rennell's life, the product of the most squalid and harrowing circumstances, would come to a premature end.

The three men who would decide his fate looked down from a burnished mahogany bench. In the middle presided Blair Montgomery, a small, white-haired man with a keen expression and sharp blue eyes, by turns wintry and amused. To his right sat Judge Sanders, whose excess weight lent his face and body a look as amorphous as his judicial philosophy, undefined by any clear principle save caution. Judge Viet Nhu was Sanders's opposite—an elfin man with salt and pepper hair and a slightly puckish expression.

Sitting at the prosecution table, Larry Pell and Janice Terrell had looked surprised when Chris, not Terri, advanced to the podium to argue for Rennell Price. Chris, dressed in a dark blue pin-striped suit made for him by a Savile Row tailor, effused a sense of entitlement and ease that one either had from childhood, or not at all.

"What the Attorney General is asking you to rule," Chris had told the panel, "is that guilt or innocence no longer counts. If you accept Mr. Pell's argument on waiver, or due diligence, or on Yancey James's conflict, you will **never** have to consider whether we're executing an innocent man." Chris's voice was tinged with disdain. "It's death by technicality, a heartless joke. And it's wrong. Killing the innocent is immoral, even when it's cloaked in legal niceties."

"Fine words," Nhu interrupted in arid tones. "But the purpose of AEDPA is to bring finality to proceedings such as these—which to Thuy Sen's family must seem infinite indeed."

Chris hesitated. Then, believing Viet Nhu a lost cause, he framed his answer as bluntly as Terri would have, hoping to engage Judge Sanders. "If AEDPA renders innocence irrelevant, then it violates at least two provisions of the Bill of Rights. 'Due process of law' does not permit us to execute a man for a crime which he did not commit. And there can be no more 'cruel and unusual punishment' than to execute Rennell Price for the perversion inflicted on Thuy Sen by Eddie Fleet."

The last, unvarnished sentence seemed to take Judge Sanders aback. "Isn't such a claim a matter for the Governor?" he asked. "If the evidence of someone's innocence is clear, then clemency provides a remedy."

Chris forced himself to answer softly and respectfully. "I'll pass over the state of politics which makes clemency so meaningless. The bottom line is this: the theoretical availability of clemency does not absolve this Court—or any court—of its duties. The

Constitution does not allow us to pass the buck for death."

"Mr. Paget's argument," Pell said with quiet scorn, "is a venture in fantasy unmoored from law. To allow a federal court to grant **habeas corpus** relief would in fact require a new trial, **not** because of any constitutional violation of the first trial but simply because of a belief that, based on newfound evidence, a jury might not find the defendant guilty at a second trial. However, it is far from clear that another jury would produce a more reliable determination of guilt or innocence, since the passage of time has only diminished the reliability of criminal convictions." Briefly glancing up at Montgomery, Pell pressed his point. "To quote Justice Fini, 'If the process is free of error, there is **no** constitutional argument, and the question of guilt or innocence is **not** before the Court.' "

"Yes," Montgomery said dryly, "we're aware of Justice Fini's views. I'm sure you're also aware of Justice Blackmun's: 'The execution of a person who can show that he is innocent comes perilously close to simple murder.' "

"But that's not this case," Pell countered promptly. "Payton Price's confession falls well short of establishing his brother's innocence. In **Burton v. Dormire,** the Eighth Circuit opinion addressed this situation in light of **Herrera.** A quotation from the Court's opinion makes it clear that AEDPA bars a claim of free-standing innocence: 'One cannot read the record without developing a nagging suspicion that the wrong man may have been convicted of capital murder in a Missouri courtroom. But Burton's claims of innocence run headlong into the thicket of impediments erected by courts and Congress.

" 'Burton's legal claims permit him no relief, even as the facts suggest he may well be innocent. We express the hope that the Governor can provide a forum in which to consider any such evidence.' "

Montgomery answered in withering tones. "Let's inject a note of realism into this rather theoretical argument. Since the reinstitution of capital punishment in 1978, when was the last time this Governor—or any governor of California—commuted a sentence of death?"

"That's not the question—"

"It's **my** question, Mr. Pell. Have the good grace to answer it."

Pell spread his hands. "I'm not aware of any commutations."

"That's because there haven't been any." Montgomery leaned forward. "Which is why **this** Court has in the past allowed us to consider evidence of innocence, in order to avert a 'fundamental miscarriage of justice.' Doesn't that fairly describe a case where you ask us to require the execution of a man who—by your own admission—would go free if we forced you to retry him?"

"No," Pell answered quietly. "It would spare this

Court a collision course with the Court whose precedent binds it, the Supreme Court of the United States. **That** Court commends the avenue of clemency. It is not the role of **this** Court to prejudge the result but to deny Mr. Price's petition, and direct his counsel to the Governor of California."

"Please respond," Judge Sanders requested, "to petitioner's argument that—absent a forum for freestanding claims of innocence—the death penalty itself violates the Constitution."

"It's nonsense," Pell retorted tersely. "A lifetime right to prove one's innocence is not guaranteed by the Constitution—"

"What about Mr. Paget's list of exonerations?" Sanders interrupted. "Shouldn't that at least induce some degree of disquiet?"

"To the contrary, Your Honor. The sheer number of exonerations proves that the system works."

Glancing at Judge Nhu, Pell gave a shrug of helplessness. "With all due respect," he said to Judge Montgomery, "there is no evidence whatsoever that **here,** in the State of California, we've ever executed an innocent man—"

"Has anyone ever tried to find out?" Montgomery asked. "Or have we literally buried our mistakes?"

Pell stiffened with resistance. "It takes all the resources we have, Your Honor, just to defend against petitions like this one. Which we do as honorably as we know how." His voice took on the weight of admonition. "The Supreme Court requires this Court to apply the law, not reconfigure it as it pleases. And what the law requires is clear: that Rennell Price's sentence of death be upheld."

Pensive, Chris finished his drink. "One purpose of making novel arguments is to encourage the Court to avoid deciding them. On its face, AEDPA doesn't allow Rennell to go free simply because he's innocent: if possible, we want to win under AEDPA, not outside it. The last thing we want to do is free Rennell by means of an argument which the United States Supreme Court thinks, however wrongheadedly, is another case of Ninth Circuit extremism."

Carlo's cell phone rang. Retrieving it from the pocket of his sport coat, he saw Terri's number flash across the screen. "Maybe the opinion's come in early," he said, quickly stabbing the call button to ask, "What's up?"

"Nothing." Terri's voice was tense but weary. "Montgomery's law clerk called—their new deadline is ten o'clock, and that's if we're lucky."

"Did he say why they're having trouble?" Carlo inquired.

"No. But take your time and meet me at home. I gave the Court our fax number."

Carlo hit the off button.

"What's happening?" Chris asked.

"A long, leisurely meal for us," Carlo answered. "Maybe some cognac. Seems like you've tied the Court in knots."

NINETEEN

BY A LITTLE PAST NINE O'CLOCK, CHRIS HAD FINISHED reading to Kit from the latest Lemony Snicket, and a temporarily amicable Elena had kissed Carlo on the cheek before proceeding upstairs. "I promised to do anything she wanted next Saturday afternoon," Terri explained to Chris as they encountered each other in the kitchen.

"And what will that be?"

"Getting our nails done. Lunch at Neiman Marcus—Elena loves the popovers. A movie, the newest teen horror film, something with a slasher. Believe it or not."

Imagining his wife soldiering through this teenage program of self-indulgence and frivolity, Chris began to laugh, mostly from relief that Terri might be allowed—at whatever cost—to assuage her guilt and make peace with Elena, however tentative and temporary, escaping for a moment the shadow of Eddie Fleet. "Mercifully, Carlo liked baseball."

"Oh," Terri continued imperturbably, "and we want your convertible. Sometimes Elena and I like to put the top down and drive around listening to CDs. Her CDs, of course. That way she can be with me without actually speaking to me—"

"Makes perfect sense," Carlo interjected, entering the room. "I always thought that Dad was best experienced as a presence."

This had been far less true of Carlo, Terri knew, than of Elena. As she often did, Terri envied Chris the generally unruffled amiability of his relationship with Carlo, a painful contrast to the tension she felt with Elena, the worry and rejection inflicted by her daughter's silences and ever-shifting moods, her hatred of Terri's work, the mercurial anger which Elena could not, or would not, discuss, the fresh wounds symbolized by the security video screen in her room. With quiet determination, Terri told Chris and Carlo, "I can't screw up our plans. Whatever happens, you two will have to cover for me. Unless there's an execution."

Chris studied her. "Even then, Terri."

"No, not then," she answered and went upstairs to Elena's room.

Checking the wall clock, Chris saw that it was almost nine-thirty. "I wonder what's holding them up," he said.

"Maybe freestanding innocence," Chris speculated. "Maybe other issues. The last moments of argument—mine and Pell's—left even Viet Nhu looking troubled."

Steeling himself, Chris had said with quiet composure, "There is, Your Honors, a final question: Does the law provide a rational standard under which Rennell Price—as opposed to all the other defendants who may be charged with a capital crime—can be executed by the State of California?"

Judge Nhu regarded Chris with a quizzical smile. "Are you suggesting, Mr. Paget, that the thirty years spent crafting California's death penalty statute have been a waste of time?"

"Worse than that, Your Honor. I'm suggesting that they've created a delusion: that Rennell Price's sentence of death is any more rational than those which the United States Supreme Court previously described as 'cruel and unusual in the same way that being struck by lightning is cruel and unusual.' "

"But hasn't the Supreme Court since provided standards under which the death penalty may fairly be imposed?"

"General standards." Chris glanced at his notes. "Principally, that the death-eligible class of murderers must be narrow enough to ensure that a substantial percentage of them are actually sentenced to death. As the data in our brief reveals, only ten percent of death-eligible defendants in California actually receive a sentence of death. Truly, Rennell Price has been struck by lightning."

Nhu cocked his head. "And you blame this lamentably meager yield on the legislature of this great state."

"And the voters." Chris returned to his notes. "California now has the broadest death penalty statute in the country. Close to ninety percent of all defendants charged with first degree murder are death-eligible, yet only one in ten are sentenced to death.

"Who are these unlucky folks? Thirty-four percent are black. Another nineteen percent are Hispanic. And the average IQ of California's death row population is roughly eighty-five—"

"In other words," Viet Nhu observed with wisp of a smile, "the only way for California's death penalty regime to be valid under current law would be to expressly confine its application to minorities of substandard intelligence. Which, of course, might create certain other constitutional problems."

Bemused, Chris could only nod. "You just summarized my argument, Your Honor. The lightning which struck Rennell Price is not, after all, an accident. It sought him out for who he is. Therefore, **this** Court must strike down **this** statute."

"What do you say," Nhu asked Pell, "to Mr. Paget's argument that the only consistency in California's death penalty regime is that it targets the disadvantaged?" Pausing, he added pointedly, "African Americans, for example. At least those like Mr. Price."

This tacit reference to Pell's own ethnicity seemed

to stun him into silence. "The short answer," he said after a moment, "is that the Court should not entertain this contention at all. In a second **habeas corpus** petition, Mr. Price is confined to challenging his individual guilt—"

"Skip AEDPA, Mr. Pell. I was looking for a substantive response."

Pell shook his head. "Mr. Paget's argument is entirely novel—"

"Novel," Nhu interrupted yet again, "may mean 'newly discovered.' I've never seen these statistics before. Doesn't that take this case outside the scope of AEDPA?"

"Even without AEDPA," Pell said in a strained voice, "in **Teague v. Lane,** the Supreme Court held that a decision announcing a new rule of constitutional law does not apply to **habeas corpus** petitioners, like Rennell Price, unless the decision says it does. The imaginary rule proposed by Mr. Paget—that California's entire death penalty statute is unconstitutional—doesn't even exist."

"So you refuse to satisfy my curiosity. On procedural grounds."

"On principle," Pell rejoined. "If Mr. Paget wishes to invalidate our entire death penalty statute, he'll have to find a newer case. Rennell Price's time has passed."

Judge Nhu contemplated Pell with a smile which did not convey amusement. "Perhaps," he said.

"So what was Nhu up to?" Carlo asked his father now. Chris looked at his watch and saw that its face read ten-fifteen. "I can't figure Nhu at all," he answered. "I don't even want to win on that argument—not with the U.S. Supreme Court waiting for us. It would throw our entire death penalty statute on the scrap heap."

"Maybe Nhu believes it should be. He's nothing if not rigorous—"

"Come on up," Terri called from the staircase. "Our fax machine just rang."

TWENTY

WITH AGONIZING SLOWNESS, THE FIRST PAGE OF THE
Ninth Circuit ruling slid from the fax machine in the
Pagets' upstairs library. Terri snatched it, summarizing
as Chris and Carlo peered over her shoulder.

"Sanders wrote the opinion," she noted.

Carlo felt a spurt of anxiety and hope. "At least it's
not Judge Nhu."

"The first issue is retardation," Terri announced,
then shook her head, unable to speak.

Taking the page from her hand, Chris started reading aloud: "Neither the legislature of California,
nor its courts, has enumerated any standards for determining whether Mr. Price is mentally retarded. Under
these circumstances, the cursory treatment accorded
this issue by the California Supreme Court is due little
deference from this Court . . ."

"All right," Carlo murmured.

Chris continued reading. "Nor, in this case of first
impression, was Judge Bond correct in finding that
Mr. Price failed to establish his retardation. Under the

appropriate standard—'preponderance of the evidence'—he has done so . . ."

Terri sat down, covering her face. "If this ruling holds up," she told Carlo, "at least Rennell's going to live."

Another sheet slipped into the fax tray. "They're on to innocence," Chris said.

Terri listened to her husband read. "As a preliminary matter, we decline to speculate on what effective counsel might have done to defend Rennell Price, when it is so painfully clear that Mr. James, effectively, did nothing . . ."

"That's the first step under AEDPA," Carlo said quietly.

"Nor can we find a knowing waiver of Mr. James's conflict of interest. There is no sign on the record that Rennell Price comprehended the complex issue to which he gave a rote response . . ."

The words brought Terri to her feet.

"As for the question of due diligence," Chris read, "Payton Price's delay in speaking out cannot be blamed on prior counsel." Taking the next page, he placed a hand on Terri's shoulder. "They're going to consider our evidence of innocence," he told her.

Mute, Terri stared at the paper in his hand.

"Keep reading," Carlo urged his father.

Chris started again. "The standard of proof was previously established by this Court: whether it is more likely than not that no reasonable juror would have found petitioner guilty beyond a reasonable doubt.

This does not require absolute proof of innocence but simply that there is sufficient evidence of innocence that this Court cannot have confidence in the outcome of the trial..."

Carlo's flesh tingled. "I think we're going to win," he murmured, then felt a superstitious fear that he had said too much.

"Under AEDPA," Chris continued quoting, "Mr. Price has satisfied the predicates which allow this Court to consider his claim of innocence. But even had he failed, the Constitution must allow him to prove—if he can—that he is, more likely than not, innocent of capital murder in the death of Thuy Sen—"

Chris stopped abruptly, reading to himself. Carlo could see his father's misgivings in the narrowing of his eyes.

"Go on," Terri urged her husband.

Chris hesitated, then began again. "By this, we mean innocent under the law, not innocent beyond a reasonable doubt."

"Yes," Carlo said.

Chris put his arm around Terri's shoulder, drawing her close. "In this case," he read to her, "Payton Price's accusation of Eddie Fleet stands unrefuted by Fleet himself. Not only was Fleet unwilling to repeat his allegations but the State was unwilling to compel his testimony through a grant of use immunity.

"Thus the only evidence of Rennell's complicity is the testimony of Flora Lewis, now deceased. In light of

Payton's statement, this testimony, in itself, cannot sustain the conclusion that Rennell Price is guilty. Indeed, by conceding that it would not choose to try this case on the current record, the State admits as much."

Carlo emitted a whoop of joy. "Nonetheless," his father continued reading, "we allow the State one month to determine whether to retry Mr. Price for the death of Thuy Sen or to allow him to go free."

Abruptly, Chris fell silent.

Terri could not speak.

"You won," Chris told her gently. But Carlo could read his fear—that by approving a freestanding innocence claim, the Court might provoke the United States Supreme Court to review the case.

Terri mustered a smile. "**We** won," she corrected her husband. "For now, that's enough."

Terri sat across from Laurence Pell in the bright but crowded Hayes Street Grill. Picking at his garden salad, Pell said with the slightest suggestion of a smile, "I guess you want me to kick him loose."

Terri marshaled her thoughts. "You really can't retry him, Larry. You can afford to let one go. Do you honestly think he's some sort of pedophile?"

"You know that's not the point." Pell placed a curled finger to his chin. "Here's the problem," he said evenly. "It's not Rennell. It's not even Fleet. It's this: not only did the Ninth Circuit treat the California

Supreme Court like **it** was retarded but they bought your freestanding innocence claim."

Terri felt her spirits sag. "That's only an alternative ruling. The opinion as to innocence also rests on AEDPA."

"The opinion," Pell countered, "is out there. If I don't take this case up to the Supreme Court, in how many other cases will it come back and bite me?"

"A while ago," Terri said softly, "you asked me if I'd ever seen an execution. Now I have. You still haven't. So let me ask you this—would you watch the execution of Rennell Price, knowing that otherwise you'd have let him go free?

"This case is about one man who's suffered way too much already. Please, don't sacrifice him to the system. Let Rennell go."

Pell considered her across the table. "No one can fault your effort," he said at last. "I'll kick it around the office. We don't need to decide today."

It seemed a lifetime, Terri thought, since she first had faced Rennell in this same plastic cubicle.

"You mean they're not gonna kill me," he managed to say, "like Payton?"

Terri searched for the proper answer. "We won, for now. The Court stopped your execution."

Rennell struggled to comprehend this. "I can just walk out of here, go back to Grandma's house?"

She has no house, Terri thought, **and there is no Grandma.** "There's one more court the State can go to," she said. "I'm hoping they choose not to—if they do, it may take months. But unless the United States Supreme Court rules against us, you'll be free."

"Free," Rennell repeated softly. "Free."

"Yes."

His smile combined incredulity with fear. "What I do then?" he asked. "Been here so long I don't know free no more. Don't know how that be without my brother."

"I know. But you've got me now."

Rennell averted his eyes, and for a fleeting moment, Terri envisioned him as a bashful child—or, perhaps, a fearful one. "Maybe I could live with you . . ."

Sometimes lawyers did this, Terri knew, to bridge a client's transition. But **she** was Elena's mother. "We'll figure it out," she temporized. "We thought you could help us at our office. Keep things neat, like you do in your cell."

"Mean I'd sleep there, too?"

Terri hesitated. "There are lots of places." She stopped herself: even a halfway house for the retarded might shy away from a man once convicted, however wrongly, of a sex crime with a child. "Not to live, I mean. Just to help you figure out the world again. There are churches, too. People care about what happens to you. I know a minister in San Francisco who may want you to live there."

The words she could not say, that Elena could never

live with him, shadowed her response. Taking his hand, Terri promised, "I'll always be there, Rennell. I'll make sure you're fine."

On the Monday after Terri's outing with Elena, the State of California petitioned the United States Supreme Court to review the case of Rennell Price.

PART FOUR

THE HIGH COURT

ONE

LATE MONDAY AFTERNOON, CHRIS, TERRI, AND CARLO met around the conference table. "No surprises here," Chris said, then began reading aloud from the Attorney General's petition to the Supreme Court. "This decision resonates far beyond the particulars of the case against Rennell Price. It is a comprehensive usurpation by two Ninth Circuit judges of the role of Congress, of the Supreme Court of California, and by extension, of the United States District Court. It conflicts with the decisions of other circuit courts. And it arrogates to these two judges the proper role of **this** Court to determine the rights available to **habeas corpus** petitioners far beyond Mr. Price."

"Yeah," Carlo remarked to Terri, "it also undermines the war on terror, promotes the teaching of evolution, and opens the floodgates to gay marriage."

Terri did not smile. "Pell is doing what he has to do—make the decision bigger than Rennell. The Supreme Court will take only cases which affect the law as a whole, and he has to persuade four justices that this is one of them."

534 / RICHARD NORTH PATTERSON

Carlo considered this. "What's been so weird is
watching Rennell become an afterthought. This isn't
about him anymore."

"No," Terri concurred softly. "It's about all the sand
we're throwing into the machinery of death." To Chris,
she said, "What's Pell's argument on freestanding innocence?"

Frowning, Chris flipped the bound pages. "This
captures the essence," he told her. "Based on the last-
minute confession of a death row inmate—an all-too-
common event—Judges Montgomery and Sanders
have abrogated Congress's carefully crafted effort to
ensure that, after thorough consideration of a prisoner's constitutional rights, a sentence of death is carried out. The result is a legal mutation: an invitation to
serial **habeas corpus** petitions, wherein piecemeal
'new' evidence of innocence is conjured by desperate
prisoners and inventive lawyers, and courts are forced
to entertain them one by one. If this opinion stands,
the fifteen years so far consumed by Rennell Price is
only the beginning, and this decision the beginning of
the end of capital punishment as we know it." Chris
looked up. "**That** would be a shame."

Terri slowly shook her head. "I can never say you
didn't warn me."

"Let it go," Chris answered quietly. "Rennell was
forty-eight hours from execution. We had to argue
everything we could."

Carlo looked from his father to Terri. "And we've
kept Rennell alive. All we need to do now is persuade

the Supreme Court not to take the case. I mean, they only grant about one percent of these petitions, right?"

"That doesn't mean much here," Terri told him. "Pell has packaged this as Armageddon, creating an absolute necessity for the Supreme Court to save AEDPA, slap down the Ninth Circuit, and pillory Blair Montgomery." Turning to Chris, she asked, "How many times does Pell mention Montgomery's name?"

Chris smiled faintly. "I lost count."

Carlo stood, stretching his arms over his head. "Can't we cross-petition on the issues we lost? Maybe the Court will look at the whole mess and decide they don't want to consider whether the entire capital punishment system is all screwed up."

"Bad idea," Terri said flatly. "We want to make this case sound ordinary, and Pell sound like he's hyperventilating. Having to defend the ruling on freestanding innocence will be hard enough."

"Terri's right," Chris concurred. "As I read the Supreme Court, Pell has got three likely votes already—Justices Fini, Kelly, and Ware. Rothbard, Huddleston, and the Chief Justice are probably inclined toward us. We have to pitch this case to the cautious middle: Raymond, Millar, and, especially, Justice Glynn—"

"All Pell needs is one more vote," Terri interjected, "and the Supreme Court will take the case. **Two** votes, and the Court can summarily reverse the Ninth Circuit—without even giving us a hearing. Our best hope is to persuade Glynn, Raymond, and Millar that this case is just about one prisoner, Rennell Price, and nothing to get excited over."

"In other words," Chris said dryly, "that the machinery of death will grind on as before. Just without Rennell."

Hearing the identity of his caller, Charles Monk chuckled softly.

"Congratulations, counselor. Been reading where you saved that poor innocent we persecuted. Must be on top of the world."

"High on life," Terri said pleasantly. "As it were. Are you really feeling all that aggrieved?"

"Oh, I'll live, too. I'm more sorry for that girl's family. No end to this for them."

"And killing Rennell would be an end?"

"For some families it is, of a kind. You never know before they execute the guy. Or in this case, the **last** guy." Monk's voice softened. "But you didn't call me to gloat, or argue capital punishment. You want something."

"Other than Eddie Fleet?" Terri answered in a pointed tone. "Betty Sims. I was wondering if you'd found her yet."

Monk laughed again. "Guess you think you haven't got the degree of innocence some judges may be looking for. Pell told me he's taking this all the way to the U.S. Supremes."

"Yeah," Terri said sardonically. "It's an outrage, what those two judges did. Pell still thinks there's at least a chance Rennell might actually be guilty, which is more than enough for him. What about you?"

"Me? I'm sitting here looking at some crime scene pictures—double murder of a mom and kid in the Mission District, domestic probably. Killed with a knife. A whole lot nastier than lethal injection, though at least it came as a surprise to the folks in these photographs." Monk paused a moment. "About Betty Sims, she's nowhere in the Bayview. I don't have much time these days, and my guess is she's long gone from San Francisco. But I'll poke around a little more."

"Thanks," Terri said, her voice revealing more relief than she wished. "Guess you're more curious than Larry."

"Maybe about Fleet," Monk answered. "You know how cops are. Never a **good** reason to hide behind the Fifth Amendment."

With this remark—perhaps, Terri thought, a tacit jibe at Larry Pell—Monk got off.

"Betty Sims?" Johnny Moore asked Terri. "Still can't find her. In fact, I've still got nothing concrete that says Eddie Fleet likes little girls."

"Well, he does," Terri snapped. "Take it from **this** girl."

"I'm turning over every rock I can find," Moore answered patiently. "But a lot of bad things happen to kids no one ever knows about—at least until it's too late."

Terri stood. "We may need this, Johnny. I don't want it to be 'too late' for Rennell." She paused, speaking in a lower voice. "Or for Elena."

There was a long silence. "I understand." Moore's tone was sober and measured. "Anything else?"

"Yeah. Tasha Bramwell."

Moore hesitated. "Sure you **want** me to find her?"

Surprised, Terri realized that, in her anxiety, the question had not occurred to her. "Why not? It seems to me she's a missing piece."

"But if she knew Rennell was innocent, wouldn't she have said so? Instead she lied—which we've always assumed she did for Payton. What if Tasha knows something about Rennell that you don't want to know?"

"Then I guess I'll have to live with it," Terri answered.

TWO

On a December morning when a cascade of moist snowflakes stuck to the ground and crippled much of Washington, Callista Hill arrived at the Supreme Court shortly after seven o'clock. By now, three months into her year of clerkship, Callista barely noticed her surroundings. But when she had first begun they'd stirred a sense of awe: four floors of marble, linked by spiral staircases, and lined with statuary and busts of the Chief Justices. This grandeur obscured what Callista had come to think of as a hermetically sealed environment, housing its own cafeteria, gym, library, wood shop, police force, barbershop, seamstress, print shop, curator, and of course, in-house law office. From the beginning of a workday until its end, perhaps fourteen hours later, Callista rarely ventured outside, nor did the others—including the justices—who labored here.

The rhythms of that work were unvarying. For seven two-week sessions each term—the first in October, the last in April—the Court sat for argument in the cases it deigned to hear. During each week of oral argument, the justices met in conference twice—on Wednesday after hearing oral argument, to debate and vote on the cases argued on the preceding Monday; and on Friday, to resolve the cases presented on Tuesday and Wednesday. But the periods between these sessions were equally intense: this was when the justices and their clerks drafted and polished the opinions which, for better or worse, defined the law for the nearly three hundred million Americans outside this building.

Much of Callista's day was spent coping with—or generating—a tsunami of paper: advising the Chief Justice on emergency applications for relief, often requests for stays of execution; writing bench memos to prepare the Chief to hear oral argument; drafting majority opinions, dissents, or concurrences; or commenting on the drafts of majority opinions, dissents, and concurrences circulated by the other justices—each with his or her own philosophy, style, and mode of working with clerks. Caroline Masters insisted that her four clerks be prepared to challenge her thinking and defend their own, which meant that Callista's work life, while stimulating, was even more demanding than that of clerks for some of the other justices. But there was one aspect of the Court's work so overwhelming that it mandated a pooling of resources among the nine chambers of the justices—the flood of petitions for **certiorari** in civil and criminal cases, roughly one hundred fifty every week, through which litigants defeated in the courts below pled with the High Court to hear them.

Every week, the clerks' office would roll a wooden cart groaning with cert petitions into Callista's office. Her job was to administer what insiders called the "cert pool": the division of these petitions among the chambers by rotation, wherein a law clerk for one of the justices would draft, and then circulate, a recommendation to grant or deny a given petition. In theory these recommendations were based on common criteria: whether the petition presented an issue of broad national importance; or a process which departed in some dramatic way from the commonly accepted operation of law; or was based on a decision which conflicted with the decision of the State Supreme Court, or another federal circuit, or—most remarkably—the United States Supreme Court itself. These criteria eliminated all but a relative handful: the average petition, Callista sometimes thought, had the life expectancy of a sperm. But the recommendations in the toughest cases were, inevitably, colored by the views of the justice, and the law clerk, who drafted it. Which was the reason for another of Callista's tasks—reviewing the recommendations of other chambers with a gimlet eye.

By now, Callista understood very well the ideological fissures which made Caroline Masters desirous of such scrutiny. In league with those of two other justices, the somewhat severe Miriam Rothbard and the venerable Walter Huddleston, Caroline's philosophy was moderate to liberal; their ideological opposites, led by Anthony Fini, the engaging and combative heir to

Roger Bannon, reliably included Justices Bryson Kelly, a choleric former Attorney General, and John Ware, a black archconservative whose contentious nomination hearings had made him wounded and reclusive. The Court's fulcrum was the centrists: Justices Thomas Raymond, Dennis Millar, and most important, McGeorge Glynn, who particularly relished the leverage the Court's schism accorded him. This complex dynamic— wherein the Chief Justice and Justice Fini mingled vigilance with a surface cordiality as they angled for votes in the middle—affected not only the few cases which the Court determined to hear but the many it did not. All of these dynamics made Callista's work with the cert pool both onerous and exacting, and never more so— given the justices' fraught emotions on the subject— than when the stakes presented were the life or death of a human being.

Shortly before ten, Callista turned with little relish to the contents of the wooden cart.

After a half hour mechanically winnowing the petitions into stacks, one for each of the nine chambers, the caption of the next petition caught her eye. Immediately she realized why—roughly six weeks before, she had reviewed the papers relating to a death row inmate, Rennell Price. To Callista's relief, the Ninth Circuit had granted Price's **habeas corpus** petition, terminating her work on a prospective recommendation which, had Price lost, would have plunged Caroline Masters into the vexing task of inducing four other justices to stay his execution. Instead, like a card dealt from the bottom of the deck, the State of California's petition for **certiorari**—challenging the Ninth Circuit's ruling—sat atop the stack destined for one of the Chief Justice's four law clerks.

This stack, too, was dispersed among the clerks by rotation—on each petition in turn, Callista would scribble her own initials or those of a fellow clerk. The petition in the Price case was destined for Brian Eng—among Caroline's clerks, the sole enthusiast for the death penalty.

Pouring herself more coffee, Callista pondered this complication.

She had retained her file in the Price case—the original papers, the relevant cases and statutes, and the beginnings of her draft recommendation to Caroline Masters. She could simply pass the file on to Brian. But getting up to speed would take Brian twice as long; writing the memo herself would, at least for this week, make the burden of the cert pool a couple of hours lighter. And also, Callista rationalized, she, not Brian, best understood the Chief Justice's thinking on the thorny matter of capital punishment.

Scrawling her initials on one corner of the petition, Callista reshuffled the stack.

It was past seven o'clock at night before Callista, fortified by a cheeseburger she had gobbled in the cafeteria, went to the library.

The vast room still inspired almost as much awe in

Callista as the courtroom itself—above her, three enormous brass chandeliers hung from thirty-foot ceilings filigreed with multicolored marble and plaster. She chose an empty table, relishing the silence of a Renaissance cathedral, and began her work on the matter of Rennell Price.

In due course, the memo she was about to write would, with Caroline Masters's approval, circulate to the other justices' chambers for discussion between each justice and his clerks. A memo in a capital case would receive special scrutiny—a series of abrasive and close decisions, with bruising dissents, had left both wings of the Court raw and angry beneath its surface politesse. But the Supreme Court did not grant petitions for the purpose of settling scores, or even correcting legal error: the issue to be addressed by Callista's memo was whether this case presented unresolved questions of constitutional law which resonated far beyond the fate of Rennell Price.

The authors of the State's petition and Price's response, Callista saw, understood this well—depending on whose argument she accepted, the opinion of the two Ninth Circuit judges was either a massive affront to AEDPA or the routine parsing of facts specific to Rennell Price. This divide was complicated by another factor, which made Callista's task harder: the vehemence of Judge Nhu's dissent—a virtual open letter to Justices Fini, Kelly, and Ware—whose weight Callista could not ignore.

But Janie Hill's daughter was not a fool, and neither

were Rennell Price's lawyers. They had given her much to work with—which was precisely what Callista intended to do.

At a little after ten on the East Coast, when Callista went home, but three hours earlier in San Francisco, the Paget family, including Carlo, gathered around their candlelit dining room table.

The conversation was unexceptional—a review of Elena's and Kit's days; a discussion among the three older Pagets of whom they preferred for President—until Elena asked her mother abruptly, "Whatever happened to that man, the one you kept alive?"

Beneath her daughter's cool phrasing, Terri heard a marked disapproval. "He's right where he was," she answered calmly. "On death row. We're waiting to hear if the Supreme Court wants to take the case. We hope they don't."

Elena's expressive eyes lit with challenge. "What would happen then?"

"He goes free."

Elena folded her arms. "Because of **you.** They'll just let him out there again, to do to people whatever he wants to do."

Terri hesitated, reluctant to answer.

"Or," Carlo interjected gently, "to have people do to him whatever **they** want to."

Gratefully, Terri realized that Carlo was placing his credibility, sometimes greater than Terri's own, in the service of her relationship with Elena and, perhaps, with her seven-year-old son. She watched Kit's eyes flicker from Elena to Carlo.

"Rennell Price," Carlo told his stepsister, "is retarded, passive, and pretty close to helpless. For his entire life, he depended on a brother who's been executed. For the last fifteen years, he's been on death row. Whatever limited coping skills he had have eroded, and the only other place he's ever known is Bayview and the drug culture.

"Even though we're confident he's innocent, Rennell is a marked man. The cops may be after him. So may a lot of pretty tough guys. If Rennell ends up in the Bayview, he'll be dead in a year. Probably sooner."

The matter-of-factness in Carlo's tone, Terri perceived, combined with treating her as an adult to keep Elena from snapping back. "So where's he going to live?" she asked, and then Terri saw a sudden jolt of fear and suspicion turn Elena's widening eyes back to her. "Not **here.**"

"No," Terri said quietly. "Not here. But he's going to be working at our law firm."

Elena shook her head in disbelief, tears welling in her eyes. "Then I'm never coming there again," she said. Standing abruptly, she threw down her napkin and bolted from the room.

"Come on," Carlo said to a worried-looking Kit. "You and I can hide together." Scooping up his brother, Carlo took him upstairs.

Terri remained with Chris. "I don't know how I can

ever dig myself out of this," she said at last. "And the worst part is that Elena's right—only about the wrong man. Eddie Fleet's still out there, and there's nobody to stop him. So Elena blames me for doing what Larry Pell is doing—making the world less safe."

"Maybe **I** should try to talk to her," Chris ventured.

Terri shook her head. "Leave it be, for now. I don't want Elena to feel our entire family is coming down on her."

Silent, Chris took her hand. "All these months," she murmured, "working so hard to save his life, then get him out. We're so close now—if the Supreme Court turns Pell down, we've won. And then Rennell, and all the rest of us, will have to live with it. Especially Elena."

THREE

FOR ADAM WENDT, CLERKING FOR JUSTICE ANTHONY Fini was more than an ideological calling—to spend time in Fini's presence was intoxicating, particularly when the justice, as he did so often, made Adam feel like a partner in reshaping the law into what the bold and unsentimental knew it should be, an instrument of clarity and order.

"Come on in," Fini called out, waving Adam to a chair.

As ever, Fini bubbled with life, his brown eyes illuminating a plump and amiable face. Even at his highest level of dudgeon, which could be considerable, some part of Tony Fini seemed always to enjoy himself. And unlike the quarters of some other justices, tending toward the monastic, Fini's inner sanctum was a testament to his numerous enthusiasms—a trophy commemorating a hole in one at a country club near Bar Harbor, site of his summer home; a wooden model of Fini's classic sailboat; an autographed baseball card of Babe Ruth, the archetypal player from Fini's beloved Yankees; a photograph of Fini with Chief Justice Roger Bannon, wryly inscribed "to my friend and fellow guardian of the law." It had been Fini's dearest wish to succeed Bannon as Chief, and but for the narrow election of the Democratic president Kerry Kilcannon, patron of Caroline Masters, Adam was certain that he, not the brash and sharp-tongued Callista Hill, would be the favored clerk of a Chief Justice. But Tony Fini was undaunted by this setback. "What's the most important rule of constitutional law?" Fini had once inquired of Adam.

Stumped, Adam could only shrug. "I'm not sure."

Fini had grinned. "Whatever five justices say it is." And, with this, Adam understood Fini's perspective on the Court: Caroline Masters might be Chief Justice, but whoever commanded a majority was king.

"So," Fini said dryly, "I take it some anomaly has bubbled up from the cert pool."

Adam nodded. "A Ninth Circuit anomaly," he answered. "Reversing a death sentence in the sexual molestation and murder of a nine-year-old girl, fifteen years after the fact. Among other things, the Court seems to recognize a claim of freestanding innocence on a second **habeas corpus** petition."

Fini cocked his head. "Who was on the panel?"

"They split two to one. Judges Sanders wrote the opinion, with Judge Montgomery concurring."

At the latter name, Justice Fini raised his eyebrows: in Fini's chamber, there was special scrutiny of the Ninth Circuit, the Chief Justice's former Court, especially when her mentor, Blair Montgomery, was on the panel. "Who dissented?"

"Judge Nhu."

"Montgomery versus Nhu," Fini said with a smile. "Two scorpions in a bottle." Adam heard the fondness in his voice: Viet Nhu had been Fini's clerk during his first year on the Court, and it was Fini's not-so-secret hope that, should a Republican retake the White House, Nhu would become his colleague.

"I copied the opinion," Adam said, handing it across the justice's desk. "Including the dissent."

Putting on his reading glasses, Fini scanned the pages. "From the looks of this," he said at length, "our venturesome friends in San Francisco are working some interesting variations on AEDPA. Who wrote the cert pool memo?"

Adam straightened his bow tie. "One of the Chief Justice's clerks. She tries to make the case sound humdrum, a waste of time."

"But you don't think it is."

"I think she slighted the State's petition, Mr. Justice. At the very least, there's a clear conflict on freestanding innocence between the Ninth Circuit and the Eighth Circuit in a case called **Burton v. Dormire.** That's a pretty important issue."

"Very important, I'd say."

Adam felt a spark of excitement, a tingling at the back of his neck. The keenness of Fini's combative instincts, though frequently aroused, sometimes held the added promise of pitched battle and, most gratifying of all, of some new landmark in the law on which his clerk's fingerprints, however faint, might appear.

"What would you like me to do?" Adam inquired.

"My homework. Dig into every question, Adam. Then, if you feel it's justified, prepare a thorough countermemo arguing for a grant of the State's petition." Fini tossed back the opinion in his hand. "Looks like Viet Nhu's dissent should give you a head start."

"Right away," Adam promised.

Unsmiling, Caroline Masters looked up from her work. While generally polite, she was not always gracious about interruptions, and this was such a day. "What is it?" she asked curtly.

Though undaunted, Callista decided not to sit. "I'm afraid I've attracted a Fini-gram."

"Indeed?" With a sigh at this allusion to Fini's oft-bombastic e-mails, Caroline leaned back in her chair. "Concerning what peril to our nation's jurisprudence?"

"The **Price** case, another Ninth Circuit reversal of a death sentence. I gave you the memo a few days ago."

"I remember it." Frowning, Caroline became still, a reflective figure framed by the only personal mementos on her credenza—a photograph of her daughter, Brett, another taken with President Kilcannon in the Rose Garden on the day of her surprising nomination. "The freestanding innocence question **is** a bit dicey," the Chief allowed. "I'd prefer the Court not grapple with it now. Is Justice Fini's communiqué in the nature of a polemic, or does it come with a concrete plan of action?"

"It comes with a countermemo." Written, Callista did not add, by a bow-tied and overprivileged little reactionary from Virginia Law School, quite possibly America's whitest male. "Justice Fini wants you to put the **Price** case on the discuss list."

Though Caroline smiled resignedly, Callista could imagine her perplexity. The Chief Justice's "discuss list," circulated before each conference among the justices, specified the petitions she deemed worthy of consideration. While the vast majority of petitions never made the list—and, therefore, were dead—any associate justice could request that a petition be added to the list. When that justice was Anthony Fini, what followed was often contentious: not only did Fini give no quarter but he was that rarest of justices on a decorous Court, a vigorous lobbyist for his positions. And never more so than in opposing strictures on the death penalty, for which he was an unabashed proponent— Rennell Price, whoever he was, had become less a person than a potential milestone in the law.

After a moment, Caroline Masters stirred herself from thought. "Prepare another memo," she directed briskly. "Hit all the issues raised by Justice Fini, and all the reasons not to take this case. I don't think it would be in the interest of the law or, in candor, this Court."

"How so?"

The Chief Justice considered her, then offered a rare elaboration of her thoughts. "Capital punishment," she answered, "distorts the law, imports the corruptions of politics into whether a prisoner lives or dies, and corrodes relations among the justices. Eventually, death penalty cases present so many fundamental questions that they can color one justice's view of another as a human being. I don't want that to happen to my colleagues."

Or to me, Callista could sense the Chief thinking. Caroline Masters was no doubt aware of the subterranean bitterness swirling among the justices—the rumor, for example, that after the latest approval of an execution in Mississippi, Justice Fini had referred to the Chief Justice's dissenting ally Justice Huddleston as a "hand-wringing mediocrity," and that the venerable Huddleston had labeled Fini "the only justice in memory who'd have deferred to the commandant of Auschwitz." The Chief Justice surely did not want another death row inmate to put her Court, or these emotions, in play.

"Do you want me to circulate my memo?" Callista asked.

"Only after I read it," Caroline Masters answered. "With all respect, Callista, I might want to take a hand in this myself."

F O U R

Two Fridays later, the nine justices of the United States Supreme Court gathered in the Chief Justice's conference room.

To Caroline Masters, the room combined the clubby aura of an inner sanctum with a distinct sense of history—wood paneling, a fireplace, a rich red carpet, oil portraits of Chief Justices Marshall and Jay in scarlet robes, shelves filled with books preserving the Court's prior rulings. At other such conferences, the Court had unanimously voted to bar segregation in **Brown v. Board of Education** and, two decades later, divided bitterly over **Roe v. Wade.** The two rulings, so different in conception and consequence, were ever on Caroline's mind; if she could manage to build consensus—and this task was not easy—this Court would not exacerbate the acrid cultural and social schisms which existed in contemporary America, and which made the ongoing battle over federal judicial nominations as incendiary as had been her own.

Certainly, the timeless rituals of these conferences

were crafted to preserve decorum. Each began with the justices shaking hands before they sat at a long table inlaid with green leather and illuminated by a crystal chandelier. Their places, too, were preordained: Caroline sat at one end of the table in a leather chair bearing a brass nameplate which said simply "The Chief Justice"; the opposite end was reserved for the senior associate justice, Walter Huddleston. The next most senior justices—Anthony Fini, McGeorge Glynn, Thomas Raymond—sat to Caroline's right, while the four who were most junior—John Ware, Bryson Kelly, Miriam Rothbard, and Dennis Millar—faced them across the table. The Court's newest member, Justice Millar, was stationed nearest the door, so as to pass messages or requests for additional documents to the messenger waiting outside. On the surface, Caroline thought dryly, everyone knew his place.

But the far less neutral way in which they defined their places made Caroline edgy. In the most contentious cases she, Huddleston, and Rothbard battled with Fini, Kelly, and Ware for the votes of the centrists—Glynn, Raymond, and Millar. So that today, when Justice Fini grinned and shook her hand, she thought of former Justice Byrnes's remark that the handshake reminded him of the referee's instructions before a prize fight: "Shake hands, go to your corner, and come out fighting."

Still, as the conference wended its way through the discuss list, their exchanges remained sufficiently muted that Caroline dared to hope contention might take a holiday. When they arrived at the **Price** case, she said with deceptive ease, "This one's yours, Tony."

Immediately she sensed a heightened alertness among the others, underscored by Justice Huddleston's quizzical frown toward his nemesis, Anthony Fini: challenges to a memo from the cert pool were unusual, and the sharpness of Fini's language, an incitement to controversy, was matched by the lawyerly thoroughness of Caroline's response. And if Fini carried Kelly and Ware—a near certainty—all he needed for the Court to grant the State of California's petition was the vote of a single centrist.

"To begin with," Fini said crisply, "this case involves a horrendous crime—"

"They're all horrendous," Huddleston murmured with a rumble of disdain.

Fini paused, to signal his annoyance, then continued as though Huddleston had not spoken. "—in a case which, to me, is wrongly decided and bristles with contempt for AEDPA. Not to mention whole paragraphs of result-oriented jurisprudence contrived by its progenitors, Judges Sanders **and** Montgomery."

You just can't resist going after Montgomery, Caroline thought.

"Among the more glaring problems," Justice Fini continued, "the majority concludes that the **Atkins** bar on executing the supposedly retarded applies retroactively to **habeas corpus** petitioners like Price; that it owed no deference to the California Supreme Court; that a dubious jailhouse confession establishes innocence under AEDPA; and that, regardless of AEDPA, Price had the right on a second **habeas corpus** petition to demonstrate freestanding innocence. In short," Fini concluded with disdain, "they tried every intellectual gyration necessary to bar an execution. To countenance such a shabby result is to beg for more—especially from jurists like **this** creative duo."

"Creative?" Kelly asked rhetorically. "You mean lawless."

Caroline chose to ignore this second breach of manners, another justice speaking out of turn. "Tony," she said to Fini, "do you have anything else?"

"No," Fini answered briskly. "Save that I vote to grant the State's petition."

Three votes to go, Caroline thought. "As Chief," she began, "and given that I'm responsible for the pool memo, I should respond.

"We all know the history between this Court and my former circuit. But it is essential not to personalize this matter." Her tone, though even, contained a touch of acid. "After all, I'm sure none of us believes that our Court's principal purpose is the moral instruction of Blair Montgomery."

Opposite Caroline, Huddleston smiled: in his view, distrust of the Ninth Circuit undermined his hope of saving what remained of the barriers against executing the innocent, and it was best to put this problem squarely on the table. Fini, too, smiled but sourly—he knew, as Caroline did, that the centrists did not wish to appear intemperate.

"As the Ninth Circuit's opinion noted," Caroline continued, "the California Supreme Court offered no analysis of the facts, which the State acknowledges could not—now—sustain a prosecution. The finding of retardation also hinges on the facts. And for this Court to deny Mr. Price a chance to prove, under **Atkins,** that he **is** retarded, would be to do what the Ninth Circuit is so often accused of—to go out of our way to achieve a desired result." She paused for effect. "But in our case it would be to **execute** one man rather than to save him. All of which makes me question why we want to touch this case."

The justices were still now, most soberly contemplating that: Caroline had portrayed a vote to hear the **Price** case as both spiteful and petty, an act beneath their dignity. "Which brings me," she said smoothly, "to Tony's principal concern—the passage regarding freestanding innocence.

"I make two points. First, the panel's primary ruling is that Mr. Price's evidence of innocence satisfies AEDPA, and rests on a constitutional defect at trial— a grossly incompetent lawyer who, believing Price's brother guilty, had an inescapable conflict of interest. Approving that claim is hardly revolutionary."

Glancing at McGeorge Glynn, she cut to the heart of her argument. "As for the majority's alternative grounds—that Price has the right to prove his innocence, even if the trial was fair—let me pose a question. Does **this** Court, in **this** case, truly want to say that there are **no** circumstances—no matter how compelling the evidence—under which a **habeas corpus** petitioner who is merely innocent can avoid execution?" Pausing, she held Glynn's troubled gaze. "Executing the innocent is every judge's nightmare. Nothing about the case of Rennell Price would justify this Court in enshrining such a risk."

Caroline stopped abruptly, allowing her colleagues to absorb this. After a sober silence, she looked toward Huddleston. "Walter?"

Huddleston leaned forward. "Practicing rough justice," he said flatly, "is to promote injustice. Denying innocent prisoners the right to prove their innocence is grotesque. I vote against."

Looking about the table, Caroline addressed the others in order of seniority. "Bryson?"

Head butting forward like a prow, Kelly spoke with typical brusqueness. "This case isn't about one man. It's about respecting the Supreme Court of California, and sending the Ninth Circuit a message so clear that we finally get out of the business of having to reverse them. I vote yes."

So far, Caroline thought, the tally was as expected. Addressing Judge Glynn, she reached the first moment of doubt. "What about you, McGeorge?"

Knowing that this vote could be decisive, Fini turned to Glynn with an expression far more imperative than imploring. Fingers clasped, Glynn propped his elbows on the table. "I'm very troubled by this opinion," he said at length. "Were Mr. Price's fate presently before us, I honestly don't know how I'd

560 / RICHARD NORTH PATTERSON

vote—it's the type of case which, however you decide
it, virtually assures a bad result." He drew a breath.
"Sometimes, the best way to deal with such a dilemma
is to avoid it. This Court has that luxury. With some
reluctance, I vote against granting this petition."

Caroline felt a tentative spurt of relief. But were
Fini to garner the next vote, Justice Raymond's, the
certain vote of Justice Ware would provide the fourth
required to grant the State's petition. "Thomas," she
said quietly.

Raymond glanced at McGeorge Glynn, seeming to
take comfort in Glynn's familiar aspect and, perhaps,
his colleague's inherent caution, which in Caroline's
jaundiced view, masqueraded as wisdom. "Like McGeorge," he said amiably, "I'm of two minds—perhaps
three or four. Which is probably the number of concurrences or dissents deciding this case would provoke." Facing Fini, he said, "I share your concerns,
Tony. But even if the panel's decision is a mess, ours
could be a bigger one—not to mention that it would
become the law of the land. One thing we **don't** owe
America is another piece of junk in an area like capital
punishment."

Surprised by this conclusion, much like her own,
Caroline saw Fini suppress a shrug of irritation before
he trained his gaze on the most junior justice, Millar.
Fini's eyes did not waiver when the seventh justice,
John Ware, tersely voted yes, or when Miriam Rothbard countered with the no which Caroline had anticipated, leaving Anthony Fini one vote short.

Turning to Dennis Millar, Caroline said evenly, "It's down to you, Dennis."

Lips compressed, her thin, dark-haired colleague studied the papers before him. Tense with anticipation, Caroline prepared herself for the Hamlet-like circumlocutions which, so often, preceded some utterly unpredictable conclusion. "As Tony points out," Millar ventured, "there **is** a conflict in the circuits, and the opinion **does** raise serious questions regarding several aspects of AEDPA.

"But what worries me most," Millar went on, "is that deciding these death penalty cases, especially from the Ninth Circuit, seems to trap all of us in a recriminatory cycle..."

So don't take this **case,** Caroline silently urged him. But something in his turn of phrase—"recriminatory cycle"—sounded less like Millar than like Anthony Fini. "I fear for our collegiality," Millar said in a reluctant tone. "Perhaps, as Tony and Bryson suggest, it is time to draw some clearer lines to keep these cases from our door." He hesitated, then finished softly, "To allow us to attempt this—collegially, I hope—I vote to grant the petition."

That was it, Caroline thought. She saw Walter Huddleston quiver with disgust: in a particularly telling display of his notion of "collegiality," Fini had lobbied Millar against casting the fifth vote necessary to stay an execution in another case where four justices, led by Huddleston, had granted the prisoner's petition to be heard. Then, as now, Millar had complied with Fini's wishes: one might say that the prisoner had died from a shortfall of collegiality.

Ignoring Fini's look of triumph, Caroline said calmly, "The State of California's petition is granted," and moved to the next case on the list.

Chris and Carlo were waiting at a French brasserie when Terri arrived late from the office, looking tired and distressed. "The Supreme Court is taking Rennell's case."

"Shit," Carlo said softly.

In sympathy and dismay, Chris reached across the white tablecloth to touch Terri's hand. "It's not good," he told Carlo. "At the least, it means that four out of nine justices are inclined to reinstitute Rennell's death sentence."

"Oh," Terri said, "it's a little worse than that. In eighty percent of these cases, the Supreme Court has reversed the lower court. With the Ninth Circuit, their record is twenty-seven in a row."

Carlo put down his beer, as if he could no longer taste it.

Driving toward the office down California Street, Terri heard her cell phone ring on the console where she had placed it.

The screen read "private caller." Hastily, she answered.

"See you lost again," the familiar voice said. "Time to let the sucker die, or face the con-sequences."

Willing herself to be calm, Terri answered tightly, "And what might those be?"

"The ones that happen to bitches keep huntin' for Betty Sims."

There was no way, Terri knew, to trace the call. "What if I found her? Or her daughter?"

For a moment, the voice was silent. "What if I find **your** daughter?" it asked softly. "Maybe I'd teach her, and send you the pictures. Close-ups, with her lookin' up at me, eyes as big as her mouth need to be."

The phone went dead.

Shaking, Terri pulled to the side and called Charles Monk.

He was still at the office. This time he did not challenge her, perhaps because of the way she sounded. There was little the police could do, he said, and perhaps her caller was just guessing she had a daughter, trying to strike a nerve. But if he had mentioned Betty Sims, it was time for Terri to fill out a police report.

She drove to the Hall of Justice and did that. But by then, Monk reported the next day, Eddie Fleet had vanished.

FIVE

THE SUPREME COURT HEARING WAS SET FOR APRIL.

Starting in December, when the Court had granted the State's petition, the Pagets shaped their strategy. Proving retardation alone would condemn Rennell to a life in prison; reliance on freestanding innocence might provoke a reversal of the Ninth Circuit, leading to his execution. The only clear path was arguing that their evidence was sufficient to establish Rennell's claim of innocence under AEDPA and—equally crucial—that freeing him under such a theory would in no way alter the law.

The Court would announce its ruling in June. "At least," Carlo said after a long day spent honing their brief, "we'll have kept him alive for six more months." But no one truly accepted this—the Pagets, and Rennell, had tasted freedom.

They visited him daily—Terri or Carlo or, at times, Anthony Lane. Their common goal was to raise his spirits and, with Lane's help, to prepare him for what they still hoped would come: a life outside the prisons where he had spent his life—the one where he now lived, the one where he was born—without the brother who had been his protector and betrayer. As the Pagets labored in the shadow of the Supreme Court, Rennell seemed to grow stronger. He did not know, and they had no heart to tell him, how precarious his purchase on life had become.

And so, on the surface, their lives went on, his and theirs. Rennell read simple stories which had belonged to Elena or Kit. Elena turned fourteen, and in early March, Carlo's new girlfriend moved her clothes into his apartment. The Pagets worked on other cases. There was no sign of Fleet, no calls to Terri.

Yet his specter, and that of the hearing, wound through the fabric of their lives. Elena and Kit went nowhere unattended. Looking for notoriety, self-proclaimed Supreme Court specialists tried to shoulder the Pagets aside; one predator, not fully appreciative of Rennell's limitations, wrote him in prison to offer himself as counsel. Chris and Terri gave the media a spate of stories about Rennell which focused on his innocence, not the pitfalls of AEDPA. But there was another problem wholly beyond their control: whether the Solicitor General of the United States, whose prestige was matchless, and whose mandate included defending federal statutes such as AEDPA, would file a brief in opposition to Rennell, reaffirming the President's support of AEDPA and the death penalty.

This the Pagets dreaded. "In a close case," Chris

told Carlo, "the Solicitor General could be the difference."

And so they waited.

In late March, when the San Francisco Giants opened the baseball season against the Los Angeles Dodgers, the Baltimore Orioles hosted Tony Fini's beloved Yankees. Gifted with two tickets behind home plate at Camden Yards, Justice Fini took Adam Wendt.

The afternoon was sunny, and although it was breezy and a little cool, Justice Fini did not let this spoil his enjoyment of another beginning, in his mind second only to Easter as a sacred rite of spring. Between innings he sat back with his eyes shut, half-smiling, absorbing the smells of hot dogs and spilled beer as sunlight warmed his face. Adam had never seen a man so perfectly content.

"When I was a kid," Fini said, "I'd skip school for opening day at Yankee Stadium. It was the only sin I didn't mind confessing—no God worth worshiping would fail to understand."

Adam smiled. Until the sixth inning, the newness of spring, the timeless geometry of baseball, absorbed every molecule of Justice Fini's being. Then, between the top and bottom of the inning, Fini spoke without taking his eyes off the Yankees' starting pitcher as he began his warm-up tosses. "The **Price** case, Adam. Looked at the briefs yet?"

Adam balled up his hot dog wrapper and tossed it beneath his seat. "Uh-huh," he answered. "Price's lawyers do a fairly artful job of tiptoeing through the minefield. I'd give them an A minus to the State's B plus."

Fini nodded, satisfied; that the justice now reposed such confidence in his judgment warmed Adam beyond description. Still watching the pitcher, Fini inquired, "So who wins?"

"I couldn't guess. But Price could hold the middle, Justices Glynn and Raymond. His brief does everything it can to give them a way out."

Fini pursed his lips. "Circulate a memo," he directed, "arguing that we should invite the Solicitor General to weigh in."

Adam hesitated. "In **this** administration?" he inquired with some trepidation. "The President who appointed the Solicitor General also appointed the Chief Justice."

Fini's keen eyes glinted. "True. But even **this** President, as a senator, voted for AEDPA. And there's a presidential election coming up. There are only two possibilities—that the S.G.'s office ducks the issue or, more likely, comes to AEDPA's defense. The latter could tip my less decisive brethren."

Quiet, Adam absorbed this. What made Fini exceptional was not simply the capaciousness of his mind but its shrewdness and practicality, firmly moored in the world outside the Court. A great justice, Adam saw, must be a great tactician.

Fini still eyed the pitcher. "How's Clemens looking to you?" he asked.

Adam had been watching Fini, not Roger Clemens. "Okay, I guess."

"He's one or two batters short of finished," Fini demurred with a smile. "A manager has to smell blood in the water before the sharks do."

As the guards eased Rennell Price into the cubicle, Christopher Paget's first reaction was one he had not expected—that this hulking man with a lineless face, a looming presence in the life of Chris's family, was young enough to be his son.

"I'm Chris." Extending his hand, Chris added with a smile, "Terri's husband, and Carlo's dad. You're about all they ever talk about."

Rennell's soft hand enveloped his. But the man's eyes were expressionless, as though studying Chris for clues: though Rennell's life had become his charge, Rennell Price did not know Chris, and Chris did not know Rennell. That had been better, the rationalist in Chris believed—to feel affection for this man, as Terri did, might cloud his judgment at some crucial moment, perhaps before the Supreme Court, when coolness was what Rennell needed most from him. But now Chris had needed to come here.

He did not know how to begin. "I wanted to meet you," he said at last.

Still Rennell studied him. Perhaps, Chris thought, this man was so attached to Terri that the reality of her husband, an abstraction become flesh, was unwelcome.

"Let's sit down," Chris suggested.

Slowly, Rennell did so. The deliberateness of his movements, his apparent fear of some lapse in coordination, brought home to Chris the vulnerabilities which made the idea of this man's death so difficult for Terri to endure.

"So," Chris inquired awkwardly, "how are you getting along?"

No sooner had he asked this question than its pointlessness overwhelmed him. But all the man in front of him said was "Same stuff, mostly. Waitin' to leave here."

The knowledge that Rennell was ensnared by forces he could not comprehend, and antagonists to whom he was barely more real than they were to him, filled Chris with anger and pity. But there was no way to explain this. "I took Carlo to a baseball game," he told Rennell. "Just yesterday. We were wondering how you'd have liked it."

Rennell nodded—whether out of instinct or merely to avoid speaking, Chris could not tell.

"Ever go to a game, Rennell?"

Rennell folded his hands. Softly, he answered, "Daddy never took me to no games."

Yeah, Chris thought, **too busy with that space heater—fun for the entire family.** He felt more foolish than before.

"What they like?" Rennell asked.

"Fun," Chris answered with a smile. "There's all kinds of food."

Rennell seemed to ponder this. "Food here's all the same. Sometimes, Grandma, she take me out for barbecue." He hesitated. "Before all this happen."

Chris tilted his head. "Did Payton go, too?"

"Sometimes." Rennell gave a reminiscent smile. "Sometimes she just take me. Special times, she say."

How much, Chris wondered, had Eula Price understood about his early childhood? Perhaps more than she had wished to, and far less than he had needed. But then what could she have done—there was so much damage to repair, so few resources. And therapists like Tony Lane did not set up shop in the Bayview.

"When I get out," Rennell said, "maybe you take me to a game. With Terri and Carlo and all."

Chris nodded. "They'd like that."

Rennell shook his head in wonder at the thought. "When you think I'm gettin' out?"

Chris hesitated. "Maybe June," he answered. "July, at the latest." **One way or the other.**

"July," Rennell repeated. "Sunny then. They still be playin' baseball?"

"Yeah. For sure." Chris mustered a smile. "If the Giants go to the championship, they'll still be playing in October."

Rennell hesitated, a frown of worry creasing his smooth forehead. "Where you think I be livin'?"

"I'm not sure yet."

Rennell bit his lip. "See, I was hopin' I could stay with you."

Chris had no answer. "Terri and Carlo love you," he said at last.

To his surprise, Rennell's eyes filled with tears. And then he half-stood, reaching across the table, and leaned his head against Chris's shoulder.

Feeling Rennell's hair and skin against his neck, Chris thought of Carlo, much younger, and then Kit. "They love you," he repeated softly.

SIX

PRESIDENT KERRY FRANCIS KILCANNON WAS nearing the end of a very long day and plainly had no patience for internecine warfare. "Why is this my problem?" he inquired of his Chief of Staff.

They sat in the Oval Office, two friends who were markedly different in temperament and appearance. At forty-four, Kerry bore the unmistakable stamp of Ireland, the country of his forebears—a slight but sinewy frame, thick ginger hair, a thin face at once angular and boyish, blue-green eyes which reflected the quicksilver of his moods—sometimes cold, at other times remote and almost absent, and at still others deeply empathic or glinting with amusement or outright laughter. Clayton Slade was the first African American to serve as Chief of Staff, and everything about him seemed earthbound—from his sturdy build and shrewd brown eyes to his plainness of speech and blunt determination to save his romantic and intuitive friend from his own worst impulses. With affection and amusement, Kerry had once remarked to Clayton, "Together, we make a passably good President. But don't start believing you could do the job without me."

Now Clayton smiled at his friend's annoyance. "Because your Solicitor General called me, back-dooring your Attorney General—"

"So tell them to work it out," Kerry snapped. "I'm the President, not a mediator. Or a judge."

"True," Clayton answered imperturbably. "People have to elect you. Next year you'll be asking them to do it again—this time, hopefully, by more than a few thousand votes. Given that you've already inflamed the pro-lifers and the gun lobby, you might want to embrace at least **one** of our nation's deeply rooted values."

"What?" Kerry inquired. "Executing people?"

Left unsaid were the complexity of Kerry's own feelings. After Kerry's older brother, Senator James Kilcannon, had been assassinated while running for President, Kerry—as a matter of private conscience—had asked the prosecution not to seek the assassin's execution. Yet Senator Kilcannon's death, which had propelled Kerry toward the presidency, haunted him still. "It's what Americans believe in," Clayton responded with the same air of calm. "During the last election you claimed to believe in it, too." Clayton took a brief sip of his diet cola, adding pointedly, "If you hadn't, Mr. President, you wouldn't **be** President."

"Oh, I know." Kerry emitted a sigh of resignation. "What's this contretemps about?"

"AEDPA. You voted for it, as you'll recall—"

"I try not to, actually."

"Anyhow, the Supreme Court's about to hear a death penalty case involving a prisoner named Rennell Price. You may have seen Bob Herbert's columns in the **Times.**"

Reflective, the President rested an elbow on one arm of the wing chair, propping his face in the palm of his hand. "It's coming back to me," he said. "From the evidence, it sounded like he might well be innocent, and another man guilty."

"So his lawyers claim. But that's not the crux of **our** problem." Clayton finished his cola. "The Ninth Circuit issued an opinion that can be read to soften AEDPA. Your Attorney General and the head of his Criminal Division want the Solicitor General to support sharply restricting the rights of **habeas corpus** petitioners—like Price—to prove their innocence. Your new Solicitor General is balking."

Clayton watched the President consider this: the S.G., Avram Gold, had been his personal lawyer, and for a number of reasons, the President was in his debt. "What's Avi want?" he asked.

"Avi Gold," Clayton said with a touch of weariness, "is a civil libertarian. He hates the death penalty. He hates this statute, always has. So he wants us to stay out."

"Is that such a bad idea? What if Price is innocent?"

"Nobody will go blaming **you,**" Clayton answered. "But if Avi Gold had his way, all you'd carry is the faculty room at Harvard.

"We've got capital punishment because that's what

most Americans want, by roughly three to one. The people who **don't** want it—civil rights groups and social liberals—have got no one to vote for but us. But if Caroline Masters and her Court do something funky with the death penalty, the Republicans will come after you like hell won't have it."

Kerry smiled quizzically. "Is **that** what the Attorney General wants us to say?"

Silent, Clayton fought to repress his exasperation. With an intimacy and candor the President permitted him alone, he said softly, "Don't be perverse, Kerry. I understand what you wrestled with after Jamie was killed. But the difference between your presidency and that of some Republican is way too important to put at risk. Not to mention how you'd feel about losing."

"I appreciate the sentiment," Kerry answered with equal quiet. "That's why I voted for AEDPA, after all."

The President's ambivalence was unmistakable. "I guess you've decided to hear Avi out," Clayton said.

"Both of them—Avi and the A.G. Toward the end of lunch tomorrow."

"Isn't that your time with Lara and the baby?"

"Uh-huh." Kerry smiled again. "I'm making whoever loses change his diapers."

Though named after Kerry Kilcannon's older brother, at seven months of age James Joseph Kilcannon already had his father's blue-green eyes and inquisitive expression. But Jamie's raven hair and pale skin were Lara's.

Pausing in the doorway, Clayton found them sitting on a carpet in the middle of the Oval Office. They made a lovely picture, as numerous photographers had captured: the young First Lady whose beauty, derived from her Latina mother, had—combined with talent and a fierce will to succeed—helped make her a celebrated television journalist; the infant discovering the world on his hands and knees; the President to whom this child, their first, was an endless source of wonder and delight. Shadowed by the grimness of his childhood, Kerry thought of Jamie as a miracle, for whose happiness and wholeness Kerry would have sacrificed anything but Lara. Jamie, knowing none of this, simply found his father very silly.

Now, captivated by some piece of absurd behavior by the President, Jamie emitted a gurgling laugh. "What he's going to remember about his childhood," Lara told her husband, "is wondering if his father was demented."

"He won't be the first," Kerry answered and then looked up at Clayton.

Clayton smiled at the First Lady. "The real world intrudes."

"This **is** the real world," Lara corrected. "The rest of you are make-believe."

"I've often wondered about that."

Standing, the President offered Lara his hand. "Anyhow," Kerry directed Clayton, "send in the holograms."

With this, Clayton ushered in the Attorney General, J. Theron Pinkerton, a silver-haired former Senate colleague of Kerry's from Louisiana, and the Solicitor General, Avram Gold, a mustached and be-spectacled ex-Harvard law professor who seemed to burn calories just standing still. As they made their apologies to Lara and she began gathering Jamie's toys, the President said to her, "Why don't you stick around. You may find this interesting."

Kerry, Clayton recognized at once, meant for Lara's presence to mute the antagonism between the Attorney General and Avi Gold, Pinkerton's subordinate. That Pinkerton now felt offended was plain—he sat as far from the Solicitor General as possible, barely deigning to acknowledge him. "Before we get into this," the President told Pinkerton, "I want it understood that Justice is **your** shop, not Avi's. The only reason you're here is Herbert's column, and the public controversy which may arise once the Court decides the case. I don't expect to be in any more meetings like this. On any subject."

Mollified, Pinkerton nodded. Avi Gold looked contrite—annoying Kerry Kilcannon was not for the faint of heart. The President turned to Pinkerton. "You first, Pink."

"There are several good reasons," the Attorney General began at once, "to intervene in support of the State of California.

"To start, most of our party colleagues voted to pass AEDPA. Before that, the Republicans were pillorying us with stories of mass murderers and child molesters stringing out appeal after appeal and then laughing at the victims' families in open court—"

"I remember. We weren't just soft on murderers, we were their nannies."

Encouraged, Pinkerton leaned forward, pressing his argument. "Legally, the purpose of AEDPA is wholly legitimate—balancing a prisoner's right to prove his innocence with society's right to finality. That's the essence of California's argument to the Supreme Court. Which brings me to our real problem, Caroline Masters."

Glancing at the First Lady, Clayton saw her eyes narrow with displeasure. "No one," Pinkerton told the President, "admires you more than I for sticking by her nomination after she and that damned Ninth Circuit ruled in favor of so-called partial birth abortion. But you won that nomination by a single vote. Out in the country, God knows how many votes you lost—"

"Or won," the President objected mildly. "People will put up with a President they disagree with. But they won't tolerate one who doesn't know who he is."

"Too many people," Pinkerton said regretfully, "however deluded, think they know exactly who you are—an East Coast liberal. And they don't like it.

"The probable Republican nominee is Frank Fasano, who's as ruthless as they come. A Supreme Court ruling which erodes capital punishment will give Fasano another weapon to pummel you with from now to next November. Caroline Masters **owes** you—you're the only reason she's there." Glancing at Avi Gold, the Attorney General finished. "You can't call Masters and tell her what to do. But if Avi intervenes, as I've directed, it sends a signal even the Chief Justice can't ignore. And it gives us cover in the next election."

Scooping up a wriggling Jamie, the President placed him in his lap, trying to direct the baby's gaze toward Avram Gold. "So why **shouldn't** I be reelected?" he asked Gold. "Inquiring minds would care to know."

Gold smiled at this. "Call me an idealist, Mr. President. But I believe in an America where you get reelected **and** we don't execute the innocent."

"Are you trying to interest me in the **merits,** Avi? I'm a practical politician."

"So's Mr. Justice Fini. Word is that he initiated this invitation from the Court to the Solicitor General, hoping we'd give death a little shove." Pressing his palms together, Gold fixed the President with a look of deep conviction. "I **know** you're up for reelection. But something about this case is rancid—"

"Yes," Pinkerton interjected, "the asphyxiation of a little girl during oral copulation. Price's brother admitted guilt, and there's ample evidence of his own. Tony Fini's put you in a box—"

"But what kind of box?" the President interrupted. "Last night, I reread one of Herbert's columns. I voted for AEDPA, it's true. But I'll admit to some disquiet about executing a man based on the testimony of someone who's used the Fifth Amendment to avoid questions about his own involvement."

Gold nodded vigorously. "We're not asking Congress to repeal AEDPA—let alone the death penalty. But I'm not sure why this administration should go out of its way, at the invitation of Anthony Fini, to help ensure that this particular man is executed. And if the Masters Court allows one possibly innocent defendant to escape death, it's not a threat to the Republic just because a bunch of right-wingers say it is."

It was a shrewd thrust, Clayton thought, appealing to Kilcannon's pride. When he turned to Kerry—hoping to urge caution—he saw a glance pass between the President and First Lady, the trace of a smile surface in the President's eyes.

Only the Attorney General seemed oblivious to what had just occurred. "Let's stay out of this one," the President told him. "Leave the Chief Justice to her own devices." Bending to kiss the crown of his son's head, he told the infant, "After all, Jamie, it's not like I'm coming out **against** executing innocent retarded people."

Across from them, the First Lady smiled to herself, and Clayton knew that the subject was closed.

SEVEN

THE PRELUDE TO ORAL ARGUMENT IN THE CASE OF Rennell Price was, to its participants within the Court, a minuet of indirection.

Two weeks before the argument, over a drink in Justice Fini's chambers—two fingers of single-malt scotch on ice—Fini inquired of Adam Wendt, "What do you hear about where Justice Glynn is leaning?"

"Nothing yet."

Fini considered this. "I certainly don't want to push him," he told Adam. "McGeorge likes to keep his counsel, and I respect that. But if you happen to hear anything from one of his clerks..."

Which was why, though Callista Hill did not know it, Adam Wendt glanced up from chatting in the clerks' private lunch room with Elizabeth Burke, the clerk on whom Justice Glynn relied to monitor the death list, and shifted the conversation before Callista joined them. But all Adam had learned from Elizabeth was that Glynn remained noncommittal.

This was also why—though Callista again did not know it—Justice Fini directed Adam to prepare a memo to the three other justices who had voted to grant California's petition, spelling out the reasons for a unified vote to reverse the Ninth Circuit's opinion. But Bill Faber, one of Justice Millar's clerks, found the memo curious enough to hit a button on his computer and blind-copy it to his friend Callista Hill.

The Chief Justice read Fini's memo with a reflective air. "Prepare a draft reply memo," she told Callista. "I can hear the next shoe dropping."

The next shoe, it transpired, was a Fini-gram to all nine justices, proposing summary reversal of the Ninth Circuit ruling. Its author, Adam Wendt, was startled by the swiftness of the Chief Justice's reply. "It's like she saw us coming," he observed to Justice Fini.

Fini merely chuckled.

The last item in the Court's Friday conference was Justice Fini's call for summary reversal. If he held his four votes, Caroline knew, all Fini needed was a vote from Justice Glynn or Raymond.

"A comparison of the briefs," Fini urged, "shows that the Ninth Circuit's opinion—both on retardation and on innocence—is not supported by the 'clear and convincing evidence' requirement under AEDPA. As for so-called freestanding innocence, not only is the evidence insufficient but the claim itself does not exist.

"Why waste time on argument? When a court of appeals is as out-of-bounds as Judges Montgomery and Sanders are here, the best course is to tell them so by summary reversal."

"A few weeks ago," Caroline responded, "five of us voted against hearing California's petition at all. Now you tell us, Tony, that the Ninth Circuit's opinion is such a mutation that all five of us must have been asleep.

"Is the brief filed by Price's lawyers really **that** feeble? I think not." Her voice became sardonic. "Indeed, any one of the five of us, persuaded of our wisdom, could try to muster five votes for summary **affirmance** of Judges Sanders and Montgomery. But that would be as unusual as summary reversal—which, in the rare cases where we grant it, is typically unanimous.

"Those few weeks ago, you suggested that we had to hear this case because it raised such novel issues. I think we should do just that—hear the case."

By seniority, it was Justice Huddleston's turn. "Speaking of briefs," he inquired blandly of the Chief Justice, "I gather that the Solicitor General's office has declined to enter the fray."

"That's correct," Caroline answered. "We do have a letter from Solicitor General Gold, which I've copied." She handed the copies to Justice Glynn, who, taking one, passed them along to Justice Raymond. "With respect to AEDPA, Mr. Gold believes that the panel's opinion does not undermine the statute but turns on facts unique to Mr. Price. Indeed, he suggests that an overrestrictive reading of AEDPA may raise constitutional problems best avoided by the Court."

Huddleston gave Fini a glance of veiled spite. "Hardly a ringing endorsement of your position, Tony. Certainly, it suggests we should at least hear from Mr. Price before rushing to reinstitute his execution. I vote no."

"McGeorge?" Caroline asked of Mr. Justice Glynn.

Glynn shook his head. "No," he said softly. "I find this case exceedingly difficult. Hearing argument can only help."

"Thomas?"

"I agree. Let's have argument."

With that, Caroline knew, Fini had lost this round: Miriam Rothbard would be the fifth vote against him. What disturbed her most occurred moments later, when the last Justice—Millar—voted with Justice Fini. Her antagonist had achieved his secondary aim: solidifying four votes against Rennell Price and identifying the two remaining sources, Raymond or Glynn, from whom he could secure the vote he needed to prevail.

"Summary reversal," Caroline said evenly, "is denied."

That afternoon, the Chief Justice visited Walter Huddleston in the senior justice's chambers, his comfortable redoubt for nearly three decades on the Court.

"So," the white-haired justice said, folding his hands across his comfortable belly, "you're in need of spiritual counseling."

"It's the **Price** case, Walter. Tony's gone to work on McGeorge. I don't want the law, or my Court, to go where Tony wants to take it. But I'm still fairly new here. I'm not sure of how much, or how little, to do."

"That's what Fini counts on—plus the fact that you were narrowly confirmed and still have to feel your way. But he also tries to intimidate the others with his brilliance. Your strength is that you're smoother and more patient—not that Tony sets the latter bar very high." Huddleston's tone filled with bemusement. "To me, Tony Fini is Mussolini clad in bonhomie—self-satisfied to the point of inhumanity. But he tends to genuinely like his peers, excepting me and possibly you, and to treat them with real affection. That means something to McGeorge—he's fundamentally a sweet man and, since his wife died, a lonely one.

"With respect to the **Price** case, the key to understanding McGeorge is that he's also a romantic. From his fortunate birth to his smooth career, everything in his life has conspired to make him believe that the world—including our system of justice—is fairer than it is. But if he truly believes that some case exposes a genuine problem in the way the system works, his sympathies become engaged." Placing his hands behind his neck, Huddleston concluded, "That's what **you** may need to do—make this case seem real to him. As decorously as possible."

"So what do you suggest?"

Huddleston gazed at the ceiling. "The American Ballet Theatre is coming to the Kennedy Center. Before Frances died, the four of us would always go." Pausing, he looked back to Caroline with a smile. "I'll have to clear it with Bonita. But perhaps we can sacrifice our two tickets for the sake of Mr. Price. And, of course, our Court."

EIGHT

ON THE MORNING OF THE ARGUMENT, CHRIS, CARLO, and Terri took a limousine down Pennsylvania Avenue toward the Supreme Court.

Chris was quiet. Mentally, he reviewed the precepts of his argument. Prepare to be peppered with questions, to answer each one crisply and move on. Don't expect to make your points in the order you had planned. Keep your legal theories as narrow as you can. Answer hypotheticals with care, avoiding traps. Avoid sweeping statements about justice which would draw the ire of Justice Fini. Oh, yes, and keep calm.

He was as ready as he could be. Every day for the last week, he had practiced as Terri, Carlo, and two professors of constitutional law had interrupted with question upon question. "Mr. Paget," Carlo had asked before he finished his first sentence, "are you adopting the reasoning of Judges Montgomery and Sanders with respect to freestanding innocence—?"

It was Fini's question, of course. Now, once more, Chris rehearsed the answer.

At twenty minutes before ten o'clock, the Pagets entered the Great Hall, designed to provide an inspiring entrance to the courtroom—towering monolithic columns, a lofty doorway framing a view of the justices' bench and the clock behind it.

The Pagets passed through. As the press gathered and spectators filed in, the courtroom seemed to await the justices themselves. Amidst the murmur of anticipation, Carlo absorbed a setting which, until this moment, he had seen only in photographs.

The forty-four-foot ceiling created the sense that he had entered a cathedral of the law. On the walls to each side a procession of historic lawgivers—Hammurabi, Charlemagne, Moses, Solomon, Justinian, Mohammed, and to Carlo's astonishment, Napoleon—gazed down on him like secular saints. Behind the bench was a red curtain through which the justices would enter and, above that, an ornate frieze depicting allegorical figures representing the Defense of Human Rights, the Protection of the Innocent, the Safeguard of Liberty, and of course, Justice. Carlo could only hope that the all-too-human figures who would gather beneath them would—in at least five instances—personify these ideals for Rennell Price.

He pictured Rennell again, a single prisoner in a six-by-six cubicle three thousand miles away, and wondered if their client was any more real to the justices than they were to him.

At ten o'clock, the marshal of the Supreme Court, wearing formal morning clothes, entered the courtroom and intoned, "The Honorable, the Chief Justice and the Associate Justices of the Supreme Court of the United States. Oyez! Oyez! Oyez!"

The courtroom rose as one: Chris and Terri standing at the respondents' table; Laurence Pell and Janice Terrell at the petitioners' table, to their left. Led by the Chief Justice, the justices emerged from the velvet curtain in groups of three and took the nine high-backed leather chairs behind the rich mahogany bench.

"All persons having business before the Honorable, the Supreme Court of the United States, are admonished to draw near and give their attention, for the Court is now sitting. God Save the United States and this Honorable Court."

On the bench, Chris knew, a green pad covered the space before each justice, separated from those of the others by wooden dividers. The bench itself formed three panels, two of them wings slanting from the center section, creating a well of intimacy half-surrounding the lectern from which the advocates would speak. Rocking and swiveling, the justices would perform a rite of aerobic listening to the advocates or one another, as the more theatrical among them, particularly Justice Fini, launched brainteasers and witty remarks at the embattled advocates. Within the law, it was the greatest show on earth, filled with drama, surprise, and personality, from which new lines of analysis might emerge, and a lawyer's misstep might presage disaster. When he had first come here, as a law student, Chris Paget had thought of himself and his fellow onlookers as spectators at some bloodless version of the Roman Colosseum, in which the various classes of society—the relatives of the justices, the members of the Supreme Court bar, the press, and seated farther back, mere members of the public—awaited some fatal error by one of the contesting gladiators.

Now Chris thought of Rennell, and came as close to prayer as he was able.

Flanked by Fini and Huddleston, the most senior justices, Chief Justice Masters called the case of Rennell Price, summoning Laurence Pell for his first appearance before the Court.

Advancing to the lectern, Pell looked appropriately daunted: from Chris's experience, Pell's time would move so quickly that the white light flashing on the podium, a five-minute warning, would startle him; the red light, commanding his immediate silence, would fill him with misgivings as to all he had not said. He, like Chris, would reprise the argument for years to come—one with pleasure, the other with regret. But at least they both would live.

Chris's regrets—should he have them—would be far more searing than Pell's.

Pell began with a jeremiad aimed at the Court's conservatives.

"This opinion—rendered by Judges Sanders and Montgomery over Judge Nhu's principled dissent—distorts the meaning of AEDPA and denies the California Supreme Court the deference which AEDPA requires. On both counts, this is a virtual act of civil disobedience—"

"Isn't Mr. Price's argument," Justice Glynn asked in unimpressed tones, "that we can't know **what** impelled the Supreme Court of California to rule as it did? How could the Ninth Circuit defer in a vacuum?"

"Under AEDPA," Pell answered without hesitation, "whether the opinion is one page or twenty, it constitutes a finding that Mr. Price's facts were insufficient to support his claim." Pell's voice filled with emotion. "It is well to remember—after fifteen years—what this case is really about: a nine-year-old girl forced to choke to death on semen—"

"Someone's semen," the Chief Justice interrupted caustically. "What this case is **really** about is whose. Aren't you asking this Court to 'defer' to the witness Eddie Fleet?"

"And to the jury which found him credible—"

"Before Payton Price's confession. But if we affirm the Ninth Circuit, you won't attempt to retry Rennell Price. Yet you're saying that Mr. Fleet was so credible fifteen years ago—in spite of what we've learned since then—that this Court can be sanguine about allowing you to execute Mr. Price."

On the bench, Justice Fini had turned to the Chief Justice, appraising her with a glint of humor. But Laurence Pell did not look amused. "It's a question of finality—"

"Finality to the max," Caroline Masters snapped. "But the trial you rely on was the product of Mr. James's worst efforts."

"The California Supreme Court," Pell insisted, "found James constitutionally adequate—"

The Chief Justice leaned forward. "The California Supreme Court," she said acerbically, " 'found' nothing. Answer my question, counselor—should this Court give Mr. James's performance its seal of approval?"

Pell attempted to gather himself. "The question," he responded, "is whether Mr. James supposed the conflict made any difference—"

"James admitted as much," the Chief Justice repeated with weary patience. "That means we don't have to decide freestanding innocence, doesn't it? Because the trial of Mr. Price was constitutionally defective under AEDPA."

Silently, Chris blessed the Chief Justice: with forensic skill, she had placed Rennell Price on the narrowest, and least contentious, path to freedom.

"Nothing Mr. James did or **didn't** do," Pell replied, "could have affected Payton Price's decision to confess. Therefore, his conflict did not affect the outcome of the trial, and Mr. Price cannot offer new evidence of innocence under AEDPA."

Caroline Masters summoned a smile of incredulity. "Let's grant—for the moment—your argument that a lawyer who assumes one client's guilt because he believes the **other** client guilty is good enough for both of them. Are you saying that even if new DNA evidence excluded Mr. Price as the murderer, you still can execute him as long as his original trial was okay?"

Pell hesitated. "In theory, yes. But our office would never do so. And, if we tried, the Governor would grant clemency—"

"Really? Because of DNA?"

"Yes."

The Chief Justice smiled thinly. "So it's okay to execute someone we're just **pretty** sure is innocent if his trial—however dubious its outcome—was 'fair.' "

With this, Chris thought, the Chief Justice cut to the heart of Pell's argument. Sitting to her right, Justice Glynn regarded Pell with a dubious frown.

"What I'd say," Pell answered slowly, "is that—under AEDPA—that decision should rest with the Supreme Court of California. This Court should not become the court of second guesses."

From the bench, Justice Fini nodded, briefly eyeing Justice Glynn. "Enough of hypotheticals," he said to Pell. "In reality, isn't the entirety of Mr. Price's **affirmative** evidence of innocence his own brother's extremely belated—and wholly unsupported—confession?"

"That's right."

"Does that 'confession' negate AEDPA's requirement of 'clear and convincing' evidence?"

Heartened, Pell spoke more firmly. "It does not."

"And even if you fabricate a claim of freestanding
innocence, the standard for innocence should hardly
be **less** than that of AEDPA, correct?"

"I agree."

Briskly, Chris saw, Fini had both rescued Pell and
reduced him to a prop. "Therefore," Fini prodded,
"under **any** theory of innocence, Mr. Price must fail?"

"That's correct."

"All right," Fini said with obvious satisfaction. "So,
according to Judges Sanders and Montgomery, the one
remaining impediment to Rennell Price's execution is
his claim of mental retardation under **Atkins**?"

"That's also correct."

"Which Judge Bond, Judge Nhu, and all seven justices on the California Supreme Court found unsupported by the evidence."

"Yes."

Fini cast an eye toward Justice Raymond—by
Chris's calculation, the swing vote of the Court along
with Justice Glynn. "And so," Fini continued, "as is the
case with innocence, Judges Montgomery and Sanders
stand alone in finding Mr. Price retarded."

"Yes."

"Of course," Fini interjected smoothly, "all of their
singular reasoning is irrelevant unless **Atkins** applies to
habeas corpus petitioners like Mr. Price. Does it?"

This invitation to controversy, however tempting,

seemed to give Pell pause. Carefully, he answered, "I do not believe that it does. To me, the rule of law is clear—a new principle of constitutional law doesn't apply to **habeas corpus** petitions unless this Court expressly says so. In **Atkins,** the Court did **not** say so."

Chris felt Terri tense—if he could, Fini clearly intended to use Rennell Price to construct a landmark in the law of capital punishment, imposing the death penalty more frequently and with greater stringency. "And therefore," Fini concluded, "**Atkins** does not ban the execution of Mr. Price, or of **any habeas corpus** petitioner—even if the petitioner is supposedly retarded."

"That's correct," Pell said to Fini.

To Chris Paget, three justices formed their own frieze of conflicting attitudes: Fini satisfied, Masters antagonized, Glynn torn and deeply troubled. And then the red light flashed on, and Pell's time was up.

N I N E

ADVANCING TO THE LECTERN, CHRISTOPHER PAGET felt the proximity of the justices, seated so close to him on both sides that he could not see them all at once. Experience had taught him that their questions, carried through speakers high above him, could seem disembodied from the justices who asked them, identifiable only by voice. But Justice Fini was squarely in front of him.

Turning slightly, Chris spoke to Justice Glynn. "The State of California seeks to execute a man," he began, "in a case where they executed the key witness to his innocence before the witness could be heard in court.

"Where the State's principal witness now invokes the Fifth Amendment.

"Where it refused to immunize this witness so that we could seek the truth.

"And where, it seems, all that matters to the State is 'winning.'"

Magnified by thick glasses, Glynn's eyes seemed to radiate concern. "But," Chris told him quietly, "there can be no 'victory' here. This is a tragic case of human fallibility, where all the components of human error— an appalling crime, an untrustworthy witness, a guilty brother, an incompetent lawyer, an Attorney General's Office bent on 'winning'—have brought a mentally impaired scapegoat to the brink of execution. While an almost-certain pedophile, Eddie Fleet, is free to repeat his crimes.'"

"So you say," Fini interrupted sharply. As Chris turned to him, Fini's eyes were combative, though his voice seemed to come not from his mouth but from above. "But AEDPA requires 'clear and convincing' evidence of innocence, not proof of imperfection. Where's your evidence?"

"Had Payton Price testified against Eddie Fleet at trial," Chris answered, "Rennell would not be here. Payton's confession takes the prosecution's 'evidence' and turns it inside out: there is no way a reasonable jury—then or now—could find Rennell Price guilty in the death of Thuy Sen. The Ninth Circuit was correct: James's admission of ineffectiveness, and the Attorney General's admission that they could not now convict Rennell, satisfies AEDPA. Such a ruling has no implications for **anyone** but Mr. Price—"

"Until," Fini interjected sternly, "the **next** petitioner argues that the Ninth Circuit should once more serve as fact finders, with no regard for the California Supreme Court **or**—in this case—Judge Bond's careful reasoning. Or are a federal trial judge's conclusions also beneath the Ninth Circuit's notice?"

598 / RICHARD NORTH PATTERSON

Justice Glynn, Chris noticed, pivoted from Fini back to him, seeming to second his colleague's question. "Judge Bond's ruling," he answered carefully, "relied heavily on the California Supreme Court, and therefore stands on quicksand—"

"Judge Bond," Fini snapped, "specifically found that Rennell Price's IQ was—at the least—seventy-two. Was the Ninth Circuit **also** justified in ignoring **that**?"

"That goes to retardation," Chris answered, "not innocence. As to retardation, the Ninth Circuit simply ruled that the California Supreme Court's opinion— which could have been written on a postcard—was not sacrosanct because of two IQ points." He looked toward Justice Glynn. "Indeed, this case encapsulates the reason for **Atkins**—a man who now appears innocent was set up by a man who appears guilty, and then fell victim to a legal process he never understood—"

"Isn't there a risk," Fini asked sardonically, "that **habeas corpus** petitioners like your client will start faking retardation, drowning this Court in a tidal wave of newly minted idiots?"

Despite the harshness of the question, Chris smiled. "I hope you're not referring to me, Your Honor." Interrupted by laughter, he paused. "As for the other 'idiots,' that's why the mental health profession requires evidence of retardation well before age eighteen—present in abundance here. I cannot conceive of a prisoner so fiendishly proactive that, beginning in grade school, he starts flunking standardized tests and bamboozling his way into special ed classes. Certainly not Rennell Price."

The Chief Justice, Terri saw, suppressed a smile of her own. But Fini, eyes glinting, was undaunted. "Why," he asked, "was Rennell Price—with an IQ above the threshold—incapable of knowing the difference between right and wrong?"

"He **does** know the difference," Chris answered easily. "That's why insisting on his innocence—as he has since he was eighteen years old—is so important to him. What his retardation impeded was his ability to keep the State of California from putting him on death row."

"The Attorney General," Fini rejoined, "points to the total absence of evidence that the State of California has **ever** executed an innocent man."

Chris permitted himself the briefest trace of a smile. "Proving that," he said dryly, "has never been the State's foremost priority. But the day may come when—despite their lack of interest—DNA will prove California wrong." Abruptly, his smile vanished. "Semen samples exist here. DNA technology is improving all the time. Rennell Price could be a human time bomb, Justice Fini. If this Court reverses the Ninth Circuit, this could be the case where—at last—we find out that the State of California has killed an innocent man."

At this, Justice Glynn blinked—the complicity suggested by Chris's prediction seemed to affect him physically. "The possibility of error," Fini objected, "hovers over any human process. Why should we allow that to cripple us?"

Chris stood straighter. "The proper question, with all respect, is, When do we ignore it when the consequence is death? My answer is, **Not here.** Not in **this** case, on these facts—"

"Does freestanding innocence even exist?"

Fini's questions came more swiftly now, forcing Chris to speak from instinct. "First and foremost, I rely on AEDPA—"

"But if we find that Mr. James's performance did not affect the outcome, do you **then** rely on freestanding innocence?"

"Yes," Chris retorted. "In **this** case, on **these** facts, before the State of California is allowed to execute **this** man—"

"Indeed," Fini pounced, "you **also** argued to the Ninth Circuit that—absent such a claim—AEDPA, and the death penalty itself, were unconstitutional."

Inwardly, Terri flinched—with one poisoned shaft of a question, Fini had attempted to paint Chris as an anti–death penalty zealot, whose radical theories were designed to distort the law. **"Only,"** Chris answered mildly, "if petitioners like Mr. Price are foreclosed from proving their innocence on the theory that the original verdict—though erroneous—was 'fairly' reached. But the Ninth Circuit did **not** accept this—"

"Nor did they reject it." Fini's voice became ironic. Briefly, he glanced at Glynn. "Would you say—in light of the array of inventive arguments you advanced to

the Ninth Circuit, and that Court's apparent willing-
ness to entertain them—that we owe the Ninth Circuit some guidance on this issue?"

The question, Terri knew, was aimed at the swing
justices: Fini's hope was that the case would be less
about Rennell, or even the issues before the Court,
than about the noxious combination of unruly Ninth
Circuit judges and advocates like Christopher Paget.

"No," Chris answered with renewed confidence.
"The Court's obligations are confined to my client, and
based on the opinion before it." Turning, he made a final plea to Justice Glynn. "This is not about the law of
capital punishment. Nor is it about what the Ninth Circuit might say in some future case which may never occur. It is about one man, and whether we will execute
him—"

"Thank you," Fini said dismissively.

No sooner had Laurence Pell launched his rebuttal
than Caroline Masters broke her silence. "Why
shouldn't we agree with the Ninth Circuit that this
man is retarded? Are you relying on his impressive
score of seventy-two?"

"In part—"

"The man couldn't cope," Caroline Masters cut in.
"From day one. Are you arguing that **that** was a
lifestyle choice?"

Pell hesitated. "According to our expert, it was antisocial behavior—"

602 / RICHARD NORTH PATTERSON

"Like getting himself tied to a space heater?"

Pell tried to adopt an attitude of patience. "In capital cases, virtually every **habeas corpus** petitioner portrays his childhood as a Dickensian nightmare. But that doesn't go to retardation. Both the California Supreme Court and Judge Bond found the evidence of retardation less than persuasive—"

"Oh, I know," the Chief Justice said with a wave of her hand. "Judges Sanders **and** Montgomery just got carried away by Mr. Paget's blandishments, and found Mr. Price retarded under **Atkins** and innocent under AEDPA. But did they rule on anything else?"

Pell paused, demonstrably unhappy. "Freestanding innocence—"

"As a fallback. Anything beyond that?"

"No."

"So would you agree that this Court need not issue some gratuitous advisory opinion on whatever else Mr. Price's lawyers might have argued?"

Peremptorily, Justice Fini looked from Caroline Masters to Laurence Pell. The lawyer paused again, plainly reluctant to be diverted from his argument by the chamber of horrors conjured by Fini, yet chary of offending his fiercest partisan on the Court. "Such a ruling," he ventured, "could clarify the law surrounding executions."

Caroline Masters gave him a dubious smile. "Perhaps we'd be better off proceeding one execution at a time. All **this** case requires, I submit, is for this Court to determine whether Rennell Price lives or dies—a weighty enough matter for most of us. But it does make one wonder why we granted your petition."

Nettled, Fini grimaced. Beside him, the Chief Justice finished airily, "But thank you for the enlightenment, Mr. Pell. Case submitted."

All at once, it was over. "So who won?" Chris quietly asked Terri.

Still watching the justices, she touched his hand.

TEN

THE **PRICE** CASE WAS ARGUED ON A TUESDAY, THE VOTE among the justices scheduled for Friday. But in ways small and large, the uncertainty of its outcome reverberated within the Court.

On Tuesday afternoon, Adam Wendt—finding Elizabeth Burke unresponsive—called another of Justice Glynn's clerks, Conor Farrell, and suggested they shoot some hoops on the "Highest Court in the Land," the top-floor gym reserved for those who worked in the building. Amidst the blare of rap music from a boom box which accompanied a spirited half-court game among the marshals, Adam and Conor played a leisurely game of Horse at the opposite end of the court.

Ever the competitor, Conor grinned at Adam. "Why don't we ratchet up the pressure?" he proposed. "Winner takes the loser to a Wizards game. Or are you wilting under the spotlight?"

"The disciples of Justice Fini," Adam said gravely, "never wilt—"

"Or experience doubt."

The sardonic remark brought a tighter smile to Adam's lips. "Why not this—two Wizards tickets against your justice's vote in the **Price** case. Think you can swing **that,** Conor?"

Conor regarded him with a more serious expression. "Doubt is sometimes better than confidence. And I'd never stake anyone's life on my jump shot."

"What about our legal system?" Adam retorted. "How many of these cases can this Court take? How many **should** it take?"

Absentmindedly, Conor began dribbling the basketball. "Two good questions," he answered. "I think that's what Justice Glynn's asking himself. What he's **not** looking for, I'm guessing, is a chance to make grand statements. I don't believe that's how your justice will get my justice to sign on."

Which, after graciously losing to Conor, Adam reported to Justice Fini.

"The Supreme Court," Rennell asked Terri. "What that be like?"

Terri considered this, wondering how to describe the Court to a retarded man in a plastic cubicle. "Grand," she said, "like a church, or a cathedral." Then she realized that Eula Price's modest church in the Bayview was so little like her own that the reference had no meaning. "It has high ceilings," she continued, "with marble statues and pillars everywhere, and drawings of great lawgivers. And there's a long bench for the justices, because there's nine of them."

Rennell strained to imagine this. Softly, he asked, "Those men all be wearin' them black robes?"

The question, Terri perceived, carried echoes of his trial—fifteen years ago, the last man in a black robe, Angelo Rotelli, had sentenced Payton and Rennell to death. And now only Rennell survived, his life hanging on the votes of nine other judges in robes.

"Two of them are women," Terri said. "They really listened hard to everything Chris told them about you."

But saying this revived Terri's sense of deep disquiet. As if he could hear her thoughts, Rennell stared at the table.

She covered his hand. "I've got good news, Rennell. We found you a home—living with a minister a few blocks from our house."

Rennell closed his eyes. "When those judges gonna tell us?"

"June. That's when they'll announce it."

"How long that be?"

An eternity. "Not long. Two months from now, that's all."

"Long," Rennell said wearily. "You tell that minister to wait for me, okay?"

The next morning, Terri, as was her custom, awoke at 6:00 A.M., before the others, to sip black coffee and read **The New York Times.**

As always, the **Times** had appeared on her doorstep, delivered in the hours before dawn. The only difference—which at first Terri barely registered—was that it lay flat on the front porch, unrolled from the tight blue cellophane wrapping, which today lay beside it.

Pausing, Terri looked up and down the tree-lined street. It was silent, save for the dull, thudding tread of a single jogger, running up the slope of Pacific Avenue in the thin glow of dawn. Pensive, Terri closed the door behind her, and went to the kitchen to pour her first cup of coffee and start reading at the breakfast table.

Lifting the front section from the others, she froze.

A loose photograph lay across Section B, inserted in the paper. Its image, though grainy, was clear enough— an adolescent girl on her knees, performing oral sex on a dark man with an oversize penis, his torso visible only from the waist down. The girl's hair was black like Elena's, her skin as pale.

Fighting back nausea, Terri heard her own brief cry.

ELEVEN

ON THE MORNING OF THE FRIDAY CONFERENCE, CAR-
oline Masters sat alone in her chambers, reviewing her
notes.

Three of the cases were predictable—she already
knew where the votes were and believed they would be
correctly decided. At least, none of the rulings would
deface the law, or bring rancor to the Court which was
her charge.

Unless she was lucky, this would not be true in the
matter of Rennell Price.

Idly scanning her notes, she pondered the chain of
irony and mischance, the changing tides of law,
through which one inmate, once a speck in the margins of society, had become the pawn of a fate which
dwarfed his own. Then the buzzer sounded in her
chambers, as in those of her eight colleagues, summoning the Court to conference.

As Chief Justice, it was Caroline's role to initiate the
discussion of each case which had been argued, outlin-

ing the decision under review, explaining her views as to the applicable law, then casting her vote on whether to affirm or reverse. By now this ritual was second nature, one she performed with confidence and crispness, and she strove to treat the case of Rennell Price like any other. But the sharp attentiveness of her colleagues underscored the stakes.

"The Ninth Circuit ruling," she began, "has two distinct components:

"First, that Rennell Price met the burden of demonstrating mental retardation. The effect of that ruling is simply to bar his execution."

Anthony Fini, she saw, smiled slightly—his silent way of objecting to the assertion that **Atkins** applied at all. "Second," Caroline continued calmly, "the Ninth Circuit agreed with Mr. Price's assertion that new evidence of innocence entitled him to exoneration. As the State concedes that it could not now obtain a conviction, affirming the Ninth Circuit means that Price goes free.

"There are two alternative grounds for doing so. Under AEDPA, the Ninth Circuit held that Mr. Price was entitled to introduce new evidence of innocence—his brother's confession—because Yancey James's performance deprived him of the effective assistance of counsel, and because counsel's failure to offer the confession earlier was **not** caused by lack of diligence..."

Fini's eyebrows shot up, noting what, to him, was clearly a contradiction. Ignoring this, Caroline addressed herself to Justice Glynn, a silent portrait of indecision. "In the alternative," she said, "the majority held that, where the new evidence of innocence is compelling, Mr. Price was entitled to introduce it **even** if he could not satisfy the predicates of AEDPA—which is to say, even if Mr. James's performance was adequate and, therefore, his original trial was technically fair."

Pausing, Caroline surveyed the others—Justices Ware, Kelly, Rothbard, and Millar to her left; Justices Fini, Glynn, and Raymond to her right; and, at the other end, Justice Huddleston. Leaning forward, she rested both arms on the table. "On the **Atkins** claim, I vote to affirm. Mr. Price's social history establishes, by a preponderance of the evidence, that he is mentally retarded.

"On the innocence claim, I vote to affirm under AEDPA. That means we do not have to resolve whether a freestanding innocence claim exists, or what the proper standard of proof might be." Her voice becameclipped. "To me, this case is hardly a landmark in the law. The only compelling question it presents relates to Mr. Price: will this Court permit the State to **execute** a man when it concedes that the evidence no longer even supports a conviction? And if we do, what on earth has the law—or this Court—gained? **Nothing.**"

With that, the Chief Justice stopped abruptly, nodding to Justice Huddleston. Her senior colleague spoke slowly and deliberately. "There's been much discussion," he began, "of all the deference we owe to the ruling of the Supreme Court of California. It's boiler-plate—less an opinion than a form for approving executions, with the victim's name left blank so the Court could fill it in later. I've seen a dozen of these, and they're all alike. And worth nothing.

"I vote with the Chief Justice."

By custom, the discussion turned to Fini. "Well," he said with a smile, "it's the third inning, and I'm already trailing two to nothing.

"But I should correct some misimpressions." Without overtly noting him, Fini leaned closer to Justice Glynn, speaking in a tone which combined regret with admonition. "This decision is about whether innocent victims like the family of Thuy Sen—a name we seem to have forgotten—will become our victims as well." Abruptly, his voice became biting. "In short, whether California has a death penalty at all, or whether the Ninth Circuit is allowed to practice abolition case by case.

"This last-minute confession is not 'clear and convincing' evidence of anything but Payton Price's desire to live a few weeks longer." Fini scanned the table. "Is this the first death row confession we've ever seen? They're routine. How naïve can we be? How much mischief will we let inventive prisoners do to our justice system?

"The finding on innocence is an abuse. As for **Atkins,** our opinion did **not** state—as required—that it applies to all the numberless **habeas corpus** petitioners who will now become 'retarded.' And **if** it does, it requires far more compelling evidence than that presented by Mr. Price.

"This case is **poison,**" Fini concluded with disgust. "Thanks to our system of 'justice,' the Sen family has served fifteen years in a purgatory of our own invention. The vote stands two to one."

Sitting beside Fini, McGeorge Glynn looked so riven that Caroline felt a moment's pity, followed by irritation—in all likelihood, Glynn held a man's life in his hands, and it was time for him to face it. "McGeorge?"

Gazing at the table, he rubbed his fingertips together. "I'm reminded of that hoary cliché—'Hard cases make bad law.' I find both sides equally compelling, and equally perplexing."

And so? Caroline thought. The silence among his colleagues conveyed the common assessment apparent in Fini's taut gaze—that Justice Glynn was about to decide the case. "I've never seen anyone do this," Glynn said at last, "but I'd like to reserve my vote until I've heard more discussion." Apologetically, he faced Caroline. "I **could** cast a tentative vote for the sake of casting one, but it would only be that."

Startled, Caroline considered the benefits of suggesting that he do so and encountered her own unwonted hesitance—she did not know which way Glynn would jump, and worried about being the one to force him. "No need," she said in a pleasant tone.

"If Tony, Walter, and I haven't dazzled you, there're still five of us to go."

She turned to Justice Raymond, knowing that he, too, could become the deciding vote to condemn Rennell Price. "Thomas?"

The rumpled and amiable Raymond—a self-styled practical man—smiled at Justice Glynn. "I'll tread where the brighter of us fear to go. Like you, McGeorge, I can argue this thing either way. But what decides it for me is that I used to be a State Supreme Court judge.

"I wasn't impressed then," Raymond continued dryly, "and I'm not now. We were elected; so are these people in California. We were afraid of capital cases; so are they.

"As Walter suggests, except for the name Rennell Price, the State Supreme Court's opinion could pertain to any case, and tells us nothing about this one. Until they start doing their job, someone should—even if it's the Ninth Circuit." Looking at his colleagues, Raymond finished serenely, "I vote to affirm."

Thank God for Tom, Caroline thought—a sensible man who knows his own mind and who, she felt certain, would sleep soundly tonight. But Tony Fini had clearly entertained the hope that Thomas Raymond was persuadable; it took Fini a moment to erase his scowl before he turned to his soul mate in ideology, Justice Ware.

As John Ware prepared to break his accustomed silence, Caroline pondered anew the complexities of race, the wounds sustained by John Ware in ways which she could never know. Though sometimes affable, Ware struck her as an angry man. But what made him angry was less racism than his belief that society's sporadic efforts to ameliorate it cheapened his own achievements, condemning him in others' minds—and perhaps his own—to a second-class citizenship he could no more escape than he could escape his race. Yet Ware had risen through the patronage of conservatives who, trumpeting a black man who purported to believe as they did, had taken a judge of more modest accomplishment than any number of African American judges or lawyers and put him on the Court. Knowing this, Caroline suspected, had further tied Ware in psychic knots. But there was one thing she knew for sure—for Mr. Justice Ware, Rennell Price's dilemma was far less vivid than his own.

"In my mind," Ware said tersely, "this is about the respect we owe state courts. This isn't nursery school—it's not our purpose to draw smiley faces on the margins of opinions with the most words in them. I vote to reverse."

The vote stood at three to two. As he butted his head forward, Bryson Kelly's bristles of crew-cut red hair evoked the football player he once had been. Looking directly at Justice Glynn, Kelly said, "Tony and John have spoken for me. We've reversed the Ninth Circuit in case after case, and still we have this problem. To encourage them further is weak-minded. As I used to say when I was in politics, 'Send them a message.' "

Justice Glynn pondered this, eyes fixed on the green leather pad before him. Caroline could sense the swirl of his conflicting emotions: cautious by nature and moderate by inclination, Glynn also suffered from the contradictory impulses of the sweet-souled but weak-willed—the desire to be fair without giving offense, for which he sometimes overcompensated by sudden outbursts of rigidity. How those forces would resolve themselves was as opaque as his expression.

"Miriam?" the Chief Justice said to Justice Rothbard.

Though the kindest of women, Miriam Rothbard had a look of intellectual severity; her plain wire-rim glasses and hair pulled back in a bun reminded Caroline that Justice Rothbard had been an early feminist, one of the first—and still one of the brightest—women to graduate from Harvard Law School. "Like the Chief Justice," she said to Glynn, "I started out by defending criminal cases. I never saw a defendant sentenced to death who didn't have a terrible lawyer. And yet only twice—in this Court's **entire** history—have we found that a lawyer's poor performance violated a condemned man's right to counsel."

Pausing, she glanced pointedly at Justice Fini. "Something's wrong here. Either my experience is anomalous—which I very much doubt—or this Court is pretzeling itself to let terrible lawyers become corpse valets. If any of us would let Yancey James represent him with his life on the line, I'd sincerely like to understand why."

Fini gave his friend and fellow opera buff a smile of reproof. "That's really **not** the issue—"

"Reality never is, is it, Tony?" Rothbard returned his smile with a killer smile of her own. "Only the most arid kind of abstraction could turn a drug-addicted hack into an excuse for executing a retarded black man who might as well have been representing himself."

Suppressing a smile of her own, Caroline bit her lip. "If this lawyer isn't bad enough to satisfy you," Justice Rothbard concluded, "no one is. I vote to affirm."

Caroline fixed her gaze on Justice Millar, hopeful, despite his vote to grant the State's petition, that Justice Raymond or Justice Rothbard might have caused him second thoughts. "Dennis?"

Millar, the court's ascetic, regarded her with a wistful air. "If I may say so, I find this whole discussion melancholy.

"There seem to be two very different versions of the Court—one that places trust in state courts, one that sees us as their keeper. The latter course, it seems to me, will embroil us in more contention. I vote to reverse."

So much for Rennell Price, Caroline thought caustically—the purpose of this Court is to keep its own docket tidy. The vote stood at four to four.

With deep misgivings, she faced Justice Glynn, saying gently, "The buck is passed, McGeorge."

Turning his entire body, Fini stared at his wavering colleague, willing his acquiescence. Caroline's mouth felt dry.

Glynn folded his hands, turning to the Chief Justice. "I have two concerns, and they're in conflict.

"The first is Miriam's: that a lackadaisical lawyer contributed to this man's conviction—though I'm stymied, I'll admit, by the fact that his deficiencies have nothing to do with Payton Price's failure to confess. But I'm also troubled that, by ruling for Mr. Price, we're going to encourage Ninth Circuit judges, some of them de facto death penalty abolitionists, to second-guess judges and juries who were closer to the facts."

"Suppose," Caroline swiftly proposed, "that I assign you the task of drafting a majority opinion affirming the Ninth Circuit. That way you can write it to accommodate your concerns, confining its scope to the particulars concerning Mr. Price."

Fearing her sudden effort to co-opt the fifth vote, Fini interjected, "I'm not sure that's giving due credit to his ambivalence—"

"For which," she cut in, "I'm offering a cure. In the process, perhaps McGeorge can find us **all** a way out of this mess."

"Assuming that we want one." Again facing Justice Glynn, Fini added incisively, "I, for one, don't."

As though cornered, Glynn turned to Caroline for relief. "At this point, I'm not sure I'm prepared to pick up the laboring oar."

"Then let's do this," she responded easily. "I'll draft a majority opinion addressing your qualms—"

"There **is** no majority," Fini retorted. "We're split four to four, with McGeorge still undecided.

"Let me suggest this: you draft your proposed majority opinion, and I, as senior justice among the opposing four, will draft ours. Then we can circulate them to the others, while giving McGeorge a basis for comparison and, I would hope, a resting place that pleases him." Before Caroline could respond, Fini turned to Glynn. "Would that be helpful, McGeorge?"

Glynn accorded him a look of genuine gratitude. "Yes. It would."

Fini flashed a grin. "Excellent. What say you, Madam Chief?"

Finessed, Caroline silently cursed McGeorge Glynn for his dithering. Of Fini, she inquired, "Is ten days enough time for an exchange of drafts?"

"Ample."

"Good. Then that's what we'll do." Checking her notes, the Chief Justice said evenly, "The next case is **City of Cincinnati v. Roberts.**"

TWELVE

THE DRAFTS PREPARED BY THE CHIEF JUSTICE AND JUS-
tice Fini were written for an audience of one, Justice
Glynn. Caroline's instructions to Callista Hill were
clear: apply Atkins, find Rennell Price innocent within
the parameters of AEDPA, and avoid resolving the
question of freestanding innocence. "Ground it in the
specific facts," she ordered. "No broad rulings, no
sharp edges."

Fini's directions were the opposite. "Hit all the issues, both on the facts and on the law," he told Adam
Wendt. "If Justice Glynn signs off on a broad ruling,
we've hamstrung the Ninth Circuit and changed the
face of the law. If he won't, then we've still got room to
narrow the opinion in a way that pleases him.

"One thing needs to be clear. If his brother's death
row confession is enough to exonerate Rennell Price,
there'll be no end to exonerations."

And so, exchanging drafts, the two chambers took
one case and fashioned two different realities for the
benefit of Justice Glynn.

"Amazing," Conor Farrell said to his colleague Elizabeth Burke. "Fini's written a broadside on the subject of capital punishment."

Closeted in Justice Glynn's conference room, they compared the two drafts. "I think the Chief's out-smarted him," Elizabeth said. "Our justice will never buy off on saying **Atkins** doesn't apply to Price."

Nodding, Conor read aloud from the Chief Justice's opinion: "To execute a retarded man for the crime of being convicted before **Atkins** is anomalous. If that be our ruling, then capital punishment is to the rest of all law what surrealism is to realism. It destroys the logic of our judicial system."

Elizabeth smiled. "You can tell where Callista leaves off," she opined. "That paragraph has Caroline Masters all over it."

Fini handed Adam Wendt a page of the Chief Justice's draft. Swiftly, Adam read the lines his mentor had underlined in red:

Justice Fini excoriates the Ninth Circuit for overstepping its bounds. But the perverse genius of our system is that it allows all of us to claim that everyone but us is responsible for deciding life or death.

Federal courts must defer to state supreme courts; state supreme courts to state trial courts, and when either fails to act, they point to the federal courts as the last redoubt for

correcting error. In the area of clemency, courts defer to governors, and governors to courts. And, of course, everyone who is elected defers to the voters who elect them, and who favor capital punishment.

In this antiseptic process of death by default, it is hard to fault the Ninth Circuit for looking at an inconvenient but stubborn fact: that the State of California seeks to execute a man whom the evidence no longer permits them to convict.

"If you buy this," Adam said, "the Ninth Circuit can designate itself as primary arbiter of innocence..."

"Exactly," Fini said. "If all else fails, **that's** what we sell to Justice Glynn."

At nine o'clock, returning from a solitary dinner, Justice Glynn interrupted his clerks' discussion.

"How are the opinions?" he inquired.

"Contentious," Conor said. "Justice Fini's mainly. He claims **Atkins** doesn't apply to **habeas corpus** petitioners like Price."

"Good God," Justice Glynn said in dismay. "Anthony's a brilliant man. But I wish, sometimes, that his notion of justice included **appearing** to do justice." This thought led to another. "What do they say about freestanding innocence?"

"The Chief Justice says almost nothing." Picking up

a page of Caroline Masters's draft, Elizabeth said, "There's just one sentence: 'Because Rennell Price has satisfied the predicate for offering proof of innocence under AEDPA, we need not decide whether—in the absence of a constitutionally defective trial—the law offers any avenue for Mr. Price to show his innocence.' "

"Good."

"However, she goes on to say, 'To create contention where there is none, Justice Fini ranges far afield, issuing gratuitous admonitions on irrelevant issues to imaginary foes bent on abolishing the death penalty by stealth. These tendentious disquisitions, however philosophically interesting, are unnecessary to the disposition of the case of Rennell Price.' "

Justice Glynn sat heavily. "What about Anthony?"

"He jumps right into it," Elizabeth answered. "Listen to this: 'Given Price's failure to satisfy AEDPA, addressing whether a claim of "freestanding innocence" exists is hardly gratuitous—it is necessary. Indeed, a failure to do so would cause havoc in the federal courts, inducing a steady trickle of deceitful and sadistic **habeas corpus** petitions, filed by defendants playing in a lottery of our own invention.' "

"Oh, dear," Justice Glynn said softly. "I sometimes wish Justice Fini weren't quite so vivid. If you try to kill your audience with every sentence, you're likely to succeed."

"There's more," Elizabeth answered with a smile. " 'Absent a constitutional defect in the trial itself, there is no basis in the Constitution for demanding judicial consideration of evidence which somehow materializes after conviction. It is time to put this argument to an end: truly compelling proof of innocence—not present here—would undoubtedly provoke a pardon by the Governor.' "

Glynn slowly shook his head. "That's way too peremptory," he said. "If there's one thing Americans bridle at, it's the prospect of executing the innocent."

"Justice Fini," Elizabeth told him, "doesn't shrink from **that,** either. Here's what he says:

" 'One could hazard a guess that some nontrivial number of people in prison are, in fact, innocent. But because of the tremendous resources focused on death penalty litigation, it is fair to conclude that few—if any—of them reside on death row.

" 'Any human decision carries the risk of human error. But we have not, because of that, abolished the justice system. And by comparison with noncapital punishment, imposition of the death penalty is a model of exactitude. ' "

"What does the Chief Justice say to **that?**"

Picking up the opposing draft, Elizabeth performed a fair rendition of Caroline Masters at her most mordant: " 'Whether the error rate on capital crimes is insignificant depends, we might well suppose, on whether one is a statistic. The question is whether this Court is required to adopt the perspective of the statistician. The sheer number of exonerations counsels greater humility—not to mention humanity—' "

"To which," Conor put in, "Justice Fini responds

624 / RICHARD NORTH PATTERSON

by focusing on the guilty: 'Far from being inhumane, imposing the death penalty on a murderer is the essence of humanity. It vindicates the moral order, and confirms our respect for innocent life. It acknowledges the existence of evil in the world, and confirms the primacy of personal responsibility.' " Pausing, Conor raised his eyebrows. " 'Even the debate over deterrence cannot erase one undeniable fact—once the sentence of death is carried out, the recidivism rate for that defendant is extremely low.' "

Standing, Justice Glynn gazed out the window, his worry palpable. "This divisiveness won't do," he said. "Cases like this could tarnish us as an institution.

"The Chief Justice was right. If it falls to me to find us a way out, then it does."

Over the next two days, the outcome of the **Price** case narrowed, as expected, to the vote of Justice Glynn.

The Chief Justice's chambers received three "join memos"—the traditional letters from other justices saying "Please join me in your opinion"—from Justices Huddleston, Raymond, and Rothbard. And Justice Fini, Callista Hill informed Caroline, had three join memos—from Justices Ware, Kelly, and Millar—accepting his opinion without requesting any changes. With one more vote on Fini's side, the opinion of the United States Supreme Court would be a sweeping triumph for conservatives—strictly interpreting AEDPA, barring claims of freestanding innocence, and denying **habeas corpus** petitioners the right to assert mental retardation. As with the incidental effect of this—Rennell Price's execution—Glynn gave no sign of his inclinations.

"McGeorge," Huddleston told the Chief Justice in her chambers, "has incredible leverage over the jurisprudence of death. The worry is how he'll use it."

Huddleston pondered this. "What Anthony has going for him is, to me, McGeorge's frightening level of naïveté: he has far too much faith that anyone who takes an oath and puts on a robe will do the right thing. He won't want to be seen as slapping down the California Supreme Court—whatever you do, you'll have to get around that."

Unhappily, Caroline nodded. "He's avoiding me," she informed her friend. "My spies tell me he's sitting down with Fini first."

"And so," Caroline said to Justice Glynn.

They sat across from each other over a candlelit dinner in the formal dining room of the Chief Justice's Georgetown town house—poached salmon in a white wine cream sauce, prepared by Caroline herself, accompanied by a chill bottle of Chassagne-Montrachet.

Justice Glynn dabbed his lips. "Delicious," he answered. "Or do you mean the **Price** case?"

Caroline smiled. "Both, I suppose. But now I'm in suspense about only one."

Glynn put down his napkin. "As so often, Tony went too far in framing bold—and, to me, unnecessary—principles of law. I've told him as much. The problem with your approach is that—in the guise of caution—it, too, is revolutionary."

Genuinely surprised, Caroline asked, "How so?"

"It reorders the relationship between the Ninth Circuit and the State Supreme Court, not so subtly concluding that the latter is constituted of seven intellectual and moral ciphers, whose sole concern is not justice but their own reelection."

Caroline tried to stifle her alarm. "What a perfectly formed sentence, McGeorge. It sounds like you've been doing a little drafting of your own."

Justice Glynn looked vaguely guilty. "I have," he conceded. "But only as a way of trying out one theory."

Once more, Caroline was struck by the degree to which Rennell Price had become a pawn, prey to legal abstractions and competing agendas. "Then I hope you'll try another," she answered softly. "What about this? We don't decide retardation at all. Instead you and I craft a narrow ruling on innocence that doesn't address the adequacy of the California Supreme Court's performance. We simply find that the evidence—in this **one** case—satisfies AEDPA's requirement of 'clear and convincing' evidence."

"How do we do **that**?"

"By stressing that the Attorney General conceded that a retrial would result in Price's acquittal. **That** circumstance is so unusual it has no broad implications for the law."

"No **adverse** implications, you mean. Because then I haven't signed off on any of Tony's theories, and you're reserving the subject of deference for another day."

Caroline smiled. "It's like the Hippocratic oath, McGeorge. First do no harm—to the law, to this Court, or to Rennell Price."

But Justice Glynn did not return her smile. "It's a way out," he said at last. "There's just so much to think about."

THIRTEEN

In late June, as the Supreme Court's term neared its end, the Court remained silent in the case of Rennell Price.

This was a sign of trouble, Chris guessed aloud to Terri—a deeply divided Court or, perhaps, last-minute vote switching or hesitance about the scope of the opinion. Left to speculate, Chris followed the steady announcement of opinions, their authorship rotating among the justices, until with two "opinion days"—a Tuesday and a Wednesday—left, it was possible to guess that the author of the majority opinion would be either the Chief Justice or Justice Fini. "If I'm right," Chris said over dinner on the weekend before, "then we'll know whether we win or lose depending on which one of them announces the opinion."

"I'd like to be there," Carlo said.

Chris glanced at Terri. "Maybe all of us could go."

Terri hesitated. She did not know which would be more excruciating—awaiting the decision in her office or being present at the moment when the Chief Justice named the justice who would summarize the ruling and, with that, whether Rennell Price would live or die. Whatever the result, the task of informing Rennell would fall to her.

"There's Elena," Terri said. "And Kit."

The comment did not need elaboration. The photograph inserted in her **New York Times** had yielded no fingerprints; its provenance, the police believed, was Internet pornography. And Eddie Fleet still could not be found.

"We can ask Rossella to stay with them."

Terri pondered this. Their housekeeper, as fiercely maternal about the Pagets' children as was Terri, was a paragon of caution and good sense. And during the day, Elena would be serving as a junior counselor at the day camp Kit attended, safely surrounded by adult supervisors and other children.

"I'll think about it," Terri told her husband.

On the last Tuesday morning in June, all three Pagets watched an inscrutable Court, speaking through Justices Glynn, Raymond, and Ware respectively, announce decisions in three other cases.

That night, as they ate a fine Italian dinner at I Ricchi, Terri thought of her last meeting with Rennell. "I can't come to see you tomorrow," she had told him. "Maybe for one or two days after that."

Rennell looked anxious. "Where you be?"

Terri paused. "I'm going to the Supreme Court," she admitted, "to hear the justices say what they've decided."

Rennell was quiet, his eyes hooded: Terri saw him struggling to imagine that his freedom, or death, was a matter to be announced in public, in an august setting far from San Quentin. "When they do that?" he asked.

"I'm not sure yet—either Tuesday or Wednesday. But as soon as they do, I'm getting on a plane and coming straight here from the airport."

Rennell's eyes widened at the thought. "Maybe I be free," he said. "Wonder what that be like."

For a moment, Terri did not know what to say. "Good, Rennell. Happy." She thought of the first time she had seen him, gazing out the window of his cubicle at a sliver of the bay. "You can look at the water, feel sunlight whenever you want..."

"Go to baseball games."

"Yeah," she said softly. "Go to baseball games."

Suddenly his eyes misted. "Not like Payton," he said. "Payton don't be goin' to no games." And Terri knew that, for Rennell, the idea of death was as awesome and enormous as it was for her.

Now, eating little, Terri was glad that Chris and Carlo were with her. By this time tomorrow, she would be sitting with Rennell.

"They can't kill him," she said aloud, and to her

own ears, she sounded as childish and willful as Elena, confronted by emotions too painful to accept.

"No," Carlo answered. "They can't."

The case was formally denominated **Godward, Warden of San Quentin Prison v. Rennell Price.** But when the Court's marshal called out "Oyez! Oyez! Oyez!" Caroline Masters instead began with "Justice Huddleston will announce the Court's opinion in Case Number 03-1540, **Commonwealth of Virginia v. Burrell.**"

In a state of silent agony, Terri, flanked by Chris and Carlo, listened to Huddleston drone through the obligations imposed on the State of Virginia by the Americans with Disabilities Act. Once again, Terri tried to read the emotions of Caroline Masters and Anthony Fini. Perhaps she only imagined that the Chief Justice seemed preoccupied and a little detached; she could detect no pleasure in the morning, the final such occasion until October.

At last, Huddleston finished, and Justice Fini looked expectantly toward the Chief Justice. Those assembled, spectators and the press, awaited all that remained for the Court to announce: its latest ruling on capital punishment—the much-publicized, much-anticipated matter of the prisoner Rennell Price.

"Come on," Carlo murmured.

Caroline Masters seemed to hesitate. Then, stone-faced, she said in a chill voice, "Justice Fini will announce the Court's opinion in Case Number 03-542, **Godward v. Price**..."

Sickened, Terri shut her eyes. "Today," Fini said, "in a case which began with the tragic murder of a child, this Court confirms the legacy of Roger Bannon..."

Gripping Chris's hand, Terri opened her eyes again and saw that Justice Glynn looked neither at Justice Fini nor at the Chief Justice but at the bench in front of him.

Not until Caroline Masters took the unusual step of reading her dissent, voice steely with suppressed anger, did Terri feel the blow sustained by the Chief Justice.

"To avoid this Court's responsibilities," she began, "the five justices in the majority have plunged death penalty jurisprudence down the rabbit hole of 'deference to state court adjudications,' condemning—almost incidentally—a man named Rennell Price to death by lethal injection."

Terri shivered.

On the steps outside, Terri breathed in the hot, fetid air of early summer, gazing across First Street at the Capitol, where seven years before, determined men and women, jockeying for power, had passed the law which had now ensnared Rennell. Carlo stood on the pavement, slightly apart, arms folded; Chris said nothing, perhaps remembering the argument and wondering what else he might have done.

"Fini got his fifth vote," Terri said bitterly. "Rennell's merely collateral damage."

This afternoon she must go to San Quentin to tell him. And in twenty-four hours, she guessed, there would be a new date for Rennell Price's execution.

"Come on," Chris said gently. "Our driver's waiting."

FOURTEEN

RENNELL PRICE'S EXECUTION WAS SET FOR JULY 22.

Rennell's response surprised her. At the moment she told him of the Supreme Court's ruling, he seemed unable to speak. Then he took her hand and held it in both of his; in that moment of communion, she was certain that, as frightened as he was of dying, Rennell felt her own anguish as well. It brought home to her, in a way both painful and moving, how little love he had received from anyone, how abandoned he had always been, and how grateful he had felt to have Terri and the others fighting for him now. For a long time, they simply sat together, two people fearing the death of one.

When she described this to Tammy Mattox, Tammy had smiled sadly. "A lawyer friend of mine," she told Terri, "used to do these cases.

"Few years ago, my friend came down with AIDS. The last case he had was for a retarded man they executed. Before the man died, he wrote out a 'will and testament,' leaving my friend his unused years. It was the only way he could think of to give something back."

All Terri could do for Rennell was visit him every day and—without false promises—try to keep hope alive: otherwise, she feared that the certainty of his time and place of death would slowly begin to crush him. They would seek clemency from the Governor, she assured him, keep up the search for sources of new evidence to support yet another petition—perhaps Betty Sims, perhaps even Tasha Bramwell. Perhaps, with luck, they could find Eddie Fleet, or someone else who was his victim. Rennell simply listened; watching his face, Terri remembered herself as a child listening to her mother say the rosary, words she barely understood but which, perhaps because her mother put faith in them, became a source of comfort amidst the brutality of Terri's home life. This thought underlay another of Terri's goals—to recruit a spiritual adviser to comfort Rennell in his final hours, when Terri could be with him no longer.

The sole comfort for Terri was family, and work.

Through the functionary in charge of clemency, the Governor's office sent the Pagets a letter, specifying its requirements for a clemency petition, the Attorney General's papers in opposition, and Rennell's reply. "The theme of clemency," Terri emphasized to Carlo, "is compassion—all the reasons Rennell's life should be spared.

"His probable innocence is part of that. But we're

asking the Governor to look at Rennell as a person: how he got that way, the difficulties of his life, and why a just society would spare him."

Before July 22, Terri explained, the clemency board would hold a hearing. Her hope was to gain support from unanticipated sources: in the eight months since Payton Price's execution, a fiscal crisis had plunged Governor Darrow into a bitter battle against a recall petition—fighting for survival, he seemed even less likely to risk granting clemency to Payton's brother. Recruiting those among the Governor's financial supporters who might also support Rennell—chiefly actors or writers—was not enough. And so, once more, she found herself sharing lunch on Lou Mauriani's deck.

"You didn't know he might be retarded," Terri told him. "You didn't know what Payton would say about Eddie Fleet. Now you do. If they execute him anyhow, how are you going to feel?"

Mauriani considered her gravely. "When I prosecuted your client," he answered in measured tones, "I was absolutely certain of his guilt, and that he deserved to die. For the next fifteen years, I didn't have the remotest doubt about either. About his execution, I still don't. If he did this to Thuy Sen, that should be his punishment.

"You claim that he didn't. But two Supreme Courts have held that the trial was fair, the verdict justified, the sentence warranted. Now you're asking me if I'll sleep at night if I don't turn my back on that and, far more important to me, on the family I promised justice. Tell me how **they** feel now."

"The same."

Mauriani contemplated his wineglass. "Then I don't think it's my place to help you. Whether I'll sleep well doesn't matter." Pausing, he looked up at her with candid blue eyes, adding softly, "Truth to tell, I wouldn't sleep well either way."

Driving away, Terri resolved to do the one thing which, out of pity for the Sens, she had left undone. "Payton's dead," she imagined telling Thuy Sen's sister. "The next death you watch will be that of a retarded man who may well be innocent. By the time you find out how that feels, it will be too late for both of you. Please don't let yourself become Eddie Fleet's last victim."

But although Johnny Moore dug up Kim Sen's address and unlisted number, Kim never answered the telephone, or her door. In desperation, Terri left a note explaining that she wished to meet. The only response was recorded after 1:00 A.M., on Terri's office voice mail: "This is Kim Sen," the soft voice said. "After all these years, it's almost done now. Please let me find peace in my own way."

How much peace, Terri wondered, would there ever be for a woman who could find none in the middle of the night? Kim Sen had watched Payton die, holding Thuy Sen's picture for him to see. But Payton's death had failed her; now she was placing all her hopes on the healing power of Rennell's execution. As Terri put down the telephone, a remark of Lou Mauriani's came back to her: "For some families, the defendant will never be dead enough. But there's only one way to know that for sure."

The day before the clemency hearing, Thuy Sen's sister met in private with Governor Craig Darrow. Out of respect for Kim Sen's feelings, Darrow's spokesman informed the media, he could not tell them what was said. But, the spokesman emphasized, one thing should be clear—Governor Darrow felt the pain of victims' families in a deeply personal way. No leader with compassion could feel less.

That afternoon, Terri received a call from Rossella, their housekeeper. In the background she heard Elena sobbing.

Terri felt panic overtake her. "What happened? Is she all right?"

"Except in her mind." Rossella's Latin-accented voice was soft. "She think she see a man following us from the day camp."

When Terri arrived home, her daughter's eyes were dry, her face drawn and—to Terri's eyes—drained of blood.

As Terri embraced Elena, the girl hugged her tightly. Over her shoulder, Terri saw Rossella's look of sympathy, followed by a slow shake of the head.

Terri sat her daughter on the couch, Rossella standing beside them.

Elena swallowed. "There was a car, following us down the street from camp—driving really slow. The driver was a strange man." Her voice was tight, emphatic. "When I looked again, he was still there, and then he turned the corner down Broadway. Before he did, he looked at me out the side window and smiled. The smile was sick."

"What did he look like?"

Elena's voice rose. "He was a black man, Mama. Like that man you worry about."

Terri forced herself to think systematically, like a lawyer. "How old did he look?"

Elena's brow knit. "How old would that man be?"

"Late thirties."

"Yes. That was how old he was."

"What color was the car?"

Elena thought, then looked away. "I don't remember."

Terri glanced up at Rossella. "Did you see him?"

Once more, silent, the housekeeper shook her head.

Terri took her daughter's hand. "We're going to see the police," she told Elena.

With two plainclothes cops from the Sex Crimes Unit, Monk spread six mug shots on the conference table where he once had questioned Rennell Price.

Fleet, Terri saw at once, was the third face on the

right. But his photograph, too, was a piece of history, an artifact of the time Fleet had traded Rennell and Payton Price for his own freedom. His eyes glinted with a young man's insolence, and the hint of a smile, perhaps perceptible only to Terri, seemed to play at one corner of his mouth.

Elena gazed at the photographs, her own face a mute portrait of fear and confusion. In that instant, Terri imagined Flora Lewis, staring at the mug shots Monk had brought to her living room and picking out Rennell and Payton Price.

"I think it was this one," Elena said and pointed to a photograph next to Fleet, a man Terri had never seen.

It turned out the man was dead.

That night, just before eleven, Terri softly opened Elena's door and peeked into her bedroom.

It seemed that her daughter was sleeping. Then Elena's voice came from the darkness.

"Did **he** have a bad childhood, too, Mama?"

Terri hesitated. She did not know whether the question, chilling to her ears, referred to Fleet, or to Rennell, or to Elena's own father.

"Who, Elena?"

Elena did not answer. "I want to know," she said. "Does everyone that something bad happened to have to do those things to someone else?"

Terri thought of herself and then, more piercingly, of Rennell. "Not always..."

"Maybe I'll hate men." Elena's voice was shaking now, close to hysteria. "Maybe I'll kill a man for forcing me to do things to him. Will you defend **me**, Mama?"

Elena began sobbing. Rushing to her side, Terri held her, her body stiff and resistant.

I hate you, Terri told her long-dead husband.

For some families, as Mauriani had said, they can never be dead enough.

FIFTEEN

ALONE, CHRISTOPHER PAGET ENTERED THE STERILE government building in Sacramento to speak for Rennell at the clemency hearing.

The steps were lined with reporters and jammed with pickets and counterpickets, some with signs seeking or decrying the execution of Rennell Price. The presence of two liberal film stars, a male and a female who lived together, guaranteed yet more media attention but underscored Chris's misgivings; the recall movement against Governor Darrow was growing in numbers and intensity, and more publicity might create a high-profile opportunity for Darrow to bless the execution of a child killer, burnishing his law-and-order credentials. Only new evidence of innocence was likely to serve Rennell, and Chris had none to offer. The last-ditch effort to save Rennell had become a search for Betty Sims, or anyone to whom Eddie Fleet might have made some careless remark suggestive of his guilt.

"Good luck," Terri had said as he left. But her voice was tired, and her tone held little hope.

The room dedicated to clemency hearings felt like a high school auditorium—three sections of seats sloping downward, sectioned by two aisles—and the proceedings were presided over by stone-faced mutes, a tribunal of eleven members, most of them white and male. In the front row, Thuy Sen's mother, father, and sister were equally impassive, save that Kim Sen kept glancing at a piece of paper grasped tightly in both hands.

Standing at the podium, Chris pled for Rennell's life. "Despite the terrible violence inflicted **on** Rennell Price, there is no record—either before or after prison—of Rennell inflicting violence on another living soul. Let alone a single act of sexual deviance or cruelty.

"The evidence before you shows a gentle man, confused by the world, who may very well be innocent. If the State of California executes him, our chance to prove that ends, and this will be Eddie Fleet's last, and cruelest, victory."

From the panel, he saw no glimmer of expression. Its chairman, a heavyset political functionary, gazed at some indeterminate spot above Chris's head. With an undercurrent of anger, Chris said, "I ask this board to stop for a moment—**just stop**—and look at the charade of justice the State asks you to take part in. Before the Supreme Court, Mr. Pell suggested that **this board**—not the courts—is the proper forum to consider our new evidence of innocence. Now the State tells you that the **courts** disposed of innocence, and that **you** must deem him guilty.

"Forget, the State tells you, anything we said before.

"Forget that we insisted on executing the principal witness on Rennell's behalf.

"Forget that **our** key witness invoked the Fifth Amendment and now—apparently—has disappeared to escape discovery of his own guilt.

"Forget that we refused to compel Fleet's testimony regarding the crime for which we insist on executing someone else.

"Forget that we—all of us—may someday learn through better DNA technology that Eddie Fleet has gotten away with murder, **twice.**" Turning toward the Sens, Chris finished softly, "Forget all that. Because the tragic death of a nine-year-old child demands that another life be taken, and Rennell Price's is the life **we** choose to take."

Arms folded, Kim Sen turned from him, staring at the panel. Facing them, Chris said, "The State has already taken one life, that of Payton Price. That execution had the virtue of certainty. **This** execution reeks of scapegoating and injustice, and **only you** can prevent it.

"It is 'justice enough,' I respectfully submit, to condemn Rennell Price to die of natural causes in the six-by-six cell in which—unless we can find a way to vindicate him—he will spend the next half century. Especially when his execution may prove to be yet another murder of an innocent." Chris paused. "Only **this time** by the State."

Stopping, Paget looked at the expressionless faces before him. "Thank you," the chairman said politely and called on Larry Pell.

Pell said little new. But then, Chris thought sourly, no doubt he did not need to. "As so often in these cases," he concluded, "defense counsel focuses on his **client's** suffering, rather than the suffering of the victim and her family, or the depravity of the crime committed by these two brothers for their own pleasure and amusement.

"It is well, then, to give Thuy Sen a face, and a voice—her surviving sister, Kim Sen."

In a tense silence, Kim Sen approached the podium, an almost ethereal presence. Then, with resolve which stiffened her posture, she began reading from her paper in a trembling voice.

"Fifteen years," she began. "To me, it's yesterday. Yesterday, and all the yesterdays since what these men did, where I relive, over and over and over again, the day that Thuy was murdered.

"Every day, and every night, I let my nine-year-old sister walk home from school alone. Only now, day after day, night after night, I know what I did **not** know then—that she will **never** reach our home." Voice breaking, she paused, steeling herself. "That she will die in those brothers' living room, choking on their semen . . ."

Silently, Chris implored her to stop, as much for her own sake as for Rennell's. Watching, Chou Sen bent her head in sorrow; only Meng Sen maintained his fierce, implacable stare at the chairman of the clemency board.

"Our family is shattered," Kim concluded in a parched voice, "our lives spent sleepwalking through a nightmare without end. Give us peace, the only peace you have to give. **End this.**"

Again the panel said nothing. But when Kim Sen sat, Chris felt very sure that it would give her the death she asked for.

Afterward, the onlookers—the media, the partisans of one side or the other—peeled away. Chris saw that Kim Sen stood apart from her parents, arms folded, and head bowed.

After a moment, he approached her, waiting until she looked up at him.

"I'm Chris Paget," he said simply.

"I know who you are." Her words were toneless. "Your wife leaves me notes and messages."

Chris hesitated. "I'm sorry. We don't presume to know how you feel. But please know that we feel for you." He paused, adding quietly, "It's just that we don't believe that Rennell did this to you, or that seeing him die will heal you."

Kim folded her arms, looking at him intently. Her voice was soft but bitter. "We'll all see, won't we. After he dies, if I don't feel any better, maybe I'll join your side."

Turning, she walked away.

Waiting for his flight to San Francisco, Chris did what he had never done before—sit in an airport bar.

Alone, he nursed a double scotch on ice. A bulky form sat next to him. It took Chris a moment to look over and see that it was Larry Pell.

"Do you mind?" Pell asked.

Chris shrugged. But he made no sign that he welcomed conversation.

Pell ordered a beer, sipping it in silence. Finally, he said, "I've always wondered. Why does your wife do this work, knowing she's going to lose?"

Chris turned to him. Softly, he inquired, "Do you feel better because you always win? Then maybe you can explain to me why **that** was winning, and just who it was that won."

Chris turned back to his scotch. Shortly thereafter, without responding, Pell put down five dollars for the bartender and left Chris sitting next to a half-empty beer.

When Chris reached the San Francisco airport, he called Terri. But there was no answer on her cell, or at the office, or at home.

Finally, he checked his phone for messages and found one from his wife. "I'm flying to Cleveland," she said simply. "Monk found Betty Sims."

SIXTEEN

MUCH OF THE EAST SIDE OF INNER-CITY CLEVELAND, Terri learned, had been ravaged since the riots of the late 1960s. Spacious homes had become boarding-houses for the desperate or impoverished; a once-thriving main artery of commerce was now a strip of laundries, liquor stores, corner groceries, and check-cashing businesses; the public housing was a Stalinist cinder-block monolith scarred by indecipherable graffiti, in front of which Terri saw a cluster of black kids passing a joint. But Betty Sims had found a toehold on a better life—the house she rented, though small, was on a tree-lined street whose lawns and gardens were carefully tended, a sign of neighborhood pride. It was early evening when Terri parked in front, hoping to find Sims and her daughter home, and the trickle of men and women walking from nearby bus stops bespoke an ethic of work and striving.

Terri rang the bell. After a moment, a plump, wary-eyed woman cracked open the door, fixing Terri with an expression that suggested few of the surprises in her life had been good ones. "I'm Teresa Paget," Terri said simply. "Rennell Price's lawyer."

The wariness in Sims's eyes became weariness. Yet, if anything, she appeared more guarded. "Another lawyer," she said.

"Another one. In two weeks, Rennell's due to be executed."

Sims slowly shook her head, a gesture of resistance. "Maybe he should be. But that's got nothing to do with me."

Terri tried to rein in her anxiety for Rennell, and for Elena—over two thousand miles away from San Francisco, with nothing to go on but instinct, there was little she could do to make Betty Sims talk. With a calm she did not feel, Terri asked, "Could I come in?"

Sims did not move. After a moment, she asked, "What happened to Payton?"

"They executed him."

Sims looked down. Finally she said, "Ten minutes, is all. Got to put on dinner."

As though regretting her own invitation, Sims paused before standing aside. The living room Terri entered was sparsely furnished. To one side of a plain wool couch sat a photograph of Sims and a girl whose smile did not seem to reach her eyes.

"Your daughter?" Terri asked.

"Uh-huh."

There was no give in Sims's expression; it was plain that she had no wish to discuss her child. Steeling herself for resistance, Terri ventured, "I'm here about Eddie Fleet. I know you used to live with him."

Though her eyes did not change, Sims's face seemed to twist, a spasm of anger she erased in an instant. "Used to," Sims responded tersely. "That was another time, another place. And none of your concern."

Terri hesitated, knowing all too well the emotions which might lie beneath this answer. "I think it is," she said. "I think you know what Eddie's capable of doing."

Sims folded her arms, looking hard at Terri. "What would that be?"

"What he did to the murdered girl, Thuy Sen. And what he did to your daughter."

For an instant, Sims seemed to buckle, as though Terri had hit her in the solar plexus. "Get out," Sims said softly. "We got nothing more to talk about."

She had been right, Terri suddenly knew. "Without you," Terri said, "Rennell Price is going to die, and Eddie Fleet will find himself another child to abuse. Maybe the next mother won't have an aunt in Cleveland, somewhere to run to. Maybe her only choice will be letting Eddie beat her up, or hiding in her bedroom while Eddie forces her little girl to have sex. Maybe it's okay with you that another mother and her daughter get to live with that."

"Get out," Sims hissed. "You get out this very minute."

The front door opened.

Sims's eyes widened. A girl close to Elena's age stood there in a parochial school's plaid uniform, tall and awkward-looking, eyes darting from Terri to her mother, as if she, too, feared surprises. Sims could seem to find no words.

"I'm Teresa Paget," she said. "A lawyer from San Francisco. I came to ask you and your mother about Eddie Fleet."

The girl's eyes became a well of anger, directed first at Terri, then at her mother. When Terri turned to Sims, the woman's eyes glistened with tears. "I'm sorry, baby. I'm just so sorry."

"Not sorry like me, Mama. I was all alone with him."

The girl's tone was so like Elena's that it made Terri shiver. When Terri spoke, her own voice was husky. "My client's a retarded man named Rennell Price. The State of California is about to execute him, for choking a nine-year-old girl to death as he forced her to give oral sex. We think the real murderer was Eddie Fleet. I need someone to say that Eddie likes sex with children, or Rennell will die in his place."

"Where is he?" Sims demanded. "Eddie."

For an instant, Terri considered lying, claiming that Fleet was dead. She paused, torn between her obligation to truth, her duty to Rennell, and her need to protect her own daughter. "I don't know," she finally acknowledged.

"If we do what you want, he'll find out where we are."

It was Terri's own fear. But she could not admit this. "He'll be too afraid to try," she assured the girl, cringing at her own duplicity. She needed Lacy Sims for another reason she could not admit: to prosecute Fleet for child sexual abuse, putting him where he could not harm Elena. "Please," she urged, "stop this thing from happening again."

The girl threw her backpack at her mother's feet. "What my mama say happened?"

"She didn't say. She's trying to protect you."

The girl's look at Sims was bitter and accusatory. "Yeah," she said in a monotone, "she's really good at that."

Inwardly, Terri recoiled from the emotions she had unleashed between this mother and daughter. But there was no time for regret. "What about you?" she asked. "Do you want to protect the next child Eddie Fleet comes after?"

The girl looked from her mother to Terri. "Don't do this, baby," Sims implored.

The girl faced Terri, a smile of anger and reprisal playing across her lips. "What you want to hear about?" she asked. "The first time, or the last?"

Betty Sims worked as a secretary. Though she was only ten, Lacy had a key to the apartment, to let herself in after school. The other person with a key was Eddie Fleet.

That day—the one she still had dreams about—

Lacy opened the door and found Eddie lying on the couch, dressed in nothing but boxer shorts, the pupils of his eyes like pinholes.

"Hey, sweet pea," he said softly.

Embarrassed, Lacy turned away.

She heard Fleet stretching lazily on the couch, emitting a silken yawn. "Don't need to be so bashful, Lacy. Ain't you seen a man before?"

Lacy did not answer. Quickly, she went to her room and shut the door behind her.

Sitting at the desk, she tried to brush aside the unease she felt, the sense of vulnerability. She opened her history book, staring at the chapter on Egypt.

The door opened behind her.

She did not turn. "What you doin'?" Fleet asked.

Reluctantly, she faced him. "Homework."

" 'Homework'?" he repeated. "What a girl need with that? Homework's what I give your mama whenever I'm in the mood for it."

Lacy knew—she could hear them through the walls. Seemed like Fleet liked her mother to scream; some nights Lacy willed herself to be in another place.

Now her stomach felt queasy. "Well," she said, "**my** homework's on Egypt. Got to do it."

Fleet's smile was so benign that it scared her. "Time for some other lesson," he said easily. "I'll be the teacher, you be my pupil."

He began walking toward her. Lacy saw the surface of his boxer shorts stirring and knew that no one else could save her. "Don't want no lessons," she said tightly.

Fleet's eyes turned brighter. "You do, child. You just don't know it yet."

She stood, backing away. "I'll tell my mama."

Fleet laughed softly. "No, you won't. Your mama knows when to open her mouth, and when to close it. That's what I'm gonna teach you."

Lacy began trembling. "You know what good pupils do?" Fleet inquired. "They get down on their knees, and say please. That be how the teacher knows it's time."

She felt his hands on her shoulders. Half-staggering, she fell to her knees and saw his shorts around his ankles.

Her eyes filled with tears. Gently, he cradled her chin in his hands, gazing down at her. "Know what?" he said with a ruminative smile. "You got eyes just like your daddy's."

Mute, Lacy stared up at him, scared and desperate. He took her hand and put it on his most intimate place. "You don't know your daddy, do you?"

She shook her head, eyes closing. The last thing she remembered him saying was, "Name was Payton. The one your mama turned to for con-so-lation. Just like what I've got for you."

Stunned, Terri faced Betty Sims.

She sat away from her daughter, at the other end of

her couch, a figure of abject shame. Terri waited until Sims could look at her.

"You wanted to know," Sims said in a voice shot through with misery. "You wanted to know everything."

Terri struggled with her own disbelief. "You were with Payton."

Briefly, Betty shut her eyes. "Just one or two times, a few days before those two got arrested. I wanted him to stop Eddie from beating up on me."

"Did he?"

Sims shrugged. "Couldn't do nothing from jail."

Suddenly, the logic of events long past struck Terri so hard that she felt herself inhale with a shudder. Softly, she asked. "When did you tell Eddie about Payton?"

Sims turned away. "Day or two after it happened. Eddie beat it out of me."

Silent, Terri absorbed this. Whatever the other reasons for all that Eddie Fleet had done, the sexual abuse of **this** child was a last act of reprisal. "And you told no one."

"No."

Terri turned to Lacy. "Will **you**? Will you go to the police?"

Wearily, Sims gazed at her daughter.

"Yes," the girl told Terri. "Let Mama's boyfriend be afraid of **me**."

"We need to file a third petition," Terri urged Chris by telephone. "Not only is Fleet a pedophile but turning in the brothers was more than just an act of survival. Taking Payton down felt extra good to him."

Chris was silent. "Of course," he said at last, "Pell will say that Betty has it in for Fleet, and that stories of childhood abuse are notoriously unreliable. He may even claim that Lacy's trying to save the uncle she never knew she had."

In her excitement and exhaustion, the warped logic of such an argument had not occurred to Terri. "Rennell's an uncle," she said softly, unable to define the sadness this made her feel.

"Anyhow, Terri, come home soon. We've got a new petition to work on, and Johnny Moore's got something else for you. For whatever finding Tasha Bramwell turns out to be worth."

Before calling Johnny, Terri tracked down Charles Monk, to tell him what had happened to Lacy Sims. Still no one knew where Fleet might be.

At last, after staring for sleepless hours at the red-illuminated numbers of a hotel room clock radio, Terri drifted off to sleep. The dream which came to her was Elena's, except that Terri had taken her daughter's place.

She was alone in a darkened bedroom, and there was banging on the door.

Elena's father was coming.

The door opened. Terri hugged herself, and saw his

shadow coming toward her. She prayed it was her mother, and then a man's face came into the light.

"Both of you," Eddie Fleet said in her husband's perfect English. "First your mother, and then you."

Terri woke up sobbing.

SEVENTEEN

IN THE MORNING, HAVING SLEPT LITTLE, TERRI FLEW TO Birmingham, Alabama, where Tasha Bramwell Harding, a mother of two preschoolers, worked as an accountant for a health care company.

Unlike her approach to Betty Sims, Terri did not attempt surprise—other than to place a call which, from Tasha's first reaction, was deeply unsettling. But her voice recovered its businesslike reserve, and with a note of resignation, Tasha agreed to meet Terri after work on the patio of a local restaurant.

From the plane, Birmingham had not been what Terri had expected. Though squat steel mills jutted from the valley which contained the center city, they were dwarfed by the sleek glass towers of a city on the rise, their windows glinting in the afternoon sun. The summer air was hot and moist, and a lush garden surrounded the patio where Tasha—still the slender, pretty woman of Monk's description—awaited with a look of unease.

She was in her mid-thirties now, with straightened hair, a lineless face whose oldest features were her dark, watchful eyes, and the well-tailored veneer of a professional woman. Her husband, Johnny Moore had told Terri, was a buyer for the region's largest sporting goods store, and they had found a life for themselves in a city which, while bounded by white suburbs, was controlled by a black electorate led by a thriving middle class. The place, and the woman, seemed far away from the Bayview.

Terri extended her hand. "Teresa Paget," she said.

The woman's gaze, like her hand, was cool. "Tasha Harding."

Terri detected an emphasis on the surname, as if to signal that Tasha Bramwell had existed in some other life. They ordered two glasses of iced tea, saying little, Tasha clearly sizing up the woman who had dropped into her new life, dragging the past with her. When the waitress left, Terri said bluntly, "I guess you know Payton's dead."

"Yes." Tasha's voice quivered briefly, then became toneless. "I also know he confessed."

Terri could feel a wall drop, sealing off Tasha Harding from the woman who had loved, and lied for, Payton Price. "According to Payton," Terri said, "the second man was Eddie Fleet."

A look of disquiet, its cause indecipherable, flashed in Tasha's eyes. "And you're wondering if I know what really happened. Maybe something Payton told me."

"Maybe. But not just that. Anything—anything at all—which suggests that Fleet might have been guilty, and lied to save himself."

Tasha appraised her. "Well," she said, "I'd know about lying, wouldn't I."

"That was then, Tasha. Now Rennell's scheduled to die."

Tasha was silent. Eyes hooded, she took a long sip of tea. "I don't know what happened," she said at last. "Rennell was slow, Payton's shadow. I didn't see any meanness in him. But get him on crack, and Payton wanting to do something, and who knows. Rennell might have been dumb, but he came with a man's equipment."

This stark assessment, etched with sexual disdain, brought Terri up short. "You told Monk you'd never known Rennell to have sex with anyone. And according to Flora Lewis, it was the other man she saw—not Payton—who pulled Thuy Sen off the street. Does **that** sound like Rennell to you?"

Tasha weighed her answer—less, Terri sensed, out of uncertainty than out of doubt as to whether she should answer at all. "No," she said tersely. "I still have a hard time seeing him do that."

"What about Eddie Fleet?"

Tasha gave her a long, silent look. "What's the point of this?" she asked. "I don't know what happened. I lied because Payton asked me to. Now you're asking me to guess about what I lied about. What good will that do anyone—me and my family included?"

For Terri, the last phrase sounded a bell of warning, suggesting a reluctance deeper than Tasha had acknowledged. "Look," Terri said evenly, "they're about to execute Rennell. I know in my bones he's innocent. But unless I can piece together a compelling case—any way I can—I'll have to watch him die.

"Your 'lies' didn't just help Lou Mauriani convict a guilty man, they may have helped condemn an innocent one. I'll take anything you've got to give me—any impressions or scraps of information that might help me save Rennell. I don't care what it is, and for the sake of your own conscience, you shouldn't either. No matter how you try to escape it, his death will be part of your life."

A spark of resentment flashed in Tasha's eyes. "I don't see that. Whatever Payton did to that girl wasn't 'part of my life.' It was part of his, fifteen years ago, when he left me with no one. After that, I made my own life."

Terri stared at her. Softly, she said, "Your husband doesn't know anything, does he. Nothing about Payton, or perjury, or the death of a nine-year-old girl. Nothing but that you worked your way out of the Bayview, and now you're a wife and mother."

Tasha met Terri's eyes. But silence was her only answer.

"You **do** know something," Terri went on. "I don't know what it is. But you started sparring when I asked you about Fleet."

Tasha placed a finger to her lips, appraising Terri with a mute hostility. Her body seemed to perch on the edge of her chair—as though, Terri suddenly suspected, she were about to leave.

"Don't," Terri said. "Don't do this."

Tasha stared at her. "You come here," she said at last, "and you've got no idea. All you care about is what you want. . ."

Once more, Terri thought of Elena. "I'm Rennell's lawyer," she answered. "He's all I get to care about."

"Really. Have you got a family?"

"Yes."

"Then how would you feel if I barged into your life, asking you to spell out in some court paper stuff you don't want **anyone** to know?"

Mute, Terri considered her response. "Resentful. Angry. Scared. Maybe ashamed. There are things in my life I don't want anyone to know, things I feel guilty about. But my husband **does** know." Terri paused. "I guess, in the end, what I did would depend on how I wanted to feel about myself. And whether I thought I could bury shame through silence when someone else's life is at risk."

For the first time, Tasha looked down, eyes focused on the table.

"Eddie Fleet," Terri repeated.

For a long time, Tasha was silent. Finally, she said, "I don't know that whatever I've got to say makes any difference."

"But you're not sure it doesn't."

Tasha touched her lips again, and sorrow seeped

into her gaze. "Promise me—unless it really matters, I don't want you to use this. And if you do, I want time to tell my husband." Her voice was raw with feeling. "I saw my name in the papers once, for lying. I don't want my family reading about **this.**"

Though the words held little meaning, Terri said, "I promise."

A few nights after the brothers were arrested, Eddie Fleet knocked on Tasha Bramwell's door.

She had always despised him—there was something twisted about him, something treacherous she could not quite identify, though the insinuating way he looked at her was bad enough. Since Payton's arrest, she had barely slept, and Eddie's gold-toothed smile made her skin crawl.

"What you want?"

His smile broadened. "A little conversation, sweet thing."

"Save it for the police," she snapped. "I know you lied to them about Payton. Now I may never see him outside of jail, or a coffin."

Eddie shrugged. "What's a man supposed to do, po-lice on your ass day and night. Didn't tell no lies about Payton, either. You just got to face the facts, sweet thing."

Tasha quivered with disbelief and anger. "Go away."

Eddie's grin broadened, as if he were struck by a

new idea. "Maybe I could do that. Just go away. Without me, the police won't have no case, and your man be back in your arms. Not to mention other places."

Tasha hoped she did not understand him. "Then go," she said. "No one stopping you."

He leaned in the doorway. "There's the one person stoppin' me," he said softly. "Till she sends me on my way."

Tasha's grip tightened on the door. "Consider yourself sent."

Eddie gripped her wrist. "Not quite yet."

"**Stop,** or I'll tell Payton."

"What's he gonna do," Eddie said coolly. "He's in jail, and there be only two people hold the key. Me, and you."

Tasha writhed in pain. **"Let me go."**

Eddie loosened his grasp but did not release her. "You got a choice, Tasha. Do what I want, and you'll get your boyfriend back. No one ever know but us."

Tasha could not speak. The intimacy in the way he spoke her name sickened her. "Don't need to say a thing," Eddie continued quietly. "All you need to do is let me in, and listen."

When Tasha did not answer, he pushed her inside, closing the door behind them.

"You want him back," he said. "I can see it. So I'm gonna spell out just what you need to do to make that happen."

He told her.

Undressing, Tasha willed her soul outside her body.

Eddie unzipped his pants. "On your knees," he said. "Do me like I know you did for him."

As Terri listened, sickened, Tasha bowed her head. "Eddie lied to me," she said. "I never could tell Payton. All I could do was lie when Payton asked me to. 'Cause I loved him."

To Terri, her voice was that of the younger Tasha, bereft and without defenses. Filled with her own fear and anger directed at Eddie Fleet, Terri struggled to discern the meaning of what she had just learned.

"Oral sex," Terri said at last. "That's all he wanted."

Tasha nodded.

As with Thuy Sen, Terri thought, and Lacy Sims. But though she could not yet parse the uses of Tasha's story, she felt the undercurrent of her own misgivings.

"I'm sorry," Terri told her.

Tasha shook her head. "You haven't heard it all. There's only one thing I know for sure—Eddie Fleet's as evil as any man I ever met."

The night after Payton and Rennell were sentenced to death, Eddie returned to her apartment.

This time she peered through the peephole and saw him. Tears of grief and rage ran down her face.

"I know you're here," he said through the door, voice deep but soft with laughter. "Figure you be needin' a man now, and wantin' what I have to give you."

Tasha leaned against the door, teeth gritted. **"You lied to me."**

She heard Eddie laugh aloud. "You **knew** I was. And I know you miss it from me, baby. You be comin' round."

A week later, Tasha Bramwell left the Bayview, never to return.

"I didn't want to go back there," Tasha said. "I still don't." She paused, voice quieter. "I hate the person I was. But I outran the evil of that place, the evil of that man. I don't want to go back there, dragging my family with me."

Terri placed her hand on Tasha's wrist. "If you do," she promised, "it will be to save a life."

It was two in the morning before she sat with Chris, the signed declaration from Betty and Lacy Sims spread across their breakfast table, and told him what she had learned from Tasha Harding.

"Forced oral copulation," Chris said. "Jealousy toward Payton of Iago-like proportions. There's a pattern. But you know what the problems are."

"Yes. Tasha's already committed perjury. She knows nothing about Fleet being a pedophile, or anything that bears directly on Thuy Sen's death. In fact, Fleet told her—truthfully—that Payton was involved."

Chris nodded. "And said nothing about his own role, or Rennell's. I can hear Pell now: assuming that Tasha's to be believed at all, what Fleet told her confirmed his story. He'll say the whole thing's just sexual one-upmanship between a couple of crack dealers, evidence of nothing but our own desperation."

Drained, Terri finished her coffee. "I feel sorry for her. But our only obligation is to Rennell. Should we use this?"

"Not yet. Let's hope we find something else."

The next morning, based on the declarations from Lacy and Betty Sims, the Pagets began preparing a third **habeas** petition for the California Supreme Court.

EIGHTEEN

TEN DAYS BEFORE RENNELL'S SCHEDULED EXECUTION, in a two-line opinion which again explained nothing, the California Supreme Court denied his third **habeas corpus** petition, and the Pagets asked the Ninth Circuit Court of Appeals for permission to file the petition before Judge Gardner Bond.

The Attorney General responded swiftly: the declarations of Betty and Lacy Sims concerning Eddie Fleet were irrelevant to the murder of Thuy Sen and, therefore, inadmissible at trial. Anxious, the Pagets awaited the decision of Judges Sanders, Montgomery, and Nhu, and with considerably less hope, Governor Darrow's disposition of Rennell's clemency petition.

"We've got two arguments," Terri had explained to Carlo. "First, that AEDPA leaves Rennell no suitable avenue for bringing his freestanding claim of innocence. Second—and this is critical—that we should have the same right to testimony from Fleet which the State had at the original trial. That would require California to grant Fleet use immunity so that he can't invoke the Fifth Amendment."

"First, we have to **find** him," Carlo pointed out.

"Sure. But we've got a pretty compelling argument, I think—the State can't convict Rennell on this pervert's trial testimony and then help Fleet avoid questioning after Payton swore that Fleet was the second murderer, and that he perjured himself at trial."

Out of public view, Johnny Moore and Tammy Mattox also worked to save Rennell. Feverishly, Tammy knocked on doors in the Bayview, seeking out anyone who might have known Eddie Fleet; Moore flew to Los Angeles, where Fleet had lived for a time after Thuy Sen's death, and began working from a motel in the South Central section of the city. The Pagets set up a phone bank in the office, manned by the other investigators, soliciting tips through the media and over the Internet. And despite all this activity, every day without fail, Terri spent an hour with the frightened and confused man who, despite her reports of all the Pagets were doing, felt his life slipping away, day by day, and hour by hour.

"Next Tuesday, right after midnight," Rennell told her in a hollow voice. "That's when the warden say it gonna happen."

At ten o'clock that evening, as Terri tried to sleep, Chris found a short opinion in the tray of their fax machine. In disbelief, he read the document's conclusions: by a vote of two to one, Judge Blair Montgomery dissenting, the panel denied Rennell Price permission to file a third **habeas corpus** petition before Judge Bond. The reasoning of Judge Nhu and Judge Sanders, the defector, was tersely stated: as directed by the recent opinion of the United States Supreme Court in **God-ward v. Price,** the panel would defer to the Supreme Court of California and, in light of that, could not say that the new affidavits regarding Fleet were "clear and convincing evidence" of Rennell's innocence. And even were the new evidence sufficient, it did not reflect any constitutional defect in the trial itself, and thus could not be heard.

With a leaden spirit, Chris went to the bedroom and found that Terri, aided by sleeping pills, had at last fallen asleep. Her face, for once, was so untroubled that Chris hated to awaken her. But he knew he must—both for Rennell's sake and for hers.

Gently, he touched the bare skin of her shoulder.

She started, and then her eyes flew open. "What is it?"

"The Ninth Circuit. I'm sorry, sweetheart, but Sanders flipped. They've turned us down."

In the dimly lit bedroom, Chris watched his wife struggle to comprehend what, fully awake, she knew by heart—that AEDPA barred Rennell from seeking review by the full Ninth Circuit, or by the United States Supreme Court.

"Oh, God," she said softly. "Oh, God."

Shortly after 1:00 A.M. in Washington, a call awakened Caroline Masters.

"I'm sorry be calling at this hour," Blair Montgomery told her, "but I've got some news. Our panel just denied Rennell Price's request to file a new petition."

Caroline paused, waiting for sleep to loosen its grip on her consciousness. "Callista said Price had new evidence. So what happened?"

"Your colleagues did too good a job. In Sanders's mind, further provoking Fini et al. will eviscerate our already tattered credibility. This man's life just isn't worth it."

Caroline sat up. Her bedroom, though lit by a full silver moon, felt dark and solitary. "So what can **I** do? Your order's not appealable."

"I know. But these lawyers will find some way to petition you. They're smart and resourceful, and they don't give up."

"That," Caroline answered with bleak humor, "would be immensely inconvenient. Why can't Price just die like he's supposed to?"

The next morning, shortly after Caroline reached her chambers, Callista Hill brought her the papers faxed by Rennell Price's lawyers.

At eleven-thirty in San Francisco, Terri passed Elena's room and saw that her light was on.

Gently, Terri pushed open the door.

Elena was lying atop the bed, an open book beside her, gazing at the ceiling. "Are you all right?" Terri asked.

"Yeah. Only I can't get to sleep."

"Neither can I."

Rolling on her side, Elena faced her mother. "They're really going to kill him, aren't they?"

"Probably." Terri hesitated. "How does that make you feel?"

"Weird."

Tentative, Terri sat on the edge of the bed. Softly, she said, "Rennell's not like your father. I'm sure he never touched that girl."

"Then the other man did. The one who followed me."

Terri could not answer.

After a moment, Elena looked away. "I'm tired now," she said at last.

Terri kissed her forehead and left, gently closing the door behind her.

NINETEEN

"How do Price's lawyers rationalize this?" the Chief Justice asked Callista. "Under AEDPA, Price has no right to be here."

Callista remained standing in front of Caroline's desk. "They claim that the Constitution gives this Court jurisdiction over **habeas corpus** petitions, including a claim of freestanding innocence, that can't be limited by Congress. In other words, AEDPA can't stop us from hearing a new claim."

"And just what is it we're supposed to hear?"

"They found a teenage girl who claims the State's key witness—Eddie Fleet—forced her to give him oral sex when she was ten years old. They also claim California's failure to immunize Fleet meant they couldn't cross-examine him about his own involvement in the victim's death." Callista paused for emphasis. "Bottom line, Price's lawyers say we're the last chance to stop the State of California from killing an innocent man."

"What about the Governor?"

"They're trying. But the Governor hasn't been heard from."

Caroline felt caught between her conscience and a wholly practical concern—that intervening would further inflame the tensions on the Court, pitting her against Justice Fini, to the discomfort and resentment of her colleagues. With an uncharacteristic sigh, she asked Callista, "What would you do?"

Without invitation, Callista sat. "I'm a black woman," she said bluntly. "You probably noticed. But a lot of white folks still barely notice me at all. And some that do couldn't pick me out of a lineup of other black women about my age and height. They've got no practice telling one of us from another—all they see is 'black.'

"Fleet has no credibility left—not after this latest thing against him. So we're going to execute Price because an old white lady thought she could differentiate him from Fleet looking through a window across the street? Come on. Anyone who's comfortable with **that** is way too white for words."

Despite her misgivings, Caroline smiled. "Even the Assistant Attorney General who argued the case for California?"

"Especially him," Callista answered with disdain. "Do **you** believe Price did it?"

The blunt question, stripping Caroline of legal hedges, gave her pause. "No," she answered. "But if you're Justice Fini, that's not the point."

Caroline saw Callista hesitate, torn between her sense of injustice and the fear of crossing the line between Chief Justice and clerk. More quietly, she said,

"My mama's mouthy and opinionated, and I guess she raised another one. So I have to ask this, even though I know I'm out of line: What's the point for **you**?

"Can we just sit here and watch them kill this guy? Isn't Justice Glynn's penchant for worrying too much about Court politics exactly what got Price here? What greater good is the Court serving if it sacrifices Rennell Price? And do we even have the right to ask that question?" Callista lowered her voice again. "Call me stupid—any black person in America can tell you 'justice' is hit or miss. But that's no reason for us to close our eyes."

Caroline considered her. "I guess Price wants an immediate stay of execution," she said. "Until this Court, or some other Court, rules on his new evidence."

"Yes."

"How many days until his execution?"

"Five."

Caroline glanced at her calendar. "Write this one up," she ordered. "And keep close contact with the Governor's office. I want to know what happens with clemency."

Three days passed, filled with fruitless scraping for new evidence, searching for Fleet, jumping when the phone rang, checking for faxes at the office and at home. Chris looked tired; Carlo was irritable and jumpy. No one could find Fleet.

"The Court's playing chicken with the Governor," Chris opined. "No one wants to go first."

Rennell had stopped eating. "Don't need food no more," he said to Terri. The fear in his dull eyes made Terri miserable.

"Don't give up," she told him.

Two nights before the date of execution, Eddie Fleet came to Terri in a dream. Hugging her, he said quietly, "I can't let Rennell suffer anymore. Tell me what I need to do."

When she woke, reality overtaking her, only Chris was there.

Three hours later, at the office, the fax machine emitted a letter from the Governor headed "In the Matter of the Clemency Petition of Rennell Price."

Every court available, the Governor explained, had reviewed this matter—several times—including an exhaustive analysis by the United States Supreme Court. Given this meticulous and repeated judicial scrutiny, the deplorable nature of the crime, and the wishes of Thuy Sen's family, the execution of Rennell Price could not reasonably be called a miscarriage of justice. Clemency denied.

There was no time for emotion. Swiftly, Chris and Terri sent a supplemental pleading to the death penalty clerk of the United States Supreme Court, attaching the Governor's letter, for review by the Chief Justice.

Thirty-seven hours separated Rennell from death.

On receiving Governor Darrow's letter, the Chief Justice went to Justice Huddleston.

He had read Callista Hill's memo and now reviewed the letter before looking up at Caroline. "It's like some terrible conveyor belt," he said. "Rennell Price is inexorably gliding toward the jaws of death, and one keeps expecting someone else to take him off. And no one does."

"So now it's down to me, as Circuit Justice. But I'm also the Chief Justice."

"And, as such, charged with doing what you can to lessen friction within the Court. Which involves preserving your own credibility."

"What about my own conscience?"

Huddleston rubbed his eyes. "Well," he said, "there is that." Picking up the letter, he scanned it again. "If you do decide to issue a stay, at the least you may buy him a few hours—our Court's not in session, and our colleagues are scattered to the winds or, in Fini's case, a condominium in Hawaii. That should put some pressure back on the Governor." Huddleston paused. "I'll support you, of course. But no one else may. And you'll need five votes to keep the stay in place—including one from a justice who only last month condemned Price to death. So how you spend your capital as Chief really is your call."

Caroline glanced at her watch. It was close to three in the afternoon, 10:00 A.M. in Hawaii. "Let's hope Fini's up and out already," she said. "If Price is extra lucky, Tony's surfing the Devil's Pipeline."

A little after one o'clock in San Francisco, the death penalty clerk advised Christopher Paget that Chief Justice Caroline Masters had entered a stay of execution in the matter of Rennell Price.

Chris felt little jubilation. Before informing Terri and Carlo, he called the Governor's office. To his surprise, the Chief Justice had already sent the Governor a copy of her order staying execution.

"She's playing hardball," Chris told Terri and Carlo. "Now it's up to Fini and Darrow."

At six o'clock that evening in Washington, an e-mail from Justice Fini appeared on Caroline Masters's home computer.

Fini's analysis was terse. Skirting the thornier legal questions, he called the new evidence of Fleet's pedophilia "woefully deficient" and "irrelevant to the crime of which Price stands convicted."

Immediately, the Chief Justice began typing a response. "Tomorrow," she began, "Rennell Price is scheduled to die. We must ask ourselves whether this latest evidence should give us pause before sanctioning such a dubious execution..."

At five o'clock in the afternoon Pacific time, the telephone in Terri's office rang.

It was the Supreme Court's death penalty clerk. "There's been a new order in the **Price** case," the man told Terri somberly. "By a vote of five to four, the Court has dissolved its stay in the matter of Rennell Price."

Mechanically, Terri thanked him for calling and put down the phone. Thirty-one hours from now, at 12:01 A.M., the State of California was scheduled to carry out the death warrant.

Frenziedly, Chris started trying to track down the Governor's scheduler.

At close to midnight, Terri was still in her office, preparing yet another petition in case new evidence was found. When her telephone rang, she started. Turning, she saw Johnny Moore's cell phone number.

"I've got some news," he said tersely.

Terri hesitated, suspended between hope and the grimness of his tone. "About Fleet?"

"About Fleet, Terri. He's dead."

Terri felt herself go numb, disbelief warring with relief, followed by a lawyer's sense of foreboding. "How?" she asked in a hollow voice.

"It happened yesterday morning, in East L.A. Fleet was hiding out with some woman he'd met, using a false name. According to the cops, he beat her up, then forced her to go down on him. When he fell asleep, she stuck a gun in his mouth and pulled the trigger." Moore's voice was soft. "There's a touch of poetry in that. I like to think he woke up first, if only for a moment."

Terri forced herself to think. "Dead," she repeated. "Somehow I kept hoping we could force him to confess. Trap him, some way."

"It never would have happened," Moore answered. "You had no leverage—other than Fleet, if you believe he was there, Payton was the only witness to Thuy Sen's death."

"Fleet **was** there," Terri answered. "And now they're **all** dead, the three people in Eula Price's living room."

A sense of tragedy overcame her and then, by reflex, a lawyer's logic. There was no more evidence to be had in Thuy Sen's death, or any hope of evidence. Only whatever inference could be gleaned from the reason for Fleet's own death. "This is part of the pattern," she said. "We can use it in a new petition."

By rote, Terri dictated the bare bones of an affidavit for Moore to execute and fax. Only then did she permit herself to be a mother, not a lawyer, and thank whatever God existed that Elena would be safe.

As soon as she could, Terri took her work home and went to Elena. It was nearly two o'clock in the morning, but what Terri had to tell her could not wait.

Restless, the girl stirred, lips parted as if to speak,

and Terri wondered if her nightmare of Richie had come again. When Terri touched her shoulder, Elena started awake.

"It's only me," Terri said softly. "Just your mom."

Her daughter gazed back at her, too newly awake, and perhaps frightened, not to appear vulnerable instead of guarded. Anxiously, the girl demanded, "Is something wrong?"

"Something happened," Terri answered. "Something I want to tell you. But nothing's wrong."

Taking Elena's hand, Terri waited for her daughter to collect herself. "What is it?" Elena asked.

"The man who may have followed you, the one I believe killed Thuy Sen all those years ago. He's dead."

Elena's eyes fluttered, then studied Terri with a look of hope and disbelief. "How did he die?"

Terri hesitated, remembering Elena's tortured outcry, "Maybe I'll kill a man for forcing me to do things." But nothing but truth could come to Terri's lips. "He beat a woman, Elena, then forced her to give him oral sex. So she shot him in his sleep."

Elena covered her face. After a moment, she murmured, "Will the woman be all right?"

"I don't know."

Elena sat up again. "I wanted him dead," she said after a time, "and now some other woman will pay for it. Why wouldn't it be better if they'd sentenced **him** to death?"

At first, Terri had no answer. Then she said, "It

would have been better, Elena, if they'd sentenced him to life. You'd still be safe now, and so would Rennell."

Elena did not answer.

"You **are** safe," Terri said softly. "Just sit with it for a while, and know I love you."

Mute, the girl nodded, and then Terri returned to the library, to try to save Rennell Price from a dead man, and the State of California.

In the morning, Elena appeared in the library.

It was six o'clock, and Terri was revising her petition. To her surprise, Elena stood behind her, silently rubbing her shoulders. Terri did not ask why, and Elena gave no reason. But when Elena was finished, she kissed her mother softly on the crown of her head, a brush of lips, and then went back to bed.

TWENTY

FACING RENNELL, TERRI KNEW WITH QUIET MISERY that, without some startling event, he would be dead at this time tomorrow.

Dead like Eddie Fleet, she thought.

It was nine in the morning, but her own words of reassurance sounded as rote to Terri as cocktail party patter at the end of a long day. "We're still working," she told him, "trying to find out more about Eddie Fleet. Chris is hoping to see the Governor."

After all of the procedural twists and turns she had tried to explain—clemency, a new petition to the Ninth Circuit; a request for a stay from the United States Supreme Court—Rennell gazed right through her, as though she were speaking in Urdu. All he seemed to know was that each step had moved him closer to his death, and that now death was at hand. Perhaps that was the only thing worth knowing.

She took his hand, as much for herself as for Rennell, an effort to ground herself for the long day ahead. "Rennell . . . ?"

He shook his head. After a time, he mumbled, "I was gonna be free..."

You nearly were, Terri thought. It seemed as though she were living in a dream state: between seven and eight, trying to steal an hour's more sleep, she had suddenly awakened, skin clammy, heart beating swiftly. Now her every word and gesture felt unreal.

"I'll be back," she promised. "At five o'clock. Maybe I'll have some news."

Tammy Mattox was crammed in a cluster of cubicles with two private investigators, fielding Internet tips and calls to the hotline number they had established, all the while keeping contact with Johnny Moore. "Still nothing more on Fleet?" Terri asked.

Tammy looked up, dark circles of weariness smudging the skin beneath her eyes. "Nothing new. Except that he's still dead."

Terri stood by Tammy's chair, gazing at the telephone. "You know what's worse?" she said. "We're still tracking Fleet because we know he was a pedophile. But now no one knows which one of them killed Thuy Sen. Absent an improvement in DNA technology, no one else will **ever** know. Rennell's dying from uncertainty."

Tammy shook her head. "Rennell," she amended, "is dying from artificial certainty. The system demands an end to things, and Darrow needs a ritual execution."

There was nothing to say to that, and no use dwelling on it. Terri was headed for her office when Tammy's phone rang.

Terri paused, turning back to look at the flashing phone line. Tammy waved toward the phone. "Go ahead," she said. "Maybe our luck will change."

Terri answered. "Who's this?" a woman's voice demanded.

"Teresa Paget—I'm a lawyer for Rennell Price. Can I help you?"

"More like I can help you. Hear you lookin' for dirt on Eddie Fleet."

The voice was young, Terri felt certain, its intonations African American. Swiftly, she picked up Tammy's pencil, saying, "If it's true."

"Oh, it's true. I used to watch his girlfriend's kid—she lived in the neighborhood."

This seemed meant to establish the caller's credentials. "Where was that?"

"South Central. Eddie came here 'bout the time we had the Rodney King riots."

In terms of chronology, that sounded right—Fleet had vanished from the Bayview about four years after Thuy Sen's death. Tense, Terri asked, "What do you know about him?"

"He's a pig." The voice became a low hiss of anger. "One day he come to the house when Jasmine wasn't there, and her kid was napping."

The story stopped abruptly, as though its end was

obvious. Straining to infuse her voice with sympathy, Terri asked, "Can you tell me what he did?"

"He was high," the woman burst out in anger. "Said he'd been watchin' me, knowin' I'd been watchin' him. I said he was crazy."

Hastily, Terri began scribbling notes. "Yes?" she prodded.

The woman seemed to inhale. "Said he want me to go down on him. I told him to do himself. Then he takes out a gun..."

Startled, Terri asked, "He threatened to kill you?"

"He puts it to my head," the woman continued huskily. "When I still wouldn't do it, he said it didn't matter shit to him whether I lived or died. But if I died chokin' on his come, at least it be an accident."

Terri leaned on the desk, feeling a flutter in her throat. Tammy watched her closely. "What you've told me could save a life," Terri said simply.

The woman was silent. "That's why I'm callin' you. So you can tell my story to whoever."

"Our investigator, Johnny Moore, is in South Central now. I want him to come see you—"

"What **I** need to do?"

"Just take me through what happened. Then I'll type up a statement and send it to Johnny for you to sign."

"Like for **court**?"

"It doesn't need to be long. But the Court has to know I didn't make this up."

"I **told** you, all right? I don't want to see no court—got my **own** problems with the law. Just want to see your guy not get killed. How you do that's up to **you.**"

Terri's chest tightened. "The execution's tonight," she said. "Without your help, he's going to die—"

Terri heard a click, then silence.

Quickly, she hit a button on the telephone to trace the woman's number. "Unavailable" flashed on the screen.

"What was **that**?" Tammy asked.

Terri sat on the edge of the desk. "She's gone."

They gathered in the conference room—Chris, Terri, Carlo, and Tammy Mattox, with Johnny Moore on the speaker phone.

Chris began pacing. "They'll never buy it," he predicted. "Pell will imply that we made this up, knowing a dead man can't refute it, or that our anonymous caller was a crackpot. Or maybe knew from the media what story to tell."

Terri leaned toward the speaker phone. "You have to find her," she told Moore. "Maybe she's somebody you stirred up when you were poking around. Maybe someone knows who she is, like Fleet's girlfriend—Jasmine."

"No telephone number," Johnny said. "No address. Twelve hours to go."

"Try," Terri said. "At least we've got the girlfriend's name."

After ten minutes of debate with Chris and Carlo, Terri glanced at her watch. It was 12:51.

"We've got no choice," she said flatly. "We have to request leave to file another petition with the Ninth Circuit, and send a supplemental letter to the Governor, citing Fleet's death and an anonymous call. They'll take my word for that or not—at least until Johnny finds this woman."

Carlo looked from Terri to his father. "There's no other way to do it," Chris said finally. "We've got an artificial deadline of twelve-oh-one tonight. I'll keep trying to find the Governor."

Tammy went back to the phones.

TWENTY-ONE

AT FOUR-THIRTY ON THE AFTERNOON OF JULY 21, HAVing drafted an emergency petition to the United States Supreme Court in the event the Ninth Circuit turned them down, Terri and Carlo went to San Quentin for what would likely be their final visit with Rennell.

It was a bright Monday afternoon. As he drove, Carlo intently watched the road, and yet Terri could read the distance in his eyes, an absorption in the imminent death of another human being. In the last ten months, Terri realized, Carlo had changed—he looked older, and his air of careless ease had diminished. The death penalty had killed his innocence.

"Why Tuesday?" he finally asked. "Why twelve-oh-one?"

"A death warrant's good for only twenty-four hours. They don't want an execution date to slip away..."

"So if we get a stay from the Ninth Circuit, or the Chief Justice, they'll still have time for the full Court to dissolve it."

"Uh-huh. As for why Tuesday, it used to be Friday."

Terri took out her sunglasses. "My theory is that Tuesday cuts down on out-of-town demonstrators, because they'd have to go to work the next day. It also allows three-day weekends for prison personnel, and early getaways for vacations."

Carlo did not respond. Abruptly, he said, "If they execute him, I'm coming."

Terri turned to him. "You don't ever want to see one, Carlo. Let alone Rennell's."

"**You're** going."

"I **have** to be there. That's the last place he needs to feel abandoned."

Carlo took the exit for San Quentin. "Just by you?" Softly, he added, "I don't need anyone's permission but his. If you check the list, you'll see I'm on it."

Sometime in the last few days, Terri realized, Rennell and Carlo had discussed this. "Did **you** bring it up?" she asked.

"No. He did."

They said nothing more until they reached the prison. Gazing up at the ventilator above the death chamber, Terri wondered if Chris had tracked down the Governor, and when they would hear from the Ninth Circuit. Maybe Johnny Moore would still find Jasmine.

There were seven hours left.

Inside, they met Anthony Lane and went to the cinder-block room where, until six o'clock on the day the State meant to be his last, Rennell was allowed to greet visitors.

Rennell sat alone at a folding table with plastic chairs, his arms and legs shackled, a stolid prison guard watching over him. The windowless room was roughly nine feet by ten; beside Rennell's table was another with plastic spoons, a bowl of red Jell-O, and slices of nondescript meat, snacks for Rennell's visitors. Terri could not imagine eating.

As Rennell stood, Tony Lane enveloped Rennell in a bear hug. Watching Lane over Rennell's shoulder, Terri saw him close his eyes.

Carlo hugged Rennell as well, fiercely and for some moments. When Rennell bent toward her, Terri kissed him on the forehead. He smelled like soap, she realized, as though he had prepared himself for visitors.

Rennell looked down at her. "Been waitin' here. I always knew you'd come."

The simple words pierced her. When he was a child, Terri thought, there had been no one but Payton to rely on, no parents coming to his school or keeping a promise to take him somewhere special on a weekend. His three visitors had become, at the end of his life, the family he had missed.

"Chris wanted to come, too," she told him. "But he's meeting with the Governor and waiting to hear from the courts. No one's giving up."

Rennell nodded, a trace of hope appearing in his eyes. "Chris is real smart," he said as if to comfort himself. "I can tell that."

Terri mustered a smile. "No one smarter. Except for maybe Carlo and me." Remembering Lane, she added lightly, "And Tony, of course."

Rennell leaned his head back, taking in his guests. "All you guys is smart," he said sagely. "Know you be takin' care of things."

Once more, Terri felt the gap between their desperate last maneuvers and the dimness of Rennell's perception of them. Reaching inside her suit pocket, she took out a picture she had found among his grandmother's effects—Eula Price with her arms around a bright-eyed Payton and a solemn, round-faced Rennell at roughly the age of ten. "I brought this for you," she said.

Rennell gazed down at the photograph, eyes dimming, and Terri realized that the photograph must remind him of death—his grandmother's and Payton's—and how his brother had died. "I love this picture of you," she swiftly added. "You look like a little man."

Rennell gave it back to her. "You keep it," he said softly.

Feeling wretched, Terri searched for something to say. Behind Rennell, the guard shifted his weight from one foot to the other, clearly as unhappy to be present as Terri was to have him there.

Then, casually, Carlo tasted some Jell-O. "Not bad," he told Rennell. "Strawberry. This your favorite?"

Distracted, Rennell looked over at him. "Yeah. My grandma used to make it."

"Want some?"

When Rennell nodded, Carlo put the bowl and plastic spoon in front of him. Taking the spoon in his manacled hand, Rennell put a dollop of red Jell-O in his mouth.

"It's good," he told Carlo.

Anthony Lane pulled up a seat, his bulky frame filling the chair. "It reminds me of when I was a kid," he told Rennell. "I tried to make a mountain of Jell-O out of seven different flavors. Should have seen my mama's face."

With this, Lane launched into a long anecdote which, Terri felt sure, he was inventing as he went along. But it ended well, with a description of a glutinous mass of Jell-O, worthy of Dr. Seuss, which caused Rennell to nod.

"Ugly," he said solemnly. "Bet your mama whipped you. Or your daddy."

Lane glanced at Terri. "Never did," he answered easily. "Never even made me eat it. It was **way** too ugly."

This, at last, made Rennell smile. "My brother woulda hid me."

Terri felt an emptiness in the pit of her stomach, deeper than hunger. "Bet he would have," Carlo affirmed. "Behind that bush you told us about."

Rennell looked over at him, as though touched that Carlo remembered. "That's right," he said softly. "Behind that bush."

As before, the thought of Payton seemed to surface the reality which lay before him. Tentative, Rennell took Terri's hand. "If they do me like Payton, you be there?"

"Of course," she answered firmly. "But maybe I won't need to."

Rennell did not seem to hear the last. Softly, he asked, "You be okay?"

Terri could not answer. "I'll be there, too," Carlo answered him. "And my dad, if he can. Just don't lose hope, Rennell."

Rennell turned to him again. "Yeah," he said slowly. "Maybe someday we go to that baseball game."

"Yeah," Carlo affirmed. "A Giants game, with plenty of peanuts and hot dogs."

With obvious reluctance, the guard stepped forward. "It's six o'clock," he told Terri. "You're going to have to leave now."

After a moment, Terri stood. But Rennell did not stand, as though unwilling to let go. "We can still talk on the telephone," she assured him. "I'll call you later, when you're with the minister."

Mute, Rennell nodded, his eyes fearful now. Circling the table, Terri held him close, his head pressed against her cheek. "I love you, Rennell."

Lane embraced him next. "We **all** love you."

Rennell blinked. When Carlo hugged him, Rennell said huskily, "You be my best friend now, Carlo. 'Cept for Terri."

Another guard led them out. As they glanced over their shoulders, Rennell sat at the table, craning his neck to see them. "I love you," he called out.

The man guarding Rennell closed the door. Speechless, Carlo shook his head. Tears ran down his face.

Carlo drove back to San Francisco to help Chris. Tony Lane left—he had never witnessed an execution and could not stand to witness this one. "Thank God he didn't ask me," he said, and wished the Pagets good luck.

Terri stayed at the prison, in a small, bare room with a telephone and desk, waiting for a call from Chris.

At a little before seven o'clock, the telephone rang. "No news from the Ninth Circuit," Chris said tersely. "Or from Johnny Moore. But I've tracked down Darrow. He's three blocks from our house—at Howard Shipler's, having dinner with his biggest donors to raise money against the recall. I've been promised a brief audience thereafter."

Terri had once had dinner at the Shiplers'—then, too, the Governor had been present. They had sat in a candlelit dining room with a Matisse and two Manets on the wall as Darrow spoke with the faux intimacy he reserved for those whom he hoped would become his most generous contributors. Then it struck her that Rennell, too, was having a meal, this one chosen to be his last—mashed potatoes and chicken like his grandmother had made, but with this chicken cut away from the bone, to be eaten with another plastic spoon.

"Just keep me posted," she said. "We're not going anywhere."

"How's Rennell bearing up?"

The question reminded Terri of another inmate about to be executed, this one so retarded that he had set aside the key lime pie from his last meal to be eaten after he came back. "All right," she answered. "But he's absorbed more about what's happening to him than a retarded person might. Payton brought it home—"

"Hang on," Chris interrupted.

In the background she heard Carlo's voice. "The Ninth Circuit just turned us down again," Chris told her. "Two to one, Montgomery dissenting."

Terri glanced at her watch. Less than five hours and Governor Darrow, or perhaps Chief Justice Masters, stood between Rennell Price and death.

"Carlo's already calling the death clerk," Chris assured her and got off.

TWENTY-TWO

At eight-thirty, Terri still waited for the Supreme Court, or Governor Darrow, to seal or alter Rennell's fate.

Rennell, she knew, was now housed in an execution holding cell. In the separate cell beside him would be the Unitarian minister Terri had chosen, a woman willing to give solace to those about to die, experienced enough that she would not lose her composure and make Rennell's last hours more terrible. Through the bars between them, the minister could speak to him or read aloud from the Bible or, if Rennell preferred, simply hold his hand.

Full of dread, clinging to hope, Terri sat by the telephone.

At nearly midnight in Washington, the Chief Justice and Callista Hill, reviewing Rennell Price's last petition, peered at the computer screen in Caroline's office. "Pretty thin," Caroline said. "Fleet's murder says nothing about the crime itself. The only other piece is hearsay from Price's lawyer, with no new witness she can name. Just someone on the phone."

"But if it's true," Callista countered, "Fleet came close to admitting guilt—'if you choke to death, at least it'll be an accident.' Shouldn't Price's lawyers have time to find the woman who called them? Why does the State insist on killing him tonight?"

"There'll always be something, Justice Fini would say—it's not this Court's job to wring our collective hands over every last wisp of 'new evidence.' " With an anger she knew to be misplaced, Caroline turned on her clerk. "What's the legal justification for granting a stay, Callista? AEDPA? Do you think Justice Fini and his four allies will find **this** 'clear and convincing'? And where's the constitutional violation which kept **this** evidence from coming out in trial?

"It didn't even **exist** at the time of trial, for God-sakes. **And** it's inadmissible—"

"It wouldn't be," Callista cut in, "if Price's lawyers could find this woman."

Caroline reined in her own emotions. "Callista," she said more calmly, "I went out on a limb a few days ago. The Court dissolved my stay. If I keep doing this, it will look like I'm sticking my thumb in Fini's eye. At some point I have to think about my own credibility, and not inflaming tensions on the Court. There **are** other cases."

Callista folded her arms. In the bleak light of the Chief Justice's office, she looked both sad and fierce.

"Maybe so," she answered, "but Rennell Price has only got one life."

Caroline studied her. "I'm sorry," she said at last. "But perfect justice does not exist."

"I know that."

The cool response was more disturbing to Caroline than more argument. Turning from the screen, she walked to her window and gazed out into the darkness, at nothing.

"I won't enter a stay," she said. "But call the others. Make sure they see this petition and know they should vote by two A.M. If you want to draft a short recommendation, you can."

"Thank you," Callista said simply. When the Chief Justice turned from the window, her clerk was already gone.

At nine-thirty, Pacific daylight time, Terri had no word from Chris. Picking up the telephone, she called Rennell in his holding cell.

"We still haven't heard anything," she said, as though passing on routine information, then tried to infuse some cheer into her voice. "I just felt like talking with you."

"Yeah." Rennell's voice was soft. "Preacher's here with me. But I feel like talkin' to you, too."

"Do you know what I was thinking about? Some of the good things that happened in your life."

"Like Payton?"

"Like Payton. But I was thinking about Mrs. Brooks, your third-grade teacher. She really cared about you."

She heard Rennell breathe heavily, a sound akin to a sigh. "Think she did?"

"She kept your picture, Rennell. All these years, and she still kept it. She wanted to remember you."

Again, Rennell was silent. Then he said, "Talkin' to you makes me feel better." He paused again. "I'm real tired, though. You tired?"

"A little," Terri said gently. "But I'm still waiting to hear from Chris. After that, I'll call again."

Howard Shipler's solarium had floor-to-ceiling glass walls, wicker furniture, and a full complement of miniature palm trees and exotic leafy plants. Tautly waiting for the Governor in an oversize chair worthy of the Viceroy of British India, Chris half-expected a cockatoo to appear in Darrow's place.

Instead, the Governor stepped briskly into the room, his shirt starched, his thin blade of a body erect, his eyes keen. Even in the company of such very good friends, Craig Darrow drank only soda water.

"Chris," Darrow said, shaking his hand, "I know these are some pretty bad hours. For both of us, however hard that may be to accept."

"Worse for Rennell Price," Chris answered. "He's only got two hours left, and only you can save him—"

"What about the Supreme Court?"

"We haven't heard. But I'm not expecting that they'll help."

Darrow shoved both hands in the pockets of his pin-striped suit. "But you expect that **I** will."

With effort, Chris achieved a tone of reasoned calm. "Aside from Fleet's murder, we have new evidence, an anonymous call. It's another case where Fleet—the State's witness—forced a minor into oral copulation. Only this time he used a gun, and offered a kind of confession."

"Yes," Darrow said coolly. "I read your letter myself. Have you found the caller?"

"Not yet. That's why we want more time."

Gazing at the tile floor, Darrow grimaced, then placed a hand on Chris's shoulder. "I respect what you're doing, Chris. I consider you a friend. But how many courts have looked at this, how many different times..."

"That's why they call it clemency. It's not about AEDPA, or even about standards of guilt or innocence—it's about mercy. But we're not even asking for **that**. All we want is a reprieve—a chance to find new evidence." Disheartened by the opacity of Darrow's gaze, Chris said abruptly, "Dammit, Craig, he didn't **do** it."

"So you say," Darrow answered in a tone of resignation and apology. "But so does **any** lawyer say. If I intervene for this man, it would seem as though I was doing a favor for a friend. And so I would be."

The transcendent cynicism of this answer frayed

Chris's nerves even further. "What will a few weeks' grace time cost you?"

"Quite a lot. If I'm not seen to be acting on principle."

Moving closer, Chris stared into Darrow's eyes. "What principle?" he said. "You've never granted clemency. Neither did the last two governors. Since they ran Rose Bird off the State Supreme Court, **no one** has. Because there's no money in it, and no votes.

"We don't have clemency in this state anymore. It's just another level of emotional brutality, a way station to death, exploited by governors who shut their eyes to scavenge a few more votes. You can do better, Craig. **This** is the case."

The Governor dropped his arm, and his face seemed to close. "It's only **a** case. So let's be real. Our state's economy is tanking. The right wing is ginning up a recall to run me out of office, with a tough-guy movie star waiting in the wings to front for them. You think **he's** going to be passing out clemency like communion wafers? Forget it.

"If I lose this office, all the other things you care about—education, child care programs, environmental protection—are going with me. If I do what you want me to—overruling a slew of courts—they'll make me into another Kathleen Brown, the last Democrat to run **for** governor **and** against the death penalty."

Now Chris's face was inches from Darrow's. "And you'll have done a decent thing—"

"Do you remember Governor Kathleen?" Darrow

interrupted with asperity. "Well, neither do I. She never had the chance to do **one** decent thing. So don't lecture me on moral leadership."

Chris felt the pulse pounding in his temple. Placing both hands on Darrow's shoulders, he said, "It's very simple. In less than two hours, Rennell Price lives or dies."

Almost imperceptibly, the Governor shook his head.

For a white-hot instant, Chris fought back the urge to grab Darrow by the lapels and smash him against the wall. With difficulty, he lowered his hands and reached into a pocket for a business card. Then he gently grasped the Governor's right lapel and slid the card inside the pocket of his suit coat.

"That's the warden's telephone number," Chris said. "It's a long drive back to Sacramento, Craig. At twelve-oh-one, you'll still be awake. That gives you one last chance to call."

Turning, Chris left.

A few minutes before eleven o'clock, the phone in front of Terri rang.

Hastily, she picked it up. "I'm sorry," Chris told her wearily. "The Supreme Court just turned us down, seven votes to two."

Terri felt sick. "What about Darrow?"

"I tried." Chris's voice was bitter. "He sees no future in Rennell, and so Rennell has none. Unless he changes his mind and calls the warden, it's over."

"What chance is there of that?"

"None. And Johnny Moore's gotten nowhere." His tone softened. "Carlo and I are on our way. We'll be there with you soon."

Before placing her last call to Rennell, Terri took five minutes to compose herself. When she picked up the phone again, her watch read 11:03.

"Terri?" Rennell said, voice filling with fear and hope.

"It's me." Pausing, she fought to keep her voice from breaking. "I'm sorry, Rennell. The Supreme Court turned us down. So did Governor Darrow. There's nothing else we can do."

She could not go on. In a dull voice, Rennell asked, "That means I'm gonna die?"

"Yes." Terri groped for words. "I hate telling you that, Rennell. But I wanted to say how much I love you."

"Me, too." Rennell's voice was husky. "You take care of Chris and Carlo, okay?"

The words pierced Terri's heart—somewhere, this limited man had learned to imagine, and to feel for, the two fortunate men who had learned to care for him. The irony felt devastating—its sadness, the immense waste of a human being who, fifteen years before, a jury had believed to be too callous to pity a nine-year-old girl.

"I will," Terri promised, and her voice began to falter. "I have to say goodbye, because our time is up. But only for now, Rennell. You'll see us all again."

"In heaven?"

It was what Terri, as a child, had been taught to believe and no longer could. But there was nothing else to say. "In heaven," she affirmed. "Your grandma's there already."

She heard Rennell inhale. "And Payton?"

"Yes," Terri answered. "And Payton."

TWENTY-THREE

AT ELEVEN-THIRTY, TERRI ENTERED THE WITNESS area.

The family of Thuy Sen—Meng, Chou, and Kim—clustered together, awaiting Rennell with impassive patience. As before, Kim Sen clutched a photograph of her murdered sister. Terri did not speak to them.

She stood alone, picturing Rennell. They would be issuing him fresh denims to put on in a cell next to the chamber. She imagined him with his head lowered, awaiting death as it crept toward him, second by second. Each of Terri's thoughts was excruciating—the most terrible part, the part she suffered now, was to have lost all hope.

Staring at the empty chamber, she tried to indulge herself in fantasy—the Governor relenting, new evidence emerging in this final hour. But each scrap of forlorn hope, evaporating in the merciless light of reality, left her more anguished than before.

If only...

If only Flora Lewis had not peered out her window;

or Payton had told Charles Monk about Fleet; or Yancey James had been capable and sober. Even more deeply than before, Terri felt a creeping, existential dread: the death of Thuy Sen had come to nothing but, perhaps, the death of another innocent. And then it struck her that only the prospect of Rennell's death had drawn Terri to him—if the Supreme Court had abolished the death penalty, she would have spent her energies elsewhere. Yet thousands of men, blameless like Rennell might be, would die in prison because they were too poor, too limited, too disadvantaged from birth to stand up for their innocence. For some such men, helpless and bereft of caring, death might be a mercy.

Terri felt herself shiver and then, to her surprise, saw Charles Monk and Lou Mauriani enter the viewing area.

They went to the Sens, speaking softly, Mauriani lightly embracing Thuy Sen's mother and sister. But Kim Sen seemed dissociated, barely able to acknowledge his words or touch.

Seeing Terri, Monk nodded grimly, and she read the doubt in his eyes, the expression of whatever feeling had led him to help her locate Betty Sims. But it was Mauriani who approached her.

He stood there, hands shoved in his pockets, his blue eyes cool and somber. "I thought I should be here," he said simply.

Terri nodded. The comment was ambiguous—she could not tell if he meant that he owed this to the Sens, or to their murdered child, or to his responsibility to witness the death of a man he had helped put here and now, his own career over, was uncertain that he should have. Finally, Terri said, "He's innocent, you know."

"No." Mauriani answered softly. "I don't know."

It was not an argument, merely a statement of truth, even—perhaps—an admission. And yet Monk and Mauriani had not cheated, as police or prosecutors sometimes did. They had simply used the system as it had always been used—and for the benefit, they must have believed, of Thuy Sen's family. Then Larry Pell, and the machinery of death, had taken Rennell from there to here.

Mauriani retreated to stand with Monk, near, yet apart from, the Sens.

Around them, the people of California slept, heedless of whom the State was executing in their name. In the morning, the radio or a newspaper might remind them of the worst act of Rennell's life—as told by Eddie Fleet—and they would feel that justice had been served. Some of them, comforted, might vote for Governor Darrow.

In the end, Terri knew, no one could prove Rennell's guilt or innocence. There was only one thing she was sure of—among those assembled here to watch him die, she alone understood his life.

When Chris and Carlo arrived at San Quentin Prison, a hundred or so candles flickered near the gate, lit by those who had to come to witness, or to pray. As they stepped from the car, a low fog, drawn across the bay by the inland heat of the day, left a damp chill on Chris's face.

He glanced over at his son and saw, for an instant, the scared seven-year-old boy who had first come to live with him. But the image—surely a father's imagining—was replaced by a young lawyer tempered by adversity and gripped by sorrow and anger. A different man; still the son he cherished, but changed.

Silent, they began walking toward the prison.

To her intense relief, Terri saw her husband and stepson enter the viewing area. It was 11:50, and soon Rennell Price would appear in the death chamber, the IVs protruding from his arm. Terri did not wish to be alone.

Quiet, Chris stood at one side of Terri, Carlo the other, each taking one of her hands. "How are Elena and Kit?" Terri murmured to her husband.

"Fine. Kit's asleep. Elena says she's waiting up for you."

The door of the death chamber slowly opened.

Rennell stumbled, eyes wide and fearful, guided by the medical technician who would connect his arms to the syringes. Then he looked up, gazing dully at the faces watching him through the glass. Hoping that he would find her, Terri managed a smile.

At last Rennell saw her. He seemed to pause, as though to imprint her face in some eternal memory. But when he tried to smile back, his eyes moistened. Shamed, he tried to wipe them with the swath of denim sleeve rolled back for the syringe.

"Oh, God, Rennell..."

It was her own voice, Terri realized. As he gazed up at her again, Rennell's mouth formed words but made no sound.

Carlo's grip tightened on her hand.

With palpable reluctance, Rennell faced the Sens. In a voice thick with fear and sadness, he said, "I didn't do your little girl..."

Once more, Kim held up the picture of Thuy Sen, covering her own face. Standing behind them, a reporter scribbled in his notepad.

Turning Rennell, the technicians laid him on the gurney.

Wordless now, Terri watched them strap Rennell to the table—spread-eagled, unable to protect himself, about to die. She had the visceral urge to scream, to pound the glass window and say that this must stop. And still she watched.

The reporter kept jotting notes.

As Rennell gazed at the ceiling, tears slid from the corners of his eyes. Briefly, Terri looked away and felt Chris touch her shoulder. "You gave him hope, for a time. And caring always."

Terri looked up at him. His face was set, the lines at the corners of his eyes taut and more deeply graven. "You may carry out the death warrant," she heard the warden intone.

"Never again," Carlo said between his teeth. "Never again."

Terri saw Chris glance over at him, as though to discern his meaning. Then, once more, she faced the chamber.

Through the glass, Rennell's eyes fluttered. As she had not done since childhood, Terri bowed her head and began to murmur, "Holy Mary, Mother of God, pray for us now and at the hour of our death..."

Slowly, Rennell felt sleep seeping through his body, more deep and numbing than any sleep he had known before. He was waiting for his brother, like he had done for his whole life. He hoped that Payton would come soon.

AFTERWORD AND ACKNOWLEDGMENTS

THE DEATH PENALTY IS A DIFFICULT AND EMOTIONAL subject. In writing this book, I (like Christopher Paget) found myself looking at my nine-year-old son from several conflicting perspectives: How would I feel about a murderer who subjected him to a terrible death? How would I feel if, on the eve of execution, postconviction lawyers cast doubt upon the guilt of a man whose guilt I had never doubted? And what kind of man would my own son become if he had the terrible history common to so many occupants of death row?

These questions, and others, pervade our system of capital punishment. But this emotional complexity is only the beginning: the law of capital punishment is far more complicated than I portrayed it (a Supreme Court justice once remarked to me that the only legal thicket of similar obscurity is patent law). So it is important to emphasize that the body of law I depicted is authentic. The Antiterrorism and Effective Death Penalty Act (AEDPA) is a real statute, and the cases and legal principles I cite are also real, however hypertechnical or counterintuitive they may seem; indeed, I was forced to simplify both the law and legal procedure—drastically—in order to make them comprehensible to laypeople. Even the case described by Judge Blair Montgomery to Chief Justice Caroline Masters, in which the execution turned on an administrative error within the Ninth Circuit Court of Appeals, is real—though I severely condensed its Byzantine history, which otherwise would have consumed many more pages than most readers could have tolerated.

Thus the essence of my problem was to portray the murky reality of the law with sufficient clarity to convey its pitfalls and yet be understood. Not easy. As an ex-lawyer, I find this the most difficult area of law I have ever encountered, convoluted in both substance and procedure. But the bottom line is this: much of this complexity reflects a fundamental and passionate disagreement—whether the principal goal of postconviction litigation is achieving finality or preventing the potential execution of the innocent. I hope that this novel does that conflict justice.

Given all this, I'm particularly grateful to those who gave me the benefit of their experience and expertise.

To be a postconviction litigator requires astonishing resourcefulness, resilience, and stamina—physical and psychological. I was fortunate to have the advice of some of the country's foremost specialists, for whom this is a full-time career: Anthony Amsterdam, Sandra Babcock, Stephen Bright, David Bruck, Tim Ford, Larry Marshall, Gary Sowards, Bryan Stevenson, Keir

Weyble, and especially Michael Laurence, who not only met with me for countless hours but reviewed the manuscript to help me stay true to the environment of **habeas corpus** litigation. Thanks, too, to the other fine lawyers who shared with me their experience in postconviction litigation: Eve Brensike, Vernon Jordan, David Kendall, Leslie Landau, Jay Paultz, Linda Schilling, Dorothy Streutker, and Doug Young.

A particularly fascinating area involved re-creating an inmate's social history and psychological profile. I was lucky to have the advice of Scharlette Holdman, the pioneer of social histories, as well as that of psychologist Kathy Wayland. Mental health professionals who shared their perspectives on death row inmates included Dr. Karen Froming, Dr. Ruth Luckasson, Dr. Daniel Martel, Dr. Richard Yarvis, Dr. Myla Young, and especially Dr. George Woods.

This book also required me to understand the investigation and prosecution of a capital case from beginning to end. It was my great good fortune to meet or speak with some of the most capable experts around: Drew Edmondson, Attorney General of Oklahoma and President of the National Association of Attorneys General (NAAG); San Francisco (and now San Mateo) Assistant District Attorney Al Giannini, who has never lost a homicide prosecution; California Assistant Attorney General Dane Gilette, a specialist in postconviction litigation; the legendary San Francisco homicide inspector Napoleon Hendrix; and Dr. Boyd Stephens, San Francisco's nationally renowned medical examiner. Officers Shaughan Ryan, Jimmy Aherne, and Tim Fowler took me for a ride-along in the Bayview District, and taught me some fascinating lessons in policing a difficult area. Thanks, too, to Lynne Ross of NAAG, who helped me in several important ways. I also received advice on the finer points of criminology and forensics from Dr. Peter Burnett. And I'm particularly grateful to Jayne Hawkins and Kate Lowenstein for sharing the perspectives of those who have lost a family member.

As I have noted, the law of capital punishment is bedeviled by complexity. Many thanks to those lawyers who shared their knowledge of the law, and of the system: Stuart Banner, Jim Liebman, and Stephen Shatz. I am also grateful to those who have recently dealt with these issues as clerks of the California Supreme Court, the United States District Court, the Ninth Circuit Court of Appeals, or the United States Supreme Court: Julie Bibb Davis, Veronica Gushin, George Kolombatovich, Stacey Leyton, Valerie Mark, Deirdre Von Dornum, and Claudia Willner.

The Supreme Court is an institution to itself, as powerful as it is secluded. I owe whatever success I enjoyed in rendering the environment of my imaginary Supreme Court case to Kathy Arberg and Ed Turner, of the Supreme Court clerk's office, and the legal scholars and practitioners Dean David Burcham, Walter Dellinger, Jon Hacker, Edward Lazarus, Richard Lazarus, Jeremy Maltby, and Mark Tushnet. And special thanks to Linda Greenhouse for sharing her observations of the Court.

I am also deeply grateful to those who gave me their differing perspectives as judges: Judge Thelton Henderson of the United States District Court, Judges William Fletcher and Alex Kozinski of the United States Court of Appeals for the Ninth Circuit, and especially, Judge Stephen Reinhardt, also of the Ninth Circuit. Another valuable perspective came from those who have made opposing the death penalty as advocates a central part of their lives: Richard Dieter of Death Penalty Information Center; Elizabeth Dahl, Joseph Onek, Barbara Reed, and Virginia Sloan of the Constitution Project, and Lance Lindsey of Death Penalty Focus. The prisoners' rights advocate Steve Fama imparted his unique insight into the day-to-day life of inmates at San Quentin. But there was no experience more piercing than my interview with Marvin Pete Walker, now Shaka Nantambu, concerning his existence as a death row prisoner facing the prospect of execution.

I also benefited from the following reading:

Books and Treatises

Books

Ellis, James W. **Mental Retardation and the Death Penalty: A Guide to State Legislative Issues.** Albuquerque: University of New Mexico School of Law, 2002.

Lazarus, Edward. **Closed Chambers: The First Eye-witness Account of the Epic Struggles Inside the Supreme Court.** New York: Crown, 1998.

Liebman, James, et al. **A Broken System: Error Rates in Capital Cases, 1973–1995.** 2000. The Justice Project. http://justice.policy.net/jreport.

———. **A Broken System, Part II: Why There Is So Much Error in Capital Cases, and What Can Be Done About It.** 2002. The Justice Project. http://justice.policy.net/jreport.

Rehnquist, William H. **The Supreme Court.** New York: Knopf, 2001.

Turow, Scott. **Ultimate Punishment: A Lawyer's Reflections on Dealing with the Death Penalty.** New York: Farrar, Straus & Giroux, 2003.

Articles

Bandes, Susan. "Simple Murder: A comment on the legality of executing the innocent." **Buffalo Law Review** 44 (1996): 501.

Blume, John, and David Voisin. "An Introduction to Federal Habeas Corpus Practice and Procedure." **South Carolina Law Review** 47 (1996): 271.

Bright, Stephen. "Political Attacks on the Judiciary: Can justice be done amid efforts to intimidate and remove judges from office for unpopular decisions?" **Judicature** 80 (1997): 165.

————. "Counsel for the Poor: The death sentence not for the worst crime but for the worst lawyer." **Yale Law Review** 103 (1994): 1835.

Leno, Mark. "The Ultimate Price: Is the death penalty California's best interest?" **San Francisco Chronicle.** January 28, 2003. p. A17.

Liebman, James S. "The Overproduction of Death." **Columbia Law Review** 100 (2000): 2030.

Reinhardt, Stephen. "The Anatomy of an Execution: Fairness vs. Process." **New York Law Review** 74 (1999): 313.

Schatz, Stephen F., and Nina Rivkind. "The California Death Penalty Scheme: Requiem for **Furman.**" **New York Law Review** 72 (1997): 1283.

Talbot, Margaret. "The Executioner's I.Q. Test." **The New York Times Magazine.** June 29, 2003. p. 30.

Will, George F. "Innocent on Death Row." **The Washington Post.** April 6, 2000. p. A23.

Finally, I want to thank those who read and commented on the manuscript: Laurie Patterson, Fred Hill, Alison Porter Thomas, Cheryl Mills, and Philip Rotner; and my editors, Linda Marrow and Dan

Menaker. And then there are the two publishers to whom this book is dedicated, who have steadfastly supported my belief that popular fiction can address controversial legal, political, and social issues: Gina Centrello, President and Publisher of the Random House Publishing Group, and Nancy Miller, Editor in Chief of Ballantine Books.

In concluding, I understand that writing about capital punishment will arouse a number of emotions in my readers, not all of them admiring. So, as always, I want to be very clear—those who helped me are not responsible for the narrative, or any of the often conflicting views expressed therein, let alone any errors of fact or interpretation. One person conceived and wrote this book; any fault is mine alone.

Thanks, as always, for bearing with me.

RICHARD NORTH PATTERSON
Martha's Vineyard
April 2004

ABOUT THE AUTHOR

RICHARD NORTH PATTERSON'S twelve prior novels include eight consecutive international best-sellers, all greeted by critical acclaim—for example, comparing his **Protect and Defend** with novels such as Allen Drury's **Advise and Consent** and Gore Vidal's **Lincoln.** Formerly a trial lawyer, Mr. Patterson served as the SEC's liaison to the Watergate Special Prosecutor and is now on the boards of several Washington-based advocacy groups dealing with gun violence, political reform, and reproductive rights. He lives on Martha's Vineyard.

ABOUT THE TYPE

This book was set in Garamond, a typeface originally designed by the Parisian type cutter Claude Garamond (1480–1561). This version of Garamond was modeled on a 1592 specimen sheet from the Egenolff-Berner foundry, which was produced from types assumed to have been brought to Frankfurt by the punch cutter Jacques Sabon (d. 1580).

Claude Garamond's distinguished romans and italics first appeared in **Opera Ciceronis** in 1543–44. The Garamond types are clear, open, and elegant.

LIKE WHAT YOU'VE SEEN?

If you enjoyed this large print edition of **Conviction**, look for additional Richard North Patterson bestsellers available in large print.

Balance of Power (hardcover)
0-375-43208-6 ($29.95/$44.95C)

Protect and Defend (hardcover)
0-375-43099-7 ($26.95/$37.95C)

Dark Lady
(hardcover) 0-375-40844-4 (25.95/$37.95C)
(trade paperback) 0-375-72789-2 ($14.95/$22.95C)

The Final Judgment (trade paperback)
0-679-76666-9 ($25.00/$32.95C)

Large print books are available wherever books are sold and at many local libraries.

All prices are subject to change. Check with your local retailer for current pricing and availability. For more information on these and other large print titles, visit www.randomlargeprint.com.

Hortensia Hayes

Love Veronica Webb

Aggie, Thanks
painting m

Eddie
Louie the
best. I love
You

Hazel O'Hara